THE PEACE HAVEN MURDERS

M. GLENN GRAVES

CITY LIGHTS
PRESS
– LAS VEGAS –

The Peace Haven Murders
(Clancy Evans PI Book 3)
M. Glenn Graves

City Lights Press
An Imprint of Wolfpack Publishing
6032 Wheat Penny Avenue
Las Vegas, NV 89122

Paperback Edition
© Copyright 2014 M Glenn Graves (as revised)

ISBN: 978-1-64119-600-0

To Cindy

THE PEACE HAVEN
MURDERS

THE HALLWAYS WERE AS QUIET AS DEATH. THE LONE FIGURE moved purposefully along the semi-lighted corridors as if she had some vital function related to their care. No one would have ever suspected why she was there. She did her job so effortlessly it was frightening.

This was her mission.

The room was darker than the hallway, but her eyes adjusted quickly. She waited by the closed door as the outline of the bed became apparent. She listened for sounds. The breathing was steady, insistent, and comforting, she thought.

It was time.

She stood by the bedside table and removed the tools of her trade from her pockets. The penlight helped to check the measured dosage in the syringe. Her eyes were now able to capture more of the light that was stealing into the room from underneath the door to the hall. The late night quiet was interrupted only by the rhythmic breathing of the person in the bed.

Standing at the foot of the bed, the silhouetted figure

carefully removed the sheet and light blanket that was neatly tucked under the mattress. She was methodical, but then, she had to be. Any job worth doing had to be done correctly. It had been decided. It was the moment of truth.

The penlight located the exact spot between the toes where she wiped gently the local numbing agent. It would take only a few minutes for the medicine to work. She looked toward the head of the bed to see if there would be any movement from the person in the bed. All was still.

She guided the needle carefully into its chosen spot. The figure in the bed remained motionless. The steady breathing remained the one noticeable sound in the room, in and out, in and out. So peaceful, she thought.

The syringe emptied slowly into the spot between the toes. Her hands moved quickly to fix the sheet and the blanket. The penlight indicated to her that all was normal on the bedding. She remained at the foot of the bed for another minute or two recalling the details of her mission. She must omit nothing. It had to be done right. No room for errors.

After retracing her steps from the time of entry to this moment, she returned to the side of the bed and removed a piece of paper from her pocket. It was a lovely pink and lavender, one of those generic cards with a short message and a Bible verse. The message read, *God bless you.* The Bible verse cited was Hebrews 9:27.

The card was carefully placed on the night table next to the bed. The message was positioned away from the bed so that it was not so much for the one who lay there dying, but for the one who would find her the next morning.

Footsteps in the hallway alerted her to a possible intrusion on her all but completed mission. She moved quickly to the darkness behind the large entrance door. She waited without anxiety as the footsteps became louder and stopped only a few feet from her. Her eyes were fixed on the closed door, waiting.

It opened slightly and the outline of a head looked in, no doubt checking on the person in the bed. The door closed and the footsteps walked on to another location. The figure behind the door remained motionless. Patience would be rewarded.

The breathing from the bed had altered slightly by this time and the mission-minded figure behind the door knew that her work would soon be accomplished. It had all been laid out so specifically, so painstakingly detailed, that there was simply no way for it to fail.

She opened the door of the room and peered into the hallway for signs of the person doing the room checks. It was empty. She started to leave when the distant sound of footsteps again alerted her, and she noticed some movement to her left at the far end of the long hallway. Then there were voices talking, but no signs of anyone in the hallway.

The lone figure moved to her right and made her way out of the building into the night. Her work was done. One more mission accomplished with discreet thoroughness and extreme efficiency. *Any job worth doing*, she thought. There was a slight smile on her face as she climbed into her car and drove away. It was pleasing to her to be called to this type of work. It was a noble task.

The next morning someone would find the card on the night table and read the scriptural epitaph for the woman lying dead in the bed without ever knowing that she had died at the hands of another. It would all appear to be so natural, so normal, and so usual. No one would suspect a murder or a mission. No one would really pay attention to the card on the table. Just a kind thought left there by some visitor intending to comfort the person in the room. She thought the Hebrews 9:27 reference a nice touch –

It is appointed once for man to die,

and then comes judgment.

It was 5:46 a.m. when my phone rang. I had just finished my morning workout and closed the door behind Sam. I allowed it to ring three or four times just to be sure that whoever it was really wanted to talk with me that early. The computer takes over after the eighth ring in case someone is truly serious and I'm not available.

"Are you ever coming to see me again?" my mother's voice spoke tacitly to me after I mumbled hello.

"Good morning, Mother. And how are you?"

"I'm fine. When can you come?"

"No trivial niceties, no small talk, just straight up."

"Well?"

"I don't know, Mother. I'm finishing up a case here. I have some obligations to meet."

"Sound like lame excuses to me. You know I won't be around forever."

The guilt would have been gripping except for the fact that I drove to Clancyville every month to see her. It had only been three weeks, give or take, since my last visit. I started to mention that.

"Besides," she interrupted my planned rationale, "I have something I need you to look into."

"What's going on?"

"I'll tell you when you get here. Just come. Today would be nice."

"I can't come today."

I grabbed my empty calendar and looked ahead. The Kowalski case was closed now, so my work load was non-existent. Nothing on the horizon, except my mother.

"I can come this weekend."

"See you Saturday."

She hung up before I could offer any other alternative. True to form, my mother seldom veered from her demanding nature. She was in her mid-seventies now and had been living alone for over thirty years.

"We're going to Clancyville, Sam. Gird your loins."

He snorted, which I interpreted to be a sigh, and then rolled over to continue his after-workout nap on the couch. I could tell he was thrilled.

Three days later we were driving across Virginia in my ten year old Camry. Sam was sleeping comfortably in the backseat while I was enjoying the non-city scenery. Despite my overwhelming confidence in my nearly ancient automobile, I had my eye on a newer model of a different brand. A two year old Jeep had caught my eye while I happened by a dealership last week. It was one of those so-called cream-puffs which occur all-too-infrequently but delight one's soul whenever they happen. Acceptable color, low mileage, and traded in by someone who wanted a new model. I had talked it over with Uncle Walters to get his opinion.

I was heading home because my mother had beckoned me. Friction with my mother had not yet achieved open warfare status, but we did have moments of conflict in which neither one of us liked the other. I had to believe that it all stemmed from my law enforcement career. She would have preferred that I become an office secretary for some reputable company in Lynchburg or Dan River, towns close-by to Clancyville.

I did please her when I stopped being a Norfolk cop after ten years. I did not please her when I immediately became a private detective. "Frying pan into the fire," I think she said. It was my father's blood that ran in me, so I really couldn't help myself. At least that's the way I see it.

I do see my mother's point of view in all this. She's been a widow for longer than she was married. My father had been the Sheriff of Pitt County. He had had his office in Clan-cyville, the town in which we had lived, the small town in which I grew up. It was also the town where he was killed when I was eleven. It is only natural then that my mother maintains a low opinion of law enforcement, which would include private detectives.

What that actually means is that my mother maintains a low opinion of me and my work. She is forever telling me that I should quit snooping around and get an honest job. About the only compliment she ever offers to me is something along the lines of, "You're a smart, young woman and you should be doing something productive." I receive this line of flattery as something akin to her washing the knife before she sticks it into my flesh.

I stopped at some fast food gas facility in Emporia. Sam insisted on taking a walk around back so I followed. It was early fall and the days still offered warm sunshine and cool breezes. It was a good time to be traveling into the heartland of Virginia. There were actually moments now and again when I actually missed living in Clancyville. They didn't occur often, but they come along once in a while to remind me of my formative years. They reminded me of some great joy now long since passed.

I was headed home, but I knew that it was not towards joy that I was headed. A visit with my mother was anything but joyful. Still, here I was, the dutiful daughter cruising along the corridors of Virginia's highways and byways en route to some minor disaster in my personal relationship with Mother. I could barely contain my excitement.

3

THE RIDE ACROSS VIRGINIA WAS A STRAIGHT SHOT USING Highway 58, except for the last leg. I turned northward on 29 just after lunch. Sam yawned in my ear and gently nosed me. This was his sign language.

I stopped in Tightsqueeze and took Sam behind the local Food Lion for his rest stop en route to my hometown. We shared a bottle of water as I curiously surveyed the surroundings of this middle of nowhere Virginia stop. Twenty more minutes and we would be back where I spent all of my youth, back where I had actually helped my father solve some crimes.

That seemed like another lifetime, but not mine.

The fall colors were beginning to show themselves. There appeared to be more reds than usual, but it was still early. It was a mild day in South Central Virginia; and, despite my mother's dictum, it was good to be returning to this place again.

I pulled into the unpaved driveway off of Honeycutt Lane and parked the Camry under the oak tree. Standing under it,

I strained my neck upwards to see the top of it without success. Once upon a time, I climbed that tree. A lot.

"Where's the dog?" the back screen door slammed just after the words caught my ears.

"Exploring."

"We have a leash law, you know."

"I know. He'll be careful."

"You make it sound like that dog can avoid detection," she muttered in her stage-whisper as she turned to enter the house.

He can... and does.

"I see you are still driving that red Camry. Why don't you spend some money and buy a new one? How old is that car?"

"It still runs well and I happen to like it. No need to buy a new one."

"Just like your father."

"Thank you."

"Wasn't a compliment."

"I know."

Everything was still in its place, I noticed, as I surveyed the room. It still felt like home, despite the absence of my father. The bookshelves, tabletops, and other furnishings were clean, neatly arranged, and without the clutter of my own apartment. My mother and I were polar opposites when it came to house keeping.

"Thanks for coming," she sat down in her softly cush-ioned blue chair near the bookshelf in the den.

"You beckoned."

"That's never pulled you in before."

"You sounded as if this was important."

"It is."

"So tell me. What's so urgent?"

"People are dying too fast."

"Didn't know that there was a pace to it."

"Don't get smart. I need you to investigate some deaths."

"Who died?"

"Sophie Tucker, Alice Blayne Walker, Marilyn Pearson, Rabbi Shelton, and Eli Rowland."

"You keeping a list?"

"Don't have to. These were my friends. They're all close to my age, some a little older. But they shouldn't be dying."

"Death comes to us all."

"Always with the mouth."

"How'd they die?"

"In their sleep."

"All of them?"

"To a person."

"Good way to go."

"If it's your time. This was premature for all of them."

"How do you know?"

"I go to the same doctor they used."

"And he talks to you about his ... former patients?"

"We wonder together. Secretly."

"Well, I admit it is a rather odd coincidence."

"You mean odd coincidences."

"Yeah, that."

"Your father used to say that there are no such things."

"I remember."

"So, detect."

"That all you have?"

"No."

I waited for an answer. Nothing came forth. She was staring out the window near her chair. She appeared to be frozen in time.

"Mother?"

"What?"

"Tell me all of it."

"They all were residents of the Peace Haven Nursing and Care Facility on the edge of town."

"That means they all had something seriously wrong."

"Not necessarily. In their cases it meant that they had no family willing to take care of them. Most of them, no, all of them, had mobility issues. Nothing seriously wrong. They just couldn't get around like they used to."

"Who can?"

"I can."

I nodded and waited.

"Anything else?"

"Your Aunt Mildred."

"My Aunt Mildred what?"

"She's on that list."

"Mildred is dead? Why didn't you tell me?"

"I just did."

"Now who's being smart?"

"I didn't want to be too abrupt. I know how you felt about her."

Mildred was my father's oldest sister. Of all the family members, she was the most genuine character of all. She was well into her nineties, but still as alert as any human being I knew. She was still a character and I dearly loved her.

"She was ninety-something, right?"

"Ninety-five."

"People die younger than that, you know."

"There was nothing wrong with her."

"Bodies wear out."

"True enough, but there is usually something wrong."

"Sometimes the heart gets tired and stops."

"Not hers."

"How do you know this?"

"We talked almost every day."

This was a revelation. Thirty years ago they hardly spoke, although they were civil. My mother always believed that Aunt Mildred was a horrendous influence on me. She accused Mildred of encouraging me toward police work. True enough.

"She moved to that *home* because she had fallen two or three times. Once she almost fell down those damn stairs in her mansion. I think it scared her badly and so, well, you know Mildred. She moved into the home."

"Why didn't you ask her to move in here?"

She looked angry. I expected some chastisement.

"She would have none of it. I offered. She declined. That was it."

"Sorry, mother. I had no idea that you two got along that well."

"People change, you know. Sometimes slowly, but we do change."

I nodded.

"When did she die?"

"The day before I called you."

"She's the reason you called."

"Yes."

"And you suspect something … sinister?"

"Enough is enough. Falling is one thing. Dying is quite another."

"True enough, but falls do usually mean that something is wrong inside."

"But not always to the point of death. Just investigate, okay?"

Her tone was different, not demanding, but actually asking. It was unusual for my mother to ask anyone for help with anything.

"I'll nose around a little and see if anything turns up."

"Her funeral's Wednesday, at the church. It was delayed

because she's to be cremated."

"Where?"

"Cuthbert-Boran made the arrangements."

"Soon?"

"Before Wednesday."

4

"KEITH CUTHBERT, PLEASE," I ASKED THE YOUNG WOMAN seated in the office just off of the hallway in the funeral home.

She stared at me so I smiled at her. Networking.

"He's busy right now. May I take a message?"

"No. I need to speak with him immediately."

"He's … ah… working. You can talk with Allen Boran if you like."

"I like."

"Just a moment." She picked up the receiver, pushed some numbers and waited. "Mr. Boran, there's a woman here to see you."

She cupped her hand over the receiver and tried to whisper to me. "What's your name?"

"Clancy Evans."

"Oh," she said to me, and then into the receiver, "Clancy Evans, Mr. Boran."

She hung up the receiver and smiled for the first time. I answered in kind.

"He said he would be right out. You can have a seat while you wait," she offered.

"No time to wait, Missy." She had a name sign on her desk that faced me. It read *Missy Shelton*.

"He shouldn't be long," she was trying to appease my blatant anxiety.

Before I could counter with some clever remark, an office door opened and a graying Allen Boran greeted me. He was a few years older, but still looked good.

"Clancy, how good to see you. It seems like forever since I have seen you," he said as he paused in the doorway allowing me to pass through ahead of him.

"Time passes," I said as I walked by him.

"That it does, Clancy. That it does. I extend my condolences to you in the death of your aunt." His words sounded professional, without much empathy. Perhaps he had been in this business of death too long.

"Thanks, Allen. I appreciate your kindness," I said giving him more credit than I felt he actually deserved. "I need to know if you have already cremated my Aunt Mildred."

"Let's see," he opened the right hand bottom drawer of his desk and began thumbing through some files. "Mildred Evans Keesee ...yes, Keith sent the body off yesterday," he closed the file and placed it back in the same spot in his desk drawer. Good detectives always watch things that are trivial. Most of them are meaningless. But not all.

"Yes," he continued, "she is scheduled for this morning ... Lynchburg ... ashes to be returned this afternoon or tomorrow."

"Can you stop it?"

"Stop it?"

"I want to view the body before she is cremated."

"It was her wish to be cremated, Clancy. It's in her will, one of those living will documents."

"I know. I helped her write it. I still want to see the body."

"I don't know, Clancy. This is an unusual request, you understand."

"I'm family, Allen."

"True enough, but still…."

"Call them and offer up any excuse you can. I'll drive to Lynchburg immediately. Just do not let them cremate her remains before I see them."

"Let me call and see what I can do. In the meantime, you can wait in the other office."

"I'll wait right here."

"Okay, Clancy. Give me a moment."

He flipped through his collection of phone numbers hanging on some type of free-wheeling device that looked more like a whirling dervish than an organized system. He found the number and dialed. I waited.

"Bill Maxwell, please," he spoke into the phone.

"Bill, Allen Boran here. I have a request from the family of Mildred Evans Keesee for you to postpone the cremation for a few hours. A member of the family wants to see the body before you cremate. Is that possible?"

We both waited for a reply.

"Yes, I know."

"There was a long pause. He seemed to be listening.

"Of course. I understand."

Another pause.

"She lives in Norfolk and just learned of the passing."

Pause.

"Good. Good. Her name is Clancy Evans and she will leave immediately for Lynchburg… Thank you, Bill. Thank you very much."

He hung up the phone and relayed the message to me.

"Thanks, Allen. We'll talk later, and catch up on old times."

Missy was chatting away with someone on the phone when I left her office.

"Who's Mildred's doctor?" I asked my mother.

"Jones-McCann, same doctor she's had for twenty-five plus years."

I made the call and luck was with me. At first she was reluctant to go, but after I explained the reasons, she readily agreed and we were on the road to Lynchburg in less than an hour. Curiosity is a wonderful thing.

The facility for cremation was on the north side of Lynchburg. It was mid-afternoon when we arrived. A tall young man escorted us to a stainless steel room with stainless steel light fixtures and stainless steel tables.

"Wait here," the tall man said.

We waited. Like a good detective I surveyed the room in case I would need to know more than I knew at present. Just as I was running out of stainless steel things to detect, the tall young man returned pushing a stainless steel gurney and a body. Since the gurney was covered with a white sheet I could only surmise that it was a body. He parked the sheeted gurney directly under one of the stainless steel lights and moved to a corner of the room where he stood without another word.

I removed the sheet and sure enough it was the body of my dear, sweet, eccentric aunt who had done her best to misguide me during my growing up years. She wasn't trying to make me a criminal, just develop a keen sense of impishness in direct opposition to the straight and narrow path my mother had me on. My father was somewhere in between the two women.

"What are we looking for exactly?" Jones-McCann asked.

"Don't watch many movies, huh?"

"I beg your pardon?"

"This is where the super-sleuth police detective or the keen private eye says something like 'evidence of foul play.'"

"Oh, that."

"Ever surveyed a corpse?"

"Not my specialty. I generally try to keep them from becoming corpses."

"Noble."

"There does not appear to be any surface evidence of trauma to the body," she offered after I watched her study all angles of Aunt Mildred. "You know that there was no autopsy performed."

"That's why we're here."

"We'll have to get permission to have an autopsy. And the family has to okay it."

"I'm family."

"Guardian?"

"I'll call my mother."

I pulled out my cell and the ever-quiet tall young man from the corner cleared his throat and approached me.

"It won't work in here. Besides, we have rules about cell phones in this room."

I walked outside the building and called my mother. While I waited, I wondered why there were rules about using cell phones in a room with dead people. Lack of privacy?

"Did Mildred have a guardian?"

"Yes."

"Who?"

"Me."

"You."

"Yes."

"We need to do an autopsy."

"What are you looking for?"

"Don't know until we find it."

"That sounds dumb."

"True enough, but it's the only answer I can give you that is the truth right now."

"Do it."

Despite his repeated objections, I finally won over Bill Maxwell and convinced him to give us time to perform an autopsy on Aunt Mildred. My girlish wiles even softened him enough to offer his facility for the procedure. Smooth talking devil that I am.

I made several calls from his office and finally located the ME in Roanoke who agreed to perform the autopsy. He wanted the body sent to him there, but I used more of my silver tongue arguments to convince the ME to come to Lynchburg.

The ME permitted Dr. Jones-McCann and me to join him for the autopsy after we donned the necessary garments. It was not my first experience with watching such an interesting procedure, but it was my first one in which I knew the person being autopsied. It does affect you.

"We'll run some blood and urine analyses to see if anything shows up, but the time-line could be against us finding something after three days," the ME said.

"Any needle marks?" I asked.

"Just the usual ones so far."

"But she was healthy. Why any needle marks at all?"

The ME opened her file, flipped through some pages, and then wrote it down.

"They were giving her B-12 supplement shots."

I moved to her feet to check for needle marks there. Between the toes is often a good place to hide needle traces if one is trying to hide such traces. I found nothing.

"Unless the samples we send to the lab show something in her system, I find nothing here to indicate that she was murdered. It all appears a natural death. She was, what," he picked up the medical file on Mildred. "Ninety-five. My, my. She was a healthy ninety-five, I will admit that. Atypical. I guess her heart just gave out."

"I doubt that," I said. "You didn't know my aunt."

"No, I did not. But there is no evidence on the body to indicate anything unnatural. I'll contact you when the test results are finished."

5

"WHY DON'T YOU GO OVER TO PEACE HAVEN AND DO SOME detecting."

I noticed that it wasn't a question.

"I doubt if they have preserved the supposed crime scene since no one but you thinks there's been a crime."

"But you can ask questions. You're good at that. Go over there and piss some people off by asking a lot of questions. Maybe you can stir up a hornet or two."

My mother had never encouraged my questioning skills, nor had she ever been supportive of my keen ability to anger people by poking my nose around stuff that was generally labeled as *none of my business*.

"Let me finish my coffee and I'll get right to it."

Sam was asleep at my side, not quite under the dining room table where we sat finishing up breakfast. My mother was reading the daily news from Dan River and I was wondering what questions I could ask the Peace Haven people.

"How long has the nursing home been accepting assisted living patients?"

"I don't know. Maybe two or three years. Why?"

"Seems like a good place to start."

"I don't follow," she said, putting down the paper and peering over at Sam.

"The ones who have died, the names you gave me yesterday, were they assisted living patients or nursing home patients?"

She pondered a few moments as if to measure my question.

"Let's see, Sophie Tucker, Alice … Marilyn Pearson …they had all been in the nursing home there for a number of years."

"You mentioned some men, too."

"Yeah, Old Rabbi Shelton – do you remember him?"

"He ran the Gulf Station where I used to buy bubble gum. He was married to one of my grade school teachers, right?"

"Wilma."

"Yes. She was my fourth grade teacher. Nice lady."

"She died years ago and Rabbi had a hard time going on without her. Seems like he got Parkinson's disease, or something like that, and had to go the nursing facility. No real choice as I recall."

"Any others?"

"Eli Rowland died just before your Aunt Mildred. He was also in the nursing home section. They all were, except for Aunt Mildred. You think that's important?"

"Don't know."

"Well, you're not going to learn anything by sitting here and asking me questions. Go detect, that's what you do, isn't it?"

"Some of the time."

I sipped my coffee and listened to Sam's gentle snoring.

"You ever consider getting a regular job?"

"Regular meaning anything not remotely connected to police work?"

"Regular meaning anything that doesn't have you carrying a gun and getting shot at," she fired back. Her tone definitely changed.

"No."

"You think carrying a gun makes you a tough woman?"

"Makes me feel safer. I'm tough enough without the gun."

"Or so you think."

"Or so I think."

"And why the dog?"

"Why the dog?" I repeated.

"Why do you have to have such a large dog?"

"He showed up one day and stayed."

"Why don't you get some cute little mutt to live with?"

"I take them as they come."

"You keep any and all strays?"

"No, just the ones who come and stay."

"You have a house full?"

"No. Just Sam."

"What happened to the other dog? I seem to remember that you had two."

"A friend needed a companion. I gave her to him."

"He looks vicious."

"Sam?"

I looked down at the sleeping dog beside me. He looked anything but vicious, but I could recall a time or two when he saved my life by attacking some folks on my behalf. Solid black with some white markings of distinction, he was a majestic Labrador Retriever with keen powers of observation. He also possessed some remarkable detective skills. I doubt if my mother would believe that or appreciate it.

"Only if he's awake," I suggested.

6

I TOOK MY MOTHER'S NOT-SO-SUBTLE SUGGESTION AND DROVE over to the Peace Haven Nursing and Care Facility. Like anything else in a small town, it wasn't far from my mother's house. Sam rode with me. He knew where he wasn't welcomed.

Sam was sitting in the middle of the back seat, which allowed him to peer out the front windshield. I looked into the rearview mirror, but could only see his eyes because of the size of his head.

"Do you consider yourself a vicious dog?" I asked him.

"Arrrr," he said.

"That's what I thought."

Peace Haven was a brick structure, all one level with ever-expanding wings and hallways leading out from what appeared to be a central complex. It was larger than I had imagined and quite modern. Some of the places like this around Norfolk were older and longing for a face-lift if not a complete overhaul.

Sam waited in the car while I went inside.

A smiling receptionist in the center of the large hall

greeted me. Her smile seemed to be a permanent fixture on her face.

"Good morning. May I help you?"

Her name tag had the name Holly embossed in black letters with a white background.

"Good morning. I would like to speak with the person who is in charge of the facility."

I tried to sound as if I knew what I was talking about, but so far I was unconvinced.

"That would be Mr. Mitchell."

"Okay, then I would like to speak with Mr. Mitchell."

"He's in a meeting right now."

"I'll wait."

"There are some seats over there," she pointed with an outstretched arm at some uncomfortable looking chairs lined up in front of the windows on the front of the building.

"Mind if I walk around and see what I can see?"

"Not at all. I can buzz the Nurse's Station to see if someone can give you a tour."

"A tour?"

"Yes. You know, show you around, answer some questions, and allow you to see the facility first hand. That way you can decide if this is the place for your loved one."

"I see. Oh, by all means, let's do a tour."

She pushed some numbers on her phone pad and then spoke into what was likely an intercom. A few seconds later an older woman entered the lobby from behind some large double doors typical of hospitals and care facilities. Her name tag said Evelyn.

Evelyn was calm and professional. She smiled, but not more than necessary. She carried a pleasant air with her, purposeful and controlled. Evelyn knew exactly what she was doing, without hesitation.

"Evelyn Scruggs." She offered to shake my hand. I

accepted it. "I will be glad to answer any questions you may have about our facility or about our personnel. We have some of the finest health care professionals in the area. We seek to maintain the highest standards for operating a facility of this magnitude. We take our work seriously here. I think you will see that. If you will follow me," she turned and walked through the large double doors from which she had entered moments ago. I followed her.

After nearly fifteen minutes, I was aware that Peace Haven was indeed an efficiently run health care facility for people who needed assistance as they aged, as well as those who required round-the-clock nursing care. I was surprised by the appearance of the rooms she showed me, the hallways we walked up and down, and the lounges available for the residents.

"Each of our residents meets with a doctor once a month, either their own personal physician or one of our two internists on call here. RN's work four six-hour shifts, rotating every two weeks with LPN's working eight hour shifts on three rotations. Auxiliary staff work the same time schedule as do the LPN's. The office is open every day from 8-6. Doctors are on call and we have an emergency hotline for all residents. We care about these people, Miss Evans, and we do our best to provide whatever mental, emotional, and physical care is needed."

"Costs?" I asked finally when her PR medley was where I could interrupt.

She handed me a slick folder which opened to multiple pamphlets and sheets filling both sides of the folder. A full-color, doctored-photograph of the building covered the front and back of the folder, while a larger-than-life photograph lined the inside of the folder. The inside photo was a group shot of the residents lined up in the garden area I had seen on the tour. They appeared to be happy.

"You'll find the answers to any and all of your questions about costs in that. If you would like to discuss more in detail and fill out an application for someone, then we can walk to my office and I would be happy to provide you with the specifics."

I couldn't imagine that there would be more, but in a system run as efficiently as this, I knew enough about bureaucracies to know she was telling the truth. I figured I had enough data in the folder to provide me with hours of reading material. Besides that, I had Rogers to help me with the research I would soon be starting.

"Not at this time, Evelyn. I appreciate your time and the tour. I will be in touch if my family decides to go this route."

Evelyn peered over the folder she had given me and pulled one of the brochures from the right hand side. She opened it without looking at it, pointed to a section which obviously she had memorized. Ever the salesman.

"This might be helpful for you and your family as you consider the future for your loved-one. Some facts to consider."

She gave me her awarding winning smile.

"Call us if we can assist you."

She offered her hand once more. We shook. She turned and disappeared through the double doors and left me standing in the large reception where it had first met twenty minutes earlier. Me and the folder.

Holly was still on the phone when I passed her on my way out of the building. She grinned and waved. Friends forever.

"I'M RETURNING to Norfolk tomorrow. I need to do some more snooping."

"You just got here. Can't you do more snooping around here?"

"I'm sure I could, but I need to use some of my contacts in the police department and run some computer searches. I'll return in a few days."

"And you learned nothing helpful from that sleazy nursing home?"

"It's not sleazy, and, yes, I did learn some helpful information. It appears to be a clean, efficiently run health care facility. They gave me an application for my loved one."

"Which loved one?"

"I was thinking of my mother."

"Over my dead body."

"That would be too late."

"Precisely. I'll remain right here, thank you, ma'am."

"It's always good to plan ahead."

"I still can use a shotgun, you know."

"I'll try to bear that in mind when I come to retrieve you."

"Bring re-enforcements." She wasn't kidding.

I fixed supper for us, which caused her to be in a better humor. My mother was a terrific cook. She could do it all. I could tell by her pantry and bare refrigerator that she really wasn't into cooking like the old days when I was a kid.

After Sam and I retrieved the necessary foods, spices, and other ingredients for my world renowned pasta primavera crowned with lemon-garlic chicken breast, Mother sat at the kitchen table more than willing to watch me prepare the meal.

"That's a lot of garlic," she offered without my encouragement.

"One teaspoon. You'll survive."

"Did you find anything suspicious at that place?"

"Nursing home place?"

"Yes."

"Not yet."

"So you are suspicious?"

"I'm suspicious of everyone until I find out what happened."

"Don't over-cook the pasta."

"I'm watching." She would make a good guard dog.

"I still cannot believe that you and that doctor found nothing unusual with Aunt Mildred. It wasn't her time."

"And you know this how?"

"I'm psychic."

"Sure you are. When did this power develop?"

"I've always been psychic. I knew your father was in trouble the day he died."

"That's not psychic. That's just being astute regarding the dangers of law officers."

"No, Clancy. I mean I knew that he was going to be killed."

"What are you saying?" She had my attention. This conversation had never come up before. She was talking about my one life-hero, my dad, and I was more than willing to listen.

"I'm saying that I dreamed that he would be killed. That morning I had the strongest sensation of his impending doom, if you please."

"Did you say anything to him about that?"

"Like he would have listened to me?"

"True enough. But did you say anything to him?"

"Yes, but he only smiled and kissed me like usual before he left."

"Why have you waited all these years to tell me this?"

"What good would it have done after the fact?"

"Point taken. And other times in your life, you have had these *feelings*?"

"Yes. I keep them to myself. You won't ever see a sign in front of the house for palm readings."

"I get that. But if it is real, it could be helpful, you know."

"Well, I'm telling you now that Aunt Mildred did not die of natural causes. You can bank on it."

Madam Rachel had spoken the words and now daughter Clancy was bound to prove her right. My mother the psychic. This was going to be interesting no matter what.

I CALLED ROGERS WHILE SAM AND I WERE EN ROUTE TO Norfolk from Clancyville just to give her some lead time in beginning the research into Peace Haven and the six people my mother had on her list of suspicious deaths.

"Good morning, Dearie, nice of you to check in. Are you coming home anytime soon?"

"Headed that way now."

"Good. It's lonely here in the apartment."

"Didn't know computers got lonely."

"I'm not like all the other computers, or haven't you noticed?"

"How could I not?"

"I get lonely without you and the dog."

"Sam."

"I know his name, Sweetheart, but, after all, he is a dog. Am I wrong?"

"Your logic is overwhelming."

"I knew you could see it my way. What's on the table?"

"My mother thinks that six people have died unnaturally

in the last few months and she wants me to check into it. One of them was my Aunt Mildred."

"Give me the data and I'll do your legwork"

I read her the list of names from my mother, including Aunt Mildred.

"And the name of the place where they all died?"

"Peace Haven Nursing and Care Facility."

"In downtown Clancyville or suburban Clancyville?"

"That would be the suburbs."

"I should have some info by the time you and the dog roll in here."

"Like death and taxes."

"Beg your pardon."

"Like death and taxes."

"I don't know that idiom."

"I can count on you like death and taxes. Dependable. Relentless. Always there."

"Some day I might surprise you and not be here."

"Where would you go?"

"I could crash."

"I'd have my memories."

"But I would have the data."

"Ever the romantic."

Sam slept most of the way across Virginia. I stopped a few times for potty breaks and food. Routine stops in light of my almost monthly trips for nearly three decades. I was a regular for two or three spots. A few of them had changed hands through the years. But it was comfortable to see some old faces along the way. Made the trip more enjoyable.

I arrived at my apartment in Norfolk early afternoon. Sam seemed relieved to be home, although it was hard to tell with him. He had been nearly comatose along Highway 58 except for the bathroom and food breaks, and now was searching for a comfortable spot on the couch.

"Found anything yet?"

"Just the raw data. Nothing suspicious," Rogers said.

"Print it out or tell me?"

"Quicker to tell you. Peace Haven is owned by the Sizemore Corporation. They specialize in nursing homes and assisted living facilities. Current count is thirty-three, and growing. They have five new buildings under construction across the eastern U.S. Ernest H. Sizemore, Jr. is the President of the Board of Directors. Ernest H. Sizemore, Sr. is the owner of the whole kit and caboodle."

"Kit and caboodle?"

"I'm studying the idioms. Archaic, but accurate."

"Quite. What's the net worth of the caboodle?"

"Forty-seven million."

"Yikes. Quite a caboodle."

"Quite, as you say."

"Other facts?"

"Squeaky clean so far."

"Keep digging."

"Aye, aye."

"Oh, where are the headquarters for the Sizemore Corporation?"

"Richmond, Virginia."

"Check to see if Ernest, Jr. or Ernest, Sr. have any connections to Clancyville. Those names are foreign to anything I can recall of the county residents."

"Already on that."

8

"Time to move."

"We may have a problem."

"Problems are to be solved. Explain it to me."

"Someone is asking questions about a recent death."

"Not the family, I take it."

"Related."

"Isn't that expected?"

"She also happens to be a private investigator."

"Interesting. Which patient?"

"Mildred Evans."

"The last one."

"Yes. I warned you that she might not be the best candidate at the time."

"I heard your concerns. But I still make the decisions. You just do your job and let me do the thinking. What does she know?"

"Halted the cremation and had a ME from Roanoke check the body."

"Autopsy?"

She nodded affirmatively, and then said, "Results pending."

"They won't find anything."

"I hope not."

"They won't find anything," he said sternly.

"She still could be a problem."

"Not for long. What's her name?"

"Clancy Evans."

"Oh, yes. She grew up in Clancyville. Do you know where she lives now?"

"Norfolk."

"She used to live here as I said. Bill Evans' daughter, the sheriff who was killed years ago. Not important. Don't you have some contacts in Norfolk?"

"Yes."

"We'll keep an eye on her for the time being. Keep me informed if she continues searching. I think we can make her go away."

"I was told she is good at what she does."

"I'm better at what I do. She will not be a problem. Now give me the next name on the list."

"Sarah Jones."

"Give me the details."

"Sarah Jones could be a problem."

"You're thinking again."

"She's connected to the Mildred Evans Keesee family."

"How so?"

"Keesee was a sister-in-law to this detective's mother. Sarah Jones worked for the detective's mother."

"Worked?"

"Maid, house-keeper, cook. Domestic stuff."

"Sarah Jones? She's the African-American?"

"Yes."

"Won't be a problem. It's the South."

"Still, we could skip –"

"Still? What part of me making the decisions do you not get here? You just do the job I ask you to do. Line up the contacts. I'll be in touch soon."

The woman started to leave.

"You worry too much, you know."

She turned and stared for a brief moment. She wanted to say something but thought better of it. Better to leave him boiling slightly than to cause a full-blown eruption. *He thinks he's so damn smart and efficient ... and morally superior. This is a mistake.*

On the way to her car she punched in the numbers on her cell phone and waited.

"Yo?" the voice answered.

"I have a little issue that needs some attention?"

"Got a name?"

"Clancy Evans."

There was a long pause on the other end.

"Is this a difficult job for you?"

"This one will cost you."

"I'll pay you the usual amount."

"Naw. I'll pass on this one."

"What's the problem?"

"The bitch is well connected."

"Give me a figure."

"Double."

"Too steep."

"Then Baby ... get yo-self another boy. Double, or no can do."

"By the end of the week?"

"Done. Wire me half up front."

"That's not our usual deal."

"This one's not usual in any way. You want her gone by week's end, grease some skin."

"Love the poetry," she said with absolutely no feeling in her voice.

"Love the green," he said with great passion.

9

It was something past eight o'clock and I was finishing my second cup of black coffee. Outside the sky was full of rain clouds, but nothing was falling yet. Norfolk weather. Rogers interrupted my early morning contemplation of various subjects.

"Dead end on the Sizemore Corporation. They seem to be squeaky clean."

"Too clean?"

"Maybe."

"Nothing on Ernest Sr. or Jr.?"

"All seems legit."

"Financial stuff?"

"They pay their taxes, their bills, and their employees. Nothing out of line."

"No claims filed against them?"

"Normal stuff, nothing irregular."

"Disgruntled employees?"

"One in Kansas City that was handled out of court. Two in Des Moines and one of those still pending. They seem to take care of those types of issues. No civil suits. No embezzlements. Nothing. Looks like a good place to invest money."

"You have money to invest."

"I'm just sayin'…"

"Help me think of another angle."

"Maybe this is all local."

"In Clancyville?"

"Why not? No criminals there since the 1970's?"

"Good point. But, whoever is doing this is very good at it."

"If anyone is doing anything. You have no real evidence."

"Point."

"Maybe your mother is just being herself. Aging and all that."

"Likely."

My world is quite unusual when I stop to consider that oftentimes a computer informs me of stuff I should already know. Like the condition of my mother. But since Rogers has been doing this for years now, I often take the uniqueness of my world for granted. I treat her more as an adversarial friend than some neatly wired hardware and software combination invented by my eccentric and wealthy uncle. And myself. Joint venture that proved quite successful.

The phone rang and Rogers answered it. Her programmed voice was remarkably similar to mine. When she answers the phone, our voices are nearly impossible to distinguish. My uncle did that on purpose.

"Clancy here," Rogers lied.

The voice on the other end was automatically placed on speaker phone so I could monitor the calls. Anytime I needed to take over a conversation I simply began talking. Usually Rogers would allow me that privilege. Usually.

"Some friendly advice to help you stay healthy," the muffled voice said. "Stop investigating those deaths in Clancyville. Nothing good will come of it. Especially for you."

I started to speak. I was not as quick to the response as Rogers, however. She was in full throttle before I could offer any comeback.

"Who do you think you are, you low life? You will regret the day you called here and threatened me."

"Now, now, Sweetheart, just consider this nothing more than a warning shot across the bow. It simply will not be healthy for you to continue looking into nothing."

"It must be something or you wouldn't be threatening me."

"The advice is free, Sweetheart. You've been warned. That's as much as I can do for you."

"Stop calling me Sweetheart, you scum bag. I'll have you know …."

The click of the receiver on the speaker phone was abrupt. Rogers couldn't finish her rebuttal.

"Some people's kids. Of all the nerve to call here and threaten us," Rogers was about as upset as a computer could get.

"This is a good break," I said.

"Well, I suppose it is."

"Did you get the number?"

"Of course I have the number."

She gave it to me along with the address.

"Shall I call them back?" she asked.

"No. I'll just run over and pay them a visit. Obviously we are onto something."

"Obviously. What are we onto?"

"I have no idea."

10

By the time we found the location of the mysterious caller on the north side of town, the rain was falling at a steady rate. The wind from the ocean was chilly, but not so that Sam and I had to run the heater in the car. I was eating a little package of peanut butter and crackers. Sam was helping me.

I was parked across the street and down, maybe, half a block from the entrance to the apartment building. This was the exciting work of detecting, sitting with a black Lab in a parked car with a steady rain coming down munching on peanut butter crackers. Sam's panting was fogging up the windshield. Must have been the thrill of the hunt for him or his excitement over the peanut butter crackers.

It was almost noon. There was no movement at the house that we could see. At least no one was coming or going by the door we were watching.

"Your fog is spreading to my side of the windshield."

He turned his head to my voice without comment. He was chewing.

"Why can't dogs hold their breath?"

He moved towards me and nudged me with his large nose. Then suddenly he jumped into the back seat, turned around, and rested his oversized head on the back of the front seat, still looking out of the windshield toward the door of the apartment building. Ever vigilant.

"Thank you."

He offered a heavy sigh, almost a snort. Perhaps it was my chit-chat that bothered him the most. It could have been that I was now out of peanut butter crackers and he was still hungry.

Now and then I would turn on the wipers to whisk away the accumulated rainfall. My stomach growled loudly and Sam rolled his eyes toward me.

"Another hour and then we break for lunch. Exhilarating, huh?"

He rolled his eyes back towards the windshield and presumably back towards the apartment entrance. Since Sam didn't talk much, it was hard to know what exactly he concentrated on during these stakeouts with me. We had been doing this kind of thrilling detecting together for a few years now. All in all, he was quite good with surveillance.

It was nearing 1:30 when a man walked out of the door of the apartment building and crossed the street. I took a couple of pictures with my super-duper detective cell phone before he got into a car and drove away. Sam and I followed.

Ten minutes later the suspect pulled into a diner, parked and went inside. Crooks have to eat too. I pulled the car next to his and we waited.

Twenty minutes into our wait, I could see our man coming back towards his car. Sam and I climbed out and moved towards him as if to going into the greasy spoon.

"Food any good here?" I asked. The direct approach. Nothing like meeting one's enemies head on with a 95 pound dog. And growing.

He looked straight at me and then at Sam.

"Yeah. Food's good. The dog ain't welcome inside."

There was apparently no recognition on his part of who I was.

I put Sam back into the car and headed into the diner.

"You new around here?" he asked. This was likely his best pick up line.

"Just passing through," I offered.

"Where you from?"

Oftentimes when I am trailing suspects and they don't know me, my best disguise is nothing more than my usual makeup and some feminine-like blouse. Being a woman is like traveling incognito. He had no idea who I was or that anyone of my gender would be following him. I was tempted to answer his question by saying Clancyville, but I knew the coincidence would be too startling for him and I would lose the edge I presently had.

"Raleigh," I lied. It was only a white lie, as they say, since I had once lived there for a few months.

"Here long?"

"Just food and out."

"Too bad." He got into his car and I walked around the corner to the diner. Sam and I were hungry and I wanted to end the conversation.

While I waited for the sandwiches, I emailed Rogers my photos of the suspect. By the time I had the sandwiches and was back in the car, she had some info related to the pictures. While Sam was chomping away on his cheeseburger, I listened to Rogers give me some particulars.

"His name is Michael Barnok, alias Barney Michaels, alias Mitchell Barnes, alias Bob Mitchell...."

"I get the picture. Go on."

"Rap sheet is long and adventuresome. Petty crimes. Passed some time in juvenal detention. Multiple overnights in the local lockups. Assault charges but nothing that stuck. Seems to be a low-level criminal headed for the big-time, so to speak."

"Connections?"

"Known associations … let's see, nothing that strikes a chord. Wait. Here's a name. I'm scrolling, dearie. Greg Gilroy. Oh, this is sweet. Gregory "Guns" Gilroy. Love those nicknames, don't you? Wonder what that means?"

"Need I draw you a picture?"

"No. I can connect the dots. Probably better than you."

"Address on Guns Gilroy?"

"You'll never guess."

"Our current stakeout."

"Pretty and smart."

"So the question now is, who hired these low-level thugs to threaten me?"

"I think it is more than threaten, sweetie pie."

"Maybe. But at least one of them doesn't even know what I look like."

"How do you know that?"

"I just had a face to face with him. No reaction. Well, he did try to hit on me a little."

"Maybe he was just being cool and careful."

"Some people don't know how to be cool or careful. No, Guns must be the main guy on this mission. That's why Barnok had to go get the food for them. Gopher."

"Super detective does it again."

"Just call me Wonder Woman. We'll see how this plays out."

"Where to next?"

"Sam and I will stay on the stakeout for the time being. I can process while I watch these birds. I'd like to know what their job really is concerning me."

"Anything I can be doing?"

"Yeah. Check to see if you can find any connection between Guns or Barnok and the Sizemore Corporation. Or maybe more directly...Ernest Jr. or Sr. and one of the two boys here. Call me if anything pops up."

"You're always first on my list, Sweets.

11

I MUST HAVE DOZED OFF BECAUSE OF THE SOUND OF TAPPING on my car window awakened me. Sam likewise must have been slumbering since he gulped down his lunch a couple of hours ago and his growling alarm clock never sounded to alert me that someone might be approaching the car. I had returned to my sleuthing posture near the apartment building where Barnok and Gilroy were staying, only this time I parked a block away to avoid running into Barnok again.

The tapping sound was coming from a gun barrel gently rapping my driver's side window. It's hard to act nonchalant when the barrel of a .38 is just inches from your cheek.

I rolled down the window, giving indifference my best shot. The rain had stopped, but the clouds still covered the sky.

"Yo, Baby Sister. Need some assistance?"

"No. I'm fine. Just waiting on my boyfriend to arrive."

"You be waitin' a long time. I spotted you this morning."

"He's driving in from Richmond."

"That so. He live around here?"

"Moving in. Newcomer."

"Well, consider this that old time Welcome Wagon thing. Get out of the car."

I studied the whole scene to see if he was alone. No one else was clearly visible at the moment, so I figured that this must be Guns welcoming me to the neighborhood. Barnok must have told him about me. Perhaps some male braggadocio and heightened embellishment. Just my luck.

"I'll wait here by the car. I don't want to miss him."

"Neighborhood not safe for a white lady. Now get out of the car."

He waved his gun so that I would naturally tremble in fear of the weapon.

"Where we going?" I sounded naïve.

"Look at brochures of the city."

"I should leave my boyfriend a note. He'll be arriving any minute now."

"Not likely, Honey Bunch. Now move. Slowly."

My gun was holstered in the small of my back. It was the best place I had found when I had to carry. Not altogether comfortable, but suitable for me. I got out of the car. My window was still down.

"I need to get my purse, if you don't mind," I said as I opened the back door. I knew that Sam was awake by now with all the talking, but due to his keen awareness of danger he had not shown himself to the man with the gun. Some things are inborn in some animals. The tinted car windows also helped to hide him on the floorboard.

"Here, let me assist you in that purse retrieval," he pushed me back with his non-gun hand and looked into the back seat to find my purse.

Sam lunged for the wrist of his gun hand with lightning speed. Of course, he had the element of surprise which aided considerably. He latched onto the wrist with his teeth and

Mr. Welcome Wagon dropped his gun in the back seat of my car. I drew my .45 and had the barrel against his head before he could even fathom what had just happened. I told Sam to release his wrist.

Sam's reluctance to release his captive was obvious to me. He returned to the back seat and picked up the gun in his mouth.

"Both hands on the trunk of the car," I said and backed away a safe distance from Welcome Wagon while all the time keeping my eyes on him.

"Yo, baby, I'm bleeding here and don't let that pooch slobber all over my weapon."

"You'll probably live. Both hands on the car. Lean over, feet apart. You won't be needing your gun for some time."

The rear window of my car shattered seconds before I heard the sound of the shot. The bullet must have missed my left ear by an inch or so. I was on the other side of the car when the second shot hit the roof of the car to my immediate left. I could see through the car windows on my side that Sam was crouching onto the floorboard once again. Lucky for us the shooter wasn't good at his job. Two shots, two misses.

I opened the backdoor of the car on my side and Sam joined me. Despite the ineptness of the shooter thus far, I feared he might get lucky if Sam stayed inside the car. He emerged from the car with the gun still in the clutches of his teeth. Backup.

Welcome Wagon was nowhere to be seen. My field of vision was limited because of the downward angle of the shooter's line of fire. Unless Mr. Wagon was really stupid, he should have been long gone.

I took the gun from Sam's teeth and wiped off the handle with my blouse.

"Try not to slobber on the guns in the future. Stay here. I'm moving."

I needed to get closer to the shooter if I was to have any chance of discouraging him. I spotted a row of trash cans about 50 yards in front of my car, up from the apartment building, but on the same side of the street as the building. I made a run, still trusting in the shooter's inability to hit anything. I estimated that the shooter was no higher than the second or third floor of the apartment complex. I fired a couple of shots in his general direction while moving towards the cans.

The shooter had time to fire one round at me, the moving target. I reached the cans unscathed. This guy must have failed Rifle Shooting 101 often. But he was dangerous since he had a gun and was firing it. I needed a diversion to cross the street. Sam was my only leverage.

"Go that way, fast," I yelled at Sam, wondering if my plan was way too dangerous for even a poor marksman.

Sam bolted. A second later, I moved quickly to the front door of the apartment building. My plan worked. The shooter had not fired a shot in my direction. In fact, I heard no shot fired at all. Sam was out of sight, so I had no idea where he had stopped running.

I entered the front door and climbed the stairs to my right. The hallway of the second floor was empty. I waited a minute or so for some sign of movement or sound, but there was nothing. I ran up the next flight of steps and cautiously peered into the third floor hallway. I listened while trying to hold my breath. Silence.

I moved from the doorway to the vending machine alcove where I could protect myself and see the remainder of the third floor hallway. No one. Nothing. Silence. I waited a few more seconds because that's what detectives who want to live usually do. Haste makes for dead detectives.

Back behind me, from the front of the building, I heard Sam barking. By the time I had rejoined him outside, he was standing on my side of the street studying a partially empty parking lot. He must have seen something, but he wasn't telling me exactly what it was. I figured that the two guys had bolted, maybe even with a getaway car, and he was pointing that out to me in his typical, silent, canine manner. Always honing my sleuthing skills.

My cell phone rang.

"Go ahead," I answered. It was Rogers.

"So what's happening to that lead?"

"They fired a few rounds at us, tried to kidnap me at gun point, but they escaped without answering in my questions."

"In other words, another normal day for you – two steps forward, one back."

"At least I am rattling somebody's cage."

I WAS SITTING BY THE WINDOW THAT FACES THE ROOF LINE OF the other buildings in my section of Norfolk. The view didn't cost that much. My office is my apartment and vice versa. I was pondering my life's work while consuming my third cup of coffee. It was early, around 7 something. Sam was in Never Land on the couch.

Pondering is good if one has time to do it. My profession often gives me time to do it. I wish it were otherwise, but one does what one can. I was in the midst of my usual conundrum within my pondering when there was a double knock on my front door. Sam raised his head as he looked toward the door. He was waiting on me to get up and answer. I obeyed.

I peeped through the view hole in the middle of the door and was pleased to see my benevolent Uncle Walters standing there in his casual three-piece suit which always looked stylish.

I hurriedly opened the door and hugged him before he had a chance to say hello.

"I should come more often," he offered.

"There's always a hug and a few kisses waiting for you here."

"I shall make a note."

"Come in."

He entered with that Bostonian air that I had come to adore. Not uppity or snobbish. Nor was it rude or egotistical. It was simply the way he carried himself, as though he intuitively knew he was important without being overbearing about it. It was the way I always believed the legendary Sherlock Holmes might have carried himself. It was a touch of class. Sophistication.

His gray-tweed three piece suit was set off by the red rose in his lapel and the scarlet tie pin which stood out against his evergreen tie with the double Windsor knot. He still carried the cane for no apparent reason other than he looked good with it. I suspected that he might have known that.

"Hot on the trail of some desperate criminals, I suppose?"

"Ever vigilant."

"Tell me about it," he laid his cane on the computer table next to Rogers and sat on the end of the couch opposite Sam. Sam raised his head, wagged his tail a time or two, and returned to his sleeping posture for the moment.

I related the events up to that point. He offered his insightful "Hmm" a few times, but made no comments until I finished the little I knew.

"You have obviously stirred someone's pot of soup."

"But whose?"

"Ah, the proverbial question. Do you think the two men you mentioned will come after you again?"

"Probably."

"Well, since you have no other leads, you will likely stay on the pursuit of the two men who tried to, ah, eliminate you."

"My thinking, too."

"And your next move would be to …." he waited for my response.

"Follow the only clues I have."

"If those shooters are smart, they will not return to their apartment."

"They don't strike me as being the brightest bulbs in the chandelier, so my money is on their return to the apartment."

"You have a plan."

"I do."

"May I assist you and give Sam a respite?"

"Actually I think I need brawn and brain for this one."

"I am highly offended. Gray matter often trumps muscle power," Walters said.

"No question. But with two less-than-intelligent low-life criminals trying to shoot me, I'm going for a highly skilled, adept shooter as well as one who uses his brain."

"Ah, that would mean the magna cum laude thug who befriends you from time to time."

"Thug?"

"You must admit he has dubious associates and habits."

"So do I. We've been known to cavort from time to time."

"No doubt, but hardly the same league, my dear."

"He's trained, smart, quick on his feet…."

"And lethal."

"It could be useful. Better them than me."

"What would your father think?"

"'Always protect your backside,' he would tell me."

"It's good to have someone you can trust."

"None better than Rosey."

"Or more dangerous."

AFTER WALTERS AND I HAD FINISHED OUR LUNCH AT THE CAFÉ down by the ocean, he agreed to take Sam on his afternoon jaunt while I made some calls.

One of the calls was to the law firm of Fielder, Young, Lawson, & Associates in D.C. where Roosevelt Washington headed up their Washington Consulting company. It was one of those mysterious internal companies that did no-telling-what for the law firm. Rosey simply said it was mostly investigations. Like I believe that.

Estelle Stevens, the long time receptionist of Washington Consulting, answered my call.

"Washington Consulting. How may I direct your call?"

"Roosevelt Washington, please."

"Clancy Evans. How are you, girl?"

"I'm good, Estelle. Hope the same for you."

"Struggling against the grain. Uphill all the way, girl. You know how it is."

"Some days. Rosey around?"

"Mr. Washington is around but very busy. May I have him

call you?" The tone of her voice changed immediately. She became the consummate receptionist.

"Estelle, this is a life and death call. I need to have you interrupt him, if you would."

"You always have a life and death situation, honey. Don't you ever have normal stuff happenin'?" Estelle, the person once more, was speaking to me. Cute how she flipped flopped.

"Not often."

"Okay, let me buzz him and see what he says." This was another usual answer from her side of the phone. Rosey, to his credit, always answered my calls. Friends.

"Clancy, love. Nice of you to call. Social or business?" Rosey said. It was good to hear his baritone voice once more.

"Alas, business."

"Muscle or mind?"

"Both. I need all of you this time."

"Life and death?"

"Heading that way."

"Local or long distance?"

"Just outside the District," I said.

"That would be … ah… Virginia?"

"Nailed it. For the moment, come to Norfolk."

"When?"

"As soon as you can get here."

"I'll use the Jag and be there late afternoon. Sufficient?"

"You're the best."

"Agreed. What else?"

"I'll fill you in when you arrive. Do bring some fire power."

"Could I have some names to play around with before I depart?"

"Michael Barnok and Guns Gilroy."

"Must be up and coming. No bells are ringing."

"None should. Your radar is set too high. Not much experience, these two. One of them for sure."

"I'll run the names and see what comes. Your apartment?"

"I'll bake a cake."

"I doubt that. Dinner's on me," Rosey said.

WE WERE SITTING in a corner of Louie's Fine Italian Food a little after 5:30. Rosey had convinced me that dining out with Italian cuisine was the best option considering all things. Walters had some obligations, called them, and left just after 5. He did agree to return and check in on Sam while Rosey and I discussed the next move. He and Sam were buddies.

"Okay, here is what I found searching Barnok and Gilroy. First, Barnok is more like an intern with Gilroy than anything else. Maybe a First Lieutenant learning the ropes, so to speak."

"First rate flunky, if you ask me. Slow on the uptake."

"I'll take your word. Gilroy is the dangerous one. It is interesting that he's the one who approached your car and left the flunky to be the shooter. That's probably why you are still alive. All sources say that Gilroy can shoot."

"Lucky for me that Gilroy is no strategist. I live again to fight another day."

"Thanks to some incompetence."

"I'll take what comes."

"You usually do."

We dined on spicy Chicken Parmesan and Ravioli stuffed with zucchini and spinach, aided by an excellent year-old Verdicchio from Northern Italy. Our tradition was usually to split the choices so that we both could enjoy a type of sampler. The Italian bread was to die for.

"I think we should pay a visit to the shooters' apartment

and see what happens," I said while enjoying my second glass of wine.

"Your vision not tainted by all that alcohol?"

"Not enough to miss the target. Always deadly accurate."

"If need be."

"If need be. Prisoners first. Corpses if all else fails."

"Should we not call in some local law?"

"They shot at me first. I have yet to raise my arms against them. I'll give them a second chance to be nice."

"And if their contract does not include that nicety clause?"

"They could be filled with regret."

"Among other things."

14

IT WAS DUSK WHEN WE PARKED TWO BLOCKS FROM THE apartment of our shooters. Rosey decided to take the front entrance while I came through the back. They knew me by sight so Rosey offered to be the face of our approach, allowing me to be the shadowy side.

The plan was to catch them off guard and gain information. Chiefly the info we needed was the name of their employer. My brief sniffing around in Clancyville had obviously shaken someone, but since I had learned nothing improper about any of the deaths as yet, I was puzzled.

What is it they think I know? Or maybe ... what is it they think I might learn if I continue digging?

Rosey had the apartment number from his search of the DMV records. My post was the back entrance of the building which also afforded me an excellent view of the fire escapes along the right side of the apartment. A well-placed tree allowed me to lean in comfort while I waited to see if any action came my way.

Rosey headed into the front door of the apartment building. He was to be the new landlord since our shooters had never seen him. I went around to the back in case our two quasi-professionals didn't buy Rosey's charm and tried to leave the back way.

When I turned the corner at the back door, an old woman with a rusty shopping cart was digging through the dumpster located about seventy-five yards from the entrance. She seemed to have found some discarded treasure but was having trouble freeing it from the confines of the trash. I figured I had a few seconds to aid her cause, so I offered some assistance.

"Get away from here." Miss Grumpy.

"I can help you get that out."

"Don't need no help."

I backed away and watched her pull and tug in vain. It appeared to be some type of dirty, brown garment with which she was doing battle.

I looked at the back door. Nothing was happening.

I turned back to see if the old woman had made any progress on her retrieval. She had a cinder block now and was standing on it so she could gain some leverage with the unwilling garment. It appeared to be a coat.

Nothing at the back door.

"I'll help you, if you let me," I said trying to sound pleasant. It was awkward.

"Stay away from me."

"Look, I don't want the coat. I would just like to help you."

"Why?" She stopped tugging and turned towards me. She was still standing on the cinder block. Before I could answer, she moved her line of sight from me to something behind me. I turned to see Gilroy coming out of the back entrance of the apartment building.

"Stop!" I yelled at him as I drew the gun from my back holster.

He froze. The rifle was in his right hand hanging by his

side. Our eyes engaged. I knew exactly what he was going to do next.

"Don't do it, Guns. Drop your weapon!"

His movement was swift and purposeful. It was a no-win situation for him. As soon as the rifle barrel started to move upward, I fired three rounds dead center into his chest. I never saw him fall. I remember only darkness after I saw the rounds hit the target. And pain.

———

I WOKE up to find Rosey sitting by the bed. It took me a few moments to realize that I was in a hospital room somewhere.

"Norfolk Medical Center?" I said.

"Good guess."

I felt my throbbing head. It was bandaged.

"Flesh wound?"

"Concussion."

"What hit me?"

"Not sure, but we think it was a cinder block."

"Ouch."

"Precisely."

"And Guns Gilroy?"

"Got away, I guess."

"Impossible. I put three rounds dead center into him."

"Yours was the only body lying around when I got there."

"What about the homeless lady with the shopping cart?"

"Never saw her. What was she doing?"

"Trying to get an old coat out of the dumpster without success."

"No such manifestation. I'll look into it."

"Maybe she took Gilroy."

"If she couldn't retrieve a coat from the dumpster, how do

you think she could pick up dead weight and put it in her shopping cart?"

"Point taken."

"And what would a homeless person do with a dead body?"

"Strip it?"

"Perhaps, but maybe do it without lifting the body."

"My head hurts."

"It should. They put twelve stitches into your thick skull."

"Only twelve?"

"It was small split, but noticeable with all the blood on the cement."

"Sounds gory."

"Nasty business you're in, you know."

"And painful."

"Since you're feeling so chipper, I'll go back to the apartment and check out the dumpster. The police will come by later and ask you many questions."

"You called them?"

"Not me. I was upstairs with Barnok when I heard your shots. The patrolman also heard your shots when he just happened to be driving by the building."

"My luck."

"Yeah. He was trying to awaken you when I came out the back door."

"The policeman who happened by?"

"That would be the one."

"They didn't arrest you?"

"Credentials. Who you know sort of thing."

"And my gun?"

"Nowhere to be found."

"Who's coming by?"

"Some fellow named Anderson, Detective Anderson, I think he said to me."

"Oh joy."

"Know him?"

"Too well. Transferred to Norfolk a few years ago from St. Louis. Been a cop for three decades, I think. No one you want to mess with too often."

"Have a lovely conversation. I'll be back with news as soon as I can find some."

"Don't leave me here too long. Oh, where is Barnok?"

"The police have him. I lodged a complaint and apparently he did not have a permit to be carrying a weapon. They also found a rifle in the apartment, so they're holding him for a while."

"Think we can question him?"

"Maybe if you're nice to Detective Anderson."

"I'm in too much pain to be nice."

15

"WHAT WENT WRONG?"

"She called in help. Some guy named Roosevelt Washington."

"And he is...?"

"Works for some law firm in Washington. I couldn't get a line on his function, but apparently he is smart and mean."

"So where are the two idiots you hired?"

"One is dead. The police have the other one."

"Dead?"

"Clancy shot him before our operative was able to help."

"And the body?"

"Our operative has taken care of that. If the police ever find the body, they won't be able to connect the dots."

"They'll know who he is and match him to Clancy's story, or did you not think of that?"

"It'll take weeks to do that. She'll be dead by then."

"You are sure of this because...?"

"Our operative is the best."

"If this ... operative ... is so good, why didn't you hire this operative first?"

"Busy in another city. Came as quickly as possible."

"Apparently not soon enough."

"Disposed of one body. Barnok is just a loose end that will be gone soon enough."

"I want Clancy gone. Is that clear enough for you?"

"She's in the hospital in Norfolk. Head injury. Our operative was almost able to take her out permanently. Except for coincidences."

"There are no such things as coincidences. Remember that. Everything happens for a reason."

"Yes, sir. I guess that means it was meant to be that the two gunmen I hired were not supposed to get the job done."

"No, it does not mean that. What it means is that because you hired two inferiors who mishandled the situation, we now have to wait longer to finish our task here in Clancyville. Your incompetence with choosing the right people to take care of this is the reason it failed. That's what it means."

"My apologies. I thought –"

"Don't apologize. It's a sign of weakness. And you don't think. I will think and plan. You simply carry out what I tell you to do. And do it better than you have thus far. Clear enough?"

"Yessir."

"This operative you hired, where is she from?"

"Los Angeles. I was told that they call her—"

"I don't need a name," he held his hand up to stop her from talking.

"Well, it's not really a name. It's what she's called… referred to, I guess."

"And what is that?"

"Diamond."

"Diamond… hmmm … She had better be as valuable as her name. Results, I want results."

"I'm told she's one of the best."

"We'll see."

MY HEAD WAS HURTING TOO MUCH FOR ME TO SLEEP. THE afternoon sun was blasting into my room and I was occupied with staring at the reflection bouncing off of the silver bars on my hospital bed when there was an intrusive knock on the door. It didn't sound friendly.

"Come in," I groaned out the words. I hated headaches.

"You decent?"

"Close enough."

Detective George Anderson came into my room with minimal enthusiasm. He was short and stocky, built like a Sumo wrestler but without the neat hairdo. His clothes always looked like he dressed in a hurry without benefit of a mirror. They all matched, if you could say that gray and white matched. His disposition fitted his attire.

"So whose business are you poking your noise into this time, Evans?"

"Good afternoon to you, too, Detective Anderson. How's life in the trenches?"

"So where's the dead body?"

"How should I know? I blacked out after I fired three rounds."

"Three? How do you know?"

"Because I can remember firing three shots."

"No evidence of that."

"Okay, then I didn't fire my weapon three times and I killed no one. Is that better for you?"

"A little. I don't have to follow up your cock and bull that way."

"You're a real trip, George. You know that?"

"I have my moments."

"Many of them. So why is it you think I am making all of this up?"

"Damned if I know, Evans. You tell me."

"Two guys were trying to shoot me. I went to their apartment to discuss it with them, and one of them ran out the back door of the building, pointed his rifle at me when I called for him to stop, and that's when I shot him three times. I blacked out and woke up here in this bed. That's all of the story I know at present. When I learn something else, I'll pass it along."

"Where's your gun?"

"Can't say."

"Can't or won't?"

"Pick your verb."

"Don't get smart."

"You don't believe me, so why should I help you?"

"I'm the police here, Clancy. I can jerk your license and you'll be out of work."

"I told you I would let you know what I find out. In the meantime, I have given you all the information I have. You have Barnok. Run the numbers on him."

"We did. Except for a lapsed permit on the gun he was carrying, he's clean."

"Except that he tried to kill me."

"Not very good at his work, is he?"

"Not yet. Can you hold him until I get out of here?"

"No reason to. We're cutting him loose …," he looked at his cheap watch, "… right about now."

"Can you loan me a gun?"

"Yeah, right. Like I would ever do that."

"You're so swell."

Anderson opened the hospital door and walked out without closing it behind him. What a guy.

"Thanks for dropping by. We should do this more often."

He waved with his right hand without looking back. Joe Casual. My enemies were circling. With Barnok released from custody and my gun missing, I felt exposed. The hospital gown didn't help either.

While I was in the midst of formulating my next move, there was a knock on the door to my expensive hospital room.

"They don't lock it," I said.

The door eased open and Uncle Walters entered my chamber of pain and horrors.

"Perhaps you could have used my help after all. Not enough brawn?"

"I was surprised."

"No doubt. Prognosis?"

"Long life despite the cinder block."

"You might want to consult another doctor. Given your profession, a long life is certainly no walk in the park."

"He's young and limited in knowledge of my involvement with crime."

"Tell me about the cinder block."

"Never saw it. I think I was blindsided. Could have been worse."

"Much, I dare say. I came by to see if you were going to live."

"You had doubts?"

"I only had questions. I have never doubted your ability to survive the horrors of evil men and their dastardly deeds."

"Women, too. They can do dastardly things quite well."

"I am sure. I also came by to bid you farewell. I must return to Boston. One of my business ventures has encountered a snag and needs some attention. If you like, I can return in a day or so. I am sure that I can handle said snag forthwith."

"My, my. I envy the pace of your handling. I can't ever recall solving anything forthwith."

"I contacted that dear, sweet lady from across the hallway of your apartment. She said that she would be happy to fed and walk Mr. Sam, your four-legged friend."

"Mrs. Murphy."

"Ah, yes, Mrs. Murphy, of course. You will take care, dear Clancy. There are people who love you." He kissed my forehead and then eased out of the room. "Call if you have need of my assistance."

I found my clothes in the closet, dressed and checked myself out without much hassle. I avoided the nurse's station and used the stairs. Since I had no car keys, I called a cab and headed to my apartment where I felt a little safer.

Sam was sleeping spread eagle on his back when I opened the door. He rolled over, wagged his tail, and then returned to his optimum sleeping position.

"I read the hospital report and listened in on the police scanner. So, tell me, how are you?" Rogers generally stayed ahead of me on current events, except my health condition. There was no streaming CNN news bulletin across the internet for her to read on that. Every other piece of information available was at her disposal. Her unique computer skills, to turn a phrase, were rather daunting, to say the least. I suppose you could also say that Rogers was self-driven and self-motivated. Understated at best.

"I'll live this time," I said.

"And their weapon of choice to conk you?"

"I believe a cinder block was chosen to *conk* me."

"I have no specifications on cinder blocks, but I can check."

"Don't bother. It requires no license to use."

"But very effective."

"My head still hurts."

"But you are alive."

"Timing is everything. I was finally saved by the cops, I suspect."

"The cavalry arrives in the nick of time just like the movies."

"When do you have time to watch movies?"

"When I'm not chasing down dead-ends for you. What else is there?"

"I should have known. Have you dug up anything I can use on the Sizemore Corporation?"

"Nothing that strikes me as useable or definitive."

"Give me what you have."

"It's too much to tell. How about a printout?"

"Print it. I'll make some decent coffee while you work."

"Sounds all too familiar to me."

I ignored her snide remarks, or tried to usually. I wonder if all artificially intelligent computers possess a superiority complex. It might go with the program or the design. Hard to say, but since I knew of no others outside of what I imagined my standup, forthright, and otherwise blameless government might be producing or utilizing, I had nothing to compare Rogers to. I decided long ago just to live with her ego. She was, after all, the best silent research partner a detective could have, idiosyncrasies aside. I say *silent* loosely.

I poured over twenty-plus pages of data on the Sizemore Corporation and picked up only tangential stuff while I consumed four cups of coffee. The most obvious thing was that this corporation was apparently not a front for some other shady businesses. As far as I could tell, they were legit. In fact, their bottom line was quite good over the past five years. With my shrewd detective skills I determined that they were probably not behind whatever it was that was happening at Peace Haven. Whatever that was. Somebody was doing something terribly wrong. I must have gotten close to whatever that wrongness was or else someone with a grudge from my past was gunning for me. Hold that thought.

"I'm going back to Clancyville," I said to Rogers when I finished reading the boring data sheets from the Sizemore Corporation.

"You and the dog?"

"Just Rosey and me."

"Oh. Him. I think he's dangerous."

"Likely. But how do you mean that?"

"Well, anyone that good looking, that intelligent, and that strong has to be dangerous in some sense."

"I'm glad you don't talk to him."

"I'm always tempted. So much to say, so little time to say it."

"Line from a movie?"

"Close proximity," Rogers said.

ROSEY INSISTED ON DRIVING IF HE HAD TO GO. NO PROBLEM
for me since he also insisted on taking the Jag. We were
cruising down Highway 58 going west. It was a warm,
slightly breezy fall day. The colors along the scenic highway
were extraordinary. I looked in the rear view mirror to check
on Sam. It was at that moment I remembered that I had left
him with Rogers. Mrs. Phoebe Murphy, my apartment
neighbor, readily agreed to check on him for his daily rounds
of nourishment and take him for walks. I left him in good
hands. Sam slept too much to get bored, but if perchance that
might happen, Rogers could always be counted upon to
engage him in conversation just to keep him alert. I missed
him. I was pleased that my friend Rosey was with me, but I
missed my dog.

"Anderson didn't tell you not to leave town?"

"Not this time."

"I am sure he suspects you of something irregular."

"I confessed to shooting someone, but he doesn't
believe me."

"No blood, no body. Must be his suspicious nature."

"Do you believe me?"

"Only because you are a woman of impeccable honesty."

"Thank you."

"And you lost your gun."

"What's that got to do with it?"

"You've never lost anything that I can remember. You're very possessive. Especially with your guns."

"They're important in my line of work."

"Mine, too."

"Besides, if they fall into the wrong hands, then I have more work to do."

"But the money keeps rolling in."

"It's not about the money. Besides, no one is paying me for this case."

"I know. Makes me wonder how you will pay my expenses."

"Keep a tab. I'll owe you."

"Like a bar."

"That'll work. You want to know the little I know?"

"All information helps," he said.

I filled Rosey in on what tidbits of nothing I had gleaned from my document reading earlier in the day. It was now mid afternoon and we were trying to arrive in Clancyville for a late supper with my mother. I called ahead to warn her of our arrival. She scared me when she sounded pleased that both of us were coming. My mother's lack of enthusiasm over most issues in life was seldom understated. I honestly believe my mother could look the Grim Reaper in the face and have a chat with him over the mechanics of his life's work. Her coolness under adverse circumstances was legendary in Clancyville.

"I forgot something important," Rosey said somewhere around South Boston.

"No backup fire power?"

"Naw. The trunk is loaded for war. I forgot to tell you that the police found a body."

"My body?"

"No, the other one."

"Barnok? The guy the police questioned and then released?"

"The same."

"What condition?"

"Dead."

"How so?"

"Head shot. From the back. Hands tied behind him. Very clean."

"Where'd they find him?"

"Virginia Beach. Some wooded area off of Highway 44."

"They take no prisoners, huh?"

"And tolerate few mistakes."

"Like missing me?"

"That could be one."

"You know I'm onto something here."

"Why do you think I'm riding along?"

"Batman and Robin."

"Sometimes feels more like Bonnie and Clyde."

"We're not robbing banks."

"But we shoot people."

"Yeah, and that bothers me. Got to be a better way to thwart our adversaries."

"We could use cinder blocks."

"You think that was them?"

"I do."

"Enlighten me."

"Tell me again about the old woman you saw rooting around in the dumpster."

"Not much to tell. She had a shopping cart. She was

standing on the cinder block so she could reach over into the dumpster to retrieve her treasures."

"Can you see her now?"

"I have an image."

"Do you see her shopping cart?"

"Yeah."

"Where is it in relation to her and the dumpster?"

"Between the woman and me."

"What's in the cart?"

"I don't know. Stuff. I think."

"Close your eyes and try to recall. You can see the cart. Is it full or half full or empty?"

I closed my eyes. "It's empty," I said.

"And the woman, what is she wearing?"

"And old coat. Something on her head."

"She's standing on the cinder block, leaning over into the dumpster. Right?"

"Yeah. I'll be a …"

"What?"

"She's wearing black flats. Street people don't wear black flats."

"Perhaps not, but they wear what they can find. Can you see into the dumpster?"

I closed my eyes again in an effort to capture the image of the old woman behind the building leaning into the dumpster trying to retrieve the coat.

"I see that it is partially full."

"Why is she standing on the cinder block? She short?"

"About average, I'd say."

"But not your height."

"No. Shorter. Five feet … six, maybe."

"Is the dumpster on the ground or on some blocks?"

"Ground."

"So the average height of a dumpster is close to five feet, maybe less. And she was average height…"

"She was using the block for leverage, I think."

"Or to hide something from you inside the dumpster, something she could easily retrieve by the added height, thus providing her with a better angle."

"You're thinking a gun?"

"I am."

"Then why did she not shoot me? Why hit me with a cinder block?"

"Maybe she had the gun hidden in the dumpster, and somehow the gun slipped down into the dumpster. If that happened, then she would have to use whatever was available. Things often happen fast as you know. Maybe she ran out of time. Tell me, did you hear the police siren?"

"Guns came out the back door. I yelled for him to stop. He turned and raised his rifle. I shot him three times. Something hit my head and all went black. I woke up in the hospital."

"No siren, huh?"

"I don't remember a siren. How long did it take you to get to the back of the building once you heard the shots?"

"Several minutes. I was in dialogue with Barnok."

"I'll bet that was stimulating."

"You mean besides his mantra of 'I ain't sayin' nutin'?"

"Besides that."

"Somewhere in my interrogation of Barnok I heard the shots. So I dragged him along with me towards the back of the building. It took us a few minutes to get to where you were."

"So you saw nothing once you opened the back door?" I said.

"It took a second or two to survey the back. I saw you and the policeman."

"What was the policeman doing?"

"He was searching your clothing. Looking for identification? Son of a gun."

"What?" I said.

"When he stood up, he had a gun in his hand. I naturally assumed it was his gun."

"Maybe it was."

"His gun was holstered. I can see it now. There was a gun in his hip holster and a gun in his hand."

"So why did Anderson ask me the whereabouts of my gun if the police had it?"

"I'd say the police don't have it."

"The policeman didn't turn it in at the station? Maybe that policeman was not a policeman?"

"What a great sleuth you are."

"Me and Holmes are tight."

"Correct grammar notwithstanding," Rosey said.

"So, if the policeman was not the real thing, and you turned Barnok over to him …" I began making some conclusions.

"Hold on there. I didn't turn Barnok over to that first cop. The second police cruiser arrived with Anderson and another detective, and I turned him over to them. The first policeman left shortly after the two detectives arrived."

"Left with my gun."

"Probably."

"And how do you think the street lady got away so fast?" I said. "Wait, I've got it. She probably hid in the police cruiser of the phony cop. You must've arrived just after she climbed into the car, and the phony cop only had enough time to retrieve my gun, talk to you to make himself look official, and then get outta Dodge."

"There you go, sleuthing again," Rosey said.

"It's what I do."

"Very well, I must say. That is, when you are not made unconscious by cinder blocks."

"I need to call Anderson," I said as I punched in the numbers of his cell phone from memory. "Did you talk with Anderson?" I said while I waited for Anderson to answer his phone.

"He asked questions and I answered them. I was actually more focused on getting rid of Barnok and making sure that you were okay."

"I'm grateful for your ... Detective Anderson," I said interrupting my intended remarks of appreciation to Rosey, "I have something to confess."

"Should I write this down and make it official?" Anderson said.

"No, just listen. The policeman who was first on the scene was not a real cop."

"How would you know that? You were unconscious."

"True. But Rosey and I have been reconstructing the scene behind the apartment building, and a phony cop makes sense of my story to you."

"These are doubting ears, but I'm listening."

"The phony cop arrives, sees the dead man I shot, Guns Gilroy. The cop comes over to me, takes my gun. While he's doing this, the street lady, the one with the shopping cart, hides inside of his cruiser because she hears your siren, and maybe she knows that Rosey is about to appear from inside the building."

"Dramatic."

"I do my best."

"And creative, too."

"Thank you. The details fit."

"To your story. But I'm looking for the truth. I'm not interested in covering up facts."

"And what would I be covering up? I told you already that I shot a man three times."

"Is this all you got?"

"I've told you everything I know."

"Plus a whole lot of stuff you don't."

"But it all fits."

"I'm not into stories. I want facts."

"Okay. Don't believe me. But here's the truth – someone took my gun after I shot a man three times. I was nearly killed in the process of defending myself."

"So you say."

I was not happy with Anderson's attitude toward my conjectures.

"Did you learn anything from Barnok while you still had him in custody?"

"Whataya think?"

"Do you think I killed him after you let him go?"

"That would have been harder to do. You were still in the hospital."

"So you believe me?"

"Some. Just not all."

He clicked off his phone before I could end with tasty sarcasm.

"The man's an imbecile."

"Because he doesn't believe your storyline?"

"That, plus … other things. Give me time, I'll think of something."

"It's a good story."

"You don't believe me either?"

"Of course I do. But then, I'm your friend. I would believe you even if you were lying to me."

18

"JOE PEARSON DIED THIS MORNING," MY MOTHER SAID IN A rather flat tone as we sat around drinking coffee after supper. Besides being a former Navy S.E.A.L., an excellent marksman, tall and handsome, Rosey could cook. He prepared a great vegetable medley that went well with his baked chicken and rice dish. The bottle of Pinot Grigio we bought in Emporia went well with his feast.

"He ran the gas station downtown," I added for Rosey's benefit. "He wasn't very old, was he?"

"Sixty-nine," Rachel said.

"That's fairly young. Bad health?" Rosey inquired.

"Peace Haven," my mother said with a slight attitude.

"Mom, you can't suspect everyone who dies in that facility to be a murder victim."

"It smells funny."

I looked at Rosey for some help in persuading my mother that she was going too far. He raised his eyebrows without saying a word.

"Nothing was wrong with Joe," Mom continued. "He had fallen while hiking during the summer and had checked himself into the facility for some therapy for his injured hip. The man was still young and strong. No reason for him to die like that."

"Mom, people die every day. Kidneys fail. The heart stops. Strokes. It happens. It's a natural part of life."

"It feels wrong. Something is going on there, but you can't find it."

I chose not to tell her that two men tried to kill me. She already had enough issues with which to deal.

"I'm still looking into it."

"And you have found nothing."

"I wouldn't say nothing. I have some leads." I had nothing. I was trying to make her feel better. It wasn't working.

"Well, you might want to check on Sarah Jones while you're in town."

"Sarah's sick?"

"Bad back, bad hip, at any rate, she can't walk. Her family put her in Peace Haven last week. She'll be dead inside of a month."

"Don't you think you're being a little dramatic? Not everyone in Peace Haven is at the threshold of death."

"I don't like sitting around doing nothing while friends are being murdered. Just go see her if you want to see her before she dies."

Despite her theatrics, I knew that something was happening at Peace Haven. The two impotent thugs who had come after me plus the remnants of my cinder block headache were enough evidence for me that I was onto something. That doesn't even count the phony policeman and the shopping cart woman who seemed to be part of the plot. I convinced myself that telling mother all of this would only add to her theatrical performance. It was not where I wanted to go.

After we said goodnight to Mom, Rosey and I walked

around the backyard before going to bed. It was one of my Southern rituals. The night air was chilly, but the friendly confines of the yard made it inviting. I had spent many hours in this yard contemplating the situations of the world. Cheap therapy.

"If you'll go to the funeral home and see Keith or Allen, I'll go back to Peace Haven and see if I can stir up some more animosity towards me. I must have rattled somebody's cage, somewhere. I figure it was at the nursing facility."

"Could be there, or not. Small town. Word gets around. Might be you rattled some coffins."

My mother and I drove over to Peace Haven Nursing and Care Facilities late in the morning. Rosey was checking with the good folks of the Cuthbert-Boran Funeral Home. My mother drove her 1969 Studebaker Hawk. For whatever reason, she bought the car after my dad died in '73 simply because she had wanted one. She used it around town, which explained why a car that old only had 40-some thousand miles on the odometer. Mint condition, too.

"You should take this car out on the highway some," I said.

"Why?"

"I think it would help the engine last longer by driving it at higher speeds occasionally."

"The engine has lasted forty years and counting."

"Point taken. But still, it would be good for the engine to run it at higher speeds."

"Engine is fine. I have it checked every year."

"I'm sure it is. I'm just saying."

"You take care of your car and I'll take care of mine," she said with great emphasis.

We arrived at Peace Haven. Thank heaven for short trips.

"I'll be in Sarah's room while you do whatever it is you do," Rachel said and walked away. Rachel Jo Clancy Evans, longsuffering wife of Bill Evans, Sheriff of Pitt County, Virginia, killed in the line of duty. My adversarial mother. The love of my daddy's life.

Good phrase. *Whatever it is* I do. I ask questions. I talk to people. I look for clues. I look for leads. I get shot at. I get hit over the head with a cinder block. The police think I make up stories about shooting people. I make enemies. I aggravate, irritate, and sometimes obfuscate. I keep coming back for more of the same. Relentless am I. Whatever it takes. Whatever it is. Some job. Could be a personality disorder. Or a profession.

I nosed around for a good while, mostly talking with the nurses. I chatted with the physical therapist. I walked up and down the corridors looking for whatever it was I was looking for. I had no idea. As some famous detectives have said before, you will know it when you see it. I was hoping. Nothing was leaping out at the moment. Maybe I wouldn't know it if I saw it.

After more than an hour of doing whatever it is I do, I could tell that some of the nurses were annoyed by my presence. My effervescence was wearing thin. Perhaps my personality was not as charming as I had imagined. I decided to go check on Sarah and Mother.

Sarah had worked for my family for decades. I had no idea how old she was, but I guessed that she was probably my mother's age, maybe a little older. I grew up with Sarah. She was a fixture in our house. She did practically everything except cook. Not that she couldn't cook, mind you. It was the one thing my mother enjoyed doing most days. Sarah raised me as much as my mother. My dad was around until I was almost twelve. Then he wasn't. Mother and Sarah remained.

"Land a Goshen, child. You look good to these old eyes," Sarah said when I entered her room.

"About time," Mother added.

"Good to see you, Sarah," I hugged her. She was sitting up in the bed with pillows packed in behind her.

I pulled up one of those padded, nursing home chairs which looks comfortable but isn't. Mother was sitting in a straight back chair on the other side of the bed.

"So you are snoopin' around."

"Mostly upsetting the locals."

"Oh, they always need something to gripe about. Way of life for them."

"So how are you?"

"Still kickin', Child. I be around soon enough."

"Doing some therapy?"

"Day after painful day. Improving though. Leastwise that be what they tell me. All I know is that it hurts like hell when I walk," she laughed when she said it. Mother smiled.

We talked on about her family, her grandchildren, and her new great grandson. She asked about my life in Norfolk and my work. It had been a number of years since she had worked for my mother. I had managed to lose track of her for a few years. We passed some time catching up.

"Tell me about Roosevelt," she said after the discussion had waned a bit.

"He works with me on some of my cases."

"I haven't seen that boy in ... well, it's like a lifetime. Could you ask him to come visit me?"

"Sure. I'll do better than that. I'll insist and bring him myself."

She laughed again, one of those deep, alto voice, throaty laughs which seem to resonate throughout a room. It was good for me to hear her laugh again. It was home.

"No, don't do that, Child. He be a man now. Has to make

up his own mind. Just tell him Sarah wants to take a look-see at him one more time. He was such a strapping boy back when he lived here."

"Still is strapping," I offered.

"You and him...," she was fishing.

"Friends. Good friends."

"What kind of work does he do?"

"Well, sometimes after I ask a lot of questions, snoop around and get folks upset, he helps to settle them back down. He has a calming effect on people."

"That's good. Tell him to come by. So tell me about this case you're on."

I told her what I knew, and my mother told her what she suspected. We never worried about alarming Sarah. She was one of those folks who stayed quiet and collected in the midst of any calamity. She was someone whom I would love to be with when the world came to an end. We could drink coffee and chat together all the while the bombs would be bursting around us. Mrs. Cool and Collected. Unflappable.

"Have you talked with any of the cleaning people here?"

"No. Haven't seen many."

"That's because they mostly work at night. Talk with Joy Jones. She'd be the one to know what's what. I think she's in charge of keeping this place clean. She's a good worker. Talk with her."

"She work every night?"

"She pokes her head in the door of my room most every night. Some nights she sits awhile, and we talk more. Come back after 6 and I suspect she be here."

"I'll do that."

"Bring Roosevelt. A lady's got to have some pleasures in life."

19

IT WAS AFTER 6:30 WHEN ROSEY AND I GOT TO SARAH'S ROOM. We parked his Jag at the far end of the parking lot in hopes of hiding our presence from the community. Like a tall white woman with flaming red hair and a tall, handsome black man working together could hide themselves from the prying eyes of a small, Southern town in Virginia. Sure.

I insisted that Rosey enter the room just behind me. I wanted to be able to see Sarah's face when Rosey came in. Her expression changed from mere delight at seeing me again to bright illumination. If anyone could radiate sheer happiness, that woman did the moment she saw Mr. Roosevelt Washington standing next to me.

"My, oh my, oh my. Good lookin', I reckon ... you be the living end, boy."

I would imagine that she might be the only living person Rosey would tolerate calling him *boy*. I had seen some strong men go down who attempted such. I wondered if he were blushing at this point. It was hard to tell.

He smiled at her and they hugged for a long time. Old friends.

We sat and talked for a long while. I decided to wait on Joy Jones to pop her head into Sarah's room rather than go looking for her down all of the corridors. Despite the size of the town, Peace Haven was a large facility and could handle nearly 200 residents.

"So, you are not a lawyer and yet you work for a law firm," Sarah said to Rosey.

"Yes, ma'am. I investigate certain clients and situations for them."

"Like Clancy."

"Well," he smiled and stretched his arms out as if to find a more relaxed position, "sometimes our strategies for investigating are different."

"You use more force. Is that it?"

I laughed to myself at her insight. *Hard to deceive a wise old woman.*

"Some times," he confessed.

"You be careful. Those clients might gang up on you."

"I'll call in Clancy if that happens. She's good to have around, you know."

"Yeah, I know. Always has been one of those people who more often than not say or do the right thing at the right time. Maybe just lucky, you think?"

Rosey looked at me and smiled. "Maybe, but I suspect it be more than luck."

"Sure enough," Sarah admitted. "Sure enough."

The door creaked open and a black woman stuck her head in the room, looked towards Sarah, and smiled.

"Land of Goshen, it's about time you showed your face in here," Sarah said.

"What you think, I got time to waste visiting your lazy bones all day?" Joy said and lumbered over to Sarah and hugged her. Joy was a large, round woman. Her shoes squeaked when she walked. Perhaps it was the weight they were supporting.

"Joy, these are my old friends, Clancy and Roosevelt."

Rosey was standing by this point and nodded towards Joy. I stood, walked over to her, and held out my hand. Instead of taking my hand and shaking it, she grabbed me and gave me a bear hug. I felt the breath begin to leave me.

"Good to meet you, Clancy. And you, Mr. Roosevelt," she nodded towards Rosey.

"Clancy's a detective, Joy."

"You workin' a case or just visiting Sarah here?"

"Both."

"You investigating this place?"

"I'm doing some research, yes." I was surprised with her question.

"About time somebody checked on this place."

"Whataya mean?"

"Full of haints, it is. Been real restless the last few months, too."

"What have you seen?"

"Ain't seen much, Miss Clancy. But I hear plenty."

"Whataya hear?"

"Noises. Bed pans falling to the floor, people walking where they ain't no people, stuff like that. I hear a bed pan rattling around and I go to the room and it be empty. I turn on the lights and look all over that room. Nothing there. Just a strange feeling, that's all. A body could get scared real easy here, if it weren't for Jesus."

"Jesus?"

"I got Jesus with me. Protect me. Ain't worried about no haints. Got a job to do, so I do it. But I don't like all those noises. Makes a body restless, you know. Fidgety like. When it happens, I just calm down, say a prayer or two, and then sing some. The fidgety goes away and I go back to work. That'd be Jesus helping me, Clancy."

"No doubt."

"You clean any other places?" Rosey asked.

"Yessire, I do. Two banks and a grocery store. Keeps a body busy and my head above water. I got a husband on disability, so I has to take care of everything."

"You notice strange noises at the other places?"

She gave him a knowing smile and shook her head no.

"I know where you're going here, Mr. Roosevelt. You think I'm crazy or something. No, sir. Those other buildings are just buildings. No haints there. Just here. Haints roam all over this place. Got a peculiar smell, you know."

"Peculiar smell?" I asked.

"Smell of death. There be good haints and bad ones. This place got the bad ones. They smell of death."

"But you've never seen anything."

"Felt 'em once. I was mopping outside of Room 324 and heard a noise inside the room. It was Mr. Eli's room."

"Eli Rowland?"

"Yes 'em, that'd be the one. Kind old man. Always had a story for me when I would go in and clean. Always friendly. Never in a bad mood, nothing like that. So, I hear this strange noise, like someone kicking or hitting the side of the bed. Done that so many times myself that I know that sound. Anyhow, I investigate. The room was dark and I didn't want to turn the light on to disturb Mr. Eli. So I opens the door wide to let some hallway light get in and maybe see what makes that sound. I took a step inside the room but could see nothing but Mr. Eli lying in bed. Then something pushes me and I fell against the bed and landed on the floor. I heard something behind me and then suddenly the room got dark. Somebody done closed the door. I just knew that I had disturbed Mr. Eli. So I got up expecting to talk with him, but he was still just lying there. Then I smelled it. That be the first time I smelled it. That smell of death. Mr. Eli was dead for all the world. I could have fallen on his bed and it wudda made no difference. Mr. Eli was gone from this world. So then I opened his door, but whoever or whatever it was that shoved me and closed the door was long gone by then."

"Did you report this?" I asked.

"I told the boss lady, but it made no never mind to her. She believes little I say. She say to me, just do your job, do your job. That's none of your business."

"Thank you for telling me."

"You believe me, Miss Clancy?"

"I do. But I think some of the haints here might just be real people doing bad things. Anything happen recently like this?"

"Nobody shove me or nothing, if that's what you mean. But I hear things at night while I'm working."

"Every night?"

"No, ma'am. Haints must take a break now and then. Every few weeks I hear things."

"Anything unusual around the time when Joe Pearson died?"

She looked at me strangely and shook her head. Then she headed towards the door, turned and motioned with her hand for me to follow her.

"Sarah, I'll come back to check on you later, after I be finished. Nice to meet you, Mr. Roosevelt," Joy said. She nodded in Rosey's direction.

We left the room and started down the hallway. She stopped a few feet from Sarah's door.

"I didn't want to talk no more in front of Sarah. All this talk of death might scare her," Joy said.

I nodded.

"You asked about Joe Pearson. Let me show you something." Joy began walking away from Sarah's room again.

"Hold on, Joy. Let me tell Rosey I'm going with you."

I stuck my head back inside the room. "Joy and I are going exploring. You and Sarah can gossip about me for a little now."

"Maybe I can get her to tell me all of your secrets," Rosey said. Sarah smiled.

"Joy wants to show me something. I'll be back."

"Take you time, Child," Sarah said. "I got me a good looking man to talk to. You just take your time. Take your time."

I rejoined Joy and we headed off in the direction of her lead. The facility had a system of built-in night lights which I assumed came on at a certain time when the main fluorescents automatically went off. The halls were lighted sufficiently to see, but they were definitely dim. It offered an eerie atmosphere. No wonder Joy could feel the presence of haints.

I walked alongside of the large, round woman, enjoying the sound of her squeaky shoes. Her cadence of squish-squash was difficult to ignore. I was thinking of some old song that had the beat her shoe cadence provided. She suddenly stopped and whispered to me.

"I want to show you something I found just before Joe Pearson died."

"In his room?"

"No. Outside the door, in the hallway. The night before they found him dead I saw someone leave his room. Nothing unusual about that, except that while I was wiping down the fire hoses nearby, I watched the person walk away and something fell out of his pocket."

"His pocket?"

"Well, Miss Clancy, to tell the truth, it cudda been her.

Hallway was dim. But I saw something fall right out of the pocket of the person leaving that room, jest like it'a jumped out. And it did look like a man to me."

"Why didn't you call the person's attention to it? Might have been something important."

"Rules."

"Rules?"

"No loud talking after the lights change at night. If I yell, they fire me. So I waited to see what it was that they dropped. My job is to leave stuff like that at the main desk."

"So you left this at the main desk?"

"No, ma'am. I kept it. I hid it in my storage closet on that wing."

When we arrived at the storage closet, Joy looked around like she expected someone to be watching us. She unlocked the door and flipped the light switch while I stood waiting for her to reveal her hidden treasure. She reached her hand behind a stack of linens and retrieved a small box. She walked back to me while opening the box. She handed me the opened box.

Inside was an empty wrapper that had once upon a time housed a syringe.

"Could this have been one of the nurses or a doctor you saw leaving the room?"

"Maybe, but not likely. I ain't ever seen a doctor or nurse come in that time of night, unless it be an emergency. Then there's a lot of scurrying around, you know. Lots of activity when they come at night. No, this was somebody else."

"It's not unusual to find a discarded syringe wrapper in a facility like this, Joy."

"True enough. I find them all the time."

"Then why keep this one and hide it?"

"Cause that's not the kind they use here."

20

I PUT THE SYRINGE WRAPPER INSIDE OF THE PLASTIC BAG WHICH I had taken from my mother's kitchen drawer. Preserve the evidence. I took a sip of coffee while I pondered the wrapper. Preserve what might be the evidence.

"I thought my daughter was some big city detective. All you have is a woman telling you about *haints* and a discarded syringe wrapper that the same crazy woman found on the floor," my mother offered as a summation of my investigation so far.

"Look, I've been shot at. I must be rattling somebody's cage," I said it before I meant to say it.

"Well, as many enemies as you have collected through the years, that could have been almost any disgruntled client or someone you have investigated who took exception to your bubbling personality," she said wryly. She handled my inadvertent leak well.

I took another gulp of coffee. Rosey was silent as he drank his coffee. The three of us were sitting around the kitchen table the next morning after the revelations from Joy the night before. Rosey and I were contemplating the dearth of evidence while my mother was critiquing our job performance. She used to help my father in his work as the local sheriff in the same way.

"I expected more from you," she said solemnly.

She always had a way of making me feel so much better.

"Step by step, Mother. We have to take the clues as they come and go where they lead."

"Clues? You call what you have *clues*?"

"Coffee's good," Rosey said.

"I don't make the clues. I don't judge the clues. I find them, or not. That's all"

"I don't know how you ever solve anything if this is all you have to go on."

"This type of work is not for everyone," I mused.

"Ever thought about getting a real job?" she asked.

"This coffee is really good." Rosey got up and poured himself another cup. "Anyone for a refill?" It appeared that Rosey was hoping to stir us in another direction before our current discussion became a crime scene.

"Not for me," mother said. "I'm going to get changed and go buy some groceries. You two gonna stay around for a few days?"

"If it's no trouble," I said.

"No trouble," she offered. "I just have to buy some food for us to eat on." She left the room and I stared at Rosey.

"Winsome as ever," I said.

"She's worried."

"I know. She cares more about Sarah than she would ever admit. My mother does not like to show her caring side. She likes to keep that hard core surface appearance."

"Helps her to ward off the slings and arrows," Rosey said.

"No doubt."

"So where to, Sherlock?"

"Well, we have nothing on the Sizemore Corporation.

Someone hired two goons to eliminate me, or whatever their goal was. One of them is dead and the other one is likely dead, but who knows if and where. There's a cleaning lady who thinks that Peace Haven is haunted and there's the discarded syringe wrapper that is out of place."

"Don't forget the dead bodies."

"Which may or may not be connected."

"Your mother believes they are," he said.

"We have to follow the facts, not my mother's intuition."

"Sometimes intuition is all there is."

"I know and that scares me a little. It's hers, not mine."

"You feel or sense nothing?"

"I sense that something is amuck. The goons coming after me was no coincidence. It's connected. And the wrapper might be connected."

"Since the goons are gone, disappeared, dead, whatever, all we have then is the wrapper."

"And the person who found it."

"So what's next?"

"Follow the clues. You and I will take Joy and check her out. I'll start some checking on that syringe wrapper using Rogers. I have a program that can do some searching on its own while we work on Joy at this end."

"Sounds like a plan."

While Rosey was getting dressed, I called Rogers to have her begin a search on whatever she could find about that syringe wrapper. I also gave her the name of Joy Jones so she could do some background checking.

Before we left the house, Rogers was able to provide me with some general data on Joy which included her home address and some detailed directions on how to get there. Clancyville was small, but even I didn't know every nook and cranny. I certainly didn't know where everyone lived.

We took my mother's car to avoid being conspicuous in

Rosey's Jag. We were warned more than a few times to be careful in her car. The car was more of a concern that the borrowers.

"Pleasant Boulevard is over near Queen's Court. About two city blocks out from the old middle school."

"Across the tracks, right?"

"Always. Across the tracks."

We drove to the center of downtown Clancyville and turned right off of Main Street, crossed the railroad tracks still in use by the frequent trains running north and south, and headed into the black community, so named by the white residents of this Southern town.

"There used to be blacks living on the white side, but I always wondered if any whites actually lived on the black side of the tracks."

"Didn't know of any personally," I said.

"Segregation has always been an interesting concept for me."

"Interesting?"

"Yeah. While I have known of it, felt it, and sometimes tasted it, it has never angered me quite the way bigotry towards people has."

"Both come from the same source."

"True. But segregation on some level is okay, I think. Just not on all levels."

"Which level is okay?"

"Where a body chooses lives."

"Free to choose, right?"

"Absolutely."

"But true segregation will not permit that absolute freedom."

"Spoken like a true Southerner."

"Enlightened and informed Southerner."

"No doubt."

We passed the empty school building and the run-down apartment complex named Queen's Court.

"Her house should be ahead on the left," I said.

Rosey slowed the car as we passed by two or three houses in a row. They were all neatly kept with trimmed yards, small, white picket fences, and fall flowers growing in abundance in beds neatly placed around the house. The house in the middle stood out the most. It had more flowers, more yard furniture, and what appeared to be fresh paint on the house. The shutters were green and appeared to be freshly painted as well. The yard was larger, or so it appeared to us as we drove by. I counted three dogs on the front porch of the middle house, all lazily sleeping and enjoying the fall weather through slumber.

Rosey drove on by the house for another half mile, pulled off onto a dirt road and turned the car around.

"Let's go back and park on the upper end where we can stop and take a longer look at the house," I said.

"And what do you expect to see, Miss Holmes?"

"Whatever there is to see. This is the part of investigating that is so thrilling. You watch and wait and watch and wonder."

"And try to stay awake?"

"That would be the plan."

"And we be waiting for what?"

"We be waiting for something to happen."

"This could take a while."

"You bet. Then again, sometimes I get lucky."

"How so?"

"Somebody shoots at me."

"Our operative take care of Clancy Evans?"

"Not yet, sir."

"Not yet. What does that mean?"

"It means that Clancy got out of the hospital before our operative could act."

"Slow are we?"

"We thought that she would remain there a few days."

"My suggestion is that you tell our operative to get the job done quickly. I just don't want this detective snooping around. She could mess things up. We are more than halfway to the goal."

"This operative is expensive, sir."

"I don't care about the cost. Just make sure the job is done."

"I meant that because this shooter is so expensive, it's different than the other two."

"Different how?"

"I can't contact this operative. Once hired, the contract is out there. The operative will not stop until the contract is completed."

"This operative goes at his own pace then?"

"Yes sir. I can't affect that. And one more thing."

"What?"

"I followed her back here, sir."

"The detective?"

"She came with that man from D.C., Washington."

"I know where D.C. is, you idiot."

"I meant his name, sir. Roosevelt Washington. He's from D.C."

"You told me that already."

"Yes sir. She returned here with Roosevelt Washington. Do you want him taken out as well?"

"What do you think?"

"That will at least double the cost for the operative."

"Do I look like I care about that? Just get it done."

"Yes sir. I need some cash. The operative will require money up front."

"How much?"

"I am guessing it to be ten thousand dollars. That's five for each of them and then the additional ten thousand after the job is done. But I will have to call my contact and then wait for the answer. My contact is the only person I know of who has access to the operative."

The man turned quickly and moved to the wall safe behind his massive oak desk. The room was larger than necessary, and the oversized wooden desk with an adjoining high-back comfortable office chair tried in vain to fill it. There was a singular chair in front of the desk. It was much smaller than the high-backed, leather chair behind the desk. It looked uncomfortable. A tall, thin woman was standing behind the smaller wooden chair placed in front of the desk. She studied the older man as he approached the safe.

He turned the dial on the wall safe back and forth until the sound of the click was evident. He retrieved a stack of bills, counted out the appropriate amount, returned the larger stack to the wall safe, and closed the door to the safe. She noticed that the man limped as he walked to the desk. After opening one of the desk drawers, he retrieved a rubber band and a manila envelope, wrapped the money carefully with the rubber band, placed the money inside the envelope, and then tossed the small package in the direction of the tall, thin woman. The envelope landed on the large desk in front of the woman.

"That should take care of the operative for the moment."

"Yes sir."

"Tell her no mistakes this time. Just get it done."

"I will tell her contact." She turned to leave.

"Is the operative already here?" he said to her back.

"I have no idea," she answered without turning around.

"Do you know anything for sure about this operative?"

"She's the best and she's expensive," the tall woman said as she glanced back at him.

"Is it just about money for her?"

"I don't follow you," she said and turned fully to face him once more.

"That's the problem with the world today."

"What's that, sir?"

"No passion. No one cares. It's just a job."

"I was told she's the best. She must have pride in that, sir. But in her line of work, it is probably best that she not have attachments."

"Get out. Make sure it is done and done quickly."

"Yes sir."

The tall woman turned and left the room, closing the door quietly. She felt his silent rage forming and wanted no part of it.

22

AROUND 3:30 A SCHOOL BUS STOPPED IN FRONT OF THE ROW of three houses and several children exited the bus. They split up and part of them entered the first house and the remainder of them went into the third house. None of them entered the middle house. In a few minutes, the children came out of the houses they entered, and all entered the middle house.

"Grandma's," Rosey said.

"How do you know that?" I said.

"The powers of deductive reasoning."

"But no evidence to prove it."

"Absolutely none, but you know I'm right."

"I do."

After twenty minutes or so, the kids ran out of the middle house followed by Joy Jones, who stood on the porch watching the children with her hands on her hips. I counted seven children. On the side and near the back of Joy's house there was an extensive playground full of brightly colored equipment – yellow slide, red & green swings, blue & purple tunnels, and something orange that appeared to be like a climbing gym. It was all connected and looked like fun, even for me, if I had the time and the inclination. All of the children appeared to be elementary school age.

The rest of the yard that surrounded Joy's home was grass, flowers, shrubs and two or three sets of yard furniture strategically placed among the flower beds and shrubs. The largest space was given to the children and their playground.

Ten to fifteen minutes went by and another group of children joined the seven already playing full throttle. I counted five in this group. The playground was large enough to handle both groups and more. It was like having your own private park.

Half an hour later, Joy emerged from the house with a large tray filled with paper cups and a pitcher of something red. The kids all ran to meet her as she set the tray down on the table closest to the playground equipment. The children all drank the juice, placed the cups back on the tray and returned to their playtime. Joy sat down in a swing and watched them for several minutes. The perfect grandma.

"And what are we ascertaining from this?" Rosey asked.

"*Ascertaining?*"

"I read a lot."

"All those years at UVA."

"I read there, too."

"I'll bet you did. Well, Mr. Cavalier, we're learning that Joy Jones is an outstanding grandmother. She probably has trophies lining the walls of her home."

"Or photos of her children and grandchildren," he said.

"Between the trophies."

"You see anything unusual here?"

"Just one," I said.

"And that would be?"

"No way she can afford that playground stuff and yard furniture on her wages for cleaning buildings."

"The astute observer."

"Sometimes I amaze even myself."

"And this means?"

"I have *ascertained* something important."

"I can't wait."

"We have another clue."

"Hot dog."

By the time we returned to my mother's house, it was close to five o'clock and she had supper waiting. While Rosey washed up for the meal, I called Rogers to see what she had on that syringe wrapper that Joy gave me.

"Joy was correct about that brand not being used by the Peace Haven people. I checked their purchase orders for the last four years and they have bought Becton-Dickinson syringes exclusively."

"Did you learn anything about the brand that Joy gave me?"

"I'm getting to that. Kind a pushy today, are we?"

"Just anxious to get to the bottom of this."

"Or on top of it?"

"One or the other."

"Well, the brand that was found and given to you, made by Lab Express Management or LEM, is sold at Fairbanks Drug Stores. LEM is a new company that began last year. They offer quality and competitive pricing, especially to a company like Becton-Dickinson. The Fairbanks people are a small chain of pharmacies operating exclusively in Virginia and some parts of North Carolina. They have about twenty or so stores."

"Easy to get."

"That would be yes."

"A dead-end."

"Not necessarily. Would you like to know the location of the closest store?"

"Informative?"

"I'd say, oft hand, very."

"Then enlighten me."

"Lynchburg."

"And the next closest store?"

"Let's see, they have stores in Charlottesville, Richmond … actually two stores in Richmond, Fredericksburg, Virginia Beach…"

"Come back this way. Anything close to Lynchburg?"

"The closest, outside of Charlottesville, would be the Harrisonburg and Winchester stores."

"Looks like the convenient place is Lynchburg."

"Might not be a dead-end."

"I like to be helpful."

"You generally are."

"Generally?"

"Okay, you are almost always helpful."

"I would think that should be *always*, with no qualifying modifier."

"I'm allowing for the mouthy part."

"Our bantering sustains me in my dark moods. You know that I'm just pulling your chains."

"Chain. You are *pulling my chain*."

"Dearie, you have several chains. I like to pull them all from time to time."

"No doubt. Oh, I need you to do a financial check on Joy Jones. Be extremely thorough. I think she may have some hidden assets somewhere."

"I'll find them if she has any. Shall I call you?"

I thought for a minute. The creation of Rogers and her unique abilities was my closely guarded secret. Outside of Uncle Walters and me, only Sam and Rogers herself knew about it. As close as I was to Rosey, I chose not to tell him. I was still wondering why.

"Yeah. You can call. I'll treat you like an undercover source."

"Deep Throat."

"Whatever rings your bell."

"Ding." She hung up.

We sat down to eat as soon as Rosey came downstairs. My mother may not be the most winsome person in the world, but she can cook. We had enough food set before us that it appeared we were expecting two more families to show up and dine with us.

My mother sat down and bowed her head. That was the clue for us to stop talking and pray. She blessed the food and then immediately starting passing dishes. While I was a child at home, my daddy always said the blessing except for those times he called on me or my brother Scott. It was a family tradition. Daddy always said that it was important to be thankful.

"You got a call from some guy named Anderson in Norfolk. Said to tell you that they found the body of some thug … his word, named Gilroy," Mother said as she passed me the mashed potatoes.

"He say where?"

"This is not appropriate dinner conversation. You can call him after we finish. He gave me the number." End of that conversation.

23

I WAS TALKING WITH DETECTIVE ANDERSON JUST AFTER DARK. Rosey was helping Mother wash and dry the dishes. They also cleaned up the kitchen. Another feast had ended and we were stuffed. Breathing was not easy.

"A small lake off of Highway 58. One of those pay-if-you-catch-it fishing lakes. Some fisherman hooked the body and thought he'd landed a whale."

"I'll bet. How'd he die?"

"Three rounds to the chest. Almost perfect spacing at the heart. Nice shooting."

"I aim to please."

"More like you aim to kill."

"Superior training."

"Before Quantico?"

"Solid home environment."

"Raised by Wyatt Earp and Annie Oakley?"

"You'd be surprised."

"I'll just bet I would. Oh, we found a business card in one of his pockets."

The muffled shot came through the dining room window

and exploded the phone receiver in my left hand before I could ask Anderson about the business card. The truth is at that moment I forgot about the business card, Anderson, and any conversation we were having. The phone was now rendered useless, my hand was throbbing, and I was hiding behind my Daddy's old roll-top desk, since it was the largest object between me and the window through which the bullet had come. I was sitting on the floor leaning against the desk as I checked myself for any other injuries. Adrenalin sometimes deadens the pain. My quick inventory revealed that only my hand was bleeding, so I figured I had escaped another death shot.

I opened desk drawers in some desperate hope of finding something to wrap around my hand to slow down the blood loss. Bits of flying plastic from the phone must have cut me multiple times when it exploded. The fourth drawer finally yielded some unopened handkerchiefs belonging to my father and I was once again grateful to him. They must have been gifts he had received from Scott or me at Christmas when they were all we could think of or afford. I tore into the unopened box and used three of them before I had the bleeding curtailed.

"You okay?" Rosey called out from somewhere in the kitchen.

"Still breathing."

"What's going on?" my mother yelled at me as if I knew the answer.

"Someone's shooting at us."

"Don't get smart. What have you done now?"

"Just my usual charming self. Asking questions and making people happy."

We sat there in silence for several minutes. Whoever was out there could likely still be out there. Before I thought of turning out the lights, Rosey was already moving stealthily from switch to switch on his side of the house. I followed suit but cautiously. My hand throbbed.

The house was now dark and the shooter had lost some advantage. Despite the darkness, we were not completely invisible because of the street lamps coming in on my corner of the house creating spots of light now and then through the windows. I carefully moved to where Rosey and Mother were now hiding. The three of us were hunched down in the dark hallway with our backs to one of the kitchen walls. The scarcity of light in this section made us feel reasonably safe.

"He's using a silencer," I said.

"Got that part. Exploding phone receivers sometimes give that away when there are no other sounds besides glass windows shattering."

"You have an idea where the shooter is?" I asked Rosey.

"Across the street, directly in line with the kitchen window. He must be in an upstairs window looking directly into that side of the house." His Navy SEAL training was always a plus in just about any situation, but especially one like this.

"That house has been empty for months," my mother added.

"One of us needs to investigate," Rosey said.

"Draw straws?"

"Not this time. Since my tan is darker than yours and my tan lines don't show as much, I get to dance in the darkness and surprise our guest shooter. Besides, your hand injury looks to be noteworthy."

I glanced down at my bandaged hand. The blood had soaked through the three handkerchiefs.

"We need to see if the shooter is still out there as well as provide some diversion for your departure," I said.

"Yes, *we* do." Rosey was already moving toward the front door.

I pushed one of the kitchen chairs into one of the spots lighted by the street lights just beyond the kitchen. The rifle shot was silent once again until it split the chair into several pieces. I turned to tell Rosey to go, but he was already through the door and into the night.

"That chair was an antique," Mother said.

"Better it than me."

My cell phone rang. It was Anderson calling back.

"We got disconnected."

"We did, indeed. Someone is shooting at us."

"Seriously?"

"As serious as it gets. I'm here at home with my mother enjoying the darkness and hoping that the next round misses me a bit further than the first two did."

"Washington with you?"

"You bet. He's on a scouting party now. Should be back any day."

"Call the local police."

"Will when I can. Right now we're trying to stay alive and see who it is after us. Can I call you back?"

"Do that." He hung up and I closed the flip-phone.

"Friend or foe?" Mother asked.

"Detective Anderson of Norfolk Police Department. Not sure yet."

"Do you have an adversarial relationship with everyone?"

"Sam and Rosey like me."

"A dog and a black man."

"Your point?"

Even in the darkness I could tell that my mother was shaking her head in disbelief. I heard her sigh a little.

"They're family. You don't choose them."

"Hardly family, but you did choose them."

"I'll split the difference with you. The dog just showed up, choosing me to live with. Rosey and I met through Mr. Joe, and the rest, as they say, is history."

"They're still not family," my mother insisted. She sighed again, louder this time. It was her way of showing exasperation or frustration or impatience. On this occasion it could be all three.

We waited a long time in silence while Rosey was reconnoitering the house across the street. I could feel my heart beginning to slow down, but the rhythmic thumping was still quite evident. My hand was throbbing noticeably. Sufficient pain.

"Are you scared?" Mother asked.

"Of course I'm scared."

"You certainly don't act it."

"What, should I scream and wring my hands?"

"That would be one indication."

"I hurt my hand and I don't want to move it."

"You and Rosey act so calm, so methodical. How do you do that?" she said.

"I don't know about him, but my mother taught me how to act in a desperate and alarming situation."

"What are you talking about?"

"The day you and Sarah drove to the police station downtown and rescued me from captivity in the jail while brandishing your double barreled shotgun. You certainly couldn't have forgotten that little episode from your life."

"That was different."

"In what way? The man was holding me at gunpoint, the threat of casualties was quite real, and you acted calmly and methodically."

"I did no such thing. I was scared out of my mind. I even let Sarah drive the car. That shows you just how out of control I was. She couldn't drive a car. No license. No training. Nothing! Besides, I was so scared when we arrived at the jail, I tried to shoot through the window and hit the door instead."

"Well, you saved my bacon that day and you acted as if you were in complete control."

"I was in anything but control, honey."

"So maybe the key is to behave like you're in control and fool the people around you."

"Is that what you do?"

"Sometimes."

"But more often than not, you are calm and methodical. Correct?"

"I have to remain calm so I can think. If I can't think, I can't act intentionally."

"Do you ever go on automatic pilot?"

"You mean, like instinct?"

"Yes."

"At some point the instincts take over."

"Why do you think that is?"

"Survival. Life over death."

"Is that what Roosevelt is doing now, acting on instinct?"

"I hope so."

I HEARD THE FRONT DOOR OPEN JUST BEFORE I HEARD ROSEY whisper loudly, "Scout returning."

"The settlers are still hiding in the dark. Find anyone?"

"You hear any shots fired?"

"Okay. Find any traces?"

"Empty casings left behind."

"Intentional, no doubt."

"Business card."

"Think this was a warning?"

"Assassins don't fire shots across the bow."

"Poor marksman."

"Lucky miss."

"I'll take luck barring other outcomes."

"It'll be harder for him now. We know he's out there."

"I doubt if he's worried much. Hit-men usually have large egos."

"Could be his undoing."

"Also could be that he shoots well enough that he won't miss next time."

"Possibility. We'll have to dodge faster."

"Or be luckier."

"You two finished with this idle chit-chat? Someone just fired some rifle shots into my house, almost killed us, demolished two windows, obliterated my telephone, destroyed an antique chair, and scared me witless. All you can do is joke about the next time." It was easy to see that my mother was not pleased with the developments of the evening thus far. "I'm calling the sheriff," she concluded.

"You forgot to mention my hand, Mother. I injured my hand," I held it up for her to see. The bleeding had stopped so it wasn't as dramatic as I would have hoped.

"Yes, of course, sweetie, and your hand. I'll be sure to add your hand to the long list of things I am upset about," she said as she stomped upstairs to use the phone since the downstairs' phone had been decimated by a bullet.

We told and retold our story after the sheriff and his deputy arrived later that evening. My version and Rosey's version were closely related. My mother's version added the hysterical element and color. Her version sounded much more dramatic than I thought it was. The sheriff, Robby Robertson, took copious notes with his small pad and appeared to be intent on catching the would-be assassin and erstwhile antique chair killer. Robby was a good man, but he was no match for this hired assassin. I knew that if I didn't find this shooter soon, he would kill Robby without so much as an afterthought. Like baseball, there were different leagues in the criminal world. Robby was not in this assassin's league. It could be I wasn't either.

It was after midnight before we were all snug in our beds asleep. I assumed that Rosey was asleep. He generally made no sounds during the few nights he and I had worked some case together. Mom was snoring away loud enough for me to hear her from the other end of the upstairs hall through the closed doors. The rhythm of her heavy breathing finally mesmerized me into sleep.

After breakfast, Rosey and I walked across the street to re-check the empty house. Robby and his deputy had done their walk-through the night before and found nothing. Rosey had kept the empty casings and failed to show them to the sheriff. He took one from his pocket.

"I'm guessing this is a bolt-action Remington 770 with a scope and silencer. Nasty weapon."

"That's a guess?"

"Educated guess. Definitely from the Remington 700 family."

"To say the least. I'll have Rogers check it out."

"Like having your own ballistics lab."

"Maybe better."

I called Rogers and described the shell casing, took three or four photos of the casing with my cell phone and sent them along. I also checked on Sam. Sam was providing great company for Rogers. My neighbor, Phoebe Murphy, was vigilant in providing food and water for him. I was confident that he was getting more to eat than if I had been home.

She called me back in less than fifteen minutes to verify that Rosey had *guessed* right on the rifle used by the shooter.

"The Remington Model 770 comes in a variety of calibers, this one happens to be the 30.06 Springfield and is a remarkably accurate weapon."

"You sound like a commercial."

"Just details, my dear. You want more info on the weapon?"

"Sure."

"The magazine holds four rounds. The barrel is twenty-two inches long. The overall length of the rifle is forty-two and one half inches, and it weighs 8.5 lbs."

"Anything else?"

"Of course. It comes with a scope but Remington does not offer a silencer for it. They are either custom made or one would have to special order it from a rifle accessories company."

"I am indebted."

"You remain indebted to me. When are you coming home?"

"We should be returning in a few days."

"That's not an accurate time table. A few could be two, three, four, or even five days."

"True."

"So which is it?"

"I have no idea. We have clues to follow."

"Why can't you come now? Apparently it is safer here than there."

"You base that on solid reasoning? Two guys were shooting at me in Norfolk. As far as we can tell, we have only one shooter here."

"I don't recall the Norfolk two actually shooting at you."

"Oh, how easy they forget. One of them shot at me. And Sam, too. The other one wanted to shoot me."

"Lots of people *want* to shoot you."

"Make my day, Rogers. I know I feel better now."

"Just telling you the truth. That's all."

"Nothing but the truth."

"Speaking of that, the financial portfolio on Joy Jones is quite revealing. She grosses about $3000 a month with her cleaning work. She's full time at Peace Haven but has two or three other buildings she does once a week. But the item that caught my attention was the monthly deposit of $10,000 over the last several months."

"Wow. Regular deposits?"

"Well, if you mean consistent, then yes. They come each

month but never on the same day of the month. However, it is always the same amount of $10,000."

"How many times?"

"Seven."

"Give me the dates."

"What for?"

"I want them."

"I already know what you're thinking."

"Well, in that case, go ahead and tell me."

"Each deposit for the $10,000 comes two days after the date on which someone from Peace Haven Nursing and Care Facility has died."

"Aren't you the cat's meow?"

"I don't know. Is that a new metaphor?"

"Actually an old one. Never mind. Any exceptions to those deposits and those dates of the deaths?"

"Some. There are about three deaths at Peace Haven which do not match any deposit dates for Joy."

"You have names for those?"

"Of course. Phoebe Scruggs, E.Y. Rowland, and Samuel L. Shelton. None of them were on your mother's list."

"Sort of begs the question, doesn't it."

"I'd say so."

"Anything else?"

"Yeah, come home. The dog misses you."

I closed the phone and turned to tell Rosey that I was going back across the street to Mother's house. He was standing close by listening to my phone conversation with Rogers.

"Are you sure that you're talking to a computer?" he asked.

"Pretty sure."

"Sounds more like a personal secretary than a machine."

"Rogers is unique."

"To say the least. Data is voice activated?"

"Something like that."

My MOTHER WAS SITTING in a chair in the hallway. She had moved one of the living room chairs and placed it in that small, confined space.

"What are you doing?" I asked when I saw her position.

"Staying away from the windows. They might think I'm you. I don't want to get shot."

"I see. Well, I think that whoever was shooting can see well enough to know that you are you and I am me."

"There's always guilt by association," she said.

"True enough. Maybe we should move all of the living room chairs into the hallway."

"Don't get smart."

"I need to talk with you about the names you gave me," I said as I pulled up one of the living room chairs close to her chair. Rosey sat down by a window without moving a chair. He enjoyed defying the fates.

"What about them?"

"I have discovered that there have been other deaths this year at Peace Haven. Three more, in fact, than the list you provided me."

"They were not my friends, only acquaintances. Small town, you know."

"So, the only reason for the list you gave me is that they were your friends."

"I have known them forever."

"Long time. Any other association for this group?"

"Whataya mean?"

"Is this group related to one another? Club, church, gang?"

"Cute. They're all in a street gang."

"Seriously. I need to find some connection."

"Not church. Well, Mildred and I were Baptists. But Rowland was a Methodist. Different churches. Let me think… no clubs, except that Sophie, Alice, and Marilyn … and I were all in the Garden Club. Ladies thing, you know."

"Well, I'm looking for anything that connects this group other than your friendship."

"What's wrong with my friendship?"

"I'm not disparaging your friendship with these people. I just don't think someone would be killing them because they were your friends."

"Probably not. I'm not that influential."

We sat in silence for several minutes while my mother pondered the names of her late friends. Rosey appeared to be asleep although I knew he wasn't. He possessed the ability to close his eyes and rest while still being alert to everything around him.

"This is probably not it, but I seem to recall that some of them, no, wait a minute, let me think here … yes, most of them served on a jury back in the seventies."

"Most of them?"

"Okay, they all did, as I now recall. They all served on a jury."

"You remember the particular trial?"

"Of course I remember the trial. It was the most famous trial this little town has ever had."

"Oh, that trial. The J.D. Rowland trial."

"You were just a little girl when that happened."

"I was nine years old."

"You remember it?"

"Only what Daddy told me."

"He shouldn't have told you anything. It was horrible."

"Murder always is."

25

THE COUNTY COURTHOUSE, ALONG WITH THE OFFICIAL records and deeds, was located in the small town of Oxford, which was fifteen miles from Clancyville. The Clerk of Court was an acquaintance of mine named Jayne Nichols. Word on the street was that she ran the office like a well-oiled machine and knew everything about everything related to the official records on file in her office. Rosey and I were sitting in Jayne's office the day after my mother's sudden recollection of our county's famous jury trial.

"You look great Clancy. How've you been?"

"Great. And you?" Small talk never was a forte of mine when it came to former classmates on any level. In fact, small talk was not a forte of mine when it came to anyone, but chiefly with former classmates. If they didn't like me in school, why would they care how I've been now?

"Oh, you know. Billy is fine, but out of work. Got laid off from the plant. Kids are growing and going hither and yon," she said with great exuberance as she adjusted a stack of papers on the left hand side of her desk. She placed them neatly on the right side of her desk.

"Hither and yon," I said with absolutely no exuberance.

"Roosevelt, what are you doing now?"

"Advisory work," he smiled easily at her.

"Wow, that sounds interesting," she smiled back. She moved the same stack of papers from the right side back to the left side. Wow, office work can be exhausting to say nothing of demanding.

It didn't sound too interesting to me, but then I wasn't much into the language of small talk. It sounded ubiquitous. And evasive. Since I knew Rosey, I knew it was both ubiquitous and evasive.

"Jayne, we need some help finding information about a trial that occurred at the end of the 60's. May have carried over into 1970."

"Have a name of the person on trial?" she asked.

"J.D. Rowland."

Jayne was in the middle of moving that same stack of papers back again to the other side of her desk and stopped. "Oh, that trial," she said as she put the papers down in front of her, the middle of the desk. Let it not be said that Jayne didn't stay busy with her job.

"I'm working a case and I need to look at the transcript and whatever notes you have on that trial."

"Big case, huh?"

"Big enough."

"Well, that surely was a famous trial around here, I'm told. I was just a child in those days, you know. I remember my parents talking about it. Most folks thought J.D. was a hero, not a criminal," she stared at Rosey and managed a smile that was pleasant, but not friendly. It was the kind of smile often associated with small talk and Southern politeness. Contrived would be a good word for it.

"Killing two people in cold blood hardly qualifies you for a medal," Rosey said.

"Well, everybody's welcome to their opinion. It's the American way," she said. She typed something into her computer and stared intently at her screen. I wanted to say something smart and sassy, but since I needed Jayne's help, I let it slide. She would never know how fortunate she was.

She wrote down something on a piece of paper and handed it to me.

"This is the number of the trial records. You can go down the hall, last door on the right, and they will help you find that file. You may read it in that room, but the file cannot leave the courthouse. It will likely be a large folder which contains both the official transcript of the trial and any official notes retained by order of the judge who presided."

"Thanks, Jayne." I took the paper from her.

"Hope your investigation goes well."

"Thanks."

"Good to see you again," she said to me as she held out her hand for me to shake it. It must be an election year, the best I could figure. Hers was an elected position. She probably thought I could vote in Pitt County. Neither parting word nor need-your-vote handshake was offered to Rosey, but she did nod in his direction and gave him yet another of the famous Southern smiles that suggested polite, Southern prejudice. Sometimes I simply adored my hometown.

"You feel slighted?" I said as we moved down the hall following Jayne's directions to the historical records' room.

"Not yet. Her hand was clammy. Never did like to shake clammy hands."

"How could you tell?"

"The great paper-shifting act she performed in front of us. Showed a good case of nervousness. Wet palms and nervousness often go together."

"They might go with outdated opinions, too," I said.

"Likely."

We arrived at our destination. The file room was larger than I had imagined. The Oxford Court House was an old building with tall ceilings. Ceiling lights and ceiling fans were juxtaposed around the room, extended from the ceiling by long, round pipes that stopped the fixtures about seven feet from the floor. They were close enough to provide both necessary light and gentle breezes for the space. The walls, where visible, were lined with both black and white photographs of former and current dignitaries of the county and state. Many of them were dearly departed, but I recognized some of the faces in the pictures. Drabness was on full display for all who entered this gray-walled room.

One of the rows of photographs was dedicated to all of the sheriffs of Pitt County. I spotted Daddy's picture immediately. He was the fifth one from the end. He had served the county almost fifteen years by the time he was killed. I scanned the other photos and dates. His was the second longest tenure of all the sheriffs, past and present. Gerald Thornton had the longest, some forty years. Sheriff Thornton was 82 years old when he died in office in 1957. I remember him through the stories my daddy told, almost without end. Bill Evans, my daddy, had been Thornton's deputy since early 1955. My daddy was the Sheriff who arrested J.D. Rowland in 1969.

"You gonna look at pictures all day or read this file," Rosey said, breaking my train of remembrances about my father and his work.

We sat down at a table made of oak that was easily ten feet long and five feet wide. It covered the entire middle of the room. We sat down next to each other and divided the file between us. I began with the typed and bound official-looking manuscript of the court proceedings while Rosey took the disheveled papers and notes that had been crammed into the folder.

It took me only a few minutes to discover the names of the jurors. Rosey was still trying to organize his loose collection of papers.

"Okay, here is the list of those who served on the jury – J.R. Blair, Alice Blayne, Mildred Evans, Robert L. Lionheart, Joe Pearson, Marilyn Pearson, Ernestine Reynolds, Eli Rowland, Ernie Rowland, Rabbi Shelton, Skeeter Shelton, and Sophie Tucker. It appears that we might have our connection. Sophie, Alice, Marilyn, Rabbi, Eli, Mildred and Joe have all died this year."

"Seven down, five to go."

"Not without a fight."

"To arms," Rosey said softly. There were two or three office workers in the file room with us. "No other names?"

"I counted them. There are twelve names here."

"I'm sure. What about the alternates?"

I skimmed several sections of the document I had. The papers were held together by one of those extra large metal binding clips which made reading the pages a bit cumbersome.

"Okay, here we go. They had a pool of twelve alternates. Just in case, I suspect."

"Moment's notice. The trial must go on."

"M.L. Blanks, Dorothy Scruggs, Ben Shelton, Josephine Diggs, Betsy Pierson, E.R. Fitzgerald, Sr., Keith Brown, Sallie Mae Caruthers, Michael W. Sapps, J. Walton Hillsworth," I stopped reading and stared at Rosey.

"That's only ten," he said.

"Two more names on the list."

"You want a drum roll?"

"No need. They're dramatic enough. Sarah Jones and Rachel Jo Evans."

"Sho-nuff."

26

"AND YOU DIDN'T TELL ME BECAUSE...?" I SAID TO MY MOTHER during supper.

"I didn't think it was important. And ...," she paused and took a bite of food.

"And?"

"And I really didn't remember being an alternate. I never served. I was just on call."

"But you had to be a part of the proceedings on some level," I said.

"As I recall, the twelve of us, the alternates, were sort of sequestered."

"Sort of sequestered."

"They put us in a room in the court house with a loud speaker. We could hear the trial. No closed-circuit television in Pitt County in those days. They treated us a little like the real jury, tried to keep us informed and all ...of the goings-on. We were housed at the same motel as the real jury. Couldn't talk about the trial with each other or anyone else either for that matter. We just didn't get to see anything. But, we heard it all."

"Interesting."

"So Sarah was the only one who replaced any of the twelve original jurors?" I asked.

"Well, at some point, I seem to recall, there was one other juror … I can't remember which one … she seemed to be having a problem with the trial … was emotionally upset or something. They almost replaced her, but …well, I have this vague recollection that they didn't. She came around finally. Had some intermissions or something."

"You don't recall her name."

"Too long ago. I must not have known her."

"So, this Robert L. Lionheart died and Sarah replaced him well into the trial." I was recapitulating to see if I could jog any hidden memories for my mother.

"You don't remember Bob Lionheart? He ran the hobby and sports shop downtown. You used to go in there with Bill to buy fishing tackle. He was the old man who always gave you that licorice junk. You came home looking like you had been eating mud pies. Had that black stuff all over your face."

"No memory of that, well, maybe the candy, but not the man."

"Kind old man. Irony was that he had a bad heart. At least that's what I recall. He died of a heart attack. Keeled over in the courtroom. Hey, you know what, I think I have some newspaper clippings about that trial. I forgot all about those."

She left us chewing our supper food and her revelations. We could hear some noises now and then coming from upstairs. By the time Rosey and I were finishing supper, Mom was back with an oversized, cardboard box that had housed some boots long ago. She seemed pleased with herself for having found it.

"Look through this. Maybe you and Rosey can find something helpful for the investigation."

She handed the box to him.

The large box was indeed full of newspaper clippings about the trial. It was arranged in reverse order, the end of the trial and the verdict news was on top. Once he discovered this, Rosey began to go through the clippings, piece by piece, and arrange them in chronological order. That took a few minutes, and from where I was sitting, it appeared to me to be a one-person task. I was preoccupied with my piece of apple pie and didn't want to be disturbed. I don't do any baking in Norfolk, and I hardly ever eat desserts, so this was a real treat for me. Rosey was not a dessert eater at all, and I could tell that his gracious refusal of the pie earlier in the meal was a significant disappointment to my mother. She prided herself on her cooking, and rightly so. I considered asking her for another piece.

"You ought to open a restaurant here in Clancyville."

"A restaurant? What for?" Rachel asked.

"To feed people. What else would you open a restaurant for?"

"I don't know. To make money. To kill yourself."

"Well, it would be hard work," I said.

"You betcha it would be hard work. You've never worked in a restaurant, have you?"

"No."

"Well, let me tell you something, young lady," my mother's demeanor suddenly changed and she became an authority on the rigors of serving the public through the food medium. Rosey was still shuffling through the pile of clippings while we engaged in what sounded like several hundred reasons why my mother would never become a restaurateur.

"If you kept all of this newspaper history of the trial, why is your memory so vague on it?" Rosey asked trying not to sound judgmental.

"I kept it for Sarah. She wanted it. She thought the trial might be historic for the county."

"So why doesn't Sarah have it?" Rosey said.

"No room to store it at her place. She asked me to hold on to it. Said it might be informative one day."

"Talk about predictions coming around," I offered.

"Maybe informative for you two. Personally, I've never read all that stuff. Wouldn't want to. I like to forget evil things."

I finished my first and only piece of pie opting to maintain my girlish figure and joined Rosey in reading through the vast material my mother had saved for Sarah. I took advantage of his reading skills, savoring my last few bites of Mother's apple delight. By the time I had joined him, he had covered the first two weeks of the trial. I read the stack of clippings which he had already finished.

"How did you learn to read so quickly?"

"Can't say."

"Or won't say?"

"I really have no idea. It was simply there. You know, a gift. So, I used it."

"Still do."

"Only when there are copious materials which require reading."

Mother was busy washing the dishes and putting away the leftovers. I offered to help her with the chores at some point, but she told me to keep at it or I would be up all night reading that dreadful stuff. I accepted her refusal since I knew she was correct about the late night for me, chiefly because my speed reading was non-existent.

We stayed at the kitchen table, which provided us with ample space to sort out any clippings which might be particularly informative. That's another way of saying that we were hoping to find some clues. That's what detectives are supposed to be finding, I'm told.

I heard the kitchen clock strike the eleven o'clock hour. I

was beginning to doze off from the excitement of the reading. Rosey was still at it, zipping through articles three times the speed I could muster. No wonder he finished at the top of his class at law school. I was impressed, but I said nothing. Doing my best to hold the male ego in check.

"Here, read this one," he handed me a long clipping. "It's about Lionheart's death and Sarah coming on the jury. I think there's a clue in there."

"A real clue?" I said as I moved to the kitchen sink to retrieve a glass of water.

"Real as they come."

"Why don't you just tell me the clue," I said after gulping down my juice glass full of water.

"Hey, you the detective. Detect."

"I'm sleepy and tired."

I returned to the table bringing another glass full of water with me.

"Everybody got issues."

"Your sensitivity is overwhelming."

"Yeah. Read it and we'll discuss."

It didn't take long for my sleepiness to go away. The article matter-of-factly reported the death of Robert L. Lionheart, but his replacement became a center of attention. Sarah Jones was the first African-American to be a juror in Pitt County. That's not the way the paper reported it. They used the term *black*. Times do change, like words.

"I don't see all the fuss," I said after I finished reading it.

"You be a modern woman. You don't understand the trials of a black person."

"What I don't understand is the reticence of white people to accept people of all races."

"You nothing but a white, liberal Commi," he said.

"True, but I do have a hard time understanding my Southern culture."

"That be my Southern culture as well. So what did you learn from your reading?" Rosey asked.

"Well, in short, some of the folks didn't think it appropriate for a black woman to be a juror for a white person who was accused of murdering a white girl and a black man. One idiot they quoted said it wasn't proper. Hell, what's not proper?"

I could feel myself getting angry.

"You lack the finer sensitivities of the white man's point of view regarding the aboriginal black man."

"What?"

"We not be intelligent enough to make decisions regarding a person's guilt or innocence," Rosey said.

"So what does that have to do with proper or improper?"

"The fineries of Southern culture."

"The fineries," I said.

"Yes, ma'am. Those fineries extend."

"Extend to what?"

"Wrong question. They extend to where? That be the question."

"So what be the answer?" I asked.

"Everywhere. Some things are right, some are wrong. You don't cross the lines of the Southern culture without ramifications or consequences."

"You're saying that pulling Sarah out of the jury pool and putting her in as an active member of the jury was crossing lines?"

"You betcha mama it was. Some places, still is," he said.

"Is this a clue?"

He raised his right hand, formed a gun with his fingers, and then aimed it directly at my head and fired his hand gun by lowering his thumb.

"Bang," he said.

27

I WAS SITTING ON THE FRONT PORCH ENJOYING MY COFFEE AND the clear, cloudless, early morning sunrise when Rosey joined me with his cup. The box of clippings was too massive for us to finish last night, especially after all that reading from the trial proceedings during our visit to the Clancyville Court House earlier in the day, so we decided to postpone our clue-finding for another time. It arrived too soon for me.

"Morning, sunshine," Rosey said.

"Me or the actual orb itself?"

"You, of course."

"Good morning."

"Besides reading, what's on the agenda?"

"How long can you be away from your work in D.C.?" I asked.

"This be my work, precious. Wait for the bill you'll likely get."

"Same scale as last time?"

"You didn't pay anything last time."

"My point."

"No doubt the same scale."

"Let's finish the newspaper clippings and then visit Sarah at Peace Haven."

"Why don't I finish the clippings and you visit Sarah to save some time?" he asked.

"Sounds like a plan. I will expect an accurate digestion of all the salient points you glean from your close reading of those fascinating newspaper accounts."

"Salient points be my specialty. I survived Harvard Law, remember?"

"Which is why I expect so much of you."

My mother arrived with a coffee pot just in time to refill my empty cup. Rosey gulped down his last few ounces for her to refill his.

"You two up for pancakes or waffles this morning?" she asked.

"Waffles," Rosey said before I could swallow my coffee and answer.

"Sounds good," I said.

"I'll get started," she said and left.

"Curious about what you said last night...in regards to crossing Southern cultural lines. Explain to me, Mr. Harvard, why Sarah's addition to that jury was such a cultural faux pas. The whole trial was about a serious breach of Southern culture to my way of thinking."

"You close, Miss Boston U., but listen while I 'splain. Point of view. From the killer's point of view, he righted a terrible wrong. A black man dating a white girl here in South in the 1970's, that be so wrong nobody disagree except you screaming liberals. So, the crusader has righted the wrong, and likely the jury, their point of view now, although aghast at his actions, will not give him the death penalty. They want to crown him hero or something. That mean they be looking for ways to keep him alive in the state of Virginia. Everything looks good until Sarah Jones joins the team. Now for the third point of view – the community …they know that the equation has shifted. The Southern way of life has been dented once again, if not downright attacked. A black woman is now sitting on a jury against a white man. Heaven help us all."

"You should have been a lawyer."

"I am a lawyer."

"You just don't practice."

"What you think I be doing here with you on this fine, frosty fall morning?"

"Helping me find a serial killer."

"And practicing my courtroom banter."

"That, too. So, Perry, your theory is that from our serial killer's point of view, he is righting a terrible wrong because the jury found him guilty of first degree murder instead of … say, manslaughter."

"Yessim."

"And you believe that Sarah Jones contributed mightily to this verdict?"

"I do, either directly, or simply because of her presence. Either way, I believe she caused the other jurors to have a conscience."

"So why not kill Sarah first?"

"Good question. Opportunity could be the answer. Had what he thought was a fool-proof method of killing jury members. Didn't want to color outside the lines. I suspect our killer is very patient. Methodical, too. Look how long he waited to begin killing them."

"If we're correct with our diagnosis."

"That sound like doctor talk. I like *theory* better. Theory of the crime," Rosey suggested.

"So our *theory* is that our killer, our serial killer, is a crusader and seeking to correct a terrible wrong here in the Southland."

"It's a working theory."

"And you will be diligently seeking what in your newspaper account reading?"

"Somebody hollerin' louder than all the other folks."

I woofed down some waffles and left soon afterward to get Sarah's first hand account of the famous trial. It was good to have a working motive even though it could prove to be wrong. All things being equal, which they seldom are, it could be that a jury member was actually the killer. Rosey was already busy reading the pile of clippings when I left the house. Eight months worth of newspaper articles on a trial that was center stage would be daunting reading for anyone. I think he gave me the easier task.

When I arrived at Peace Haven, there was an ambulance at the back entrance where the ambulances usually parked, next to the double doors. The lights on the county vehicle were flashing.

I stopped at the nurse's station to see what was happening.

"We had a patient die sometime last night or early this morning. Are you family?"

"I don't know. Who died?"

"Ernestine Reynolds."

"Which room?"

"Oh, you can't go down there. We're waiting on a doctor to arrive. No one can go in the room, except family," she said trying to be emphatic.

"Wouldn't think of it," I said.

I walked down to Sarah's room. Joy Jones was in Sarah's room when I entered.

"Good morning, ladies," I said.

"Mornin'," said Joy.

"Hey, girl. How you doin'?" Sarah seemed bright and happy.

"I'm fine. Hope you are," I said.

"Better and stronger each day. May go home soon."

"That'd be good," I said to Sarah, then turned to Joy, "You're working late this morning."

"Oh, I had to stop by and visit with my friend Sarah. Just checkin' in on her to see if she needed anything."

"So you worked the night?"

"Yes'im."

"You see all the commotion earlier?"

"Yeah. Miss Reynolds passed away during the night. I think a nurse found her early this morning."

"Oh, poor Ernestine," Sarah said.

"Yeah, she was a sweetie," Joy added.

"She been sick long?"

"Not what you call sick. Just weak and feeble. She used her wheelchair to go everywhere in this building. She'd sit outside and smoke. Smoked like a chimney, as the sayin' is," Sarah said.

Joy nodded her head in agreement.

"Long as I been workin' here, Miss Reynolds would be somewhere in the halls or outside or in the dining area, or sitting pretty-like at the front entrance. She hardly ever stayed in the room, except to sleep. Friendly person. And she did love to smoke," Joy related.

"Know her room number?" I asked.

"412," Joy said.

"Which direction?"

"4 means the South Wing and room 12 in that wing," Joy offered. "Go back to that central nurses' station and make a hard right. You'll find it."

"Thanks."

"They're waitin' on a doctor. Probably won't let you in the room now. Has to have a doctor … you know, pronounce them dead."

"I'll use my charm. Gets 'em every time."

28

I was standing outside of Room 412 waiting on the doctor, pretending to mind my own business and failing miserably. I phoned Rosey to update him.

"That be two on your watch," he said.

"Juror number eight from the trial."

"Theory holding water."

"But no one believes us. My true-blue friend, the local sheriff, one Robby Robertson, doesn't think our conspiracy theory has any merit."

"As in old people die in nursing homes daily," Rosey said.

"You nailed it. He told me that there was no reason to check into it, that my mother was simply being overly dramatic."

"Your mother?"

"Dear old Mom."

"Rachel Jo Evans, being dramatic," he said with emphasis.

"Proves he doesn't know my mother," I said.

"Credibility gap or they're all complicit."

"All?"

"The whole town."

"Yikes. Let's go with our credibility."

"What you mean *our*, white woman?"

"Cute."

"I have a notion," Rosey said.

"Let me hear your notion."

"From the pages of the detective books, crime novels, and how-to-solve-'em manuals, I recall a time-proven technique."

"I'm listening, Boston Blackie."

"Hey, watch those racial slurs."

"No slur, Kingfish. Real name of a detective."

"Long ago and far away."

"Very. Early television."

"B.R.W.?"

"BRW?" I said in confusion.

"Before Roosevelt Washington."

"Yeah. B.C.E. as well. But I read a lot."

"Me, too. But I just read the hard stuff."

"So, tell me the technique of your notion."

"Follow the money."

"We're doing that with the computer."

"Phase two – follow the person who got the money."

"I thought we did that," I said.

"We do it again. Till something breaks."

"Your notion, you follow. Her shift is over and she should be leaving any minute now."

"And you?"

"Me and corpse number eight are just waiting on the doctor."

As soon as he clicked off, a middle aged woman in a white coat appeared in front of me. She was wearing a white badge with dark blue letters that informed me she was Dr. Harriett Burchette. Her entourage consisted of two nurses with name tags and a young black man who had no name tag, but appeared to be muscular.

"I'm sorry for your loss," she said to me very sympathetically.

"Thank you," I said, trying to sound earnest.

"You must be her daughter. I'm Dr. Harriett Burchette. You'll need to wait here just a little longer. I'll call you when I'm finished. You want to see her, correct?"

Except for the fact that a woman had died, I was actually enjoying this. I love the assumptions people oftentimes make. So far I had not lied to gain access to the room and body. I was simply playing along with Dr. Burchette's postulation.

"I do."

"It won't take long."

"Thank you," I said and stepped back from the door allowing the doctor and her entourage to enter the room.

I decided early in my gumshoe career that if people want to make erroneous suppositions which aid my investigations, then I can let them without qualms. Of course, there is always the piper to pay when they find out that you have deceived them. It's never pretty. But it usually speeds up things for me and my routine.

While I waited to examine the body of the lady whom the doctor thought was my mother, I reviewed what little I knew about this case. Under my careful watch as a super sleuth, there had been two more deaths. Eight people had died all told, and they were all connected to that trial in 1970. I had some suspicions about Joy, but nothing solid. If it wasn't for someone trying to kill me, I would really be groping for facts to prove that I was on to something. The local police didn't suspect anything sinister going on, and neither did the people of Peace Haven. I surmised that Chicken Little must have felt this way.

I could feel my phone vibrating. It was Rosey calling.

"Why aren't you busy reading?" I said.

"Finished."

"And nothing to do?"

"Waiting on orders."

"Let me call you back," I said as I watched the room door open and Dr. Burchette emerge with her little group. She addressed me in somber tones and acted concerned.

"Would you like to be alone for a few minutes?" She was still using her sympathetic voice. How kind of her.

"Thank you," I said.

"We'll be out here if you need anything," she said.

I entered the room and gently closed the door behind me. I knew my ruse would endure only so long. I worked quickly.

I checked the room for anything that might be a clue. The floor was spotless. The closet had only a few items of clothing. There were some toiletries on the sink. The small chest of drawers next to the bed had some more personal items. Nothing looked out of place.

I found what I was looking for on the moveable swivel table that had been pushed back into a corner away from the body. Next to the cup of water and straw there was the card which read, "God bless you" on the first line. The second line was more to the point – "It is appointed once for man to die, and then comes judgment." I put the card in my pocket.

I checked poor Ernestine Reynolds for needle marks in the usual secret spots that many drug addicts use to hide their habits. Just under the bend of her left big toe I found a red spot. There was a drop of blood that had clotted. It looked like a botched entry point. I photographed it with my hand-dandy phone. If only Sherlock Holmes had had one of these. But he solved ninety-nine percent of his cases without one, so I doubt if it would have helped him to improve his technique. I also noticed that she had had regular shots in both arms. In her case, if you are going to kill her with an injection of something, you might as well use the regular route to hide your devious work. It would be much like hiding something in the open. Last place you would suspect.

I uncovered her face to see if I remembered her when I lived in Clancyville long ago. Her face seemed kind and generous. I could imagine that as a young woman Ernestine would have been quite attractive. She was still handsome in my opinion. She certainly didn't appear to be old. Even though her face was vaguely familiar to me, I had no definitive memory of her.

As I pulled the covers back over her head of Ernestine Reynolds, the door opened and the doctor entered, followed by her ever-present followers.

"Have you had enough time?" she asked.

I nodded without speaking, trying to hold back my contrived emotion.

"We have to call the funeral home. Do you have a preference?"

Before I could answer, there was a knock on the opened door. A young man was standing by the entrance.

"My name is Jack Reynolds. I think that's my mother… here," he hesitated and then pointed to the body under the sheet on the bed.

I moved swiftly through the open door and pretended to be crying as I passed Jack Reynolds. I hurried down the hallway. The last thing I heard the young man say was, "I don't have a sister."

I had enough time to disappear and return to Sarah's room without being seen or apprehended.

I eased open the door and found Sarah snoring silently. Joy had gone. I called Rosey and updated him on my findings.

"Joy Jones just left after her night shift work. Think you can tail her just to see what there is to see?"

"Wild bear live in the woods?"

"Buster, in my line of work, I find wild bears just about everywhere."

"You're not supposed to reason through my metaphorical humor," he said.

"Call me when you get something."

I left Peace Haven immediately, not wanting to be caught by Dr. Burchette or her entourage in case they were now searching the facility for the imposter. I had another clue to add to my growing file; but, like the other ones, it was nothing more than a loose end that led me only to believe what I already suspected. Somebody was getting away with murder right under my nose.

My phone vibrated in the ashtray of my car's console as I was arriving at Mother's house.

"She didn't go home," he said.

"Where did she go?"

"Don't know. Haven't arrived yet."

"In hot pursuit?"

"You betcha. We're really out in the country this time. Old Highway 29 going north."

"Let me know when you arrive."

"If I can. You know how sporadic cell phone service can be. By the way, she drives an old Mercedes. Something from the 1970's," Rosey said.

"And this means?"

"She got good taste."

29

Rogers was not happy when she learned that we were not returning to Norfolk today. She seldom used subtle ways to display her frustration with me. I figured that Sam was handling this disappointing news in stride. He was likely asleep on the sofa.

"You're needed here," she said emphatically.

"More so here."

"I need you here."

"This coming from a self-reliant, independent and technologically advanced machine?"

"I am not as self-reliant as you believe."

"What's Sam doing?"

"Whataya think he's doing? And don't change the subject."

"Yes ma'am. Look, we'll be back in another day or so. But for the moment, there's been another murder and I need to stay."

"You working on clues or hunches?"

"Sometimes they're the same thing."

"With you. Many detectives, I have read recently, actually have solid clues to work from."

"I am not part of the many. I work with what I have. Speaking of which, what do you have for me by way of *clues*?"

"Alas, I have nothing," Rogers confessed.

"Empty as a pocket, huh?"

"Metaphorically speaking, you could say that. Actually I have quite a lot of data that could be processed if only you would provide me the correct parameters."

"I'm sure you do. My bad. I'll get back to you when something further develops. In the meantime, remain vigilant."

"Give me something to go on."

"Okay. Let's see… how about checking into Joy Jones' prior employments."

"How far back?"

"Start back around 1970."

"I'm on it."

I thought I could hear her network gearing up before she turned off the phone line. The world would likely be more transparent if everyone owned a computer like Rogers. But on second thought, if the villains of the world had something like her, then my work would be even harder. Her secret was worth preserving.

When I entered the house, my mother was nowhere to be seen or heard. I took a walk to clear my mind, not that it was overly cluttered with an abundance of clues to run down. I did need to rethink what little I knew and what I might delve into next. I think this is what other super sleuths refer to as making a plan. I never took much stock into making plans. Most cases I have ever worked led me along and I merely did what came naturally for me. I nose around and ask questions. I rattle a few cages. I disturb the equilibrium. I make a nuisance of myself. I touch a lot of nerves. Generally my style of aggravating people is sufficient for uncovering the truth. If I agitate folks long enough, they usually do something stupid just to get me off of their backs.

I missed Sam. I now wished I had brought him along this trip. His presence had a way of helping me think through the stuff that clouded my mind. The two of us would often debate the finer points. I talked and he listened. Best male listener I have ever known.

There was a warm breeze blowing at my back and the fall colors were still coming along. Nothing extravagant as yet, but they soon would be. Clancyville had some great, old maple trees mixed in with some ancient oaks, which created a picturesque landscape along most streets. Some memories from my girlhood never diminished.

I thought of Sarah as I walked along. Occasionally she and I would walk the streets of Clancyville whenever my mother would have one of her famous tirades over something my brother Scott or I had done. Sarah would say something like, "Let's walk, Miss Clancy. Time to skedaddle." We would rush out of the house and down the street before my mother ever knew we had gone. By the time we returned, she was in control of her faculties and no longer seeking blood vengeance. Sarah had done this often enough that the memory was burned into my databank. She had no doubt rescued me from my mother's invectives, or at least salvaged the top layer of skin that covered me.

Now I had the daunting task of keeping Sarah safe from whoever was trying to eliminate the jurors from that infamous trial long ago. Eight people were dead. All were former jurors in that trial. Two of them were killed right under my nose. I could as yet prove nothing. I was still waiting on the toxicology report from Mildred's demise. They were dying too fast for modern science.

I turned down another street, not really thinking where I was going. Just walking and pondering the little I knew. I had a woman who was somehow connected, but I had no hard evidence to suspect her of anything specific. Yet, she had lots of money pouring into her bank account around the time of each of the suspected murders. Lots and lots of money, as far as she was concerned. I had a syringe wrapper that this same woman had discovered and given to me. Why would she do that if she were involved? Throw me off the scent? Is she that smart? And I had one of those ubiquitous cards often left by ministers or other church people when they visit folks in nursing homes. Somehow this one seemed different. The message on the card was not soothing to my way of thinking. It had to be a clue. I wanted it desperately to be a clue.

On the surface, I had nothing. Nothing solid, just a lot of circumstances. Circumstances that were only loose ends. I could feel that it all connected, but I could not make the connections as yet. And I had the fact that someone was trying to kill me. Whoever was behind this had sent out some goons to eliminate me unsuccessfully. Then, had sent out, perhaps, someone with a little more skill and stealth, to finish what the goons could not do. Perhaps this second killer was indeed a professional. The rifle of his choice pointed in that direction. I was lucky to be alive. Cinder blocks and cartridge shells were adding up. I had the suspicion that I was getting closer to whoever was behind all this, all the while some assassin was getting close to me. The most frustrating thing of all was that I had nothing that I could put my hands on to prove anything.

Sam, where are you? What would you tell me to do next? Where would we go? I need your direction. I need your nose. I need your uncanny ability to stumble onto the next thing. I feel like I am sitting at a dead end sign after coming down this long road.

The cell phone interrupted my wishful thinking.

"Whataya got?" I said. It was Rosey checking in.

"Mansion in the countryside. Appears to be a rather large estate type place. White fence around a few hundred acres, stuff like that."

"Her first stop."

"Her only stop, so far. She drove up to the house and then walked around towards the back. I followed her with my trusty private-eye binoculars as far as I could see her."

"Still inside?"

"As far as I know. I have to assume she went inside, unless she met with someone on the back porch or in the yard under a shade tree. I'll snoop around to see what I can see."

"Veranda, "I said.

"Beg your pardon."

"If it's an estate, they would not refer to it as a back porch. My mother has a back porch. If the house you are viewing is a mansion, then it's a veranda."

"Sorry 'bout that. I be ignorant of white folks and yo culture. I calls it like I sees it."

"Just updating that Harvard and UVA education."

"I 'preciate the schoolin', ma'am."

"No other news?"

"Nothing. I'll just wait here and see what happens next."

"Who owns this estate?"

"No name on the box. Let me see …. 5-4-9-7 is the number."

"You still on Old Hwy. 29?"

"No, we turned off of that and are on White Horse Lane. That would be 5497 White Horse Lane."

"Be careful snooping," I said.

"You're talkin' to a trained S.E.A.L., lady."

"Yeah, like I said, be careful there buddy. I'll check that address for ownership. Might be helpful."

"You don't mean another clue, do you?"

"One can hope."

30

THE EIGHT TALL WINDOWS SHOULD HAVE ALLOWED THE ROOM ample light, but the darkness was ever present since there was no benefit from the unlit massive chandelier. It could have been the sad, heavy gray, wormy chestnut walls which thwarted the light each day. There were also a few thousand books lining the shelves which fought against whatever light entered from the outside. In addition to the three, dark cherry tables established around the room, there was an excessive cherry desk in the center. When he sat in the black leather, high-back chair at his immense desk, his back was to the tall windows and his face was toward the center door that led to the hallway. Another door, to his right, led to the gun room. The third door, to his left, permitted passage to the master bedroom suite when it wasn't locked from the other side.

He sat in his high-back chair without benefit of the chandelier's light. He was staring out one of the many windows, nursing his pain and anger. He was stroking the back of one of the two Pekinese dogs sitting in his lap. One was asleep. The other was enjoying the attention she believed necessary for her well being. Despite the attention he was giving to the contented dog, the man in the black leather chair was lost in his own self-imposed trance. His insatiable dream of vengeance was close to completion; satisfaction would soon arrive along with its related companion, exhilaration. He contemplated sweet revenge. Once upon a time he actually thought that joy might return to his world, but not now. Perhaps it was too much anger over too many years. Maybe it was simply nothing more than that miscarriage-of-justice conviction that roamed the corridors of his mind. For whatever reason, joy had long since passed from all possibilities. Revenge was his only true companion during the long, dark nights and the intolerable, dull days, and they were intimate.

There was a knock on the door to the hallway. The sleeping dog was roused. The one being stroked made no movement at the sound from behind her.

"Yes?" he said without turning his swivel chair to face the sound.

The door opened. It was Marie, his housekeeper, maid, and nurse. She took one small step moving just inside the threshold. She spoke softly as if afraid at interrupting him.

"Miss Saunders is here."

"Show her in."

A tallish, thin woman slid easily through the doorway past the maid. The woman was wearing a dull gray suit with low, black heels. Her starched, white blouse stood out from the gray suit and the heavy gray walls of the room. Her salt and pepper hair leaned heavily towards the pepper side. The stern expression on her face seemed to be permanently fixed.

When the maid closed the door behind her, she stopped about ten feet from the desk. There was an awkward distance between them.

"I want you to stop the hit," he said. He slowly swiveled his chair around to face the thin woman.

"I don't believe I can," she answered hesitantly knowing that it never was fruitful to deny him any request.

"Why not?"

"It's a contract."

"Void the contract."

"It doesn't work that way. It goes until the job is done."

"Call her and tell her to stop."

"I can't."

"Why not?"

"I have no way of calling her."

"You set up the contract. Why can't you stop it?"

"I contacted her through a mutual acquaintance in Chicago. The number given me to call initially is no longer valid. Throw away cell phone. It's the way she does business."

"Do you know what she looks like?"

"No."

"You could follow Evans and hope to spot her."

"I'd have to have a death-wish, sir. No one tries to follow an assassin. I am told no one talks to them, no one contacts them … they are ghosts, if you please. She could be anyone. I have no idea who she is."

"This is absurd. There has to be a way to stop her."

"You have changed your mind about Evans?"

"Temporarily. I want some time to pass. She's getting close, too close. I don't think she realizes just how close she is. I want to back off for a while. That's all."

"But if you back off, will that not allow Evans more time and opportunity to discover your identity?"

"Are you questioning me?"

"No, sir. Just posing a possibility. Evans is smart."

"But not smarter than me."

"No, sir. Perhaps we could turn her attention elsewhere."

"What do you mean?"

"We could create a distraction. Something that has

nothing to do with what we are actually doing. A diversion. We could draw her attention away from Peace Haven and create some additional work for her."

"You have an idea?"

"I do."

"Let me hear it."

It was dusk and Rosey was strolling along the streets of Clancyville with me. Mother had fixed another delicious meal for us and we both could feel the weight gain.

"Do we know yet who owns the property on White Horse Lane?" Rosey said.

"A retired minister named Robert Lee Rowland."

"That's quite a spread for the reverend."

"So you say."

"So I say. Yes, ma'am. We're talkin' serious money to buy such a place. How do you suppose the reverend came by all of that?"

"Playing the market?"

"Could be. No law against preachers owning stock. So what's his connection with Joy Jones?"

"Mother thinks that Joy worked for Reverend Rowland once upon a time."

"Old friends?"

"I have the computer doing some research on Joy Jones' employment, but we might need to check out any specific connection between those two."

We walked along a couple of blocks without talking. The street was quiet. Some leaves were rustling because of the slight breeze tonight. It was peaceful and calm. This was the way I remembered Clancyville.

"Question, super sleuth," Rosey said. "By your theory there are four jurors left on this hit list. One of them is Sarah Jones."

"Correct."

"Is Sarah the only one of the four remaining living in Peace Haven?"

"Good question. No. One other lives there, J.R. Blair."

"And we have no idea the order the killer has selected for the victims."

"Or if there is an order."

"Or if our theory holds water."

"It has so far."

"True enough. But more to the point, is the killer waiting until each of the old jurors ends up in Peace Haven and then kills them? Leaving a lot to chance, don't you think?"

"I hadn't thought of that. What are you thinking?"

"Why Peace Haven? Why not just kill each one of them somewhere else?"

"In other words, what is the connection with the jurors and Peace Haven?"

"Super sleuth does it again."

"And this is important because?"

"If the killer wants to actually kill these people, after all these years, he seems to be leaving a lot to chance by waiting until they arrive at Peace Haven. In the world of possibilities, some of them may not make it to Peace Haven, or could possibly go elsewhere to live out their days. In other words, there seems to be too much stock in Peace Haven to make sense here."

"I'm impressed with Harvard reasoning."

"You shouldn't be. We should have considered this."

"True. But we've been busy with some murders and dodging bullets."

"I think we checked our brains at the door, though. I feel stupid, like we've missed something significant in all this."

"What do you think we missed?"

"I'm thinking that there is a vital connection between the killer and Peace Haven."

"You going psychological on me here?"

"Maybe. But if the shoe fits...,"

"Okay. Where to next, Rosey my man?"

"You be the detective. I jus cum up with idears."

"But this is your theory. So you need to create some strategy."

"I need time to think."

"Good. I'm returning to Norfolk tomorrow to get Sam. He can help us think."

"The dog."

"Only Sam I know right now. Besides, this will give you some alone time. You can start thinking while I am away. And ..." I paused to construct my next idea.

"And what?" he said.

"Two jurors in Peace Haven and two elsewhere. I think we need to stay close to both of the ones in Peace Haven for now. If you keep an eye on J.R. Blair, I will ask my mother to stay with Sarah. At least we can prevent any unnatural demise for those two. If your psychological angle holds sway, then the two jurors not currently living at Peace Haven are quite safe for the moment."

"I'll begin tonight. Take no chances."

"Agreed. It may take some convincing, but my mother is a good watchdog."

"I would approach her from a different angle."

"No doubt. One more thing. I need to borrow your car."

"The dog don't ride in no Jag."

"Wouldn't think of it. I'll leave your car in Norfolk and return in mine."

"I be grateful. Likewise the car be grateful, too."

I WAS WRONG ABOUT MY MOTHER. SHE READILY AGREED TO stay with Sarah. I did have to convince her that she could not carry a shotgun with her into Sarah's room at Peace Haven.

"I see no reason why I shouldn't have something to protect myself from this killer," Rachel said.

"No, Mother. The people who run the place would certainly take exception to a gun-totin' mama sitting in the corner with a shotgun draped across her lap."

"I wouldn't sit in the corner."

"Well, that solves the problem immediately."

"I don't need your sarcasm. You want my help or not?"

"I need your help. But you can't carry a weapon with you."

"Not even a handgun?"

"I thought you hated handguns."

"This is an emergency," she said.

"Truly. But I think it's a bad idea for you to have any type of weapon in that place."

"You have a weapon."

"I have a license and I have training."

"You don't think I can fire a gun?"

Our conversation was going in the wrong direction quickly.

"You are more than capable of shooting a gun. That's not the point here. The administration of Peace Haven would call the police if you had a gun with you. The police would come and arrest you, and then I would have no one to keep an eye on Sarah. It would defeat our purpose."

"Oh. I hadn't thought about that. But what if something happens? What if someone comes in during the night? How do I protect Sarah as well as myself?"

"If you see them, scream, throw a bed pan. Noise is your best ally. They certainly won't hang around if you are awake and making noises. Remember, they don't kill with a gun. These have all been cloak and dagger murders, all on the QT, hush-hush. They use a syringe."

"I get the picture. I'll do it."

"Thanks, mom. Rosey will be in another wing of the facility with J.R. Blair."

"I never did like that old man, but I don't want to see someone kill him. If he'd just die a natural death…"

"Mother! That's a horrible thing to say."

"Well, it's true. He's an old coot. Nobody likes him."

"But he doesn't deserve to die just because he's unpopular."

"He's a mean man with mean dogs and he hated children. Don't you remember all the times he would sic his dogs on you and Scotty? They almost got you two more than once."

"He wasn't the kindest man in town, but we had fun going through his yard and trying to avoid the dogs."

"So you and Scotty actually provoked him?"

"That might be too strong a word. Teased would come closer to reality."

"Whatever. Here I thought you two were innocent all these years."

"Mother, I am sure that you have used many words to describe your two children through the years. *Innocent* would not be one of the words you could use with a straight face."

HALFWAY across the state of Virginia I called home to let Rogers know I was coming in late. I got a busy signal for each of the three times I punched in the numbers. This was unusual in that Rogers had the phone system set up so that multiple calls could come in simultaneously. I waited thirty minutes then called again. Same result.

I then called Phoebe my down-the-hall neighbor who knew everything about everything that was going in a nine block radius of our apartment complex. If something was happening, she would know about it. She was also supposed to be feeding Sam each day.

No answer.

Whatever was happening, it couldn't be good. I speeded up in an effort to get to Norfolk a little quicker. Highway 58 had a few speed traps along the way, but I decided to chance it since this could be something serious.

I was passing through Franklin when my phone rang.

"You need to get home quick," Rogers said.

"I'm en route now. What's going on?"

"Someone has taken the dog."

"Say again."

"Someone broke into the apartment, two of them, a man and a woman. They used that dog catcher apparatus – a pole thing and a round hook-like head restraint – and took Sam."

"Anything else?"

"Nothing else."

"They took my dog and left everything else?"

"That's what I said."

"Are you sober?"

"Of course I am sober."

"This makes no sense."

"I don't make up your life, you know. This has just happened. If you could consider all of the things that happen to you, and all of the things you get yourself involved in, then I surmise that this makes perfect sense. In your world."

"Did you record anything?"

"Does a wild bear live in the woods?"

"You've been listening to Rosey too much."

"I pay attention to all conversations. Of course I recorded it. I activated the keyboard scanning device that your precious Uncle Walters created as well as the internal camera. The stupid thieves actually looked into my monitor so that I got marvelous photos of their mugs. And... I am pulling up records on them right this moment. Let's see, the male thug is named Jack Russell. The woman is Marilyn Saunders. Either name ring a bell for you?"

"Nope. You got anything else on them?"

"I'm running the prints of the woman. She actually tried to use my keyboard. Can you imagine that?"

"I am aghast. The nerve of some people when they break and enter." I smiled when I recalled the silly argument I had with Uncle Walters when he insisted on installing the scanning device within each key on Roger's keyboard so that she could activate it if anyone ever broke into my apartment and tried to retrieve information from the computer. I thought was ludicrous that such a thing would happen, and even more so that someone might want any data I had collected. Silly me.

"Do I detect some sarcasm in your voice?"

"Mild humor," I said.

"This is no laughing matter. They took your dog."

"Yeah, I got that. Can you play the recording for me?"

"Is the Pope Catholic? Of course I can play the recording for you. Here, listen to this:

>   *"...no, you go that way,"* the woman's voice said.
>   Sam was growling in the background.
>   *"Bring the hook closer,"* the woman spoke again.
>   *"Ah....gottcha, you mangy mutt,"* the male voice said.
>   Sam was growling louder now.
>   *"You take him out to the truck and I'll leave the note on the computer," the* woman said.

"That's the whole conversation," Rogers said. "Except for the clicking on the keyboard. That's when I shut down her access and she couldn't type and use the monitor. I was still recording, but she just couldn't access anything. Oh, it was awful. I can't stand for some strange person to touch my keys."

"Miss Sensitivity," I said. "Anything on the prints yet?"

"No…yeah, here it is. Russell has a record, but nothing serious. He lives here in Norfolk. Oceanfront Boulevard. That's 2428 Oceanfront Boulevard. I think it's an old apartment complex."

"I'll check it out. And the woman?"

"Well, surprise, surprise. Her residence is 921 Leftwich Street, Clancyville, Virginia. Imagine that?"

"Imagine that."

33

I CALLED ROSEY TO UPDATE HIM ON THE SAM KIDNAPPING.

"It's a diversion, you know. Throw you off the scent or distract you."

"It won't work."

"It might. Depends on what they do or threaten to do."

I was sitting at the computer watching the tape of the woman once more. I had the sound turned down while I spoke with Rosey.

"They left no note. Nothing. If it's a kidnapping, why not leave a note?"

"Maybe they'll call and provide you with instructions."

"Okay. So, I'll sit tight for a while. In the meantime, I want you to do something devious."

"My middle name."

"In the morning, find Joy before her shift ends. Around 7 or so. She usually stops in Sarah's room to check on her. Since we suspect her of something, not sure what, let's use her in case she actually is working with the killers in some capacity. She could be the inside person who is helping them.

Let's be real tricky here. Let's ask her to stay with J.R. and you go check out the house on Leftwich Street. See what you can find out about this Marilyn Saunders person. Anything will help at this point."

"Isn't using Joy to watch J.R. like asking the fox to guard the hen house?"

"Yeah, but if she is the inside person, I doubt if she would do anything while she has the responsibility of keeping an eye on a patient. She's certainly smart enough to realize that."

"You're assuming that she will agree to help us with J.R.," Rosey said.

"I think she will. If we are correct about her involvement, then she would want to get us off her trail, and this would be a good way to make us think she is not the one."

"And is that what we are going to be thinking?"

"Unlikely."

"So, we be out-foxing the fox, so to speak."

"You have a way with words. See what you can find at the Saunders' house."

"Aha. This be excitin'. We has another clue."

"And which clue would that be?"

"A woman who lives in Clancyville is involved in dog-napping Sam in Norfolk," Rosey said.

"Racking up those clues, are we? How come we're no closer to solving this crime?"

"We be slow and thorough."

"You got that right. I'd vote for fast and sloppy at this juncture."

"No, ma'am. Fast and sloppy too often means careless. No place for careless in this business. You get careless, you get shot. Sometimes you get dead. Remember the cinder block."

"It made an impression. I'm not changing tactics. I just want some results."

"Me, too. I'll check out the house. You keep checking on what you have at that end. Let me know if you need me."

I folded the phone and put it back in my pocket. I turned the sound up on Rogers at the moment the picture of Marilyn Saunders disappeared from the screen in front of me. I could hear some rustling of papers, like someone was searching for something. Then I heard what sounded like someone writing.

"I think she wrote something when you closed off the computer to her. What do you make of that last segment? Play it again."

She did.

"It is definitely the sound of someone writing," Rogers said.

"So where's the note?" I said as I looked around the apartment.

I felt stupid when I spotted it finally. It was thumb tacked to the back of the door to my apartment. I read it without touching it:

WE HAVE THE DOG. IF YOU WANT THE DOG BACK ALIVE, STAY IN NORFOLK. DO NOT RETURN TO CLANCYVILLE. IF YOU FAIL TO OBEY THESE INSTRUCTIONS, THE DOG DIES. THERE WILL BE NO SECOND CHANCE ON THIS. STAY IN NORFOLK OR THE DOG DIES.

I retrieved a hand towel from the kitchen and took the note down, trying to preserve any prints she might have left. Since I already knew who she was, it was of little help in the long run, I thought, but just in case I had missed something, I decided to do it the right way. I put the paper in a gallon size plastic bag and sealed it. Crime Solver 101.

"Read me the note," Rogers said. "I want to hear the whole thing."

I read the note. She took a long time before saying anything.

"You okay?" I asked.

"I was just wondering if there is any way you could arm me."

"Arm you?"

"Yes. You know. Get Uncle Walters to rig up some type of apparatus whereby I could fire a bullet or throw a knife and protect myself. And the dog."

"And be headed towards a life of crime, no doubt."

"Be serious. I'm no criminal."

"And there's no way I'm even addressing what you are suggesting. You'd probably shoot me instead of some thief."

"Not intentionally."

"That's my point. No, I am not arming you with anything other than the surveillance equipment you already possess. Besides, you already have provided me with enough information that the police can arrest these two with ease."

"If I had a gun, I could have stopped them from taking Sam."

"You and my mother. You did enough. Believe me. I am grateful for the data I have on this. I'll find Sam. You're not worried, are you?"

"Computers do not worry. We are above such emotions. I merely suggest to you that there are certain inherent weaknesses in my current system. I was only advising an upgrade of sorts."

"I'll get back to you on that. In the meantime, call Detective Anderson for me, use my voice, and ask him to meet me over on Oceanfront Boulevard. I'm heading that way now. If he has any objections or possible delays, call me so I can stay informed. Oh, see if you can find out where this Jack Russell guy has worked. It could be helpful."

"On it. Oh, you might want to reconsider arresting Saunders and Russell," Rogers said.

"And why is that?"

"I am thinking that dog-napping is a misdemeanor. There'd be a lot of paperwork, but in the end they would get out with a slap on the wrist. The B&E would add some weight, especially for Russell who has a rap sheet. But in the end, you have accomplished nothing and they got what they wanted."

"And what did they want? Sam?"

"Unlikely. They merely wanted to distract you. A diversion."

"You're the second person who has suggested this."

"I'm flattered," Rogers said.

"Why are you flattered?"

"You referred to me as a person. Made my day."

"Slip of the tongue."

I found the old apartment complex on Oceanfront Boulevard and located the number. I parked in front of an apartment three doors down and watched number 2428 to see if anyone was coming or going. All was quiet until my passenger door opened and Anderson sat down in the front seat.

"I don't do burglaries anymore," he said.

"You need more flexibility in your work ethic."

"Homicide provides sufficient flexibility. People can be quite creative with murder these days. So what's happening here?" Anderson said.

"What you see is what you get."

"That bad, huh? So, who is it we're watching?" he asked.

"Male. Jack Russell. Know him?"

"No," he shook his head. "From Norfolk?"

"Yeah. Short record. Must be a newcomer to the criminal world."

"And you know this how?"

"I'm a detective. I know things."

"Sometimes you know too much. I would ask you as to how you gain access to police data."

"Sources."

"If I find a source that is feeding you from my department, I'll have his head."

"Your support is encouraging."

"How long you been here?"

"Twenty minutes."

"You got a plan?"

"Don't need a plan. Using my technique."

"And that would be?"

"Sit and wait."

"How long?"

"Until something happens."

"What if something doesn't happen?"

"I sit and wait a little longer, and then go home. Sometimes I spend the night in my car. Just sitting and waiting."

"You need a life."

"Tell me about it."

"We could force the issue."

"You mean storm the Bastille?" I said.

"It's a plan."

"He's got my dog."

"Means a lot to you, doesn't he?"

"The dog, yes. The thief, not so much."

"I meant the dog. So, we just sit here and enjoy the ambience of your car and each other's aura?"

"We could discuss sports."

"You know sports?"

"I can tell the difference between baseball and football."

"Impressive. Tell me your thinking on this Russell guy," Anderson said.

"Well, if Sam is inside there, then Mr. Jack Russell will have to bring him outside sooner or later, or clean up whatever mess is made. Most folks don't like cleaning up. So, he has to come out."

"If the dog is inside there."

"That would be the *if*."

THE DOOR OPENED AND JACK RUSSELL WALKED OUT, GOT IN his car, and backed out of his parking space.

"You up to some hot pursuit?" I asked Anderson as I started the engine.

"Let's boogie," he said.

I've done my share of tailings through the years. Most of them offered a challenge just driving through regular traffic. Once they made you, the game was afoot and did, in fact, become much more difficult. Ten minutes into our hot pursuit I had the feeling that Jack Russell knew we were tailing him. Point of fact, Jack Russell was leading us around.

"He knows we're back here," I finally said to Anderson.

"Yeah. Since we left his apartment."

"You're good at this."

"Years of practice. Notice how he keeps us in his rear view mirror. Stops at all the caution lights so as not to lose us. Drives the speed limit. Nobody does that unless a patrolman is following you and you're trying not to get pulled over. It's too perfect."

"Maybe he's been to the defensive driving school," I said.

"Let's eliminate the Primrose Path. Smells like a trap, or he's just stalling."

"You have a plan?"

"Start over."

"When in doubt."

"Take me back to my car. I go do some real police work; you go home and make some coffee."

"That your whole plan?"

"Every detail."

"So, Russell now thinks he has won."

"Probably. Sooner or later he will make a mistake."

"In the meantime?"

"Enjoy the coffee."

"Is this the way you do hardened criminals?"

"No. I don't always have the luxury of time. I got folks at the top pushing me for results. You're a freelance type. You got no one pushing."

"I got me. I just don't push me that hard. Could be a character flaw. But I live with it."

"If the dog's worth it."

"He's worth it."

I dropped off Anderson at his car and returned to my apartment.

"Where's Sam?" Rogers asked.

"No idea."

"You gave up too easily."

"Not yet. Working on Plan B."

"What happened to Plan A?"

"Russell knew we were tailing him. Anderson and I both had the feeling that he wanted us to follow him."

"In other words, you think that Russell was leading you into a trap."

"Maybe. I don't know if he's that smart."

"You think he has the dog?"

"Can't say. Maybe he does, or maybe what's her name has him."

"Marilyn Saunders," Rogers said.

"Yeah. Her."

I was sitting on the couch in the spot where Sam usually enjoyed his daily siesta. I was on my third cup of coffee when the phone rang.

"Put it on the speaker phone," I said to Rogers. "You answer it and I'll do the talking."

It rang two more times before Rogers answered it. After I heard a loud click, I said, "Clancy here."

"Any leads on Sam?" Rosey's voice was clear.

"Nope. But I did find the note."

"Ransom?"

"Not really. Just threatened me to stay away from Clancyville or else."

"I get the picture. You get anything from Jack Russell?"

"A run around. Literally. He wanted me to tail him. I was playing into his hands."

"Reverse the game."

"I'm listening."

"Don't play his game, make him play yours."

"Go on."

"Go back to surveillance on this Russell guy. I'm sitting here watching Saunders' house on Leftwich Street. If she shows up, I'll call you back. Once we know that they are split, we have them where we want them."

My wheels started turning.

"I'm beginning to form a plan," I said.

"Now I'm worried."

"They're following orders."

"Agreed."

"Once we know that they are separated, we can attack

each of them. Divide and conquer, or something like that. Was that your plan or did I thwart yours?" I said.

"I don't feel thwarted."

"What was your thinking?"

"Who's the leader between these two, Jack or Marilyn?"

"She is."

"Agreed. So, you get to strong arm poor old Jack. I'll follow Marilyn to see if she leads us anywhere significant. Could be she has to make contact with Mr. Higher Up. If she dilly-dallies, I get to strong arm her too."

"And again, ladies and gentlemen, the Harvard graduate comes through with a plan. Except for that dilly-dally part. That must be from UVA."

"Wahoo."

Norfolk can be beautiful in the fall, but it seldom lasts too long. In honor of the brief beauty that had descended upon my fair city, I decided to do my surveillance on the Hog. I doubt if Jack Russell would be expecting anyone on a bike to be on a stakeout, must less tailing him if I had to. It was an idea.

I spent most of the afternoon watching the front door of his run-down apartment complex. He obviously was not yet successful at robbery, or else his stealing was limited to animals. I'd say the payoff on stealing dogs would be low. Not everyone would go to the lengths I would go to get their dogs back.

Late afternoon he emerged from his hovel, got into his car, and drove off. Naturally I followed.

Being the super sleuth I knew myself to be, I finally deduced that he did not have Sam or else his apartment smelled funny and looked disgusting by this point. Once I made this deduction, I felt freer to actually use force to help Jack understand the error of his ways.

He pulled into a drive-in that had looked new back in

1959. I parked my bike by the bathrooms on the right side of the building and waited for him. Fifteen minutes or so later he came out carrying a box and a drink. I followed him back to his apartment.

I decided not to allow him time to finish his evening meal. I could hear the television blaring through his paper-thin door. I slowly turned the door knob to see if he kept it locked. Poor Jack, he was much too trusting in such a rough neighborhood. I pulled the Glock from my back holster and entered his place.

"Hello, Jack. Nice to see you again."

He had a mouth full of French fries so he couldn't respond coherently to my greeting.

"Never mind the chit chat, Jack. Just stay in your chair. I'll talk first. You finish your supper."

He mumbled something that I couldn't decipher.

"Shouldn't talk with your mouth full, Jack. Manners. So missing these days."

He spit out some fries and finally spoke to me. "Who the hell are you?"

"My, my. Is that anyway to treat someone holding a gun on you? And someone you already know. Surely you haven't forgotten the person whose dog you kidnapped."

His expression was priceless. I think I must have been the last person on earth he expected to come walking through his front door. If I had been a more trusting soul, I would have thought that I had cornered the wrong person. His face showed that he had so many questions, and for a brief second, I almost felt sorry for him.

"Shall we start with something simple, Jack? Where's my dog?"

"I don't know nothing about no dog," he said. His expression of shocked innocence had abandoned him. He was assuming the expression of ignorance. Lying was not his strong suit.

"Jack, we can do this easy or we can do this painful. I'm not one of those folk who will sit here for an hour or so torturing you. I will, however, begin shooting your kneecaps, one at a time, of course, until you start screaming and begging me to stop. You only have two kneecaps, so this will not take very long. Now, if you do not answer my questions quickly or honestly, then the pain starts. It will start for you, more or less, about two seconds after I ask my next question. Am I communicating with you sufficiently so far?"

Poor Jack did not really know what to say to my wonderful speech. I doubt if he thought it so wonderful.

"Listen, you stupid broad, I'm not talking to you about anything."

I pulled out the silencer for the Glock from my jacket. I attached it to the barrel and shot him in his right kneecap. He spilled what was left of his sandwich and fries when he grabbed his knee with both hands.

"You shot me!"

"Of course I shot you. I told you I would shoot you. Now, are you ready to help me answer my questions, or do I have to shoot you in your other knee?"

"No more shooting," he said. "What do you want to know?"

"I already told you what I wanted to know."

"Damn, this hurts."

"Of course it hurts. You may never walk again. Well, check that. You may walk with a limp the rest of your life. If I shoot you in the other knee, you may never walk again. Wheelchairs have some technological advances these days, however."

"She's got the dog! Saunders took the dog!"

"Where?"

"How the hell do I know?"

"You were partners."

"Partners? Are you kiddin' me? That broad don't partner with no one. She gives the orders, pays me, and I'm outta the picture."

"Well, almost out. Where do you think she took the dog?"

"She drugged the dog and said something about that holding him until they got to where they were going."

"But she never said where."

"Never. She just needed another body to help her steal the dog."

"Wow, I hope she paid you well. You need a lift to a doctor or hospital?"

Jack was not very happy when I left him in his apartment. I did suggest a tourniquet on his upper leg to control the bleeding. I think he was more concerned about the pain he was in than the fact he might bleed to death.

I called Rosey from my place.

"You shot him?

"Of course I shot him. I didn't kill him. I just inflicted some acute pain on his knee cap. He'll make a full recovery, but there could be a decided limp."

"Decided."

"You discover anything?" I said.

"Several items. The woman came home late morning. She drives a green truck. No sign of a dog. And she is still in her small house. I was waiting on you to call me."

"So what's your plan? We have divided them, or they have divided themselves."

"I doubt if shooting her knee cap is my first choice. But I will go talk with her now. You want me to take some photos?"

"No, thanks. I will defer to your judgment on that matter. Since Jack told me she had Sam, and I happen to believe him, she either has him there at her place or she has him housed somewhere else."

There was hesitancy in Rosey's answering. I knew him well enough to know an unnatural pause when I heard one.

"You're thinking," I said.

"Sort of."

"Dare I ask you what you are thinking?"

"Better not this time. I don't want to say it."

"Then by all means, don't say it. We'll cross that bridge when we get to it."

"I'll call you back after my dialogue with Marilyn Saunders. Should be enlightening."

"I doubt it to be otherwise. I'm on my way back to Clancyville. Now that we know what we know, my geographical placement does not really matter for Sam's health. I'm returning in the Jag."

"Please drive carefully."

"Concerned for me or the car?"

"Don't make me answer that."

36

"WHY DO YOU HAVE TO GO BACK TO CLANCYVILLE?" ROGERS asked me.

"Connect more dots."

"Can't you connect them from here?"

"Wish I could. Sometimes you have to look people in the face in order to do any real connecting."

I love debating with a computer. Not everyone has such a privilege. Then again, not everyone had Rogers.

"And you're returning when?"

"When I need to and when I have more answers. People have been killed in that nursing home, and I have to put an end to that."

"If you can."

"You have anything yet on Marilyn Saunders?" I asked.

"Still looking. Many of the folks you have me check on fly low under the radar, you know."

"That's what makes you so valuable."

"Don't flatter me," Rogers said.

"Can't take a compliment?"

"Not if it's condescending."

"Didn't intend it to be condescending. Sherlock Holmes should have been so lucky as to have someone like you. He never would have needed Watson if you were around."

"That's fiction. I'm nuts, bolts, circuit boards, and brains."

"And a sexy voice."

"Is that any way to talk to a lady?"

I MADE excellent time across Virginia. I must have been lost in my thoughts the entire way. I was worried about Sarah. I was worried about Sam. And, I suppose, I was worried about my mother. I seldom worried about Rosey. He was such a smooth, cautious, and well trained combatant, that I could find no reason to be overly concerned about his welfare. I probably even courted the idea of his being invulnerable when I certainly knew better.

It was late afternoon when I pulled the Jag into the driveway. Rosey was sitting in my old tire swing near the garage.

"Miss me?" I said.

"Missed the Jag, too."

"I took good care of it."

"I know."

"So what were you apprehensive about?"

"No apprehension. Just missed driving her."

"Her?"

"Yeah. She's a *her*."

"Why do men name their cars after women?"

"Missed that psychological course, did you?"

"Some Freudian slip or other?"

"Wouldn't know. The Jag has no name."

"But you referred to it as a *her*."

"Yep. She's a *her*. My girl."

"Makes no sense."

"Doesn't need to. It's my illogical logic."

"Well put."

"Besides, you have a thing that's a *her* as well."

"Oh, that. Well …" I started to explain, then thought better of it. I trusted this man with my life, but some secrets are better kept secret. Rogers and her *skills* would certainly qualify as need to know. Even Rosey would understand that, if he knew what I was keeping from him. At least I hope that he would.

"What can I say?" I tried to sound defeated.

"Touché."

"Ah, touché. Now that I have been out-parried, update me on what you know."

"More like what I don't know."

"Whichever you have."

"I've watched the house where Saunders lives and I've seen no sign of Sam."

"Done some snooping, have we?"

"Some. Late night recon. If she has him, she has him somewhere else."

"Other contacts she's made?"

"Nothing significant, unless you call the post office, the grocery store, gas station, and a quick trip to Lynchburg as significant."

"Could be. Depends on who she saw and why she went to those places."

"Right. Stamps, bread, milk, cheese, and cantaloupes. Gasoline and some ladies underwear."

"Thorough, aren't you?"

"I aim to please. Every stone uncovered."

"No wind, snow, hail, nor rain motto as well?"

"I don't like snow. I can handle the others. You get the snow detail."

"So where to now?"

"Well, your mother is at the nursing place. I took some liberties and moved Sarah into the room next to J.R. Rachel has a nice chair in the hallway between rooms."

"How'd you convince Peace Haven to do that?"

"Charm."

"No threats?"

"None intended. One complaint, however."

"From whom?"

"The *whom* would be J.R. He didn't like having a black woman that close to his room."

"But you convinced him otherwise."

"I be mighty persuasive when I needs be."

"Yes, you can. What about Joy Jones helping us watch these two patients?"

"She was hesitant, but agreed to help some during her off hours."

"Did you pick up anything in her hesitancy?"

"Not really. Her hesitancy seemed legit. She said it had to do with some family issues, but that she would work around it to help us out."

"So, if we have Joy on board and my mother is okay with her guard duty, then we're free to chase rabbits."

"We are."

"Any ideas on the whereabouts of some rabbits?"

"I'd say the high cotton."

37

"He's in the garden," she said to the tall woman at the front door. "Come this way and I'll direct you."

"I know where it is," she said more sharply than necessary. "I can find my way."

Marie bowed slightly and tried to show no anger at the slight. She didn't like that woman and she wondered why her boss had anything to do with her. She reasoned that some people simply had no redeeming virtues.

The preacher was walking the two Pekinese around the massive flower garden. They were both on leashes to prevent escape. Despite the acreage he owned, he would never trust the dogs to roam freely for fear that they would leave him. He heard foot steps on the inlaid brick walkway, and turned in the direction of the sound.

"Did we achieve the diversion we sought?" he asked.

"Not entirely," she confessed.

"What does that mean?" he said.

"People are staying around the clock with Blair and Jones. Our inside contact says that it is impossible to proceed."

"Impossible? Don't talk to me about impossible!" he shouted at her.

The tall woman backed away slightly. He allowed the dogs to guide him along the path of the roses. When he moved a few feet away, the woman cautiously followed him at what she deemed a safe distance.

"We will simply change our procedures. There are four left, correct?" he said.

"Yes."

"What's the situation of Shelton and Rowland?" he said.

"Both are at home for the time being. The Rowland family is considering Residential Health Care because of mobility issues."

"Then focus on Rowland. Offer some incentives if money is the issue. Give them your strongest recommendation for RHC. I want results. I want this done," he said impatiently. "I refuse to allow some big city detective come along and ruin my ...," he stopped abruptly from what he was about to say to her. He allowed the dogs to guide him towards some newly planted Japanese Irises. He had spaced the rhizomes evenly around the area he had allowed for these unique flowers. The ground still showed signs of being worked. The male dog, Russell, sniffed at the ground and immediately began to dig where the preacher had carefully placed his rhizomes. He yanked on the leash with more force than the tall woman thought necessary. The force of tug dragged the helpless dog several feet away from the flower bed.

The dog yelped in pain. The female dog, Ruth, trotted over to see if her brother was okay. She sniffed him all over just to be sure.

"Stay out of that bed, Russell," he said as if he expected the dog to answer.

Both dogs stared at the preacher. Neither of them wagged a tail. Russell meandered toward another section of flowers, looking back at the preacher with some fear and much caution.

"Now what was I saying?" His question was not addressed to anyone in particular. He might have even been talking to himself, something he frequently did in the absence of people.

"I will not be prevented in carrying out this divine plan. This is something which God wants me to accomplish for him. This is all his timing. We are on a schedule here. Do you understand me?" This question was addressed to the tall woman. He had turned to look at her as he spoke.

She had heard the words before. Many times. Still, the force of his tone this time caused her to move away from the sound of his voice ever instinctively. She understood the divine plan of which he spoke, and had accepted it. More than that, she had adopted it as her own mission. She agreed with him. A time of judgment had come to those twelve people. This judgment was justice, a justice that was meted out with some measure of mercy. They were all old and some were dying already. The only question was why the preacher had waited so long. Since she was a little girl she had worked for the preacher. There were odd jobs around his other house, before he had moved to his estate. Once he was here, there was more that could be done, should be done, needed to be done. Once his wife died, her hours were increased so much that she practically lived on the estate. But he never asked her to come live with him. She had her small hovel in town. It wasn't much, but it was hers. He had helped her buy it. It was her home, he had said.

"What are you waiting for?" he asked her, interrupting her thoughts.

"I'll get right on it."

"Tonight," he said.

"But if they refuse RHC?"

183

"Make it so appealing that they cannot refuse. Whatever it takes. Win them over. Get it done."

"You don't think waiting a few days after RHC has begun would create less suspicion?" she asked knowing full well that acting so impulsively would definitely cause some questions.

"Tonight!" he yelled at her as he yanked on the leashes of both dogs simultaneously. She didn't notice if the dogs had done anything to merit his action. She only saw them fly ungracefully through the air a short distance and land on their sides. They both yelped. She wondered if the dogs shared her feelings about this man. Ever since this divine judgment had begun she had more fear of him than she did respect. There were times when she felt as if there was a leash around her neck. At first he only had to ask her to help him. Now, months later, as his obsession had increased, she was a reluctant participant despite her philosophical agreement regarding the justice behind this divine judgment. If he would let her, she would carry it out. She would accomplish it her way. She was rational and methodical. She planned carefully. This new plan was out of line. She could foresee difficulties.

She bowed slightly, backed up two or three steps, and then turned and left him standing near the small pond at the center of the garden. The two dogs were resting now. No more exploring for them for fear of reprisal. The preacher watched the woman walk away and wondered if she had the right attitude to finish this holy task. He would pray for her, but also he would check to see if he could continue to count on her. This was much too important to leave into the hands of someone undependable and less than vigilant. How dare she question his plan. How dare she have the audacity to question God's mission. He would pray for her soul. He would decide what to do if she failed him.

38

It was late-afternoon and Rosey and I were sitting in his Jag on White Horse Lane. We both watched Marilyn Saunders go into the mansion owned by Preacher Rowland, and then twenty minutes later return to her car and leave the mansion.

"We have another clue," Rosey said.

"Yeah, but what does it mean?"

"I don't interpret them, I just notice them," he said.

"We can connect her with Preacher Rowland on White Horse Lane."

"True. But we know nothing about him, do we?"

"I know a little from stories around town and my mother, of course. He's a legend in our county. In fact, his reputation extends throughout south central Virginia. Well known and well loved."

"Is that it, the sum-total of your knowledge of this man?"

"The sum."

"Run his name through your computer and see what pops," Rosey suggested.

"Yessire," I said, saluted, and made the call to Rogers.

Saunders turned out of the driveway and headed back in the direction of Clancyville. Rosey began following her a safe distance back.

Rogers answered my call.

"Did you run Robert Lee Rowland through your database?"

"Of course."

"Give me all you have," I said.

"Don't I always?"

I was afraid to answer for fear that Rosey would get suspicious from what would sound like a conversation between two people.

"Hey, don't I always give you everything I find?" she repeated trying to force a reprisal from me. I refrained.

"Go back forty years," I said.

"Are you alone?" Rogers asked.

"No."

"Oh, I see the problem. We have to sound like a person talking to a machine, do we?"

"That's correct."

"Okay. That male thug is with you?'

I wanted to ask her if she had been talking with my mother, but I knew better.

"Give me a few minutes and I'll call you back. People searches don't usually take too long," she said.

I hung up without another word. Saunders was definitely returning to Clancyville. We followed her to her house, watched her park and go inside. The trail was getting colder by the minute.

"We're running out of clues as to where Sam might be," I said.

"You worried?"

"A little. We know from an unreliable source that she had the dog when she left Norfolk and returned here."

"Unreliable, but we did threaten him."

"A bit more than threaten, I'd say," Rosey said.

"Okay, so we can assume that under duress he told us the truth. Still, she could have stopped anywhere along the way and turned Sam loose or placed him somewhere between here and there."

"Lot of land. Think he'll find his way back home?" Rosey said.

"Given enough time, yeah, I do. But not if he's being locked up somewhere."

"What would you do with a dog if you had no place to house him as a prisoner? And, let's say that you were acting on orders from someone else to steal the dog. The person who ordered you to steal the dog doesn't want the dog around, so you have to find some place where the dog cannot escape in order to use him as collateral … or leverage."

"You've thought a lot about this."

"I think a lot about everything. That's why I'm good at what I do."

"What is it you do?" I asked.

"I help people like you who have lost their dog."

"So what is your summation?"

"Saunders would likely drive through Dan River coming from Norfolk, correct?"

"Coming from Norfolk, yes. She would skirt the town, but still be close to Dan River."

"I assume that there is an animal control facility there?"

"There is, and wonder of wonders, it's on the east side of town."

"She'd have to drive right by it?" he asked.

"No, but she would drive close to it."

"Let's go to Dan River and do some checking."

"Nothing happening here," I said.

"Nothing visible to the eye."

We headed south to Dan River to check out the Pitt County Animal Shelter. I called ahead to see if they stayed open past five o'clock. We were in luck. They were open until 6:30. I had one other question related to our search for Sam.

"How long do you keep dogs brought in as strays?" I asked the lady on the phone at the animal shelter.

"Unless the dog is showing signs of aggression, we generally keep them for two weeks. We try to find homes for them, but there are simply too many dogs for that. Some are claimed, of course, but many are not."

"Then you exterminate them?"

"We put them down," she corrected me.

"Oh, that sounds better. Same result, but it does sound better," I said. "Thank you for the information."

The lady hung up without saying another word. I think I ruffled her feathers. She could join the very large club begun in my honor.

When we neared Dan River and the animal shelter, Rogers called and gave me what she had on the preacher.

"The Reverend Mr. Robert Lee Rowland started and ran the Clancyville Divine Church of the Savior for 45 years before he retired in 2000. Born in 1923 in Duley, West Virginia, he moved back and forth from Virginia to West Virginia until he went to college in 1941. He married Cybil Maloney of Kentucky in 1945, and they had three children – Andrew Jackson Rowland; Nancy Ann Rowland Shelton; and Jefferson Davis Rowland. Andrew was born in 1948 but died in the summer of 1952, the victim of a hit and run while riding his tricycle. The family was living in Richmond at the time. The driver was never found. Nancy Ann was born in 1950. She married Herbert "Hubie" Shelton of Riceville, Virginia in 1968. She currently lives in Richmond with Hubie. They have four grown children. The third, Jefferson Davis, was born in 1952 and died in 1971. He was arrested in 1969, charged with the murder of two teenagers, Samuel Tilley and Barbara Ann Smith. Sam Tilley was black. Barbara Ann Smith was white. They had been secretly dating. Apparently J.D. took exception to this interracial relationship, killed them, and was found guilty. He was sentenced to die by lethal injection after a lengthy trial of 8 months. J.D. died at the Richmond facility on February 14, 1971."

"Any more background on Preacher Rowland?"

"He's a Civil War buff and supposedly has a remarkable collection of Civil War artifacts. Cybil died in 2007, just a few months after the new house on White Horse Lane was completed. Is that enough for now?"

"Well, it certainly connects some dots, that's for sure."

"You talking to me?" Rosey said.

I had a momentary lapse. I closed the cell phone and told Rosey what Rogers had found out.

"I'd say that Preacher Rowland is connected, wouldn't you?" he said.

"Not buying the coincidence, huh?"

"No such thing, I told you before."

"It's certainly worth paying Robert Lee Rowland a visit," I said. "Besides, I want to see the inside of that mansion on White Horse Lane."

"Me, too."

39

We arrived at the Pitt County Animal Shelter in Dan River a few minutes before six. The lady at the main desk checked her records to see if a dog matching the description of Sam had been brought in anytime yesterday.

"Yes, here's one. Large, black Lab was left here sometime in the early afternoon. It says here that he might be vicious, and that he had attacked some people earlier that day."

She looked up at us and waited for us to say something. The silence was awkward.

Finally, I said, "May we see the dog?"

"If you want to," she said. "Follow me."

She led us through a heavy, green metal door and we followed her past some offices and storerooms along a hallway towards the back of the building. We passed through another green, metal door at the other end of the hallway and into a large room full of cages which were full of dogs. I tried hard not to feel anything for the caged animals. It was difficult.

"We keep the larger breeds out here," she said as we left that room and entered another area, larger still, with ground cages and more exposure to the outdoors. "We try to walk them as much as possible, but we are understaffed and the number of animals is growing."

I nodded and quietly appreciated the problem she had. I was hoping to help eliminate at least one of her concerns.

"This is Beulah," she said as we came upon a slightly overweight young woman whose Pitt County Animal Shelter uniform did not fit her too well. In addition, the uniform was dirty and her shirttail was out. She did, however, look very comfortable.

"Hey, folks. Looking for a good pet to take home?" Her dress belied her personality.

"They're wanting to see that Lab brought in yesterday, the one I told you to be careful with that he might be vicious."

"Oh," Beulah said and laughed. "Yeah, he's vicious alright. He attacks food. But he's my buddy. Come on, I'll show him to you. He'd make a great pet."

"You can follow her," the lady from the main desk said. "I have to get back up front and close up." She left us with Beulah.

We followed Beulah out the back door into the courtyard. Sam was sitting in the little shade that was created by the roof line of the building. When he saw me, he sprang to his feet and bolted towards us. Beulah stepped in front of me as if to protect me from the charging dog.

"It's okay," I said to Beulah. "He knows me." I moved alongside of Beulah and allowed Sam to put his front paws on my shoulders and lick my face. I say *allowed* as I had any method of stopping him short of shooting him.

"I'd say he does know you," Beulah said. "I had to convince him I meant him no harm before he would lick me. How'd you lose him?"

"He was stolen."

"Wow. Why would someone steal him and then drop him off here?" she asked.

"Long story, Beulah. Doubt if it would interest you very much. Thanks for taking care of my dog."

"It was my pleasure. What's his name?" she said.

"Sam."

"Good name. Sam, it's been a pleasure to know you and have you stay with me. I'm glad you have a good home." She put her hand down in front of him to shake hands. Sam extended his right front paw and they shook. He then quickly licked her face and Beulah laughed. "I would have taken him home if no one had claimed him by the end of the two weeks. No dog deserves to die like this, but we have laws and …, well, we have to follow them. But I could tell he was special. I let him roam around the yard without restraints because I knew right away I could trust him. But don't tell Susan. She'd get all bent out of shape. Miss Rules, you know."

"It'll be our secret. And thank you again."

"Anytime. Sam, you come back to see me."

Sam gave her what I surmised to be an appreciative look as we headed back to the front of the building.

"You'll need to stop at the desk. Susan will have some forms for you to fill out."

Thirty minutes later we were headed back to Clancyville and I was feeling much better.

"You owe me," Rosey said.

"I do. Sam does too."

"He owes me twice."

"Twice?" I said.

"He's riding in my Jag. Dogs don't ride in my Jag."

"He likes riding in your Jag."

"Don't get too attached to it," he said to Sam.

Sam licked Rosey's ear and then continued to stare out

the front window as if he were looking for something or someone in particular.

"I think we should drive by Marilyn Saunders' place. I think Sam would want to speak to her, don't you?" I said.

Rosey smiled at me. I could tell he liked the idea.

"Better save that meal for another day," he said.

THE RESIDENTIAL HEALTH CARE VAN PULLED INTO THE driveway of the home on Highland Drive a little after one o'clock in the afternoon. A tall woman emerged from the passenger's side wearing a nurse's uniform and carrying a clipboard. She walked to the front door purposefully as the driver of the van opened his door and got out. The driver, a black man of medium height wearing a white technician's uniform with the initials RHC clearly evident over his shirt's front pocket, slid open the side door and took out a wheel chair and a black bag. He left the wheel chair sitting next to the van. He carried the black bag to the front door where the tall woman was standing. They waited for someone to answer the door.

An elderly lady finally opened the door and greeted the two people from Residential Health Care as if she had been expecting them. The tall woman and the black man entered the house and sat down on the sofa in the living room. The lady of the house, Mattie Rowland, sat down in the high back blue chair next to the sofa. The blue chair was no match for the sofa's blue color. The incongruent colors were only obvious to the tall woman.

"Mrs. Rowland, I am Marilyn Saunders from RHC and this is Mr. Jones. We're here to do the final paperwork on your husband and prepare his room for our services," the tall woman said.

"Thank you for helping us," Mattie Rowland said to the two people sitting on her sofa.

The tall woman smiled but said nothing in response to this opening remark.

"We certainly could not afford your service without that grant you offered us," Mattie continued.

"I need you to fill out these papers here," the tall woman said as she handed Mattie the clipboard with several forms attached. It all looked very official.

The tall woman and the black man watched Mattie begin the process of filling in the lines on the multiple forms. The black man glanced over periodically at the erect Marilyn Saunders, but the tall woman kept her focus on Mattie Rowland. Her only concern was the job at hand. There was no compassion in her stoic demeanor. The black man crossed and uncrossed his legs multiple times. The comfortable couch made him even more uncomfortable. While Mattie Rowland slowly, methodically filled in the blank spaces on the sheet in front of her, the black man's eyes roamed the living room taking in the arrangement of Mattie's home décor. He was not thinking of the ambience of Mattie Rowland's living room. He was wondering if the tall, thin woman had any concern for these people.

"I don't know what this means," Mattie said after several minutes of work on the form. "Question number 8 here," she pointed to the line on the top sheet and looked up at the tall woman. "What should I put in the blank as the reason for the decision to use RHC?"

"Invalid husband," the tall woman said flatly without emotion.

"Invalid?" Mattie said. "I don't like that word *invalid*. That's not my word."

"Then use any word you like."

"Well, could you give me a better word than *invalid*?"

"How about *incapacitated*?" the tall woman said with some slight irritation in her voice.

"I don't know what that means," Mattie said.

"It means your husband cannot walk without assistance, use the bathroom without help, and has trouble eating without another person assisting him," the tall woman said trying hard to control her annoyance with this unnecessary ruse. She had a job to do and wanted to complete it expeditiously.

"Well, all of that is true, of course. But, I can't spell that word. Do you have something simpler?"

"Put down that your husband has problems with mobility," the tall woman said, controlling herself. Her voice had no emotion in it except impatience.

"Oh, that's better. I like that. I can spell that, too."

The two people sitting on the sofa continued to watch Mattie Rowland as she filled in the forms. She had other questions which the tall woman answered without feeling. Mattie left the living room two or three times to look in on her husband who was resting, and to check on the bread she was making in the oven in the small kitchen in the back of the house.

"The timer on the stove is broken," she confessed as she returned to her seat next to the sofa. "But I'm almost finished here. Just another two or three questions. So many questions to answer. Why is there so many forms to fill out?"

"Blame the government," the tall woman offered. "They force us to ask all of these things. Regulations, just more and more regulations. Somebody is always adding to our work load. Most of it is unnecessary, but it's the law. It's demanded of us and we have to comply," she said with the ever-so-slight feeling of annoyance in her voice.

It was as if Mattie had inadvertently touched a nerve of some sensitiveness in asking her innocent question. The black man even noticed the difference in the tall woman's voice. He knew that she was lying, but her words sounded as if she were telling the truth on some level.

Mattie finished the forms and handed them to the woman.

"May we see Mr. Rowland now?" the tall woman asked.

"Well, he's still resting. He always takes a little nap after lunch. He's awfully tired these days."

"We have to see the patient, Mrs. Rowland. We have to set up his room for our therapy to be any value to him," the tall woman said.

"I understand. Let me go back and see if I can wake him."

The tall woman almost smiled and nodded agreement as Mattie got up and left the room. She slowly walked down the short hallway to a back room. The floor creaked and popped as she slid along the uncarpeted hardwood floor. The black man looked at the tall woman and gave the impression he wanted to say something to her, but didn't. The tall woman stared at the papers on the clipboard she had in her lap. The writing appeared to be that of an early adolescent, someone learning to write cursive and not too sure of themselves about forming the letters. She thought how funny it is that we begin our writing lives with an awkward script and more often than not end our lives with the same type of script.

"Miss Saunders," Mattie said in a loud voice from the back of the house, "would you come in here please?"

Marilyn Saunders got up and walked confidently in the direction of Mattie Rowland's voice. At the end of the hallway she could easily see that Ernie Rowland was in a bed in the room on the left. Mattie was standing on the left side of the bed next to him. Ernie was not awake.

"I can't rouse him," Mattie said. "Would you see if you can wake him up?"

Marilyn Saunders moved closer to the man lying in the bed. She approached him from the right side even though there was less room to do so. She put her left hand close to his nose and mouth to see if she could detect any air coming out. She felt nothing. She shook the patient and waited to see if he would open his eyes and speak. Nothing happened. She shook him again and waited. The patient was very still. She felt for the pulse on his left hand. Nothing. Marilyn knew enough to check for the pulse around his neck. She could find nothing pulsating.

"Henry," she called out to the black man still in the living room, "come in here." It was an order, not an invitation.

"Check Mr. Rowland for vital signs?"

Henry stared at her in disbelief. He was thinking that this was not part of what he had reluctantly agreed to do. He stared at the man in the bed who was not moving at all. Henry looked over at Mattie who was just standing by the left side of the bed without comment. She was waiting for Ernie to wake up. It was more than obvious to Henry that Ernie Rowland was not going to wake up.

"He's dead, Miss Saunders," Henry said after he barely touched Ernie Rowland's wrist.

The tall woman's first reaction was disbelief, but that quickly changed to relief when it crossed her consciousness that she would not have to perform her duties on this day, this time, to this person. Natural causes had taken some desperation out of her life and she was relieved. She composed herself quickly.

"Mrs. Rowland, I think you need to call the funeral home."

Mattie moved her eyes slowly from Ernie's body to Marilyn Saunders who was still standing on the right side of the bed.

Her eyes were empty of any expression. It was as if someone had removed her personality from her body without asking her permission. She felt numb. She had no idea what to do next. There was no way she was going to call anyone at this moment.

"Grab her, Henry. I think she's going to fall," the tall woman directed.

Henry quickly moved from the foot of the bed to the left side and placed his strong hands on Mattie's fragile body to steady her and keep her from falling. He guided her to the only chair in the room and helped her to sit down. His help seemed to be more kindness than duty, but it went unnoticed because was Mattie Rowland was in shock. She would remember little of what was done for her the rest of the day.

"We need to leave," Saunders said.

"We has to call... someone," Henry said.

"You call," she said to him.

"They knows my voice. I used to work for them some. Too many questions if I calls."

Marilyn Saunders sighed loudly and walked back towards the front of the house looking for a telephone to use. She finally found one on a kitchen wall almost hidden by the cabinets and some furniture that made the already small kitchen even smaller. There was no phone book evident anywhere so she rifled through several kitchen counter drawers before she found one. She dialed the number for the Cuthbert-Boran Funeral Home and waited for someone to answer.

"Cuthbert-Boran, may I help you?" the voice said much too politely.

"I'm calling for Mattie Rowland. Her husband, Ernie, has died and she's here at the home on Highland Drive. Could you send someone over to help her?"

"We would be glad to help her. May I ask your name?"

The only thing the voice from Cuthbert-Boran heard after the question was the sound the receiver makes when someone has hung up the phone.

Saunders looked first at Mattie to see that she was now almost completely in shock and non-responsive. She then looked at Henry whose eyes met her glance as if on cue.

"We need to go. Now," she said.

Henry walked briskly out of the room. He glanced at Mattie quickly before he disappeared down the hallway. There was nothing more he could do for that poor woman, he thought to himself. He felt sorry for her despite the fact that this was the mission all along. It just happened in this unplanned manner. It was the strangeness of life.

Saunders was lost in her own thoughts as she walked out of the room and down the short hallway toward the front door. She knew that her employer was not going to be pleased with this turn of events. Revenge was still his cup of tea and death by any means was not the end he desired the most. He wanted to take the lives of those whom he hated, not have them die from natural causes.

Saunders paused as she was passing through the threshold. She thought she heard someone crying as she closed the door to the house on Highland Drive.

41

Sam and I returned to my mother's house sometime mid-afternoon after taking a long walk down to the river and back. It had been many years since I had walked that road. Sam had never been to the river, so I decided that he might benefit from some roaming time since he had been restrained by both Saunders and the animal shelter. One used to freedom can only handle so much captivity. He ran more than I did along the way to the river. In fact, I didn't run at all while he chose to run quite a bit. He also decided to jump into the river. I refrained from such ecstasy chiefly because I knew the water to be quite cold this time of year even though the warmth of the fall sun belied the temperature of the water.

Rosey was still cleaning the Jag as we entered into the yard from our latent pilgrimage. Rachel was sitting on the steps close by watching him work.

"Well, the adventurers have returned," Rosey said.

"Sam, here, had the adventure. I simply wandered down memory lane for some cheap therapy."

"Chase any rabbits?" he asked Sam.

Sam shook his whole body as if on cue to answer the question with a negative. He was still slinging water after multiple shakings along the way from the river back to the house.

"No rabbits," I said, "just running and playing in the water."

"Sounds like fun."

"For dogs," I said.

"Humans, too," Rosey added.

"Not this time of year," my mother said as she walked down the few back steps of her house.

"Sarah okay?" I asked Rosey who was to check in on her earlier this morning.

"Yeah. She's doing fine. I brought your mother home and got Joy to fill in for her for a few hours."

"I insisted on coming home. Keeping vigil for hours on end is not something a body can endure for long at my age," Rachel said.

"At any age, Mother."

"Well, you young folks have an advantage."

Rosey and I looked at each other knowing that we had passed *young* a few miles back. He smiled at me.

"Joy agreed to keep an eye on J.R.?" I asked.

"Reluctantly," my mother said. "Seems she has a hard time with his obvious dislike for people of color. Sitting in the hallway between rooms was tolerable she said."

After all these years my mother still surprised me from time to time. When you think you finally have someone, like a parent, finally figured out, they say or do something which causes you to have to rethink your pigeon hole. My mother had grown up using the word Negro to refer to African-Americans or people of color. However, in my lifetime, she had used only the term *black*. I think the change from Negro to black occurred when Sarah Jones began working for our family. Until now, I had never thought it possible for my mother to use any other term than black. She never found it necessary to adapt to new terms as they came into vogue.

I decided against making any comment regarding her usage of *people of color*. I imagine that Rosey's presence had something to do with that. He could handle anything my mother would say, but I still thought better of exploring my mother's growing vocabulary at the moment.

"Do you think J.R. is safe with her?" I asked tongue-in-cheek.

"Sarah told me that Joy has a temper," Mother said, "but I believe Sarah's level-headedness will prevail over any severe conflict that might erupt."

"She could stop a fight which might develop?" I said.

"Without a doubt," Mother said. "Even in her weakened state. The woman has a constitution of steel."

I smiled as I remembered that rescue scene from my early life when Sarah drove our family car while Mother literally road shotgun down to the city jail to rescue me from the throes of an irate man bent on destroying my mother's precious little girl. I doubt if my mother would recall the incident in such terms. That was my memory.

"Oh, the phone's ringing," Mother said and turned quickly to re-enter the house and answer it before it stopped. All calls in the south are important, even the ones which are not.

"What's our next move, Sherlock?" Rosey asked.

I was watching Sam sniff around the yard from my perch on the tire swing. I was almost too big to sit comfortably inside the tire, a fact that was not lost on me for obvious reasons. While I did consider myself to be in good shape for a woman of my age, I also knew that time had a way of adding inches and pounds even with the best of physical conditioning routines.

"I'm waiting," I said.

"For?"

"Don't know. When it shows up, I'll tell you."

"Is this a detecting posture?"

"Pretty much."

"And your solution rate?"

"High enough."

"High enough for what?"

"For people to keep hiring me."

"You have no goals, no aspirations towards improvement, no self-motivated incentives for betterment?"

"Is this a survey?"

"Honestly. I don't get you sometimes."

"My daddy always said that when you get to a fork in the road, take it."

"He was quoting Yogi Berra, love."

"I know that. But I never heard Yogi say it. Only Daddy."

"So we're at the fork in the road?"

"You betcha."

"Which one of our options are we going to take now?"

"Don't know yet. But we will take one."

Mother came out the back door and let it slam. Still surprising me. Before I could comment on her deportment regarding slamming doors, she had some startling news.

"Virginia Lee just called to tell me that Ernie Rowland died earlier today."

"One of the jurors on the list," Rosey said to me.

"How'd he die?" I asked.

"Heart attack, most likely, Virginia Lee said. She gave me as many details as she had, which were considerable, but nothing you want to take to court yet. Seems as if he died of natural causes in his own bed at home."

"No kidding," Rosey said.

"Poor old Mattie. She's beyond distraught, Virginia Lee

said. Still in shock. I probably need to fix something and go over there."

"I assume that Mattie is his wife?" I said.

"Yes. Married over 60 years, I think. Some such large number. Imagine finding him in bed that way. Tried to wake him and couldn't, as the story goes. I'll find out more details when I go over. The rumors will be wild around town. I need to get in on the early details so as not to be misled by all the add-ons and embellishments which surely will come with all the re-tellings."

My mother had a keen fix on life in the rural south. Clancyville was almost an archetype when it came to understanding Southern culture. Embellishment was an art form in this culture. No one considered it lying or even fibbing. It was just something that was done. If a man walked five miles to see a doctor, then by the time the story got around town, he had walked maybe twenty miles. If a person died peacefully in his bed at home, then by the time the story is all over town, he likely lay there two days or more before someone discovered him and then they imagine some kind of horrendous death attached to that man's passing. Dying in your sleep is not an exciting story. The devil is truly in the details, especially in this culture where I was raised.

"I think we should take this opportunity to go see the Reverend Mr. Robert Lee Rowland and speak with him in person," Rosey said.

"That's a wonderful idea."

"You really think so?"

"Truly. We have some time before we need to get back to Sarah and J.R. Let's see if we can ruffle some feathers."

"This could be fun."

42

THE TALL WOMAN STOOD IN FRONT OF THE HUGE DESK AND waited for a response from the man seated in the high back leather chair. The two dogs were sitting by the windows intently looking at something moving around in the flower garden outside. The woman could hear every beat of a large clock resting on top of a large armoire behind the man and to his right. Despite the size of the clock and the armoire, the room dwarfed the furniture. In fact, the tall woman felt small in this room.

"I am not pleased," he said finally.

"But he is dead. He's as dead as the others."

"But … not … by … my … hand," he said, emphasizing each word.

"It was out of my hands. I suspect the man was already dead by the time we arrived. Hard to say."

"Tell me again what happened. I need the details."

"The old woman was filling out the papers and finally finished. She left us to go check on her husband in the back bedroom. After a few minutes, she called for us to come back. When we entered the room, he was not moving. I checked for a pulse and found none. I called Henry to come back and asked him to check for a pulse. Henry found no pulse. We determined that he was dead. I called the funeral home because the old woman was in deep shock and nearly collapsed. Henry put her in a chair. She was like a zombie. She couldn't function."

"And you called the funeral home?"

"I did, but I gave them no name, other than Ernie Rowland."

"Do you get the paperwork she was filling out?"

The question hit her hard. She had failed to retrieve the paperwork that the old woman had painstakingly worked on for at least some thirty to thirty-five minutes. She couldn't remember where the paperwork was. She had made a mistake and left it. The sudden death of the man had caused the whole scene to shift and she forgot that pivotal detail. It was that simple. She was caught.

"No," she said.

"No?"

"I must have left it."

"You left it."

Her anger was rising. The man could be incorrigible at times. Most times. She could feel her face getting flushed. No doubt it was turning red, she had that characteristic. The color emerged immediately when something like this would happen. No way to hide it.

"Everything changed when we found the body. I lost track of the paperwork."

"Can they trace it back to you?"

"The papers? No way. There're just papers that Residential uses to admit people into the program. They're generic. Nothing specific on them, except the information about the client."

"But they are a loose end, correct?" he asked.

"Yes. It was a mistake. It won't happen again."

"You had better be right about that. I can't believe that he died on the very day we had chosen. Talk about bad karma. Bad luck. Bad something."

The tall woman could tell that he was more than unhappy, he was moving slowly towards rage. Whatever was driving him was something beyond anything she had ever seen before. He was taking vindictiveness to another level. In her opinion, dead was dead, no matter how it occurred. Obviously, that was not his philosophy.

"Let's move quickly now. What about Skeeter Shelton?"

"He seems to be rather healthy. My research indicates that he takes good care of himself. He doesn't smoke, drink, or eat fried foods. Walks every day. He could easily live to be a hundred."

"Not if I have anything to do with it. No word yet from that Diamond person?"

"No."

"Takes her own sweet time. Is there no time limit on these things?"

"Apparently not. When it is done, she will contact us in order to get the rest of her money."

"It seems that this latest strategy of ours might work after all. We take care of Skeeter Shelton, then all we have to do is finish our work at Peace Haven. Maybe by then the contract on our obstacle will be finished."

"I suppose so."

"It's up to you. I want you to take care of Skeeter Shelton."

"There's no way to inject him. He's not bedridden."

"Do it some other way. Justice will prevail no matter her method. I want them dead. I want them all dead. Do it now!"

43

THERE'S AN INTERESTING ROAD CONFIGURATION ON THE WAY to White Horse Lane. I only mention it because it is a place where accidents are just waiting to happen; however, for some odd reason, only a few wrecks ever occur at this spot.

We were on our way out to see The Reverend Mr. Robert Lee Rowland. Rosey, Sam and I nearly made some dubious history. I don't know the history of the road, that is, which came first, the road and then the train tracks or the other way around. The engineers either dug a tunnel to make way for the road or another set of engineers created an archway to allow the train tracks to pass over the highway. Whichever came first is of little consequence in the aftermath. The problem is that whoever constructed what is now there made a one lane road through the short tunnel under the train tracks. To make matters worse, if you're traveling south the road arrives at the one lane tunnel after a sharp curve in which it is impossible to see around; and therefore, quite impossible to see oncoming traffic. Sometimes people like to drive faster than necessary as they come around that blind curve. They can likely be running close to fifty miles an hour when they enter the small tunnel. If you are approaching the tunnel from the south heading north, you at least have time and a short distance to look ahead and notice oncoming traffic from the sharp curve, but just barely. If an oncoming vehicle is traveling faster than fifty miles per hour around the blind curve heading into the one lane tunnel, then you have, say, three seconds or so to decide whether you can safely enter the tunnel and make it to the other side before life as you know it has come to an abrupt end.

Some days life can be challenging just by traveling the roads of Pitt County even if no one has a contract on you.

As we were approaching the tunnel, Rosey was driving the Jag and he could easily see that the tunnel and the road from the tunnel to the sharp curve were clear. It also appeared to be clear from my vantage. Sam was lost in his own thoughts, but still was looking straight ahead. We proceeded. As soon we entered the tunnel, a car came around the blind curve traveling more than fifty miles per hour. Rosey was forced to slam on his brakes and back up at break-neck speed to avoid what would have been a nasty head-on collision.

Sam tumbled through from the backseat toward the windshield because he was perched in between the two front seats. Rosey was strong enough to move Sam's bulk just enough to grab the gear shift in the middle island and move it to reverse quickly to avoid being hit by the oncoming vehicle. At the same time, he was strong enough to stop Sam's momentum and prevent him from crashing into the windshield. Rosey's reaction time was impressive. His one-arm strength to stop a 95 pound dog traveling at least 40 miles an hour was also quite impressive.

"Is that driver crazy?" Rosey asked me, no doubt rhetorically. "That was too close."

I was looking at the driver of the car. She was more

interesting to me that the fact we almost kissed vehicles. Sam was having difficulty regaining his balance after his fall forward over the gear shift. He found both his composure and a more suitable posture after we stopped a safe distance from the one lane tunnel. The other vehicle speeded on past us as if we had made the more serious error.

"You didn't recognize her, did you?"

"Are you kidding me?" he asked. "I'm trying to stay alive here."

"Marilyn Saunders."

"Really?"

"No kidding. I'd recognize her face anywhere. Wonder if she was coming from White Horse Lane?"

"She's been there before."

"She wasn't driving a green truck."

"Could have been a rental used just for Sam," Rosey said.

Sam growled softly as if he understood who it was we were discussing.

"Is this a clue?" Rosey asked.

"Not much of one. Maybe only a reinforcement of something we already knew."

"That's not a clue?"

"Well, maybe a little one, but I don't know if that counts."

"Is there some official scorekeeper like in baseball?"

"I think each detective is supposed to keep a running tally himself," I said.

"You do that?"

"Never."

"Explains a lot."

"Probably."

We were thankful that the rest of the trip to White Horse Lane was uneventful. Sam decided to lie down in the back seat instead of sitting up to watch where we were heading. I think the sudden stop discouraged his desire to look out the windshield.

This time we drove into the long, circular drive and parked the car near the front door. I told Sam to remain in the car and he offered no objections.

Rosey rang the doorbell which turned out to be chimes which were clearly audible outside. A young woman answered the door. She was dressed in what I decided was a maid's garb.

"May I help you?" she said.

"I'm Clancy Evans and this is Roosevelt Williams. We would like to speak with Mr. Rowland, if we may." I was using my best manners to gain entrance.

The woman, dressed in a knee length black dress with a white collar attached to a matching placket that ran down the front of her outfit, opened the door wider and gestured with her head for us to enter the colossal hallway. The black shoes she wore had soft soles which squeaked some when she walked. The black and white apron she sported tied in the back. Picture perfect.

Once you enter, you feel dwarfed by the size of the wall behind you through which you just passed. The tangent walls to the front entrance wall were equally as tall, some three stories, but were not as long because of the stairways that spiraled upward to the next two floors on both sides. Immediately above the entrance door was a moose's head the size of a wooly mammoth, or so I guessed, having never seen a wooly mammoth's head. Large would have been an understatement to describe the moose's cranium. Paintings were hung all around the hallway room depicting scenes from what I surmised to be the Civil War.

I was trying to decide how the oversized moose's head fit into the Civil War theme when the young maid broke into my yet unsuccessful pondering.

"I will ask if he will see you," she said and walked away from us, moving under the divided stairways towards what I guessed to be the back of the house. As I continued my survey of the hallway the size of my apartment, I noticed an expensive looking uncomfortable sofa-like construction along one wall adjacent to Mr. Moose. It encouraged me to continue to stand and wait.

The sound of the maid's rhythmic squeaking shoes had almost faded when Rosey interrupted it. "This feels like a museum."

"Looks like one, too. Civil War?"

"Be my guess. That would be my great, great Uncle Stonewall Jackson up there," Rosey smiled as he pointed the famous painting of Jackson crossing some river.

"Not enough greats to be your uncle," I said.

"Oh, that's the problem. Better go back and check the family Bible once more."

"You think this is his hobby?"

"Obsession," he said as we both took in the rifles, maps, handguns and uniforms all displayed in floor cases and wall cases mixed in with the paintings which covered nearly every available space. "And this is only what we can see in this area. Think he has more or is this all?"

"Maybe we'll find out. Here comes our answer," I said as the maid approached.

"He will see you both. Follow me."

"Thank you," Rosey said politely.

We walked for what seemed like a few minutes as we followed our guide along more hallways and past rooms in which we could tell that the Civil War theme was still prevalent at each turn of our journey. He obviously had not run out of artifacts from that conflict.

At long last our guide knocked gently on a closed door

and we all waited for some response from that inner sanctum.

"Come in," a voice said from somewhere inside the chamber.

Our black and white dressed guide opened the door for us and gestured for us to enter. She closed the door behind us, shutting herself out of the room, and squeaked away.

Seated behind an extremely large wooden desk was the famous Robert Lee Rowland. I had seen him on one other occasion in my life, but he had been much younger then. It was my daddy's funeral back in 1972. He was not the preacher of record for that occasion, but he certainly made himself known and greeted all who came as if they were long, lost cousins he hadn't seen in several years. It appeared to me that he behaved as if he was running for some political office back then. I remember that well. The bad taste left in my mouth from that occasion was still present with me now.

Two dogs were sitting in his lap like small statues. They watched us intently as we walked to the available chairs several feet in front of the wooden desk. It seemed odd to me to have the chairs so far away from the desk. I judged the distance to be something close to twenty feet. The room allowed for such a configuration, but cultural patterns dictated a closer arrangement. Evidently the man liked his space as well as his importance. Perhaps the two were intertwined.

"Please be seated," he said. "I would get up, but the dogs get a little unsettled if I move about too much. So, forgive my impoliteness at not standing for you. You are most welcome in my humble home."

Humble home. I pretended to cough gently to stifle the laugh. Talk about pretentious.

"How may I help you?"

I wanted to ask him to define *mansion*, but my breeding

helped to contain so early an attack on his pretentious absurdity.

"I'm Clancy Evans and this is my friend, Roosevelt Washington. We were hoping you would talk with us about the trial of your son," I said.

He stared without emotion directly into my eyes. He was pausing for effect as much as for word loss. He rubbed the backs of both dogs as he seemed to ponder the reason we had come to call on him.

"Clancy Evans, daughter of Bill Evans. Hmm. My son's trial was a long time ago," he said. "I like to put such painful memories behind me. No sense holding onto the bad stuff of life. People make mistakes. Sometimes they answer for their poor choices. There is forgiveness and justice given to all who seek it. I don't really know what I could talk to you about in that regard."

"Well," I said, "there seems to be someone in the community that is holding grudges. The people who served on the jury for your son's trial are dying unnaturally. I count nine of the twelve who have died this year, going back a few months. Recently, four of these have died. We were hoping that you might help our investigation by shedding some light on what you recall or what you may have heard."

"Investigation. I had not heard of any investigation, nor had I heard of anyone linking these deaths with that trial."

"Well, if you look at who has died and the fact that some of the deaths are rather mysterious, it would appear that someone is out for revenge."

"My, my. Who hired you to do this investigating?" His voice showed interest but his body had not shifted even the slightest bit from his position of stroking the backs of the dogs and watching us keenly. His eyes shifted from Rosey to me and back again. He had a kind of regular movement with this, one that was studied and precise, not careless or distracting.

"No one officially hired us. I am looking into this as a courtesy to my mother."

"Oh, your mother. And she thinks that something irregular is going on with all of these deaths?"

"We all do," I said firmly.

"Some of these folks who served on that jury would be rather old at this point, would they not?"

"Yes, they would. But many of them were still quite healthy. Some of the recent deaths appear to be intentional."

"My, my. You have proof of this?"

"Nothing substantial."

"Have you been to the sheriff? He would be the one to do the checking," he said.

"Yes, we have talked with him and he is checking some things for us."

"Well, that is certainly good. I still don't know how I might be able to aid you here."

"Do you recall anyone who was extremely upset after the trial ended?"

He thought for a few seconds and then said, "Many people were surprised at the verdict, and some, yes, were upset. But I don't believe anyone would have been upset enough to, what, wait thirty years and then begin to murder the jurors. That does sound rather ridiculous, does it not?"

"It is unusual, to be sure. But that appears to be what is happening," I said.

"You are Roosevelt Washington, is that correct?" he addressed Rosey for the first time.

"I am."

"You are credentialed quite well, Mr. Washington. The University of Virginia and Harvard, is that right?"

"So far, so good."

"Does all of this sound reasonable to you and your studied mind?"

He phrased his questions quite well, but I had to wonder if there was not some slight hint of sarcasm in his tone, just enough for the good preacher to enjoy his sparring with us.

"Mr. Rowland," he said, "it is my belief that murder is hardly reasonable, and that revenge is often served best when served cold for some."

"Insightful, young man. Very insightful, but from what you have told me you do not appear to have any substantial evidence that what is happening here is murder."

"We have enough to keep snooping around," I said, "and you can bet that we shall continue to do so."

"Well, in that case, I wish you well. I hope you get to the bottom this. And, for the sake of the remaining jurors, the three souls left, if someone is out there killing off these good folks, then I certainly hope you stop them before it is too late."

He sounded as if he meant what he said, but then he had had years of practice using his voice to convince folks of what he was offering. I had to admit that I was impressed with his style. He was smooth and confident. Maybe too much of both.

"I am sorry that I cannot be of more help to you in your endeavor. If you think of something else I might be able to help with, please do not hesitate to call me or come by. I always enjoy guests here in my home."

He pushed a button on his desk. The maid person who had escorted us in returned promptly and opened the door, this time without knocking. Rules of the house.

"Please show our guests out, Marie. Thank you both for coming. It is a pleasure to see you again after so many years away from our village."

"Thank you for your time," I said to the preacher. He

nodded and continued to stroke both of the dogs as he remained seated in his high-back leather chair.

"Quite a collection of period memorabilia you have gathered here, if I do say so myself," Rosey quipped as he stood and moved a little closer to the man seated behind the wooden desk.

I watched the preacher's controlled demeanor change slightly. It was as if he felt threatened as Rosey moved toward him.

"Perhaps one day I shall have the opportunity to show you the entire collection, Mr. Washington. Another time, however."

"Another time," Rosey said.

"This way, please," Marie said as she motioned for us toward the doorway of the large room.

44

"He didn't insult you directly," I said to Rosey as we arrived at my mother's house. He stopped the car suddenly. It was unlike him to show anger. His lack of control was oozing.

"No matter. I'd rather have him call me a sonofabitch than to sit there and listen to that polite dribble, knowing that his speech is filled with double entendres. The man is an ass, pure and simple."

"Nothing is pure and simple."

"Okay, but he's still an ass."

"No argument from here. But what do you think?"

"About him?"

"About his involvement."

Rosey took a deep breath and climbed out of the car. He let Sam out and closed his door without slamming it. That was a good sign. He was gaining control back. He walked over to the tire swing, seated himself on top of the tire instead of inside it, and pondered my question.

"He could be the one," he said.

"Do you suspect him?"

"Best lead we've had so far. Powerful enough. Motive sufficient. Thinks of himself as smarter than others. Ego, power, and motive. Could be a deadly combination."

"One more ingredient."

"That would be?"

"Divine right of kings," I said.

"Yikes. I forgot the theological angle. It's not always present, you know."

"But, when it is, it can be rather difficult to overcome."

"May not be able to overcome it. May have to obliterate it," he said.

We walked up the back steps and smelled supper cooking. Mother was busy watching over the several pots cooking away on the stove. She was in her element. Rosey turned to me as we entered the kitchen.

"Anything in particular cause you to come up with his divine right?"

"Just his whole aura. More or less adding things up rather than spotting something. He perceives himself to be a powerful man who does what is right. He is intelligent, to be sure. And he is very much in control. You did notice how he questioned us about our process for the investigation."

"I noticed."

"He is very much a control person. He is the man in charge… of everything. If he turns out to be our man, I would be surprised if his personal theology is not connected to the motive."

"If he is the man," Rosey said.

"Thought you might want to eat early so you could get over the nursing facility and stand guard over Sarah and J.R.," Mother said from across the room.

"Good idea," I said. "Did you learn anything of substance from your visit with Mattie?"

"Oh, that poor dear. Her husband, Ernie, God rest his

soul, died just when the people from Residential Health Care were there getting Mattie to sign some papers. She was still emotional and distraught, but she showed me the papers that she was filling out. Couldn't remember their names and who could blame her. She had a vague recollection of two people there helping her."

"Helping her with what?"

"Well, I assume they called the funeral home. Mattie said she didn't remember calling the funeral home."

"Did the folks from Residential Health Care stay with Mattie until the funeral home arrived?"

"I don't know. I didn't ask her that. Is that important?"

"Maybe not, but it would have been kind to stay and help her, if she needed it," I said.

"Oh, she would have needed it. She was in no state to function like that, even by the time I arrived. She had a hard time remembering where the kitchen was. I gave the plate of deviled eggs to her and she headed towards the bathroom with them. No telling what she would have done with them if I hadn't caught her."

"So they called the funeral home and then just left?"

"Can't say, but you're a detective. Go detect. You have some time before supper will be ready."

I used the newly installed telephone in the den, just off of the kitchen and the dining area to call the funeral home. It was late, but since they had at least one new body, I figured someone would be around.

"May I speak to Allen, please? This is Clancy Evans."

I waited for the person on the other end of the line to find Allen.

"Clancy, Allen here. How can I help you?"

"Just curious about something related to Ernie Rowland's death."

"Okay. I don't have any information as yet. I just got the body this afternoon," Allen said.

"I meant the circumstances surrounding his death, not his actual death. Did you take the call concerning his death?"

"No, I think Missy Shelton probably took that call."

"Did she happen to tell you who placed the call?"

"No, I don't believe she did. I have no memory of that. Is that important?"

"Don't know until I have the answer. Is Missy still there?"

"No, she left just a few minutes ago."

"You have her home number?"

He gave me the number.

"Thanks, Allen. Sorry to bother you. I know you're busy."

"No bother, Clancy. Call anytime."

I dialed the number Allen gave me for Missy Shelton. It rang four times and then some cutesy answering machine message took over, Missy and her children singing some gosh awful song. I left my phone number after the beep. I refrained from singing my number. I do have some limitations.

We ate cornbread, beans, and cabbage for supper. Despite my mother's sharp tongue and acerbic wit, she had the skill of a master chef, or at least I always thought so growing up. Rosey must have thought so too. He was on his second helping of everything before I finished my first.

"We don't eat like this in D.C.," he said.

"What do you eat like?" Mother asked.

"Salads and fish. Salads and chicken. Salads and steak."

"We could have salad and meat, if you prefer," she said.

"I do not prefer. I love what you fix, Mrs. Evans. You're an excellent cook."

"Don't flatter me. I just throw together whatever I have in the cupboard. Whatever comes out, that's what I eat."

"Well, you certainly do an excellent job of throwing it together."

"You must want something," she said to Rosey.

"Nothing but another piece of cornbread."

She passed the plate of cornbread to him. "Nothing here worth making over. You got any complaints?" she asked me.

"Not yet."

I had the feeling that some dart from Mother was headed my way when the phone rang and interrupted whatever dig was about to emerge from her vast storehouse of insults. Saved by the ringing of the bells.

"I'll get it." I was hoping it was Missy calling back.

It was Missy and she was as chatty as ever.

"This is Missy and I'm returning your call."

"Clancy Evans, here, Missy. Thanks for calling back."

"No problem, Miss Evans. Sorry we weren't around to talk with you when you called. We take the girls out to Dairy Queen now and again. They like those burgers the folks out there fix, so we try to splurge a little and treat the girls to some genuine deluxe Dairy Queen hamburgers and some French fries once a week. They also like their strawberry milk shakes. It sort of keeps the girls happy, if you know what I mean."

She paused to breathe and gave me the chance to interrupt her enthusiasm.

"Missy do you remember who called you about Ernie Rowland today?"

"Well, I certainly remember the call, like I always remember when someone calls to tell me that someone has died. It's awful to have to receive those calls, but someone has to be there to answer the phone and I figure it might as well be me, and I do consider it a sort of ministry, at least that's what my preacher says it is and he should know, right?"

"But do you remember who the person was you talked to about Ernie?"

"They never told me their name. Many times folks don't give out their names when they call. Sometimes I guess 'cause I know so many people around here and I recognize their voice and all, but this time I didn't recognize the voice, but I do think it was a woman who called, I just didn't know her voice, she could have been a distant family member or something like that, but I didn't get a name. Is that important? Did I mess up?"

"No, Missy. You did fine. I was just curious about who was in the home helping Mattie when she found Mr. Rowland."

"Oh, I heard through the grapevine, so to speak, that it was Residential Health Care who was there when she found the body, so it could have been someone from that place who called us. You might try calling them, they have offices in Dan River. They're nice folks and would be happy to help you. I'm sorry I couldn't answer your questions ... Put that down, Marcie! Don't you hit your ... I'm sorry, Miss Evans, I have to go. My girls need my attention. You know how children are, always needing some attention and testing their parents. Is there anything else?"

"You wouldn't happen to have the number for Residential Health Care in Dan River would you?"

"I certainly would," she said and then rattled it off as if she was expecting me to ask.

"You have all work related telephone numbers written down like that?" I asked.

"Oh, no, Miss Evans. I have the ability to remember numbers real easy like. Since I was a little girl, I can recall just about every telephone number for all of my friends, ex-boyfriends, and stuff like that. I have no idea how I do it, but

I just do. It comes in handy at work as you might imagine," she paused once more to breathe.

"I might indeed imagine the handiness of such a gift. I am impressed, Missy. Thank you for your help."

"Oh, you are most welcome…Marcie!!" she yelled into the receiver. "I do need to go now, Miss Evans."

I was grateful that she paused once again for a breath and I said goodbye after thanking her once more.

I was tired. The woman could talk. So young and yet so full of words.

"Learn anything?" Mother asked.

"Nothing definitive," I confessed.

"You never learn anything definitive. Why don't you and Rosey go on over to Peace Haven and do something constructive. If you can't solve these murders, at least you might be able to prevent another one from happening."

Despite her caustic charm, I had to admit that she was right. We were getting nowhere and all the while people continued to die around us.

Mother insisted that we head over to Peace Haven even though we offered to help her clean up and do the dishes after supper. She flatly refused.

While en route I called Residential Health Care using Missy's information. It was after hours, but someone answered finally on the sixth ring.

"Can I help you?" the voice said.

"I was calling to check on the two people who were here in Clancyville today helping the Rowland family with your program."

"You've lost me," the voice said.

"Ernie and Mattie Rowland were about to enroll in your program for home health care. You had two people working their case. Apparently, Mr. Rowland died during the interview process," I explained.

"We have no one working any Rowland case in Clancyville. Who did you say you were?"

"My name is Clancy Evans. I was simply calling to thank the person who stayed and helped Mattie Rowland after they found Ernie in his bed. That's all. I wasn't trying to get anyone in trouble. I just wanted to thank them personally for their assistance."

"Well, they must be working for some other company. We had no one in Clancyville today, and we don't know anything about any Mattie or Ernie Rowland wanting our services."

"Sorry to have bothered you. My error. Must have been another company. Thanks for your help."

They hung up without responding. Short and less than sweet.

"You look lost," Rosey said.

"Not lost, just floundering on a detail."

"Floundering?"

"It's what I do best when lose ends come flopping by."

"Flopping … is that detective jargon?"

"Must be. I seem to encounter it a great deal."

"And the loose end that flopped by…?" Rosey said.

"Residential Health Care rep said that they had no one in our fair town today working the Rowland case. In fact, they don't have a Rowland case here in Clancyville."

"That deserves a wow-ee. So what are you thinking?"

"I'm thinking that our mastermind killer was going after another juror who was not a resident of Peace Haven."

"He has broadened the playing field."

"Quite."

"Wow-ee."

"HEY, WHY DON'T YOU GO ON HOME AND GET SOME REAL sleep?" Rosey said. The sound of his voice woke me from my half-slumber, half-awake state. I was sitting in one of those tall-backed, cushioned, uncomfortable chairs always available in nursing or hospital facilities for the visitors. No doubt they were designed to be uncomfortable to keep people from staying too long.

Sarah was snoring gently. Apparently the sounds of her sleep were what did me in.

"You checked on J.R. recently?" I said.

"A few minutes ago. Deep sleep and snoring loudly."

"I think I will go and let you have the first night shift. How about I return around 2 a.m.?"

"Two it is. Take care of my car…and yourself," he said.

I slept peacefully in my old bed at Mother's. Sam slept on the floor nearby. I set the alarm for 1:30 and went to sleep quickly.

Just before two a.m. I arrived at Peace Haven to relieve Rosey. All was quiet there. Sarah was still gently snoring while J.R. was fretting about something in his dreams. The night was uneventful thus far. After Rosey left, I moved the uncomfortable chair into the hallway between the rooms for my guard post.

It was after eight when I saw Joy enter Sarah's room. I was more than willing to devoid myself of the chair-bed modeled after something used by the Spanish Inquisition a few years back. I moved my limbs slowly as to not do permanent damage by stretching after the five hours of nocturnal torture. I followed her into the room.

"How you folks doin' in here?" she said

"Hey, good morning," I said behind her.

"Good mornin'. Everyone okay?" Sarah was still sleeping away, although when I checked in on her earlier, she had been busy rolling from left side to her right side multiple times.

"I think all is well here. You want to check on Mr. Blair next door?"

"Not really," she said with a mischievous smile, "but I will."

I stretched for a few minutes more. My muscles were yelling obscenities at me from the self-imposed agony of sleeping in that chair from Hades. I recall frequent waking and napping during the hours since my return to relieve Rosey. There is nothing restful about keeping a vigil in a nursing home.

Joy stuck her head in the door and said, "Miss Evans, you needs to come quickly. I think something is wrong with Mr. J.R."

I followed her into the next room. Sure enough J.R. was in trouble. The man was convulsing, violently shaking the whole bed. The corded button for the nurse's station was wrapped around one of the side rails. I pushed it twice, hard. A voice from the speaker above his head answered, "May I help you?"

"Room 240. Mr. Blair is convulsing. He requires medical attention. Send someone down here quickly," I said.

I tried in vain to stop him from shaking so violently. It was obviously beyond my expertise. I was afraid that he might shake himself off of the bed into the floor despite the side rails. Something white was oozing from his mouth. One of his legs slid off of the bed and I grabbed it and put it back on the bed.

"Joy, you hold his chest down and I will hold his legs. Hopefully the nurse will be here soon," I said more from desperate hope than assurance.

I moved quickly to the end of his bed and put both hands on his feet. Something stuck me, like a sharp pen prick.

"Ouch!" I said and moved my right hand from his foot to see if I could find what I had inadvertently touched. An object was sticking out from between his big toe and first toe on his left foot. There was a box of plastic gloves on the night table, so I grabbed two and put them on. I removed the short, metal object from between his toes. It was a broken needle. It appeared to me that someone had broken off the needle of a syringe while injecting something into his foot. Despite my lack of knowledge concerning medical procedures, I knew that between the toes was not the usual spot for injecting patients with their meds, to say nothing of leaving a broken needle in the foot.

While still holding onto the broken syringe, I removed the plastic glove from my hand over the object, wrapping it completely in the one glove, and placed it in my pants pocket. I was hoping to preserve some possible prints, just in case the person who injected him had tried to remove the broken needle. At any rate, I had another clue.

"What you got there?" Joy asked.

"Don't know. Probably nothing. I'll have to check it out," I said. I was reluctant to tell her more than I thought she needed to know.

J.R. Blair stopped convulsing and lay perfectly still. I was checking for a pulse at his throat when the nurse came in. I moved aside to allow her to do her job.

"What did you do to this man?" she asked.

"Whoa there, Queenie," I said, taken aback by her question. "Let's get your facts straight. I came into this room, found this man shaking violently, called you and you just arrived. I've been trying to help him for five minutes or more. I'd change that tone if I were you."

"Sorry, but he's dead now. I need to know if you did anything to him?" she asked in a kinder voice.

"We held him down to keep him from jumping out of the bed; and, just now, we tried to take his pulse."

I looked at Joy and held off on telling the nurse about removing the broken syringe needle from the foot. "That's whut she did," Joy said.

"So you found him convulsing and then he just died?"

"That's the short version. I found him convulsing, tried to hold him into the bed, you showed up, then he died."

She pushed the button for the nurse's station and spoke to the monitor on the wall behind J.R.'s head, "We need a doctor in Room 240. Then call the funeral home."

The nurse ushered us out of the room and closed the door.

"You can't go back in there, but I need you to stay close so the doctor can talk with you."

"We'll be next door, Room 242. My friend Sarah is in this room," I pointed to the door of Sarah's room.

"Just don't leave. The doctor will definitely want to speak to you."

"I'll be here."

"You both need to stay," she said more to Joy than me.

"I'll be with her," Joy said and pointed to me.

The nurse walked away briskly.

"I don't think she believed you," Joy said.

"The world is full of skeptics. I'm one as well. Too many liars and not enough truth tellers, I suppose."

"I guess you be right on that," she affirmed. "You gonna tell them about that syringe breaking off?"

"Not yet. Need to know basis."

Sarah was sitting up in her bed when Joy and I entered the room.

"What's all the commotion out there?" Sarah asked.

"J.R. Blair is dead," Joy said before I could find a way to ease into the truth. Not sure how you soften the fact that the fellow next door has just died a violent death and he was likely another victim of murder.

"Oh, my Lord Jesus. Say it isn't so, please. What happened?"

"Don't know yet. The nurse is waiting on the doctor to come check him out."

"But we were all right here, right here in this room, not twenty feet from him. Did you hear anything?" she asked me.

"Nothing. But it must have just occurred," I said as much to myself as anyone else. I was pondering the situation, trying to rewind the several minutes before I discovered J.R. convulsing.

"Merciful God," Sarah said, "it could have been me. I could be next. They could come after me, child. They will come after me, child," Sarah said, suddenly realizing the danger she was in.

"It's okay, Sarah. I'm right here. I'm not leaving you."

"Clancy, dear Clancy, what are we gonna do?"

46

I SPENT THE NEXT HOUR OR SO TRYING TO CONSOLE SARAH. IT was easy to understand her anxiety. My count had reduced the number of jurors down to only two. All but one had died at Peace Haven. It was Sarah and Skeeter Shelton now. Skeeter was not a resident of Peace Haven, but Sarah definitely still was. She could easily be the next intended victim, although that fact was not certain since I had uncovered the unusual details around Ernie Rowland's natural death. Still, I had to focus on Sarah. I could never forgive myself if something happened to her while I was on watch. That would not be acceptable. I simply would not allow anyone to harm my dear, dear friend.

I called Rosey to update him on this turn of events.

"And you have the piece of syringe needle?" he asked.

"I do."

"And where are you to get it tested?"

"Good question. Dan River or Lynchburg would be the closest places available. Too far to go to Norfolk."

"You're thinking prints, right?" he asked.

"I am."

"What about having it tested for trace residue – whatever was in the syringe that was injected into J.R. Blair? You might have better luck with that than with prints," Rosey said.

"The *what* could lead us to the *who*."

"Be my tack. Either one could ultimately lead us to the other, I hope. But in this case, that inch of metal is not going to reveal much of a print, if any at all. And when you removed it with the gloves, you likely smudged whatever portion of a print might have been on it to begin with."

"The insightful investigator strikes again."

"Ever vigilant."

I closed the cell phone and sat down next to Sarah. We talked for another half hour. When I was satisfied that she was adjusting to the desperate situation occurring, I looked up the number of Dr. Jones-McCann and called her.

"Clancy here, doctor."

"Another autopsy?"

"Not this time, but I do need your assistance."

"I'm listening."

I told her about the broken syringe needle and what I was hoping to find.

"Bring it over to my office. I'll have it sent off today. I can do a preliminary check, but the lab in Lynchburg will do a much more thorough job for you."

"Thank you very much," I said and closed the phone.

"You lookin' for some type of poison?" Sarah asked.

"I believe so."

"No ideas?"

"Too many options. It's a killer's veritable cornucopia. Need to narrow the field. Maybe the broken needle will help."

"I don't think I want to stay here any longer, Clancy," Sarah said. "You think they'll let me leave?"

"Moot question," I said. "You and I will work something out."

I heard voices in the hallway and suspected that the doctor had finally arrived. I opened Sarah's room door and found myself staring into the face of Nurse Ratched, the charming one who questioned my integrity earlier in the morning. I recognized her as the one who had entered J.R. Blair's room just after he had stopped convulsing. Her name tag read Evelyn Guinn.

"I thought you had gone," she said.

"You asked me to stay."

"I didn't think you would."

"Here I am, Evelyn."

"The doctor is examining the body next door. When he is finished and makes his determination, I'll come get you and you can tell him what you did."

"The anticipation is getting the best of me," I said and shut the door.

I heard Sarah laughing from behind me. It was good to hear that sound once more.

"You always did have a mouth on you, child," she said.

"You think I was rude?"

"Borderline. You always had a way of getting next to people and ruffling feathers."

"My Evans' charm."

"More 'n likely it's that Clancy charm. You got your brains from the Evans' side, but your mouth comes from the same place Rachel Clancy got hers. I been around a long time, Clancy girl, you think I don't know both of them families? My, oh my, the stories I could tell."

"We'll have to do that some day. I'd like to hear some of your stories."

"Not my stories, girl. They be your stories. You just don't know 'em yet."

When the doctor finished his work with the body of J.R. Blair, he knocked on Sarah's door and I joined him in the hallway along with Joy. His name tag read *Dr. J. Miles Sinclair*. He asked his questions, and we answered. I told him the whole episode, leaving out the broken-syringe-in-the-foot part. A girl has to have her secrets. He was much nicer than Nurse Ratched, so I rather enjoyed talking with him. I tried to keep his feathers smooth. For some reason my character flaws were not as evident with him, and I actually believe he thought I was telling the truth. Now and then I would eye the good nurse Evelyn standing a few feet away from our conversation. Her expressions suggested to me that she was still not convinced of my story. He basically asked Joy the same questions and her answers more or less matched mine. At any rate, our conversation with the doctor finally ended and the medical entourage left with him.

My cell phone rang. It was Rosey.

"Your mother's car is gone," he said.

"Where'd she go?"

"Nowhere. She's right here with me."

"Who took the car?"

"Don't know."

"You mean the car's been stolen?"

"Good detectives never rest."

"She didn't leave it somewhere and forget where she left it, did she?"

"You want to ask her that?"

"No."

"Neither do I. I think someone absconded with her car."

"Begs the question of why?"

"They needed some wheels."

"Unlikely. My mother's car is not a hot item for car thieves. They'd do better stealing and stripping down bicycles."

"You're cruel."

"I've driven it for most of my life. I should know."

"But it runs. Gets her from A to B and back again."

"Running interference for her?"

"Defending her choice of cars."

"This coming from a Jag owner. Speaking of which, wonder why they stole a Studebaker and not the Jag."

"Locked, and state-of-the-art alarm system. Somebody try to steal the Jag, the alarm wakes the neighborhood and notifies the D.C. police," Rosey bragged.

"Doubt if the thieves knew that. Did you call Sheriff Robby?"

"Just got off of the phone. Gave them the plates' info and the description."

"Shouldn't be too hard to find. How many Studebaker Hawks could there be in greater Clancyville? It's not like the car will blend in with all the other rattletraps roaming the streets of our village."

"Point. Anyway, the local authorities are checking into it."

"No doubt. Well, isn't that a fine turn of events. With everything else we have going, we now dealing with petty thievery."

"I think that's grand larceny," Rosey said.

"I think you are over-rating the car's worth."

"Not to your mother," Rosey said.

47

"THERE'S A CHILL IN THE AIR, MARIE. CLOSE THE WINDOWS. Ah… leave a gap in the curtains behind me, so I can see out a little."

"Yes sir." Marie closed the drapes except for a small section directly behind the massive wooden desk. "You want me to bring you the dogs?"

"No. Just leave us alone."

The tall thin woman stood several feet away from the front of the desk. Although rigid and quiet, her eyes followed every move Marie made. She relaxed ever so slightly as soon as Marie closed the door and was gone.

"Is it done?"

"Yes."

"I would rather not know your method, you understand."

"Yes."

"Down to one."

"Yes."

"It will all be accomplished soon, correct?"

"Hopefully."

"That's not the answer I desire."

"The last juror is guarded closely."

"Always?"

"24/7."

"Talk with our assistant. Maybe she can do something under the radar."

"I will."

"I don't want any miscues at this point. Justice must prevail. I have waited a long, long time for this to happen. This is divinely appointed, you know."

"I have heard you say that."

"You sound skeptical," the old preacher said.

"I am not a religious person. I have questions."

"About the justice for those ungodly jurors?"

"No. The jurors were wrong. My questions have only to do with any divine influence."

"I am a man of God, a spokesman, like the prophets long ago. God gave me this mission, this divine mission to carry out. To do justice. To bring down the haughty, the proud, the arrogant, the infidels. These people had no moral ground on which to stand to judge my son for what he did. He was purging absolute sin from our community. No black and white should ever be mingled. This is the word of the Lord," his voice reached a fever pitch.

"Yes, sir."

"You don't believe in God, Miss Saunders?"

She was hesitant, afraid that her ideas would cause him to explode in self-righteous anger. She was searching for the right words.

"I have lots of questions," she confessed.

"Perhaps we should talk about this when the mission is finally accomplished."

She could see a way out now. She relaxed and felt more at ease, but not completely. She never experienced total ease in his presence. That was quite impossible. She never quite understood the man despite the years she had worked for him.

"That would be good, sir. I would like that," she lied.

"Good. Any word about Diamond?"

"Nothing.".

"You believe she is still out there?"

"I do."

"Why would she stay at it?"

"She's a professional. Relentless. Never quits."

"Sounds as if you know her well."

"No sir. Only by reputation. My contact told me that there is none better."

"Let's hope so. And soon. For my money, she is taking entirely too much time to get this private investigator off the trail. One more death and it really will not matter anyway, I suppose."

"I have no control over the timing of her success."

"I know, I know. You've told me that. I don't like it. It worries me when I do not have control over what is happening. She's a loose end."

"The detective or Diamond?" Saunders was having trouble following the conversation.

"Both. But I was referring to the shooter."

"The last juror could be difficult to handle as long as the detective is around. Once she is gone, then our work is made much easier. It all goes together, it seems to me."

"I suppose you are right," he said as he turned away from her face to look out the narrow gap that Marie had left in the curtains behind him. "Sometimes I feel as if God is impatient with me and won't let me see the promised land of satisfaction. You know anything about Moses, Miss Saunders?"

"A little. He led the Jews out of Egypt, I think. Wrote the Ten Commandments. That's about it."

"We have much to talk about, Miss Saunders. Your

biblical education is sorely lacking. My fault, I fear. But all in good time. No, Moses was a stalwart leader of the Israelites. Great man. Perhaps the greatest of all in history, except Jesus, of course. Moses was a commander, a lawgiver, a judge, and a dispenser of justice. Moses was God's right hand for many years. You understand that, Miss Saunders?"

"I understand your words, sir. It seems that you admire him greatly."

"Oh, absolutely, Miss Saunders. Absolutely. I have tried to model my life after Moses. I feel in some ways as if I have been a modern day Moses. And that worries me a little."

"Why's that?"

"God only let him see the land of promise, Canaan, the land of glory, the land of fulfillment. Moses died and never got to cross over into the land of hope and anticipation. He only saw it from a distance."

"We're about to cross over, sir. We're very close now. Another day or so, and I think you will be in your land of justice."

He turned back from the curtain gap to face her. He stared into her eyes for a few seconds before speaking. She noticed a gleam in his eyes.

"Correct, Miss Saunders. We are close. I am about to cross over. Go finish the job. I shall pray for your success."

She nodded slightly, almost a bow as she backed away to the door. As she walked down the long corridor towards the front door of the mansion, she decided that she wanted nothing more to do with this man after this was all over. Saunders believed the preacher to be mentally unstable. She had never noticed it before now, at least not to this degree. He was mad, she concluded. He was out of his mind and her level of fear was growing, especially when they were alone in that large room.

Marie was waiting by the front door. Saunders exited and

Marie closed the door behind her. Saunders concluded that she did not want to have that conversation with the preacher about God when this whole episode was over. She would leave town and go far away. She would go away and he would never find her. No one would find her unless she wanted to be found. That would be her plan. It felt good to have a plan. Maybe going away was her *promised land*. She smiled to herself as if she finally understood something of what the old preacher was saying.

48

IT WAS LATE AFTERNOON WHEN ROSEY ARRIVED TO RETRIEVE me from Peace Haven. He stood in the threshold of Sarah's opened room door.

"You ready for some relief?" he asked.

"And how," I said. "Only there is to be a slight change in our schedule."

"Okay. Let me have it."

"You and I are leaving together, and Sarah is going with us."

"Oh, good. I love togetherness. They're setting you free, are they?" he smiled at Sarah and she easily returned it to him.

"Not entirely. They don't know I be leaving this place," she said.

"Oh, this is a breakout."

"Something like that," I said. "I didn't want to announce our departure to the officials here."

"Are we doing this now?"

"Yes, sir. We are packed and ready to roll," I said.

"Front door?"

I smiled at him. "Even I am not that brazen. We're escaping through the side entrance, where the ambulances park. Used for entering and exiting via those medical vehicles."

"Oh. And the alarms?"

"Not on those doors."

"But they don't open from the inside, do they?"

"They do now."

"You've been playin' around with stuff again, huh?" he asked.

"I've been a busy little girl. Let's get outta here."

Rosey led the way with Sarah. She was still wobbly with walking, but he had an arm around her and I knew Sarah didn't mind that at all. I followed, carrying her packed suitcase. It was just before supper time and everyone was preoccupied with either the first deliveries or preparation for the meal. There were enough distractions for us to make a clean getaway.

"Ooh, I like this car," Sarah said as we drove out of the parking lot, heading towards Mother's house.

"Me, too," Rosey said.

"Let's swing by Dr. Jones-McCann's office. I have a clue which needs to be checked and re-checked," I said.

"Yes, ma'am. Forthwith."

Mother was pleased when our caravan of three arrived. She had been baby-sitting the dog for too many hours. But at least I think there had been some bonding between them. At least now she was talking to him.

"Sam, get back. Let them in," she said as we marched up the back steps in single file. Rosey still had a steadying hand on Sarah's backside to make sure she got up the steps and inside the house safely. Sarah stopped and hugged Rachel on the porch before entering the house.

"Sam, how are you?" Sarah said. Sam sat down and

extended a paw to Sarah in his formal method of greeting old friends. She took it and they shook.

After we had all settled into our seats of choice, Mother quizzed us concerning Sarah's presence. Sarah and Mother were on the couch together. Sam was lying on the floor in between their feet.

"They released you?" Mother asked Sarah.

"Not knowingly."

"You just walked out and left?"

"Something like that," I said.

"Why?"

"Thought it'd be safer here," I said. I left the part out where Sarah had asked to leave Peace Haven. Sarah was quiet on the subject. Our little secret.

"A whole lot safer, I hope," Mother said.

"You take the guest room upstairs, the one close to my bedroom. That way I can keep a close eye on you," she said to Sarah.

"Thank you, ma'am. I hope this won't be any trouble."

"No such thing," Mother said. "Good to have you back home again."

"It feels like home," Sarah said.

"It is home," Mother said emphatically. "Oh, Ben Pickeral found my car."

"Good," I said.

"Not really," Mother added. "Whoever stole it drove it off into a gulley out near Mossie's Point, near where your uncle used to live, Rosey."

"Badly damaged?" he asked.

"Don't know. Haven't seen it yet. The sheriff told me there was blood all over the front end."

"Blood?" I asked.

"They believe it was involved in a hit and run."

"They know who or where?"

"Unfortunately, yes. Poor old Skeeter Shelton and his caregiver were run down. The caregiver was transported to Lynchburg General by helicopter. Skeeter was taken to Cuthbert-Boran."

Sarah looked at me immediately. I could see the fear in her eyes. "I'm the last one," she said. "I'm next."

"Don't get ahead of yourself. You're safe here," I said, hoping to allay her fears a little.

"You have to find who's doing this, Clancy. You have to stop them," Sarah said.

"We will," I said, unconvincingly, even to myself.

"Well, you haven't done such a hot job so far," Mother offered.

Thanks, Mom. Always nice to have someone like you in my corner. Mrs. Encouragement. I had nothing to say to counter her opinion since she spoke the truth, even if I didn't want to hear it.

"Where's the car now?" I asked.

"I think they towed it out to B&R Auto Repair. Shelby has a fenced in, locked area to protect his vehicles. Sheriff said it was the only safe place to keep the car while some outsiders checked it out," Mother said.

"Outsiders?" Rosey asked.

"Robby asked for help from both Lynchburg and Dan River. I think some investigators from Lynchburg came down to see if they could find anything," Mother said.

"Likely some crime scene techs," I surmised out loud.

"I suppose," Mother said, "but he didn't say exactly what they would be investigating."

I motioned to Rosey with my head and he joined me on the back porch.

"Let's go check out the car and see if we can find anything ourselves."

"I'm game," he said. "Your mother takes no prisoners with

her opinions."

"Never did, never will. I'm used to it by now, but I admit it stings occasionally. I wish she had more faith in me."

"Like me," he said.

"Like you."

49

SHELBY'S PLACE, B&R AUTO REPAIR, WAS LOCATED ON OLD Highway 29 North out of Clancyville. It was remote since only one side of the road had businesses once you passed out of the town limits, and Shelby's was only the third business in a half-mile stretch. Across from Shelby's crowded, dirty buildings and fenced-in car lots was a steep bank and train tracks running along the top of the steep bank. Trains still ran north and south through Clancyville. Years ago the town was a significant stop along the rails. That was before the old train station on Main Street was torn down and discarded. The only sign of rail life these days was the red caboose placed across from where the train station stood. It was more like a museum than any actual evidence of trains. An occasional train passed through town bellowing its whistle to remind folks of another era. It was the periodic interruption of twenty-first century life by what was considered a defunct past by many.

It was a little after 6 o'clock in the evening when Rosey and I arrived at Shelby's place. Shelby was just leaving when we pulled in. Shelby locked his dirty office door and met us at the Jag.

"I don't work on sports cars," he said to Rosey.

"Don't need any work," he said.

Shelby looked at me, studied me for a few seconds, and then said, "Aren't you Bill Evans' daughter?"

"The same."

"Well, well. Good to see again, Clancy. Been years."

"At least. We need to see my mother's car."

"You're a big city detective now, huh?"

"Some would say less than that. I work in Norfolk."

He moved towards the car lot to our left and motioned for us to follow. He had a key chain that held more keys than a high school custodian. As he led us to the fenced area, Shelby flipped through them searching for the correct key. He found the one he wanted and unlocked the padlock. He moved the gate just enough for a body to walk through. He left the padlock hanging on the chain link fence.

"Close this and lock it back when you're finished. I'm late for supper. Hope you find whatever you're looking for. Car's in good shape. I think the bumper is dented slightly, but nothing else seems out of whack. I'll check it out real close as soon as the cops are finished doing their thing," Shelby said.

"Thanks, Shelby. We'll lock it up," I said.

He walked away without another word.

"Trusting soul," Rosey said.

"Solid reputation," I said.

We walked into the lot and searched for my mother's Studebaker. We heard Shelby's tires spitting rocks as the truck pulled onto the highway from his graveled parking area. It took a few minutes to find the car. The fenced-in area was full, but we located it finally near the back.

The blood was still evident on the bumper. Shelby was

right about the car. None the worse considering what had happened. I took a photo of the bumper.

"They don't make 'em like this anymore," Rosey said.

"Nor should they."

"Let's not be too hasty. This was a well built car."

"Why didn't you buy one then? Instead of that Jag thing."

"Don't get testy. It has to do with lines and curves and important things."

"Lines and curves? Sounds like you were looking for a female relationship."

"Wouldn't argue the point."

"Men," I said and shook my head.

I saw Rosey go down before I heard the report of the rifle shot. He had been standing close to me, but I was moving away from him to look at the back of the car when the shot came. We were both on the ground and waiting for another shot or sound. No movement from us, and nothing else happening for the present.

"You okay?" I said.

"I'll live."

"You hit?"

"Arm. Through and through."

"Which?"

"Left. I can still shoot."

He crawled over to my location behind the Studebaker.

"Aren't you glad this car is made solid?" he said.

"Tickled pink. You spot the shooter?"

"Across the road, up on that bank, straight across from us."

"Our rifle friend has returned?"

"Be my guess. I need to move over there," he said and pointed towards the front entrance of the car lot, "so that you can get out the back entrance," he nodded in the direction of a gate twenty yards away from our position.

I looked at the locked gate now behind us.

"And how do you expect me to get out that locked gate back there?"

"Womanly wiles."

"You have other ideas?"

"Yeah, I will begin firing as soon as I get to where I am going, and you will have plenty of time to clear the gate."

"It's at least eight feet high," I said in protest. "You want me to climb over?"

"That or fly."

"Talk about being a sitting duck."

"Don't dilly dally once you get up there."

"I think we need another plan," I said.

"If you move at the first sound of my gun firing, and as tall as you are, you should have no trouble clearing that fence in a matter of seconds. Now stop arguing and get ready climb quickly."

He slid along the parked cars in the back of the lot towards the gate through which we had entered. A shot ricocheted close to Rosey's head. I was watching closely. Another shot ricocheted off the chain link fence behind him. The shooter was narrowly missing him. I wondered if it was intentional misses. Rosey continued toward the front gate.

Another shot shattered a windshield close to Rosey's position. The shooter was definitely following Rosey's trek to the gate. I would have fired in the direction of the shooter, but he was too far away for my gun to do any good. Rosey had another fifty feet or so in order to reach the front entrance. He stopped and motioned for me. I took his gesture to mean it was now my turn to move. Ah, the fun of being a big city detective.

As soon as I moved towards the back gate of the lot, Rosey opened fire. Several rounds gave me ample time to go up and over the gate in seconds, none the worse for the wear.

I was aging, but I still had some climbing ability leftover from my vigorous youth. Lucky for me that Shelby didn't have barbed wire across the top of the gate like he had all along the rest of the fence. Rosey was still firing in the direction of the shooter as I made my way along the outside of the lot. There was a small grove of trees and a creek behind Shelby's lot and I used the bank of the creek and the trees as cover to move along in a direction towards the town and away from Rosey's position. I traveled about two hundred yards hoping to get some distance from the shooter's peripheral vision.

I emerged from the little forest and the shallow water bed at the far end of the last row of Shelby's used cars. I had to cross the highway without benefit of cover here. Rosey stopped firing and I thought he was either reloading or dead. I waited for an opportunity to cross the road.

After a minute or so, Rosey opened fire again and I made my break. By the time that I was breathing heavy on my perch atop the embankment, I had crossed the highway and had climbed the challenging hill in a matter of seconds. I was about three hundred yards down from where I suspected the rifleman to be. A thicket of dying honeysuckle provided some ground cover for me as I slid along the front side of the ridge in the direction of Rosey and the shooter. After a hundred yards or so, I decided that my advance might be better served if I crossed the tracks and climbed down the short ridge on the backside of the train tracks. That way I would not be quite as vulnerable to whoever was up ahead trying to kill us. Now and then the rifleman from my side of the highway would fire a shot towards the car lot. I assumed by this that Rosey was still alive enough to be drawing fire.

I noted that Rosey would pause for a minute or so, either reloading his weapon or shifting positions, and then engage the rifleman once more. Moving along as quickly as I could, I made good time on the back side of the ridge towards the target. I estimated my target's position by the shots being fired. It was really nothing more than guesswork.

I crawled up the short ridge slowly, hoping to surprise the rifleman from behind. At least that was the sort of strategic haphazard plan I was putting together as I left the car lot and meandered my way to this particular position. Think on the fly so to speak.

It is not often that my planning works to perfection, but on this occasion I was spot-on with the shooter's location. As I quietly and slowly climbed to the train tracks so as to see along the top of the ridge, I spotted the shooter not more than a hundred feet slightly to my left. He was dressed in camouflage attire, top to bottom, and wearing a dark green watch cap while leaning against a tree on Rosey's side of the tracks. I decided to use the train tracks for my final approach. With the Smith and Wesson 360 drawn, a loaner from Rosey, I balanced myself on the steel railroad track on my side of the ridge. I was more or less behind the shooter, away from his peripheral vision. Still, I was overly cautious in my movements, time and again, stopping to gain some breath, to re-balance myself, and to re-evaluate my surroundings. Concentration is a must at this point of a hunt especially when the prey has a weapon. I had to look both at my feet on the rails and at the shooter ahead of me now on my right. Each step was the same – down at my feet to be sure of my footing, then up at the shooter leaning against the tree. Now and again he would fire in Rosey's direction. There were long pauses between his shots. Rosey was not affording him a clear target. Despite the weight of the revolver in my hand, it was the sufficient fire power I desired at this moment. I had only five rounds, so I couldn't engage the rifleman in a gun battle. I either had to kill him or hope that he would succumb to my significant advantage behind him with a .357 aimed at him.

I stepped cautiously from the steel rail to the soft dirt of the ridge.

"I would suggest that you make no sudden moves, but that you slowly toss that rifle down the embankment in front of you. This .357 is fully loaded and more than capable of injuring you to the point of death if I fire only one shot," I said to the shooter now about thirty feet in front of me.

He raised his right arm without turning around, lifted the rifle slowly with his left hand and tossed it down the bank directly into a thicket of ground cover, a mixture of darkening kudzu and wild plants dying off after the early frosts.

"Now, back away from the bank and the tree towards the train track. Turn slowly towards me. I hate shooting people in the back, but I will if you do anything but what I say."

He took one step away from the tree and slowly turned in my direction. His face was much softer than I had imagined, although I had not an inkling of a notion as to what he might look like. I was too focused on staying alive and keeping whatever advantage I thought I had over him.

"Take off the watch cap," I said.

He removed it and his long, brown hair fell onto his shoulders. He immediately became a she. Talk about wow moments in the history of gunfights.

"Isn't this is a delightful turn of events? I don't suppose you would give me your name," I said.

"Not a chance," she answered.

"Who hired you?"

"Negative on that too," she replied.

"Well, let me see if I can ask something you might be willing to tell me," I said and paused. I decided to move no closer to her for fear that she might actually be quicker at some close-in, hand to hand combat technique way beyond my skill level. I had the .357 pointed directly at her head and the thirty feet in front of me. I liked my odds, but wanted nothing nearer since I suspected her to be a trained assassin.

"Were you hired to kill both my friend across the road and me?" I asked.

"Finally a question I can answer. Yes."

"Package deal, or separate contract on each of us?"

"Simultaneous contracts. Double the money," she said.

"I'm flattered to be in the same price range as Rosey. He's a much better prize."

"Perhaps, but you were the mark. Still are. He was in the wrong place, wrong time. Not important to me. Nothing personal. It's what I do."

"So good to meet a true professional these days. Okay, here's the problem. I don't want you to kill me, nor my friend. And I really don't want to kill you either. So, the way I figure this, if I let you go, you will continue to stalk me and try to earn your money. Correct so far?" I said.

"Correct."

"And if I turn you over to the local law, you would likely escape from their custody because ... well, you're you and they're them, if you get my drift."

"I do. I will."

"You see the problem. I suppose I could take the time to escort you to Lynchburg or Dan River. Their jails and police are of higher quality, if you please. But I imagine that you have been inside some very fine facilities and left those facilities without proper paper work."

"I have. And will again."

"Clancy, jump!" Rosey's voice yelled from down the embankment, behind the shooter. Without thinking, I followed his frantic and forceful instruction and jumped down my side of the train tracks, down the short hill from the ridge, down away from the female assassin. As I rolled, I heard two shots fired and then the gigantic explosion which sent rocks, cross-tie pieces, and mutilated vegetation descending on top of me. I correctly guessed that my conversation with my adversary was finished for the moment. At present, I was more concerned with counting fingers, toes, and other vital body parts which belonged to me. That would have to wait, however. I found myself completely covered under the barrage of dirt, rock, and splinters of wood and shredded foliage. I suspected that whatever advantage I had over my female counterpart was now gone.

50

By the time I came to my senses and at least some awareness of where I was, Rosey was removing debris off of me and asking me if I was okay.

"I suppose. I haven't had time to take a complete inventory," I said.

"Well, you can talk and think. That's a start," he said.

"I'll probably do that when I'm half-dead."

"No doubt. You almost were all dead."

"What happened?"

"He had a trip-wire attached to his boot which was attached to his buried land mines some twenty feet out from him, all around the top side of the ridge. I fortunately saw the wire as I was climbing up the bank behind him while you two were talking. The setting sun reflected by the wire, or I never would have seen it. I wouldn't be talking to you now except for Mr. Sun. How close were you standing?"

"Probably thirty feet or so. Maybe less."

"Close, Sherlock. Too close for comfort."

"And here I was worried about her hand to hand combat techniques."

"Beg your pardon?"

"Her hand to hand combat skills… I was concerned, so I kept my distance."

"Her?"

"Our rifleman is a woman," I said. "You didn't see her?"

"Saw the target. Fired twice, hit the target twice, saw the target fall. Gender is not even secondarily an issue. Came to you instead of …the target."

"True S.E.A.L. Reckon she's dead?" I asked.

"Let's go see."

"Cautiously. She seems to be a careful planner. I don't want to stumble into another mine field, if you know what I mean."

"I do," he said.

We climbed the short hill and moved slowly around the circumference of the shallow pit that was created by the land mine explosion moments ago.

"Where did she fall?"

"Over there," he pointed to a spot some ten feet from the tree against which she was leaning earlier.

We walked in that direction, making sure that we circumvented the radius of her land mine circle. If anything, she was neat and exact, so it was easy enough to follow the logic of her thinking.

There was no body. We searched in vain for some sign, some evidence that she was down and out of the picture.

"There's blood over here," Rosey said after a few minutes. "At least I hit the target."

"You had doubts?"

"No, just wanted some evidence. But I can't believe she's still alive."

"Know the location of the hit?"

"After I yelled for you to get out of the way, my target began moving to her left. I put one in her left side as she dove to the ground. The second shot likely hit her in the left thigh because of her quick movement. She's hit all right. I don't miss very often at such a distance."

"Just checking, no offense meant at your shooting skill. Can we follow the blood trail?"

"Sho' nuff," Rosey said and started off down the embankment towards Shelby's auto shop.

"Look for her rifle, too. It should be in this area," I pointed to the spot where I recall her tossing the weapon.

We found no rifle. We did find blood, more of it, in the place where I had remembered the rifle falling. We continued down the hill and blood trail was evident all along the way.

"I think she's bleeding badly."

"Injured animal. Very dangerous."

The blood trail led us across the highway and back towards the spot where Shelby kept his used cars in front of the fenced in lot where the Studebaker was housed. There was a gap between two cars and more blood.

"Think she stole one of Shelby's?"

"Or was smart enough to park her own vehicle in that space," Rosey said.

"Either way …."

"Either way."

We headed back to my mother's and I nursed my minor injuries. I had managed to receive some cuts and bruises which hurt, but nothing serious. My face was dirty from wallowing around in the thicket, plus the blood was starting to dry on my cheek and forehead.

"Think she'll go after Sarah?" Rosey asked.

"No. She's after us."

"You know that … how?"

"She told me."

"Oh. And you trust her because…."

"No reason not to. Two contracts, one for you and one on me."

"Different prices, though."

"Sorry. Same price."

"I am offended. I should think a good looking African American male, highly intelligent, skilled in all manner of martial arts and warfare, graduate of UVA and Harvard—"

"Okay, okay. I get the idea. I'd be offended, too. But she probably doesn't know all of that, or didn't when she took the contract. Next time, she'll ask for more."

"Next time? Won't be no next time, Sister."

"I see. Sure of yourself, are we?"

"Hide and watch."

"Plan to do that, at least."

"So, we have an assassin after us and someone entirely different after Sarah."

"That's the fact, Jack. At least we now know what she looks like, and that she's a she, and good at her profession," I said.

"Uh, not so good, but wounded. *She's* a wounded animal," Rosey said.

"Makes her dangerous. I still wouldn't discount her abilities."

"She's come close, but missed us so far."

"Luck."

"Maybe for you, but not for me," he said.

"Let's add angry to that dangerous assessment," I said.

"If she's a true professional, she won't have an emotion like anger. It's not personal. She's hired. Accepts the contract, takes the money, and goes about her business."

"And now she's wounded."

"She'll crawl into a hole and wait for some healing. I nailed her twice. She'll require a day or two, maybe more. Then she'll come after us again."

"You think she requires medical attention?"

"Yeah, I do. But she won't sit in the waiting room bleeding all over the furniture. Someone might notice, even in Clancyville."

"Unscheduled nocturnal visit, then."

"Be my guess."

51

It was dark when Rosey and I walked into the living room of my mother's home and found Sheriff Robby Robertson and his faithful deputy, Ben Pickeral, talking with Mother. Sam was pretending to be asleep at her feet. Sarah was not in the room. More than likely she was resting in one of the bedrooms upstairs, listening to the conversation.

I was still wearing some of the debris from the explosion on Business Highway 29. Truth is, I looked a bit frightful. At least Rosey said as much in the ride home.

"Have you been looking for buried treasure, Clancy?" Sheriff Robby said.

"I was involved in an explosion."

"Should I investigate?"

"Might turn up something. One never knows. What do we owe the honor of your presence?" I said.

"Just asking Rachel Jo some questions about her car, the one we found that had run down poor old Skeeter."

"He wants to know my whereabouts yesterday when Skeeter Shelton was killed," Rachel Jo, my mother, said.

"You suspect my mother?" I asked.

"No, not really. But I have to ask. You know that."

"Sure. Did you tell him?"

"I did. I also told him that if I wanted Skeeter out of the way, I wouldn't use the Studebaker to do it."

"Well put, Mother. And you found other prints in the car besides Rachel's?" I said.

"No. Just hers. And yours."

"So any other evidence?"

"Well," Robby sighed as he scratched his balding head with the hand that wasn't holding his official Yankee cap, "we found some stuff at the crime scene, but nothing where the car was ditched. By the way, the keys were still in it."

"I always leave the keys in the car," Rachel said.

"Always?" Robby said.

"Most of the time. This is Clancyville. Who's going to steal my car, the only Studebaker in town? Everyone knows that's my car."

"Well, apparently, whoever wanted to kill Skeeter Skelton stole your car," Robby answered.

"I suppose I need to ask you now if you believe me about someone killing off the folks at Peace Haven." I asked.

"It looks suspicious," he said.

I saw Rosey roll his eyes. Sam sighed heavily for some reason. The ever vigilant local authorities were on the hunt. The crime would certainly be solved forthwith.

"Two people were not at Peace Haven," Ben Pickeral offered to the conversation. Ben usually said nothing, just sat quietly listening and thinking about whatever it was that Ben thought about during official investigations. He had the same technique during unofficial investigations as well.

"Good point," I said. "I think whoever is behind all this is hurrying up the procedure. Impatient or worried, one or the other."

"Because we might be on to them?" Ben asked.

I almost laughed out loud, but managed to stifle it. No sense insulting the local cops when not absolutely necessary.

"No doubt," I said. "Hot on the case."

"Well, when you get some real evidence that I can use, Clancy, you come see me," Robby said as he stood. "In the meantime, you mind telling me where that explosion took place and if you think it is related to all of this?"

"I'll tell you, but I don't think it is directly related to all of this. Tangential."

"Beg your pardon," Robby said.

"Hazards of my profession, Sheriff. Meant to throw you off the scent."

"Oh. But since it was an unauthorized explosion, I have to check it out. Where'd this happen?"

"Highway Business 29 North. Across from Shelby's place. Up the embankment, and look for a tree that's been there for a while. You'll see the hole nearby that was left."

"Any ideas on what caused this explosion?"

"Land mines," Rosey said.

"Land mines," Robby said, repeating Rosey's pitch. "Anything damaged?"

"You mean besides my bruises, scratches, and clothing?"

"Besides that."

"Some ground and a portion of the train track," I said.

Robby rubbed his chin as if pondering my words. He stood and Ben followed suit. Robby moved slowly and methodically. He might not be the brightest bulb in the chandelier, but he wasn't stupid by any means. He noticed Rosey's arm was heavily bandaged but the dark, red stain had penetrated the several layers of wrappings which Rosey had secured around the wound with my able assistance.

"That from the explosion as well?" Robby asked.

"No. Another injury."

"Should I know about that?"

"Not unless you want to fill out lots and lots of forms for the rest of the evening," Rosey said.

"I'll get back to you on that. In the meantime, Rachel Jo, when the car comes home, keep the keys in the house somewhere."

"Sure thing, Sheriff. With this growing crime spree, I'll probably have to start locking the doors to my house as well."

The sheriff and his faithful deputy turned in unison to leave.

"You gonna ask me, Robby?" I said.

"Ask you what?"

"Where I was when Skeeter Shelton was run over."

"Why would I ask you that?" Robby said.

"Because my prints were also found in the car."

"Oh. Yeah. Must've slipped my mind. Where were you?"

"Seriously?"

"You brought it up," he said.

"I was busy at the Peace Haven home."

"Busy doin' what?"

"Figuring a way to smuggle my friend Sarah Jones out of that place," I confessed.

"You devised a plan, I'm sure."

"I did."

"Successful?" he said.

"She's upstairs. Safe and sound. Now you're satisfied of my innocence?"

"Regarding Skeeter's death, I was before I asked you. But I'm not so sure of you being innocent of much at all."

I smiled as the sheriff and his deputy walked out the back door. Only in rural America. I couldn't imagine a conversation like that with the police in Norfolk.

When the room ambience changed after the departure of Andy and Barney, Rosey and I told Mother the whole truth about our adventure at Shelby's. By this point I figured she needed to know what was happening.

"Sounds like whoever is behind all of these murders is serious about finishing it off."

"That means Sarah is at risk, no matter where she is."

"You sayin' I'm at risk, too," Mother said.

"Yes, ma'am. We have to think that way. If you are standing between the killer and his intended victim, you will be removed. Permanently."

"I don't want Sarah going anywhere," Mother said.

"Me either," I agreed. "I believe she is safer here than anywhere else."

"You have any good leads?"

"No, but we have lots of rabbits to chase and some working theories," I said.

"We do rabbits well," Rosey said.

"And theories," I said.

"We have one theory," he said. "But it's not well developed."

"But it has plausibility."

"It has that. But no evidence."

"I have a plan."

"Better than what I have," Rosey said. "You want to share?"

"Okay, Rachel, you now get the gun you wanted. Since we are convinced that we're up against violent people who will do anything to kill, get one of Dad's rifles and have it close. You might need it."

"I know just the rifle I'll use," she said.

"Rosey, let's stay on Saunders. She's obviously involved, we just don't know how much. My guess is that she's a puppet to the preacher, but we have nothing to connect him, except what Saunders might yet do."

"Stalking is good."

"Sam and I will go courtesy calling."

"On whom, may I ask?" Rosey said.

"Our first stop will be a visit to Mattie Rowland."

"I'd wait until after the funeral," Rachel said.

"That's tomorrow?"

"Yes."

"Then I'll hold off a day or so and go offer my sympathies."

"And ask questions," she said.

"I'll be gentle. She'll never know I'm investigating anything."

"Like me," she said. "I'd never know you are investigating anything."

Sam raised his head as Rachel walked out of the room and went upstairs. His expression of bewilderment matched mine as we stared at one another for a moment. I shook my head in disbelief. Sam shook his head as if to clear the cobwebs of sleep as well as puzzlement.

Rosey was smiling, highly amused with the interchange between mother and daughter.

"She has your charm and wit," he said. "Fallen apples from trees, there's nothing like it."

52

THE NEXT MORNING SAM WAS SITTING IN THE BACK SEAT centered between Rosey and myself. His preferable position for peering. We were parked on Washington Street, just down from Saunders's home on Leftwich Street. Rosey and Sam were busy watching her driveway and house, I was on the phone with Rogers. As far as Rosey was concerned, I was entering data via my cell phone, like a diary. Actually, I was permitting Rogers' acerbic diatribes to go unanswered while I was forced to maintain a cool, unruffled composure.

"The least you could do would be to call and let me know that you are okay," Rogers said.

"After our encounter with the assassin, we returned to my mother's house. She was being interviewed by the local sheriff, Robby Robertson and his deputy, Ben Pickeral."

"Frank and Ernest are up to their necks in murdered bodies and they're trying to pin this on your mother."

"I informed the sheriff about the explosion across from Shelby's auto shop and they left to check on that."

"They still are skeptical of your sparse evidence, are they not?" Rogers said.

"The evidence we have gathered is chiefly circumstantial," I said.

"Except for the attempts on your life, which seem to be more prevalent."

"Check on known female assassins operating out of the big cities like Chicago, New York, Dallas, Los Angeles, and Salt Lake City."

"You did connect the dots, didn't you, Miss Super Detective?"

"If you find anything of substance, call me," I said.

"That assassin is probably that old bag lady at the dumpster who knocked you senseless with the cinder block. Forget about that already?"

"Interesting," I said.

"Sure is, Sweetie Pie. See, I'm not just another pretty face around here. You should trust me more, ask me what I think, and call me with updates on your whereabouts and what's going on with your charmed life," Rogers said. She was on a roll.

"Thanks for the connection," I wanted to say more but thought better of the idea with Rosey half-listening to every word.

"Sarah and Rachel okay?"

"Update on Sarah Jones ... staying with Mother instead of the Peace Haven facility since she is the last remaining juror from that trial of 1970. She is safe at present."

"Mother doing guard duty?"

"Everything is under control at present."

"Yeah, right. Like you could control your mother. Give me a break," she quipped.

"Call me with any updates. End of notes for October first," I said as a way of saying goodbye to Rogers.

"Call me regularly," she demanded just before I closed the phone.

"So tell me what is *interesting*," Rosey said. "Seems to me that everything we do nowadays is *interesting*."

"The computer suggested that our assassin is the same person as the bag lady by the dumpster who crowned me with the cinder block."

"Suggested?" he asked.

"Okay, logically deduced from the data I had entered. Poor choice of words," I said.

"Interesting choice of *word*," he replied. "Suggested…. hmmm."

He was pondering while he continued to watch the driveway about four hundred yards from our parked position on the side street. We were located on the north end of Washington Street. Despite our vigilance, nothing was happening at Saunders' place.

I had an idea, so I flipped open the phone and searched my data base for the number.

"Whatever did we do before the invention of cell phones?" he asked.

"Use more gasoline driving around looking for pay phones," I said as I listened to the ringing in my ear.

I have a long-time and experience tested theory of investigating. If nothing is working, do something different. It's quite similar to another axiom of shrewd investigating which is if one day you find yourself in a hole with a shovel, stop digging. Climb out of that hole and go dig somewhere else. Basic stuff.

"Good morning! Isn't life beautiful? How may I help you?" the sweet, syrupy voice on the other end of my cell phone said.

"Jessica? This is Clancy, Clancy Evans."

"Clancy Evans. My goodness gracious, how in the world have you been? It's been such a long time since I have seen you to talk with you. How long has it been, dear? It must be at least fifty years. Has it been fifty years, Clancy?"

I exited the Jag. It was a warm, sunny October day and the car seemed to be more confining than usual.

"Not quite, Jessica. I'm not that old yet."

"Well then I guess it couldn't have been that long. But it sure seems like fifty years. It is so good to hear your voice after all those years. How are you, dear?"

"I am fine, thank you, Jessica. And how are you?"

"Never better, Clancy. Never better. Life is good. In fact, life is great. I just turned 96 and I am walking at least 6 miles each day around Clancyville. You know it's a three mile circle around town from my house and I walk it twice each day. The winter time is more difficult to navigate, but I manage to get around most days of the year. I especially love the spring and summer, the flowers and trees blooming, the warm breezes blowing...it's just so wonderful to be alive and all—"

Jessica was the original walker in Clancyville back in the 60's. Before walking became fashionable for exercise, Jessica Thompson was walking in her high-top black and white tennis shoes. Nearly everyone in Clancyville thought she was wacko. Her nickname became Weird Jessica while she was still in her fifties. Now that she was well into her nineties there was little scuttlebutt around town referring to her as wacko; however, she was still referred to as Weird Jessica. It had become a term of endearment rather than a term of scorn. However, Jessica did have one other trait which never became endearing. She knew everything going on in Clancyville and she loved to talk about whatever it was she knew.

"I need some help, Jessica," I interrupted her soliloquy.

"Of course you do, dear. How may I assist you?"

I leaned my backside against the Jag and felt the window on my side of the car do down. Rosey was getting curious.

"I need to know what the word on the street is regarding the hit and run death of Skeeter Shelton," I said.

"Oh what gruesome stuff that is, Clancy. I never thought I would live to see the day when honest, hard working folk would be run down on the streets of our little town. They say it wasn't an accident, you know. Not at all. Intentional, they say. And of course no one in their right mind believes it was your mother, Rachel Jo. Dear, sweet Rachel would never do such a thing as that. I mean, she has her moments and can be forceful, as you know, but she would never run down someone in that Studebaker of hers. She's a much better driver than that. And she would never willingly run over someone walking along the street. Many a times I have seen her driving along when I was walking and I never feared for my life one instant. I mean, Rachel might shoot me if she took exception to something I said or wrote, but never run me down with her car. You agree with me, don't you?" she finally stopped and breathed. I jumped to get my next sentence into her slightly one-sided conversation with me.

"So, what's the word about who might have done this?" I said.

"Well, now that is an intriguing question, Clancy. This is only what I have heard, mind you, merely friends sharing with friends, if you get my drift, but the word is that Henry Smith had something to do with it."

She stopped talking after only a couple of sentences. I was not prepared to respond so soon in the quasi-dialogue going on between us.

"I don't remember anyone named Henry Smith," I said.

"He's the son of Joy Jones, lives across town on the other side, out past where the old elementary school used to be. Out there near Queen's Court, you know the area."

"Yes, I know the area. And I know Joy."

"Well, Joy raised three boys and two girls in addition to

271

Henry. She had a husband, Carl Jones, but he died early in life and left her with all those kids to raise. She did a good job of it, too. But Henry was the unlucky one, you might say, the one who never could find a place, something to hold onto. Henry was the child she had before she met and married Carl. Smith was her maiden name, so that's the name she gave the child. Henry never quite fit in with the others, although Joy tried. Henry was different. Just couldn't find his place, you know. Lots of folks have that problem. They just never seem to fit. Good people, but without a purpose, without something that drives them and gives their life meaning. Silas Marner has the same problem. You ever make that observation, Clancy?"

"Often."

"Me, too. And it's true. Sad, but true. Anyhow, that was Henry. Her other children all got good jobs and are working hard to this day. But Henry, well, Henry has gone from job to job. Does odd jobs for folks. I heard that Preacher Rowland took him in a few years ago and has provided some work for him off and on ever since."

"Preacher Robert Lee Rowland?"

"The same. He has that big house out beyond Blue Mountain Estates. I think he must own some 400 acres out there. Lives on White Horse Lane, or something like that. I've driven by a few times, but never been inside his new house. Anyhow, he's the one who gave Henry some work."

"So how does Henry tie in with this hit and run?"

"Word on the street is that Henry stole your mother's car, the one that was used in the death of old Skeeter."

"You're saying that Henry was driving the car that killed Skeeter Shelton?"

"No, not me. This is the … ah … word on the street, as you say. I hear things from time to time, as you know. Still try to keep my wits about me and listen to what's being said

THE PEACE HAVEN MURDERS

and all. But no, Henry was not driving the car when it hit Skeeter. Henry just stole the car," she said for clarification.

"So you're saying that Henry Smith stole the car but was not driving the car when Skeeter was killed?"

"That's true," she responded with the shortest sentence I ever heard her deliver without additional commentary.

"Sounds like you have more than one source for your information."

"I can see why you are a good detective, Clancy. Your mother brags about you all of the time. Why it's almost shameless the way she talks about you being a great detective off in Norfolk and all."

I had a hard time with that one. My mother seldom talked about anyone, let along me. And one thing about my mother was that she never bragged about anything or anybody. I was beginning to have doubts about this source of information regarding Skeeter's death.

"Maude Jeffers saw a dark figure steal your mother's car," Jessica continued. "She watched from her kitchen window that night. It was very late, she said, but she had to get up and take some medicine since her legs were killing her. Her kitchen window looks out into the back of your mother's house, out where she parks that Studebaker. Maude said she saw someone out there, sneaking around and then get in the car and drive off. She knew it wasn't anyone that was supposed to be there that late. So when the car left from where your mother parked it, the thief drove it straight up towards Vaden Drive where there's a street light. That street light is almost directly in front of Maude's house where her kitchen window is on the front, you know. Anyway, she said it looked a lot like Henry Smith."

"Jessica, that's a long way from Maude's kitchen window to that corner of Vaden Drive. I can see how she could look out her kitchen window and see someone around the back of my mother's house. But that street light is almost twice the distance from there. Maude couldn't possibly identify someone at that distance," I commented.

"Yeah, she did or so she said. She has binoculars."

"Binoculars?" I said.

"Yeah, she uses them to keep up with things. And another thing, Henry was good with his hands growing up and all, and had the reputation for stealing when he was young. Mostly cars, I'm told. And I'm also told, by reliable sources, that Studebakers would be no challenge to steal, even without the keys in them."

It was no secret, apparently, that my mother kept the car unlocked with the keys in the ignition most of the time. In fact, I couldn't recall a time when the keys were not in the car. Stealing it would have been no challenge at all.

"But how does all of this prove that Henry wasn't driving when Skeeter was run down?"

"Well, all of this does not prove that. But what Elsie Dalton saw does."

"Ah, another source. What did Elsie see?"

"Elsie saw a tall woman get out of the Studebaker and run away after Skeeter and his nurse were lying all over the sidewalk. She ran off so quickly that Elsie never got a good look at her, but she knew that it wasn't Henry Smith. Wasn't Henry at all. The woman was white. You know that Maude and Elsie are good friends. They talk all the time."

"And you told all of this to Sheriff Robertson?"

"Not a word. He never asked me. Besides, Robby and his family don't speak to me since I wrote that piece about them a few years back."

"Did Maude or Elsie talk to the Sheriff?"

"Yes, they both did. They told him everything they saw."

"Do you think he believed them?"

"Probably not. He thinks we're nothing but a collection of nosey old women. And crazy, too."

"Well, Jessica, you are nosey."

"I like to think that some of us desire to stay abreast of what is happening in our neighborhood. I write, you know. The newspaper likes my column and the things I know about the community. You did remember I am highly regarded in some circles as a reporter?"

"Yes, ma'am, I remember. You've been reporting on community affairs for many years now. I hope you won't write about all of this."

"Too late. It's coming out in this week's edition."

"You named names?"

"No, that would make me libel. I just tell stories and infer a lot, you know. My style of reporting to the newspaper."

"Yeah, your style. Thanks for the information, Jessica."

"Anytime, Clancy. Do come see me."

"I will, Jessica. I may even have more questions for you. Thanks again," I closed my cell phone and put it away.

"Well, sounds like you were gathering info," Rosey said.

"We have some clues."

"Real, live clues?"

"I think. But we also have some problems."

53

I WAS SITTING ON SOME BOXES STACKED UP AGAINST WHAT amounted to my mother's car garage staring into Maude Jeffers' kitchen window. A light above the window was on and I could see a figure standing in the window looking out with binoculars. Rosey was sitting atop the tire in the tire swing nearby staring at his Jag. Our day long surveillance was empty of substance. A full day of doing nothing did provide us the opportunity to rest up from our bumps and bruises and gunshot wounds. Plus, the information I had gleaned from Jessica Thompson presented us with some new insights if not outright clues to ponder and debate.

"Why is it you believe these women and their ... gossip?" he said.

"If only half of it is true, then there is something there."

"Which half?"

"It doesn't matter. Here's the thing – since I do not believe in coincidences, I find it particularly interesting that Henry Smith's name surfaces in conjunction with Preacher Rowland as well as with a tall, thin woman who just happens to fit the description of our Marilyn Saunders. That's a bit too much for me."

"Particularly interesting," he repeated. "So, Sherlock, which cage do you want to rattle next?"

"I called Rogers and asked for some data on Henry Smith. I don't expect much; but, since he is likely in the system somewhere, I expect her to come up with something that might corroborate what the gossip ladies have shared."

"One can hope."

I could see Maude Jeffers standing at her kitchen window watching us in the dim light. I waved at Maude. She moved quickly away from the window. I think I surprised her for the moment. I had no doubt that she would return soon and resume her clandestine activity.

I turned my attention to the Vaden corner that Jessica had mentioned. I watched a car pull up to the corner and turn. I could clearly see into the car because of the angle of the street light. It was Billy Bob Gleason out patrolling the night, looking for whatever it was that Billy Bob was looking for in his late model Ford pickup. Another senior citizen dragging main, so to speak, remembering the good old days of his now spent youth.

"Maude does have a clear sight from her window to the corner."

"Do tell."

"And with binoculars … I think it is possible for her to see into a car that stops there and then turns."

"And this proves?"

"She could have seen who she said she saw."

"Henry himself."

"Precisely."

"So, we are off on the hunt once again. Let me guess. We will pursue with vigilance Mr. Henry Smith to see where that trail takes us," Rosey said.

"That would be the trail."

"Now or tomorrow?"

"Time draweth nigh. Let us be off."

"With vigilance."

We drove out to the section of town where Joy and her children were living. Sam accompanied us. In fact, he all but insisted that he go along. By the time we arrived, Rogers had informed me that Henry Smith had been listed as unemployed for the last year or so, and that two years back he had been arrested for petty theft. His bail had been posted by none other than Robert Lee Rowland, the man in charge of changing lives. It would stand to reason that Henry might feel indebted to Reverend Rowland. More connections. So many facts, so little evidence. Maybe one day the whole puzzle would fit together. A picture was forming, and I believed that I had a motive, but until someone did something really stupid so that I could see them, I really had nothing. Something was missing and I had no idea what that was.

Rogers gave us Henry's current address, so we knew which house to watch. It happened to be the one singular house across the street from Joy Jones' home and the other small houses all aligned along her side. Henry was still an outcast from the family.

It was after ten o'clock. We stared at the window where a light was on until sometime after midnight. The light went out.

"This could be a very long vigil," Rosey said.

"Such is my life of crime solving."

The front door opened and a man walked down the few front steps, and got into the Ford Fairlane parked in the unpaved driveway next to the house. The car backed out into the street, and then headed off in the direction of downtown Clancyville.

"Then again, maybe not so long," Rosey said as he started

the Jag's engine and followed the old Ford. "That's a nice car he's driving."

"Nice?"

"You know, well-built engine, smooth lines, good quality car of the sixties. Durable. And the fact that Henry, we suspect, is still driving it, all speaks for itself."

"Expensive?"

"For some, it might be a collector's item. But, a good mechanic could have restored the car. So, no, not really expensive. Just a good choice of cars."

"Speaks to his character?"

"Speaks to his craftsmanship, if he's the one who either rebuilt the engine or restored it," Rosey said.

"He's known for working with his hands."

"Fits the profile."

We followed what we believed to be Henry's Fairlane to Leftwich Street. It pulled into Marilyn Saunders' driveway and drove around behind her car garage, parking out of sight from the road. We pulled down Washington Street to our spot from earlier in the day and waited to see what might develop.

"How do you know so much about cars?" I asked.

"I only know what I like."

"And you like Fairlanes?"

"They're okay. Another time, another place, I might have owned one."

"Is this is a man-thing?"

"Probably."

The lights of the small house were on when we arrived. It was after 10:30 and nothing was happening. The streets were quiet and there was only an occasional car driving by on Leftwich. We were the only traffic on Washington and we were parked. I heard a dog barking off in the distance and had an idea. So did Sam. He sat up and growled in low tones.

"Easy, big guy," Rosey said quietly to him.

Sam waged his tail once. He sat perfectly still and growled once more, this time in a lower tone. Like a growl whisper.

I had an idea. Detectives are supposed to get ideas now and then. Mine come less frequently.

"We need some surveillance."

"I think that's what we be doing right now," Rosey said.

I turned to Sam who was now back to resting in the back seat, "We need you to go over to that house and observe," I said to Sam and pointed through the windshield to the small house we had been watching. "The house with all the lights on. See what you can see. And don't go off chasing after that dog barking in the other direction. Stay on point."

It seemed to me that he nodded and stood up, ready for me to let him out of the car.

"He understands all that?" Rosey asked.

"Of course he does."

"What other language does he speak?"

"I don't know. I've never had the occasion to use anything but English. Perhaps another time I will use Spanish or French and see what happens."

I got out and opened the back door of the Jag. Sam headed off in the direction of the small house. "Stay out of sight," I said in a stage whisper as he trotted towards his destination.

"You know you're crazy, don't you?" Rosey said.

"Absolutely. But what has that got to do with anything?"

"Talking to a dog as if he's human. Talking to a machine, over the phone no less, as if it is human. And where do I fit into this equation?"

"I talk to you as if you are human as well. What's your complaint?"

"No complaints, except for the salary I'm drawing on this case."

"You're getting the same salary I'm getting. Equal pay for equal work, I always say."

"Yeah, you always say that. And the pay is always the same. Do you ever do anything but pro bono?"

"Sometimes I work for less."

We both watched Sam approach the house, sniffing along the way. I assumed he was trying to pick up a scent. He checked each bush and every tree in Saunders' yard. He marked his spot near the metal garage. We watched him move stealthily towards a window of the house and look inside. Sam walked from window to window on the side facing our view, spending only a few seconds at each. I assumed that either his vision was obstructed or that there was nothing of real interest to him since he moved along so quickly. He disappeared around the back of the house.

"How long have you known this dog?"

"A few years."

"And you didn't train him?"

"We discussed it, but I never really saw the need."

"We discussed it?" Rosey asked in a voice that possessed the obvious quality of incredulity.

"Sam and I talked it over. He really saw no need for it, and I concurred."

"You are absolutely out of your mind. And that's a fact, Jack."

"Opinions vary."

Sam reappeared to us on the far side of the front of the house. He was now standing on the little house's front porch, staring into the singular front window. He paused there and remained stationary. He sat down and continued looking into the window.

"Reckon he is taking notes?" Rosey asked.

"I don't think I like the sarcasm in your voice."

"I've never had a dog like that."

"Jealous?"

"A little. Is it that you just assume to know what he is thinking or is there some genuine communication going on between the two of you?"

"We have our moments. I think we both read each other's mind."

"No doubt. He doesn't talk much. Does he ever bark?"

"Only when he has something to say."

Sam got up and meandered over to the other front window on the other side of the small porch. There was no light on in that window, but he seemed to be watching something. He jumped off of the porch, sniffed another bush or two, and then broke into a run back to the Jaguar. I opened the back door and he climbed in.

"Good job, Sam. Did you see anything of interest?" I asked.

"I can't wait for this report." Rosey said under his breath.

Sam raised a paw and touched my shoulder. I looked into his noble eyes and saw that he had seen something.

"Well, Captain America, it is time for the two of us to go have a looks-see."

"I'm still waiting on Sam's report."

"He's already given it. I told you he didn't talk much, but I forgot to mention that we use hand signals a lot."

"I shall remain skeptical and impressed."

"A paradox."

"Precisely," Rosey said as we exited the car and headed towards Saunders' house.

"Blow the horn if you need us," I said to Sam.

"Has he ever blown a car's horn before?" Rosey asked me as we crossed Leftwich.

"Not as I recall."

5 4

THE KNOCK ON THE BACK DOOR WAS SO SOFT SHE ALMOST missed it. She was sitting in the small living room watching television. She waited to see if the sound would repeat itself.

It came again, very softly. Like a shy knock.

She opened the back door and greeted the black man with a half smile. He nodded and entered the kitchen.

"Do you knows what he wants next?" he asked her as he followed her into the living room.

"Yes," she said without facing him.

The tall, thin woman returned to her favorite chair in front of the television. The black man sat down on the brown couch and waited for some type of explanation or plan.

She appeared to be watching whatever was on the set in front of them, but her eyes showed a distant stare that belied the direction in which she was looking. Her mind was not on the television show. She was thinking about the preacher and the way he treated her. If the black man had had any powers of intuition he would have come to the conclusion that the woman was angry. In fact, there was great rage behind her eyes, but that was not yet discernible on her face.

The black man slowly became a part of the ambience of the room. He was waiting for her to explain their next job. The woman was silent, lost in her growing anger mingled with dissatisfaction. At some point, the man thought he heard something outside the window of the small living room. His eyes drifted to the thin, white curtains and caught a glimpse of some shadowy thing that moved on the other side of the window.

He got up, walked to the window and looked out. Nothing that he could see moved. He waited to see if his eyes might permit some type of vision as he stared into the darkness. The television light had blinded him and he didn't have the patience to wait it out.

"Something wrong?" she asked.

"Thought I heard something," he said as he slowly eased back into the confines of the brown couch.

"Night sounds," she said emptily. She continued to stare at the television show without paying attention to it.

"Thought I might've saw somethin'."

"Sit down and let's talk," she said. "There's nothing out there. You're just nervous."

"I'm scared," he confessed.

"You're a big boy. Why are you scared?"

"I'm scared of the same thing you scared of."

"I'm not scared any more," she said with a hint of anger in her voice.

He noticed the change of tone, but didn't know what it meant. He looked at her from the side. She appeared to be watching the television.

"You watch this show often?"

"No."

"So … talk to me. Tell me a plan," he said.

"He wants us to take care of the last juror."

"Gonna be hard."

"We're to break into the house and kill her."

"Dat all?" he asked.

She turned to look at him. He seldom said or did anything that even suggested a bit of humor. He smiled at her.

"That's what he wants," she said.

"Gonna be real hard," he said.

"And dangerous. Too many in that house."

"And a dog, I think."

"Yeah, there's a dog," she said. "I doubt if the dog likes me. We've already met once."

"I don't like dogs."

"He probably won't like you either."

"I feel better already."

"You must be in a good mood this evening," she said. "Humor is not your strong suit."

"I got paid. I have money. I feel good. Money makes me feel good. I don't get suits, strong or weak. You get paid too?"

"I don't care about the damn money. I am tired of this whole thing. Lots of people have died just because he wanted them dead."

"What you be sayin' now?"

"I'm saying enough is enough."

"You can't just quit, you knows. It ain't that simple."

"Yeah. It's that simple."

"He a powerful man. And he's a man a' God. We just can't walk away. I don't think he gonna like that."

"He won't like it, but he may have to accept it."

"I don't like the sound of this."

"I'm tired of doing his bidding. I feel like a slave."

He started to say something, but decided against it. They both sat in silence for several minutes. The only sound in the room was the nocuous noises coming from the television set. The direction of their conversation scared him. He feared the preacher, and now the woman was beginning to upset him. He wanted her to say something, to break the horrible silence between them now, but he was frightened of what she might say next, what she was thinking. She stared at the television while his eyes searched the barely decorated living room for something to ease his troubled mind. The empty walls offered no solace for him. A cross, a picture of Jesus, or even some statue of the Virgin Mary would have helped. There was nothing there. Empty walls. Colorless. Dark.

The sound of a board on the front porch creaked, and the black man turned around and looked out the singular window. He thought he saw a dog looking into the window. His mind must have been playing tricks on him. All that talk about that dog in that house probably made him see things, or so he thought. The woman was still silent. He got up and walked to that window to get a closer look.

There was nothing there by the time he arrived.

"Still hearing things?" she asked.

"I saw something lookin' in the window."

"You wanna go outside and check it out?"

"No. It's probably nothin'. I jus' a little nervous, that's all."

He sat back down on the brown couch. He noticed it was not a comfortable place to sit. His eyes searched the room in vain for another place to sit. There were no other options. He remained quiet for a few more seconds, afraid of asking her specifically what she was thinking.

"Are we gonna break into the house and kill that woman?" he said, fearing her words.

"I'm not."

"I has to do this alone?"

"If you do it at all, you will have to do it without me. I'm finished."

"He won't allow you to quit, you knows."

"Yes he will. I will explain to him."

"You playin' a dangerous game, Marilyn."

He seldom ever used her name. It surprised even him as he said it. She turned away from her distant stare at the television screen and looked at him, as if for the first time. It appeared to him that she was really looking at him now. A smile spread across her face unlike anything he had ever seen from her. He sat motionless. He was waiting, but he had no idea for what.

"That's the best part, Henry," she finally said to him. "That's the best part. The danger is worth the price of admission. I think I finally feel alive for once in my life."

"You scarin' me."

"I don't mean to. I'm leaving now. You do what you have to do. His orders are that she be killed. If you want to do that, then go ahead. I'm finished. I going to see the preacher and tell him that. Shall I tell him that you are following orders?"

Henry thought for a long time. He didn't know what to say to her. She was serious, he could tell that. He thought about what he had to do in order to kill the woman. He was not good at planning. A different type of fear suddenly engulfed him and he sat frozen on her uncomfortable, brown couch. He was afraid to take the next step.

The sound of the back door closing startled him out of his trance and he suddenly realized that the tiny living room was empty. The woman was gone.

"Marilyn!" he called out, but only the sound of his fading voice returned to him. She had left. Whatever she intended to do with the preacher, say to the preacher, was now set in motion. He knew that his job was clear enough. There was a woman staying in Rachel Evans' house who must die. If he did this, he would be paid handsomely. It wasn't personal. He didn't even know the woman. No one had given him a name.

He had only been told that she was the last one. She was the last juror that the preacher wanted killed. It would be easier with Marilyn's help, but that was out of the question now.

He heard a small clock strike somewhere in another room. It seemed a lonely sound to him. He thought about the money. It would be good to have more money. It was just another job, he told himself. Just another job.

55

Rosey and I stood on the backside of the house, just to the right of the deck that covered nearly two-thirds of the back. It was so dark I couldn't see Rosey who was standing next to me. I could hear him breathing softly.

"That's Saunders," I said as we watched the tall woman shut the back door and walk towards her car.

"Where's Henry?" Rosey said.

"Who knows? We have to decide," I said.

"We have to decide what?"

"Do we split up?

"Split up?" he asked.

"Yeah, you know. I take Sam and the Jag and follow her. You stay on Henry."

"Oh, that kind of split up. I don't think so."

"It's a plan."

"Yeah, but not a very good one."

"What's wrong with it?"

"Okay, you take the Jag and follow Saunders. Wherever. Not important. But then Henry comes out, gets into his car and drives off in another direction. I'm supposed to run after him and hope that he drives slowly enough for me to keep up? Or better yet, I accidentally run into Henry and ask him to give me a lift?"

"Oh, didn't think of that."

"No, you did not. So here's another plan, better plan. We stay together and follow her."

"And the reason we're doing this…?" I asked.

"It's my Jag and Saunders is likely the playmaker in this duo. Henry follows orders."

"Okay, but I think the real reason is that you don't like the idea of following someone on foot, you being lazy and all."

"That may have something to do with it," he said as he ran towards the Jag after Marilyn had pulled out of her driveway. I ran closely behind Rosey as we trotted to the Jaguar.

"She's going north, towards Lynchburg," I said when we were several car links behind her.

She then turned off onto Old Highway 29, through the short, dangerous tunnel, and out towards the preacher's estate in the northern part of Pitt County.

"Awful late to be calling on the preacher," Rosey said.

"You think that's where she's heading?"

"Best guess. And her attitude is different."

"And how do you know this?"

"She's driving faster. Usually she's a deliberate driver, going the speed limit, methodical. She's doing ten miles over the speed limit. She's in a hurry."

"Perhaps the preacher called an emergency meeting."

"Perhaps, or maybe Saunders called an emergency meeting with him."

"We'll find out soon enough," I said.

"Sho' nuff."

Saunders' car slowed and turned into Preacher Rowland's long drive. Rosey slowed the Jag and waited for Saunders to get closer to the house before turning into the drive. We watched her taillights become smaller and then suddenly her brake lights came on and her car stopped.

"What's she doing?" I asked.

"I don't know."

Her car lights went out and it was instantly black. Rosey quickly turned off the Jag's lights and we sat in the road in the darkness. There was no moon so it was hard to see at first. There was a row of lamps near the front entrance of Rowland's mansion which provided a sort of backlight for us to view Saunders and her car. As far as we could tell, she was simply sitting in her car in his driveway with the lights out.

Rosey pulled the Jag off of the highway onto the shoulder near the driveway entrance to the mansion. He left the motor on.

"You have a plan?" he asked me.

"I'm working on it. I would welcome any ideas from the former Navy S.E.A.L.," I said in an intended pleading voice.

Rosey put the Jag in gear and road the shoulder of the old highway down to a dirt road about five hundred yards from Rowland's entrance. He turned left onto the road and parked the Jag.

"We'll go on foot since this is likely her destination. It will be easier to maneuver. We'll move closer to Saunders and her car, and then wait to see what she does next."

"I want Sam to come, too."

"Can he keep his mouth shut?"

"Few better."

We cut through the trees that lined the road and into the open field which I am sure that Rowland called his front yard. It was probably no more than five acres, give or take. Even without a moon, the lampposts near the front of the house provided us with ample light for moving safely towards Saunders and her vehicle.

Rosey stopped our trek across Rowland's front lawn

about fifty yards from Saunders' car. Her motor had been shut off. She was sitting very still in her car. We found a spot next to one of the large trees between the shrubs which helped to form the line around his long drive. The pattern of tree, shrubs, tree, etc., fashioned Rowland's landscape theme all the way to the oval portion of his driveway. The trees and shrubs fanned out and simply ended at the edges of the oval drive when the drive turned toward the house. Stylish. He obviously spent a good bit of money on landscaping his country home.

"Now what?" I said.

"Nothing. We wait. The fun part."

"Fun, yeah," I said as I tried to find a comfortable spot against the tree bark to rest my back. I wasn't having much success. Sam lay down in the grass near the tree next to my feet. I could see his shadowy figure from the lights do his typical circle dance in search of just the right spot.

"Time check," I said.

"Twelve fifty-two," he said. "I should have asked Sam if you could keep your mouth shut."

"Wise guy. I'm resting my eyes. Wake me when there's some action," I said.

"Roger."

We had a long wait. I slept for some time. I imagine that Sam slept too, but I had no way of knowing for sure. He could play the game of possum as well as any animal I had ever known.

Rosey shook me at some point.

"I need you to watch while I sleep some. It's two-thirty. Nothing's happening. Saunders is still sitting in her car."

"She must not have made an appointment. You think she's waiting for the light of day?"

"Good guess. Breakfast at six, perhaps. Wake me at 5 if I'm not awake by that time."

"You got it."

I think Rosey was asleep before the period was solidly on the end of his last sentence. I marveled at his ability to control his body that way. Sam got up and moved closer to me. I couldn't see his eyes, but I could sense that he was looking at me, asking something.

"Whatever you need to do, just do it quietly," I whispered to him.

He moved away and I could no longer see him. I suspected he was answering the call of nature somewhere off in the shrubs below us. Always considerate.

The night sounds were somewhat subdued despite the warm evening. There was nevertheless a chill in the air and I moved closer to Rosey to share some of his warmth. It only helped my left side. I could have used Sam for the other side. He was still gone on his necessary excursion.

I rehearsed over and over what we knew about the case in an effort to stay awake. I plotted each step, each small item that was providing us with some kind of clue, but nothing was clicking. We had no word yet on what substance was found in that broken syringe, if any. We had a connection between Saunders and Henry and the preacher, but it was tenuous at best. Everything was circumstantial in tying Robert Lee Rowland to the murders. I had nothing on tying Saunders or Henry to the murders that took place inside Peace Haven. In fact, I had no real evidence that those deaths inside the nursing facility were murders. My mother believed them to be unnatural, and I was following her lead. In fact, I actually agreed with her. At present it was nothing more than a feeling, an intuition, a high degree of suspicion. The evidence was sparse and leading us nowhere. The only thing that truly convinced me of this whole ghastly ordeal being planned and executed was the presence of the hired gunman who was trying to eliminate me and Rosey. If she had not come along, I would have practically nothing to go on. At least for the poor souls who died at Peace Haven. The hit and run did give us more evidence, but so far there was little more than rumors abounding to tie some of the players to the crime. It was frustrating. A game of watching and waiting.

Such is the life of an investigator. We spend most of our hours investigating and hoping to string together some clues in order to keep from being clueless. It's a funny job, and sometimes deadly. Some days I wish that my father had been able to warn me against such a profession, but then, he had no idea that his baby girl would enter into such work because of him. I learned from the best, but he had no idea he was teaching me such skills.

I took out my cell phone and pushed a button on the side to light up my dial. It was nearly five o'clock, so I awakened Rosey. He came to fully awake and alert, as if he had only closed his eyes for a moment. Amazing.

Dawn was creeping onto the scene as the mansion nearby became silhouetted in front of us. The sun would be coming up in the direction of Rosey's Jag. It would be a while before that would happen.

"Where's Sam?" he asked.

I looked around and realized that I had not seen him since he asked to be excused a few hours ago. He didn't come back.

"I have no idea."

"I thought you could depend on him," Rosey said.

"I can. And I do. He'll be back."

SARAH JONES WAS SITTING UP IN THE BED WITH THREE PILLOWS behind her. The light on her bedside table was still on, but Sarah was asleep. Rachel was sleeping in the rocking chair across from Sarah, which was in the corner of the room between the front window and the side window. The fully loaded 30.06 was resting dangerously across her lap with her right hand resting on the stock. Her left hand was lying across the barrel in an uncomfortable position.

The two ladies had been reliving some past experiences until a few moments ago. Rachel had been rocking to the rhythm of the some vague memory when she had fallen asleep. Sarah was chattering away about some crazy escapade that Clancy and her brother Scott had gotten themselves involved in without noticing that her conversation partner had dozed off. Before she could finish the tale to her own satisfying conclusion, she had succumbed to the silence of the night in her upright position in the bed.

A distant sound awakened Rachel in the corner. She held her breath while she waited to see if the sound would come again. She was slowly coming to her senses and hoping that she could tell from where in the house the noise was coming. It came again. She could tell that it had come from downstairs. The pace of her heartbeat increased.

Cautiously, she stood up from the rocking chair with both hands firmly gripping the rifle. She quickly and silently exited the open door of Sarah's room without awakening her, and walked to the hallway rail where she could look down and see a portion of the dining room downstairs. She had left a light on in the kitchen so that there was something below her to aid her eyes as she waited to see if any familiar face would emerge. She was expecting Clancy and Rosey and Sam to return from wherever they had gone; however, she had little idea of when that might be.

Rachel was in the shadows by the balcony rail not far from the head of the stairs when she first saw the man approach the steps at the bottom. It was not Rosey, nor anyone else she recognized. He was coming upstairs. Her heart began to pound even more rapidly. She glided back into the darker shadows towards her own room which was down the hallway from Sarah's. She was now completely out of sight in the small corner of the hallway leaning against the door that led to the attic which was just to the right of her own bedroom door. She tried to inhale in order to control the rapid pace of her pounding heart. She feared that the man might hear her heart beating. Breathing was difficult.

The man slowly ascended the stairs and moved to his right towards Clancy's old room and the guest room where Rosey was sleeping when he slept. He passed the bathroom which was directly in front of him after he emerged from the stairs. He checked both bedrooms without apparently finding whatever it was he was searching for. Or whoever. He briefly stopped and looked into the small bathroom as he moved around to Rachel's side of the hallway.

Rachel exhaled gently and felt some better, but her heart

was still pounding much too rapidly to suit her. Her right index finger was now resting on the front of the trigger guard for her weapon. Her left hand was holding onto the barrel of the rifle waiting for the approaching danger to come towards her room.

The man turned down the short hallway that led to Rachel's bedroom. The room where Sarah was sleeping was on his immediate right. The lighted room beckoned him. As he was about to enter through the open doorway, the hardwood floor cracked just in front of Rachel. No doubt the man's own weight had caused the noise, but it stopped him from entering the room. He paused and peered into the darkness of that end of the hallway. He was staring directly at Rachel without seeing her. The light from Sarah's bedroom allowed her to now see that the man held a small gun in his left hand. Rachel held her breath in hopes that she could stop whatever sound she would make in the natural process of breathing. She prayed he would turn away from her soon so that she could exhale and breathe naturally once more. She was running out of time. Her breath would explode from her mouth and lungs any moment.

The man finally turned away from Rachel's corner and entered Sarah's bedroom. Since the light was still on it would be easy for him to see the woman lying in bed asleep, propped up by the pillows. He disappeared from Rachel's sight.

Rachel eased carefully along the wall towards Sarah's doorway. She first heard Sarah's voice after she arrived at the threshold.

"Henry Smith," Sarah said, "what in the world are you doing here?"

"I didn't know it wuz you, Misrez Jones. Maybe I got the wrong room," he said.

"What in the world you doin' sneakin' around this old

house so late at night? What you lookin' for, boy? And what's that you got in your hand there, Henry?"

He lowered the gun which had been pointing directly at her.

"I got a job to do, Misrez Jones."

"And what would that be, Henry?"

"I got to kill someone."

"Not much of job, Henry. Who you gonna kill?"

"I was told that the person I wuz to kill was stayin' in this house. You alone, Misrez Jones?"

"What if I am? Did you come here to kill me, Henry Smith?"

"I don't rightly know, ma'am."

"Well, what if I am the one, Henry? Are you still gonna kill me?"

Henry was holding the gun, but it was simply hanging there on his left side. He became aware of just how heavy the small gun was. His head was down. His eyes simply could not meet hers on any level. He was thinking.

"I needs to kill the last one, Misrez Jones."

"The last what, Henry?" She continued to say his name as if to connect with some faded past memory that the two of them shared. She could remember him as a teenager, wandering around the streets of Clancyville, mostly alone, acting as if he had no home. Truth was, Henry never had much of home. He was the outcast, even in his own family. That she knew right well.

"I think it's the last person who served on a jury long time ago."

"Who told you to do this, Henry?"

"I better not tell you that. I might get some folks in trouble if I talks too much. It's a job, Misrez Jones. You understand that?"

"But what kind of job? This is bad stuff you're into, Henry. You gonna take my life?"

"Are you the last one?"

"I certainly am, Henry. I'm the last one alive. And you're gonna kill me, for what? Money?"

"Yes, ma'am. I took the job for money."

At that moment Henry Smith became aware that someone was standing in the doorway of the room. Perhaps Rachel had made some sound as she moved through the threshold and into the room. He slowly turned his head to the right and saw a woman standing there holding a large rifle which was pointed directly at him. He was still holding the small, heavy handgun in his left hand, and it was pointed downward, towards his feet. He dare not take his eyes off of the woman with the rifle.

"I can't allow you to shoot my friend," Rachel said. "If you think for a moment that I will not pull this trigger, then you will be making a terrible mistake."

"Yes, ma'am," Henry said without moving anything but his lips.

"Now don't even flinch or you're a dead man. This is a game rifle and it will make a hole in you too large to sew up. I don't want to shoot you. You understand me? The last thing I want to do is to shoot you. But, I will. Do not doubt me for a second."

Rachel was calmer than she had ever imagined being in such a situation, not that she ever imagined a situation like this. She was calm and frightened to death. Her great fear was that this man standing only a few feet from her would lift his left hand and try to shoot her. Bill had always told her that if you are in a situation with another person and they have a gun and the likelihood is that they intend you harm, you cannot hesitate. It is fatal if you do. Bill must have told her that a hundred times. She now knew why. She stood resolute, but with great fear.

Henry let his eyes fall to the floor in front of him. This was a terrible position to be in. He never thought of anything like this. He simply believed it would be easy to break into the house and kill whoever it was he was supposed to kill. He never thought about it being someone he knew. And he certainly never thought about having to decide whether or not he could move fast enough to shoot a person aiming a rifle at him.

He really did need that money. For him, it was a lot of money. Maybe he could get away with it, shoot both of them and leave town. His mind was racing, as fast as Henry's mind could race. He had to decide.

He slowly turned his head to the right and looked at the woman holding the rifle. She seemed to be calm, as if she had done this before. For Henry, it was all about the money. He knew what he had to do.

57

THE TALL, THIN WOMAN PUSHED THE BUTTON ON HER WRIST watch to check the time in the dark. It was close to four o'clock. She was growing impatient waiting on the sunrise. She wanted to break in and get it over with, but she knew that the preacher had alarms everywhere on the property. So, she waited for the morning, for his breakfast time. She had come calling at that early hour before. He would not be surprised at her presence. That could be her advantage.

The gun was lying on the passenger seat next to her. There was enough light from the lampposts strategically placed around the semi-circular driveway for her to see the weapon. She took it in her hand and felt the cold steel. She placed the gun against her cheek and it felt good. This was a solution. Maybe not the best one, she thought, but at least, it was a solution.

She had loaded the gun earlier in the evening, long before Henry had arrived. She had made plans. Enough was enough. It was time to do something about the heavy weight around her. It was restricting, much too restricting.

Her mind wandered to the aftermath, the time when it

would be all over. Where would she go? What would she do with freedom, a new life? She smiled at the possibility of extreme joy. She had never known real joy, or, for that matter, satisfaction. She accomplished her tasks well enough, but they had been simply for him. She had found no fulfillment doing his bidding. It was a job, nothing more. But with him gone, out of the way, out of the picture, she would be seeking contentment for herself. It would be different.

She played the scene over and over. She imagined what it would be like to stand in front of the man and force him to cower, make him do her bidding for once. Something surged inside of her. Excitement came to her for the first time in a long time. Perhaps the first time ever. She would have to be calm in order to do this, but the anticipation of it was thrilling indeed.

It would all be such a surprise to the preacher. He would never dream of her doing anything like this. That was an advantage for her. She wondered how many shots it would take. How many bullets would she have to use or how many would she want to use? Maybe that was the real question.

She located some anger stored deep within regarding the preacher. It was a long ago, far away memory of an event that occurred between them. She had buried it of course. She was forced to bury it. Life had to go on, and he seemed to be willing to make it up to her in his own sick sort of way. He had told her at the time that he was weak and that he meant no harm. He told her that he had cared for her, that she was special to him. Special.

It was a lie. All of it was a lie. He simply found a way to use her to do his bidding whenever he wanted something done, something he didn't have the courage to do.

Something moved off to her right, some distance way, and she could not tell what it was. Perhaps it was an animal.

Goodness knows he had enough land here for hundreds of wild animals. She wondered if he tried to control them, too.

It was nearing five when she checked her watch again. Another hour or so and the dawn would be breaking upon her new world, new possibilities, new way of living. It was thrilling to entertain such thoughts. She regretted that she had not thought of this before. Maybe it was all of the killing that she had been connected with over the last few months that finally gave her the idea. She felt stupid, but worse than that, she felt used.

Matters were now in her hand. She would do it. She would free herself from this despicable person who called himself a man of God. It would be over soon. She sighed and put the handgun back on the passenger seat next to her. It was a great comfort to have it so close.

SAM MAGICALLY APPEARED out of nowhere and startled me. He licked my face and sat down on his haunches as if to report in from his patrol.

"I told you he would come back," I whispered to Rosey who had been awake for the last half hour.

"Ah, but what mischief has he been involved in since he left?"

"You have no faith."

"That would be accurate. He's a dog."

Sam walked over to Rosey and put a paw on his arm.

"What does he want?" Rosey asked.

"He wants to shake hands with you. It's like a contract. He'll do his part and you do yours."

"Are you kidding me?"

"Moi? No sir, I would not jest about so serious a matter. His word is binding."

"His word?" Rosey whispered incredulously.

"Well, whatever approximation exists in the canine world. That would be his bond. Shake his paw if you want him to trust you," I said.

Rosey shook Sam's paw. Sam moved closer and licked Rosey's face.

"You're in," I said.

"And you know this, how?"

"He never licks anyone unless he trusts them. Never. No exceptions."

"He told you all of this?"

"Observation. I'm a detective, you know."

"Yeah, I keep forgetting that. So where do you think Sam here has been roaming?"

"Probably around the estate, the back side of the mansion, checking windows, stuff like that."

"And you have never trained this animal to do any of this?"

"On my word as a lady. Don't say it, just trust me."

Rosey was silent as he crossed his arms on his chest. Sam lay down next to him. It was another sign of relational posturing on his part. Sam seldom made mistakes in sizing up people. Of course I knew Rosey well enough to know that I certainly trusted him. Sam had to perform his own ritual to get to that point. Once there, he was there.

"She's definitely waiting on the light of day," Rosey said.

"Figured that. Wonder why she drove out here so early? Why not wait at home and then come out for breakfast or whatever?"

"Don't know. Suspect it to be a case of anxiousness."

"Or nerves," I said.

"That, too."

58

SARAH JONES FINALLY RELAXED WHEN SHE REALIZED THAT THE loud crash was the sound of the gun falling onto the hardwood floor at the end of her bed. Henry was not going to shoot her, and neither would Rachel shoot Henry. To her credit, Sarah felt sorry for Henry. So alone, so mistreated, so used, and so confused in his life. Perhaps if someone had only loved him, then maybe Henry would not have been involved in all of this mess.

Rachel still held the rifle on the man standing at the end of the bed. She recalled that Bill had taught her to always be alert for another weapon when the first weapon was dislodged and taken. Most killers had a plan B. Henry was not like most killers. He barely had a plan A. He sat down in the rocker without asking for permission. He was a defeated man, and troubled. However one might describe Henry Smith at this moment in time, it would assuredly be understated.

"Can you reach the phone, Sarah?" Rachel said.

"Yeah," she stretched across the bed to the phone and grabbed it. "You want I should call Robby?"

"He would be the one."

"You know the number?" Sarah said.

"By heart." Rachel told her the number.

Sarah dialed and waited. Rachel could hear the sound of the phone ringing through the receiver from across the room. Somewhere around the eighth or ninth ring, a sleepy voice answered.

"Sheriff Robertson here," he said angrily.

"Sheriff, this is Sarah Jones. You need to come over to Rachel Evans' house. Someone broke in and …" she hesitated. She didn't want to make it sound worse than it was at the moment, at least for poor Henry's sake. She knew that he had come to kill her, and maybe would have killed Rachel, too. She didn't want to say all of that to the Sheriff over the phone.

"And what?" Robby said. "Are you alright?"

"Yes, we're okay. We took the gun from him."

"The gun?" he said in more of an awakened voice. "Who is he?"

"It's Henry Smith, Sheriff. He came here to harm me."

"Where is he now?" Robby said.

"He's sitting in the rocker in the corner of the room."

"Why didn't he try to run away?"

"Rachel has a rifle on him. He's not gonna run anywhere, Sheriff. But we need you to come over here and take over. We're both a little tired. Rachel's a little edgy, if you know what I mean."

Robby Robertson said nothing else as he slammed the phone down and quickly dressed. He would be en route within ten minutes.

"I assume the Sheriff is on his way," Sarah said to Rachel.

"Good."

Rachel took a long look at Henry Smith sitting in her rocking chair in the corner of the bedroom. He appeared to be a fragile man, maybe so fragile that he was starting to break. There were tears flowing down some of the lines on his tired face, but no sound was accompanying his emotion. Fear kept her from being sympathetic. She found it impossible to have sympathy for someone who wanted to kill another person, especially a friend of hers.

"Why won't you tell us who's behind all of this?"

"All of what?" Henry said, wiping both of his eyes on his shirt sleeves.

"The murders?"

"I never killed nobody. I stole your car, Misrez Evans, but that's all. Marilyn and I went to a house to kill a man, but he died natural before we did anything to him. I never killed nobody."

"So you didn't run down Skeeter Shelton and his nurse?" Rachel said.

"No, ma'am. That wuz Marilyn driving."

"What about all of the deaths at Peace Haven?" Rachel said.

"None of me, Misrez Evans. I laid no hand on no one. No time. I just did what Marilyn Saunders told me to do, mostly."

"So, Henry, child, why on earth did you come here to kill me? Why didn't that Saunders woman come to do it if she did all of the other killings?" Sarah asked.

"She said she'd had enough. Enough was enough, that's what she said. Plain as day. Enough wuz enough and she'd have no more doings with it. She told me to take care of it. And I would've too, if it hadn't been you, Misrez Jones. I couldn't kill you. You were one person that wuz always kind to me. Always kind to me. Even back when I wuz a stupid kid, you wuz kind."

"Land of Goshen, Henry. How on earth did you get mixed up in all of this?"

"I just worked for …," he stopped. He knew somehow that he must not say the name.

The doorbell rang and then there was rapid, repeated loud knocking. Rachel backed away from Henry without taking her eyes off of him. She had come too far to let her guard down now. She stopped at the bedroom door.

"Come on in," she yelled in the direction of the stairs.

Sheriff Robby Robertson emerged in a few seconds at the door to the room. He quickly surveyed the situation and then drew his gun. Rachel took her finger off of the trigger and allowed the barrel of the rifle to point down to the floor. Sheriff Robertson crossed in front of her and handcuffed Henry Smith.

Rachel and Sarah hurriedly told Sheriff Robertson what had happened. He listened while he cuffed Henry Smiths wrists behind Henry's back. Robby just kept saying, "Hmm." He nodded a lot as well.

"Henry, you're in real trouble this time," the sheriff said.

"Yes, sir. I knows it. Real trouble."

"Ladies, I'll come back and get your statements. In the meantime, don't go anywhere. I need to lock Henry up and get some paperwork started on this. But I will be back, probably early morning, to get your statements. You can tell me what happened then."

"It's simple enough," Rachel said as she crossed the room towards the foot of the bed and laid the rifle on the bedspread with the barrel pointing to the front window. "I convinced Henry Smith not to shoot my friend Sarah here. He was more than willing to comply."

The sheriff looked at her, then at Sarah, and then moved Henry through the door and down the steps without saying another word.

59

"SHE'S MOVING," ROSEY SAID.

I looked towards the parked car from behind the tree we had used for a pillow for a few hours. Sam lifted his head and stared in the same direction.

We waited until she was standing at the front door. I wondered if she would ring the bell to announce her presence. Off in the distance I thought I heard some chimes sounding. Soon enough the maid came and opened the door, allowing Marilyn Saunders to enter the mansion.

"Let's split up," Rosey said. "I'll go through the front entrance. You go around to the back, go to that room where we met with the preacher, the one with all of the windows. One of those windows is likely open and a place for you to get inside."

"What about Sam?" I asked.

Rosey's look led me to believe that he was not about to answer that question. We were both running now and Sam was stride for stride with us. Rosey stopped at the main entrance and waited. I continued on my trot to the far side and Sam came with me.

"I'll give you three minutes to get in place," Rosey said loudly.

It's funny how your mind starts to race when the adrenalin begins to flow freely. My immediate focus was this fast approaching early morning meeting between Saunders and the preacher. As Sam and I trotted towards the backside of Rowland's country home, I thought of Mother and Sarah and suddenly felt this need to call them and check in. Henry Smith was also on my mind. Where was Henry and what was he doing? Too much was happening too fast. It was hard to know what to do. Perhaps the best you can do is to simply play the hand that is dealt, or so they say. One day I must take up poker to see if those analogies were any good. Maybe they sounded better than they were. At the moment my hand was full of wild cards.

Two minutes later, Sam and I rounded a back corner of the house and could see the large room with the more-than-enough windows lining the entire side of the building. I could see that people were in the room. The only one I recognized at first was Saunders.

I slowed to a trot and moved cautiously along the side trying to avoid detection. I could now see that Preacher Rowland was sitting at his large wooden desk with Saunders and the maid standing by the door. They appeared to be talking to him, or to one another. It was hard to tell from my angle.

The problem at hand was that there was no way I could enter the room through one of those windows without being detected. The good news was that one of the long, rectangle windows was in fact opened enough for me to enter. Sam followed suit.

I finally came into the view of Saunders, who appeared to be frightened when she saw me. She turned and started to leave the room just as Rosey entered. He encouraged her to stay.

"We have a situation here," Rosey said.

I looked over in the direction of Preacher Rowland and could now see that he was slumped in a chair, lifeless. I assumed he was not asleep. We detectives know these things.

"Oh, my," I said. "Sleeping temporarily or is it a more permanent slumber?"

I walked over to the preacher and felt for a pulse. There was nothing, either at his wrist or his neck. "Appears to be of a more permanent nature," I said.

I noticed a magazine on the floor beside him and an empty glass on the desk in front of him.

"So, ladies, what happened?" Rosey said.

"I just got here," Marilyn said. "I have no idea."

She sounded as if she were telling the truth; but then, that's another thing that we detectives must never do. We must never believe anyone is innocent of anything. The other thing we have to believe is that everybody is capable of lying.

"Okay, so ….Marie is it?"

"Yes, ma'am," the maid said.

"Can you tell us anything?"

"I came in after his breakfast to give him his medicines."

"What does he take?"

"Normally I give him potassium and insulin."

"How do you give it to him?"

"Both are injections."

"You are a nurse?"

"Yes, LPN. I'm working on my RN certification."

"You said, *normally* you give him potassium and insulin."

"Yes, ma'am. His doctor recently added some weekly B-12 shots. I give him those twice a week, following the doctor's instructions."

"So, today you gave him an injection of potassium, an injection of insulin, and another injection of B-12."

"Yes, ma'am."

"One after another?"

"Yes, he prefers them all at once. I give them along with his prescription pills."

"What else did he take?"

"Mainly heart meds and a daily vitamin."

"The epitome of health," I said.

"Yes, ma'am, considering his age, he was doing well."

"Except for the diabetes, bad heart, and low potassium."

"I think he has been living with those conditions for a number of years."

"There's an empty glass on the desk here."

"He likes to drink pomegranate juice with his pills."

"Anything else?"

"That I administer to him?"

"Yes, did you give him anything else this morning?"

"Just a magazine."

"Tell me what happened after he had taken his medicines?"

"I gave him the three injections. I then set his pills down in front of him next to his pomegranate juice. I handed him the magazine ... then the doorbell rang. Miss Saunders was at the door, I let her in and we walked back to the room. I knocked and told him that Miss Saunders was here to see him, but there was no answer. I knocked again and again. He told me never to open the door until he answered. So, we waited in the hallway. It was several minutes."

"It was a long wait," Saunders interjected.

"Go on," I said to Marie.

"After we waited a long time, like she said, then Miss Saunders told me to open the door, and I did. We came in and found him like that, like he is now," she said as she looked at the lifeless body of Robert Lee Rowland.

"He was okay when you left him to go answer the door?" I said.

"Yes ma'am. I think it he was reading the magazine."

"How much time passed from the moment you gave him the drink and your return with Miss Saunders?"

"I can't say for sure. I would have to guess."

"Okay, what would be your guess?" I asked.

"Maybe fifteen minutes."

"That's a long time between placing a glass of juice and some pills in front of Mr. Rowland, walking to the front door of this house, and returning with Miss Saunders."

"I didn't leave the room right away."

"Okay, tell me what you recall doing."

"I put his drink on the desk. I gathered up his breakfast dishes and put them on a tray. He asked for a magazine. I walked over there," she pointed to a table that appeared to have several magazines displayed, "found the magazine he wanted, and brought it back to him."

"What was Reverend Rowland doing at this point?"

"He was drinking his juice."

"And taking his pills?"

"I would assume so."

"Then what did you do?"

"I heard the doorbell ring, so I picked up the tray of dishes and left him. He was looking at the magazine when I left the room."

"Had he finished his drink?"

"I didn't notice."

"Is this his glass?" I pointed to an empty glass on his desk.

"Yes, that's the glass I gave him."

"Is this the same size glass you give him every day?"

Marie nodded.

"It appears to be at least eight ounces," I said.

"It's a ten ounce glass. He likes a lot of juice for breakfast."

"Where did you go when you left the room?"

"I took the dishes to the kitchen and placed them near the sink. Then I went directly to the front door."

"Did you do anything else in the kitchen before going to the front door?"

She thought for a moment, then said, "Not that I can recall. I think by that point I was in a hurry to answer the door."

"After you opened the door, did you and Miss Saunders remain at the door for very long?"

"I didn't open the door directly. Reverend Rowland instructed me to look through the peep hole to see who was outside wanting to come inside. He told me that you could never be too cautious."

"You recognized Miss Saunders?"

"Yes. I opened the door and she entered. We walked together back to his room."

"Then you and Saunders came back here and waited outside for Reverend Rowland to answer your knocking."

"That's correct."

"You think you waited five minutes?"

"Maybe. That seems to be a long time, but we did wait several minutes."

"Miss Saunders finally told you to open the door, and when you opened the door and entered, you found the preacher just like he is now?"

"Yes."

She seemed genuinely shocked to have found his body there. It all sounded plausible, but then again, that's another one of those no-no's for detectives. Nothing is really plausible until all the evidence is gathered.

"And you are positive that this is the glass that you gave to

Reverend Rowland and it was filled with juice?" I said to Marie as I took a handkerchief from the pocket of my jacket.

She nodded without saying anything. She seemed to be slightly emotional, but still under control.

I placed the handkerchief over the glass then picked it up.

"Marie, would you happen to have a large plastic bag I could have for this glass?"

"In the kitchen. I'll get you one."

She retrieved a gallon size plastic bag and I placed the empty glass inside the bag and zipped it shut. I then put the plastic bag into my coat pocket.

"Do you still have the syringes you used this morning?"

"Yes, ma'am. They're in the kitchen on the tray of dishes I removed from this room."

"Show me," I said. As I was leaving the room, I nodded at Rosey as if to pass a signal to keep any eye on Marilyn Saunders. He nodded back.

"Sam, you stay and keep these lovely people company."

Sam offered a low growl. I couldn't tell whether it was an affirmation or a disagreement.

As I entered the kitchen Marie pointed to the tray of dishes on the counter by the sink. Sure enough there were three syringes. Two of them were clear plastic, but the third one was an amber color.

"I've never seen a syringe this color," I said.

"Yes, ma'am. They're used when some medicines are light sensitive. It sort of protects the medicine and keeps it from breaking down."

"Which medicine was this?" I said as I held up the amber colored syringe using my trusty handkerchief.

She hesitated in her answer, moved over to the tray of dishes and reached for the other two syringes.

"Don't touch those syringes. Evidence. Could have prints on them besides yours."

"Oh," she said.

"You have three more plastic bags? Smaller ones, this time, please."

She opened a drawer, took out three medium size plastic bags, and handed them to me. Using my trusty handkerchief, I put the amber colored syringe in one and the other two clear plastic syringes each in its own bag. I handed her the three plastic bags with syringes.

She studied them briefly and then handed them back to me.

"The amber one had the potassium," she concluded.

"And you remember this how?"

"Well, notice the largest syringe there, that's for the B-12. The other one, the one for the insulin, is marked on the side. That only leaves the potassium."

"Where do you fill the syringes?"

"I always fill them here in the kitchen."

"Where do you keep the medicines?"

"In this cabinet," she moved towards the double sink and started to open the top cabinet to the right of it.

"Don't touch that. Let me open it."

I put the three bags of syringes in my other coat pocket. Balance with the glass. I then tore off a paper towel and used it to help me open the cabinet without adding my finger print to the collection already there. Inside the small, narrow cabinet was what I suspected to be Rowland's collection of meds. I used the paper towel to pick up the different bottles to examine them. I checked the pills while I was at it. Nothing but thorough.

"Where is the potassium?"

She hesitated, and then replied, "I finished it this morning."

"So where is the empty bottle?"

"I threw it away."

"You didn't need it to renew the prescription for another round?"

"It was the last refill in the cycle. The pharmacy keeps records, you know. They can fill it without the bottle being taken to the pharmacy."

"Where did you throw it?"

"In the trash can under the sink."

I opened the doors under the sink and took out the small trash can. Some of the items in it looked disgusting and I failed to see the honor of putting my naked hand into that mess. Besides that, there could be some evidence there and I really didn't want to violate any potential crime scene.

"Do you have any plastic gloves?"

Marie opened a drawer nearby and took out two gloves from the box. She handed them to me. Just my size. How fortunate.

I put on the gloves, dumped the trash on the floor and luckily found the empty potassium bottle without having to rummage through the despicable collection of yucky stuff. Yucky is my favorite technical word in all crime scene investigations.

"I need another plastic bag."

I put the empty potassium bottle into the bag, placed it in the pocket with the syringes, and escorted Marie back to the study where Rowland's body was found.

"Did you touch the body?" I asked Marie after we had arrived.

"No, ma'am."

I looked over in the direction of Saunders. I couldn't read her expression.

"Miss Saunders, did you touch the body?"

"Heavens no," she said emphatically, as if I had asked her if she baited her own hook when fishing.

"Well, indeed, we do have a situation here. Let's call

Robby Robertson and see if we can find some answers. Shall we?"

I called Robby and he arrived about twenty minutes later. I decided to let him have his crime scene. I did however look around the room while we waited for his arrival. I found nothing suspicious. There seemed to be something missing, but I couldn't get it in my head as to what that might be. I noticed Sam walking around the room sniffing at every nook and cranny. It dawned on me that he smelled the Pekinese twins that Preacher Rowland owned.

"Where are the dogs?" I asked Marie.

"I don't know," she answered.

When Robby arrived, he had plenty of questions to ask all of us. Ben Pickeral was with him, so we knew that good law enforcement would hold the day and all would be well. I know I felt better with both of them there on the job. We detectives also have an arsenal of humor. Well, the good ones have such an arsenal.

I told him my story, that is, the reason that Rosey, Sam and I were there. He scratched his head and said "uh huh" and "hmm" a lot. He failed to ask us what time we had arrived at Rowland's estate, and neither of us volunteered that information.

Marie told him the same story she told me earlier. At least she had a good memory. Failing that, she was likely telling the truth. At any rate, I believed her. Rosey looked skeptical, but he remained quiet. Sam sat down in a corner and faked sleep.

Saunders related the same story she had given us, but she left out the part about arriving last night and waiting in her car until daylight. While Saunders was answering Robby's questions, I took out the plastic bag with the potassium bottle inside and examined it. The date on the bottle was for two days ago.

"Let's all go down to my office and see if we can get this sorted out," Robby said.

Robby moved towards me and held out his hand. "I believe you have some evidence that is vital to this investigation."

I handed him the potassium bottle bag. I reached into my pocket and gave him the three bags of syringes. I hesitated for a moment, smiled at him, and then waited to see if he would ask for anything else. Like playing Crazy Eights. I was hoping to hold onto the glass and have it tested.

"And the glass?" he said without smiling.

I gave him the glass and he walked away without another word.

"Are we under arrest?" Saunders asked.

"Not yet. But don't get too excited. I may yet arrest all of you. Something does not smell right here."

I had a wisecrack just waiting to be voiced, right on the tip of my tongue. Rosey must have suspected such because he elbowed me just as I opened my mouth to add some mirth to the dismal scene. When I looked at him, he shook his head. "Bad idea," he whispered.

"Did I miss something?" Robby asked as he looked in our direction.

"I think you have it covered, Sheriff," I said.

We all walked out to the cars in the front of the house. Sheriff Robertson told Deputy Pickeral to put the two women in the back of his squad car. He then told Ben to call the funeral home and have them come out to verify that Reverend Rowland was indeed dead, and to take care of the body. He told Ben to wait at the house for their arrival.

"You might want to hold off on having Cuthbert & Boran work their magic on Rowland's body," I said to Robby.

"And why is that Evans?"

"You might want to autopsy the body to see what kind of poison may have been used here?"

"Oh, poison is it? You know this for a fact?"

"No. But the autopsy might reveal some important information about how Reverend Rowland died."

"I know that Clancy. Just leave the case to me. Would that be too hard for you?"

"Not at all, Sheriff. Just merely making a suggestion."

"Can I trust you two to drive straight to my office? I've had enough of you Evans' women being involved in dangerous events for one day," Robby said to us.

"What does that mean?" I said.

"It means that your mother was holding an intruder in her home at gunpoint."

"She and Sarah are okay?" I said.

"They're fine. They're fine. Listen, you two come straight to my office."

As he walked around his car, I saw him lean into the open back window and speak to Marie. I moved closer so I might hear what was being said.

"Aren't you Joy Jones' youngest daughter?" he asked.

"I am," she said.

"And Henry Smith is your half-brother?"

"Yes, sir. But my mother doesn't claim him."

Robby smiled at Marie and patted her on the arm. I thought it was a strange encounter considering the whole situation that had just unfolded. I filed it in my super-duper detective memory log in case I might need it someday.

"What do you make of that?" I said to Rosey when we were alone.

"Don't know. Maybe nothing more than a small town Sheriff being friendly."

"I don't know. It didn't seem to be right or something."

"What, the question or the touch?"

"The question was okay, I suspect. Just substantiating information that he thought he had. Nothing wrong with that. But why the pat on the arm? It seemed out of place considering everything else this morning," I said.

"The whole world is out of place or haven't you noticed?"

"Outta place in Clancyville."

60

IT WAS STILL EARLY WHEN EVERYONE GATHERED AT Clancyville's so-called police station. It was on a backstreet off of the main drag in the area one could humorously refer to as *downtown*, the heart of the city. The front of the building had absolutely no character, nothing but a brick facing with a door. Windows were obviously scarce at the time that the building was formed. It was one of those unfriendly, uninviting buildings in which the only time you would want to go inside was the time you had to go inside. Official business.

"Ben, take this," he handed him the bags of syringes, potassium bottle, and the drinking glass. "Put these in large, separate envelopes and send them to the lab in Richmond. Have all of them tested for whatever."

Ben took the five plastic bags and walked out of the room.

"Everybody sit down. I'm going to get to the bottom of this," Robby said.

The office complex was composed of an outer office and

an inner office. The outer office was the home of the secretary whose main job was to fill the coffee pot and answer the phone. We were a good hour or so away from her scheduled arrival. There was no fresh coffee made and it was unlikely that the phone would not be an interruption for a good while. Ben Pickeral also had a small desk in the corner in this outer room. It was good that Ben was a small man since his corner of the room was mostly insignificant.

We all sat down except for Rosey. He leaned against a wall by Ben Pickeral's empty desk. Saunders and Marie took the chairs available. I sat on the corner of the secretary's desk. The Sheriff cut a side glance at me, started to say something, but then apparently changed his mind. He exhaled loudly.

Ben entered the room after he had swiftly handled his envelope chore.

"Ben, make some fresh coffee," the Sheriff said. Ben scurried out of the room once more.

"Miss Saunders, tell me why you were at the reverend's home?"

"I was there on a business matter," she said.

"What sort of business?"

"That's personal, Sheriff."

"Maybe. Maybe not. What kind of business were you and the preacher involved in?"

"I'm sort of a personal secretary for him. I take care of all kinds of matters. Have been for years," she said.

"I see. So, what time did you arrive at his home?"

"Around 6 o'clock," she lied.

"Okay," the Sheriff turned the angle of his head in my direction, "Miss Evans, tell me your story."

"Which part?"

"The part that relates to this serious matter before us," he answered.

"Rosey, Sam and I were following clues. The best clue we had was associated with Saunders here and Henry Smith. We were tailing Henry and followed him to Saunders' place. After an hour or so there, Saunders left. We decided to follow her."

"Who's Sam?"

"My dog."

"Your dog?"

"Yes."

"He normally work cases with you?"

"Is that relevant?"

"Maybe, maybe not. But it certainly is odd."

"Why? You have Ben. I have Sam."

"You comparing the two?"

"Not really. Sam is smart."

Robby wrinkled his forehead as if frustrated with my answer. He exhaled loudly again.

"Ben, is that coffee ready yet?"

"Almost," Ben said.

"And you have no idea where Henry Smith went?" he asked me.

"Not until you mentioned him just before we came here from Rowland's home," I said. "He was still at Saunders' house when we left to follow her."

"But I told you nothing of Henry Smith."

"True, but you did tell me that you discovered my mother holding a man at gunpoint in her home earlier this morning."

"I did, but I never told you it was Henry Smith."

"You didn't have to. I suspect that Henry went there to kill Sarah Jones."

Marie gasped when I said that. She put her hand over her mouth and I watched her eyes open wider. Saunders had no emotion, nor did I expect her to have any.

"That's another matter," Robby said.

"Not really, Sheriff. This is all related, it all comes back to Preacher Rowland and Marilyn Saunders here. I'm not sure where Marie fits into this. She's a new chapter."

"Indeed," Robby said as he walked over to the coffee pot sitting on a table by the entrance door to his office. He poured a cup. It was one of those cheap coffee makers that don't allow you to stop the brewing process when you remove the carafe. Each drop made a sizzling sound on the hotplate below while Robby held the carafe in his hand. He offered none of us coffee. Good old Southern hospitality.

"Follow me, Clancy," he said.

I followed him from the outer office into his office. He closed his office door and pointed to a chair in front of his desk. He made no move to sit at his own desk, so I sat on the corner of it. He stood by the closed door.

"Tell me what you have," he said.

"Basically, I have already told you just about everything I have. But here's what little I know as of this moment. Rosey and I were doing surveillance on Henry. We followed him to Saunders' place late last night, a little before midnight. Then, around 12:30 or so, Saunders left. We were forced to choose since we had only one car to follow in. We decided to follow Saunders since we had already concluded that she was the brains between the two of them. My theory is that Preacher Rowland was giving the orders which Saunders was carrying out."

"You think Saunders killed those people in the nursing home?"

"That one is harder to answer. I don't believe Saunders did the actual killing in Peace Haven, but I do think that Saunders had an inside person. My guess is that Saunders gave the orders to someone who had access to the rooms, someone who would not appear out of place, someone who could come and go easily from room to room. The orders didn't originate from Saunders. She was like Rowland's foreman. 'Personal secretary' is what she called it. He gave the orders; she found the people to carry them out. She found the people to do his dirty work," I said.

"Proof?"

I shook my head, "Nothing that would hold up in court. Lots of facts, lots of loose ends, but nothing that ties it together."

"You think Saunders killed the preacher?" he asked.

"I don't know. From what she said out at the mansion, and the way she said it, I have some doubt that she killed him. Apparently, if she is telling the truth, he was already dead when she got there."

"So, Marie killed him?"

"Maybe. I think Marie was doing her normal duties and something went wrong after Preacher Rowland received his daily medicines."

It then dawned on me what could have gone wrong. It was one of those moments when you are investigating a particular case and the investigation is going nowhere. Then, suddenly, some breeze blows by you or a twig snaps, and you know. Or, as in my case most of the time, I think I know. It all falls together in one beautiful, horrible moment. The answer is there and all I usually have to do is go to the source. Something must have appeared in my eyes or my expression when this happened.

"What?" Robby said.

"What do you mean *what*?"

"You look like you know something."

"I've told you what I know. Now you can tell me what you know about my mother, Sarah, and Henry Smith."

Sheriff Robertson told me their stories and what he

found when he arrived at the house. I was relieved, of course, and also rather amused at my mother. Apparently my father had taught her well. Perhaps she was better with a gun than I had imagined.

"May I go and see my mother and Sarah?" I said to the sheriff.

"Stay close. I may have more questions."

"You gonna hold Saunders and Marie?"

"Yep. They're going nowhere. Material witnesses or something like that."

"May I have a moment or two to speak with Marie?"

Curiosity was evident on his face. I had the impression he wanted to refuse my request. He took a sip of coffee, studied me for a moment or so, and then overcame whatever reluctance he was nursing. He nodded.

"Go ahead. But in this room," he said as he opened his office door and asked Marie to come out. Marie entered and he exited. He left the door open. I closed it behind Marie.

She sat down without my asking her. Her hands were folded in her lap. She was scared and I felt some pity for her.

"Do you know what happened?"

"You mean to Reverend Rowland?"

I nodded.

"No, ma'am. Not really. I did everything I usually do. I cook his breakfast and then I give him his pills and his injections after he finishes eating. The only injection I added this morning was his B-12. I follow the same routine each morning. He does not like to vary his schedule. He's a disciplined man."

"Are all of his meds filled at the local pharmacy?"

"Yes. I pick up the prescriptions myself. He gave me clearance to do that. I keep all of his medicines on hand at the house. Everything except the vitamin is a prescription."

"He must trust you a lot."

"Yes, ma'am. I expect he does … or did. But I have training for this. Like I told you earlier, I have my LPN license. He hired me to be his household nurse and manager. I think he knew that he might one day need my skills. I hope to become an RN soon."

"When you said that you keep his meds on hand at the house, you meant Rowland's house, right?"

"That's correct. But, I also have some B-12 at my own house. My mother takes it, so we keep an ample supply on hand for her."

"Have you ever used her prescription for Reverend Rowland?"

"That would be dangerous," she said.

"True, but have you ever done it?"

"Are you going to report me if I say yes?"

"No," I said. "I simply want to know if you have ever utilized your mother's prescription for your employer."

"I did it once. The pharmacy shorted us a dosage and I didn't realize it until he was out of his B-12. It happened last week. He's only been taking the B-12 for about three weeks. I didn't want him to miss a dosage, so I got some of my mother's B-12 to use. She keeps extra stuff on hand anyway. Our house is like a regular pharmacy."

"What type of stuff did your mother keep?"

"Lots of medical supplies – extra gauze, tape, droppers, ointments. She always wanted to be a nurse, but she couldn't afford to go to school. She had too many mouths to feed. That's what she always said. We used to tease her about having the Joy Jones Drugstore."

"Did this happen with any of his other medications?"

"What do you mean?"

"Did you ever run out of any of his other prescription medications and be forced to use another source, like your mother's supply?"

It seemed to me that she flinched at my question. I could not tell for sure; but, at any rate, she took longer than I thought necessary to answer my question.

"No," she said.

61

I CALLED MY MOTHER'S DOCTOR USING THE DOCTOR'S PRIVATE cell number after Rosey and I had listened to Rachel and Sarah tell us over and over of their early morning ordeal with Henry. It was certainly a dramatic encounter and Sarah's version was much more detailed than Mother's. Despite the fact that Sarah was the one threatened by Henry, she had a better recollection of the events, or so it seemed to Rosey and me. My mother focused largely upon the bare facts in her three tellings while Sarah offered side commentary to embellish the desperate details. I discerned by reading between her lines that my mother was not enamored with the possibility that she might have had to kill a man. It is a sobering truth that has often surfaced in my life as well. Solving ghastly murders is one thing in my profession. Facing the too-frequently occurring situation of having to shoot someone is an altogether different animal for me.

"Dr. Jones-McCann speaking, may I help you?" the voice on the other end of the phone said.

"Clancy, here, Doc. I need some information."

"I have a minute or two. Go ahead."

"If I were planning to kill someone with a prescription medication and my choices are insulin, B-12, and potassium, which one would I choose?"

"I don't like the question."

"Granted. But do humor me. There is a method in the madness."

"No question. Potassium. Too much of it stops the whole system. Shuts down everything."

"How much?"

"Depends on a lot of factors."

"What if I wanted to be certain it would do the job?"

"As in overkill?"

"Well said, Doc. Yes, to make sure that the person died from the dosage."

"One would use potassium in a concentrated form."

"If I injected it into the person, how long would it take?"

"Minutes. But again, it depends upon the health of the person being injected. But, I would fathom an educated guess to be 25 cc's. That should be more than enough to shut down the average human. You on to something?"

"Yes, I am. I think I know how the good preacher died."

"What good preacher?"

"Robert Lee Rowland."

"Hadn't heard this. When did he die?"

"Sometime early this morning."

"Was he in Peace Haven?"

"No. He was home. Died shortly after breakfast while reading a magazine."

"Doesn't sound like a typical murder that you would involve yourself in, Clancy."

"Doesn't, does it?"

"Care to elaborate?"

"You his doctor?"

"No. I heard through the grapevine that he didn't trust

331

female doctors, so I was definitely out of the loop for him. Just curious, that's all."

"Well, the truth is, Doc, I have no idea what killed him. I am spinning some theories, nothing more. There was no visible sign of any dastardly foul play, so I am looking into other means of getting rid of one's enemies."

"Suspects?"

"Several. I didn't like him much myself, but I did not do the deed. There are several suspects, even when I eliminate myself. Someone else beat me to it."

"Would you have done the deed otherwise?"

"Good question, Doc. That's a really good question."

6 2

Rosey and I drove over to the Peace Haven home after stopping to drop Sam off at Mother's house. She seemed genuinely happy to see him, if it was possible for my mother to show genuine happiness. It was not a trait I looked for in her. Maybe she was just glad to be alive. That would fit.

"Do you think Nurse Ratched will be happy to see you?" Rosey said.

"As much as ever," I said.

"When did the light bulb come one for you?" he asked.

"Well, believe it or not, it was Robby's question to me. As I was answering it, it all came together. At least the part about who killed Preacher Rowland and who was behind the murders at Peace Haven."

"You mean besides Preacher Rowland."

"I do. It was all his idea, his plan, his plotting, his revenge. He just had enough people under his control to pull it off."

"He almost got them all," Rosey said.

"Yeah, I know. Too many people died."

"But you're still not going to tell me what you figured out?"

I had him curious and I liked the position he was in. It wasn't often that I could stay a jump ahead of this man, my friend, Mr. Roosevelt Washington. But, I would enjoy this for a while and try to make it last a little longer.

"Some things you just have to figure out for yourself."

I thought I detected the slight curving of a smile at the corner of his mouth, but I could have been mistaken.

"I'm hurt that you can't confide in me something of this nature."

"Get over it."

He parked the Jag in front of the building and we entered. It was close to mid-day on a Saturday. The place was buzzing with visitors, if it ever could be said to be buzzing. We walked through the maze of wheelchair patients being pushed around the entrance hall by visiting friends and family members. There were patients using walkers with family or friends offering assistance. There were some who were shuffling along on their own, alone, no one visiting with them. They had come to the lobby out of curiosity or some need to be in the midst of the crowd. Maybe they were hoping to conquer the loneliness the institution offered them. I noticed that the visitors were mostly women, but there was a spattering of men in the mixture.

Rosey and I meandered our way through the web of people and arrived at the nurse's station at the hub of the main lobby. From there the building spread out in four different directions much like a sprocket with its four spokes.

"Nurse Ratched?" I said to the first person who actually looked at me. She was seated at a portion of the round desk. Her name tag read Eileen Biggs. Eileen appeared to be in her early thirties and was already establishing herself in the proud tradition of Nurse Ratched. Somehow in the transition from human being to worker at a nursing care facility, she had lost both pleasantness and friendliness. Smiling was simply out of the question.

"Who?" she said as my interruption of her busyness was stopping the world from turning that exact moment.

"Nurse Ratched," I said again, hoping my humor would win the day for Eileen.

"We have no one by that name here. You have the wrong facility. Do you have a patient here you wish to see?"

I looked at Rosey who was simply amused that I had taken my humor this far with an obviously unwilling participant. Eileen was an established woman of significant proportions and she appeared to be the kind who did not suffer fools gladly. It was blatantly obvious that I was going to lose in this attempt to get her to smile or display any sort of helpful personality traits. Eileen was a rock. A real trooper. Held her ground with the force and magnitude of a bull elephant. Humorless.

I smiled and finally acquiesced. Eileen was now looking at me through eyes of steel and absolutely no hint of a smile.

"Beg your pardon," I said, "I had the wrong name. The person I'm looking for is named Evelyn Guinn."

"Oh. Well, yes, Mrs. Guinn does work here, of course. She's my supervisor. What's the nature of your business?" she asked unpleasantly.

"The nature of my business is with Nurse Guinn," I smiled broadly at her.

"I will need to know why you want to see her because she will want to know why you want to talk with her when I talk with her." She actually said that with a straight face.

"Tell her it's a matter of life and death."

"It usually is," she muttered as she waddled off in search of the great one.

Within minutes Eileen and Evelyn were walking towards us, bookends of a troubled disposition. The singular difference between these two dispassionate people was that Nurse Ratched was half the size of Eileen. Bull elephant, baby elephant.

"Whataya need?" Nurse Ratched said in her usual abrupt tone.

"Fine, thank you. And you?" I said.

"Okay, okay. Look, I'm busy here. You see all these people? This is a serious job and I take my work seriously."

"Do tell. Believe it or not, Nurse Guinn, I actually take my work seriously as well."

"And what work would that be?"

"I find murderers and stop them from killing. Preferably before they have a chance to kill again and again."

"You a cop or something?"

"Or something. I'm an investigator, a private one."

"And why are you telling me all this?"

"You have a murderer on your staff."

"Are you joking with me now?"

"Not in the slightest. Can we go someplace and talk privately?"

"Follow me," she said and headed quickly off in the direction from which she had come.

Rosey and I followed her keeping to the brisk pace she set. Her office was down a hallway in which there were no rooms for the residents. There were people walking along, up and down, walkers and wheelchairs, just like in the other halls of the facility.

The sign on the door which she unlocked read "Evelyn Guinn, Head Administrative Nurse." We followed her into the office. Rosey closed the door behind us.

"Now, tell me what all of this is about."

I explained to her all that had happened and what we had

learned in the last twenty four hours. I told her who I suspected of killing the patients.

"That's ridiculous," she said.

"I'm not really here to convince you of this. I simply need to know if she had access to your medical supplies."

"No, absolutely not. There is no way she could have gotten into those locked closets and locked cabinets inside of those closets. Impossible," she said it so emphatically that I was almost willing to believe that I had made a mistake.

"Who has the keys?"

"I do."

"Anyone else?"

"The Duty Nurse has a set of those keys."

"I assume that you keep your set with you."

"I do. All the time. Never leaves me. Never."

"And the set for the Duty Nurse?" I asked.

"That set is hidden by the assignment roster at the central station for nurses."

"How many duty nurses are there?"

"Four."

"And you trust them all," I said.

"Of course I trust them all. They wouldn't be duty nurses if I didn't."

"And no one has reported the keys missing at any time in the last several months?"

Evidently my question hit something that had been absent from our discussion so far. Her answer to my question was not as forth coming as her other answers. She had this look of sudden awareness that seemed to strike her across the bow. She was defeated by the ever-vigilant ace detective doing her job of asking relentless, probing questions.

"Oh, my," she said in a quiet tone. "Nurse Ingram came to me late one afternoon back … when was that? … February? It could have been that long ago…Anyway, she came to tell me that she could not find the keys to the medical supplies. But they turned up the next morning, back in the spot where they were supposed to be. I never thought anymore about it."

"So they were missing for some twelve hours, give or take?"

"Could have been twelve hours," she said.

"And you probably did an inventory of the supplies the next day?"

"I don't remember," she said.

"If the keys were missing on a Friday afternoon, say, is it likely that there would have been no inventory taken the next day?"

"No. Not until Monday morning," she said.

"So, the normal procedure would be to have an inventory the Monday following the missing keys?"

"Not likely. Things go into high gear every Monday. It was probably overlooked. Can you tell me what was taken?"

"Don't know yet. We're still waiting on lab tests to determine what type of poison was injected into the patients who died here. But there would have been a number of syringes."

"We use a lot of syringes here," she said. "It is difficult to keep an accurate count of those things. We do the best we can, you understand. But we absolutely do not keep any type of poisons in our medical supplies."

"True, but you do keep some drugs that if given in a large enough dosage would act as poisons."

She nodded reluctantly to my point, "Yes, that's true."

I looked at Rosey and he shrugged.

"Is she working today?"

Nurse Guinn shifted some papers around on her desk apparently looking for a schedule. After moving several files and shifting papers from one side to the other, she finally found a document that gave her the answer.

"Let me see … yes, this is her weekend to work. She's supposed to be here today. You want me to call her in?"

"Do you ever call her to come see you?"

"No, I don't usually call her into my office. I go looking for her."

"Then we'll go looking for her," I said.

63

My cell phone rang. It was Rogers. I had called her earlier in the day to update her on all that had happened since our last conversation.

"The lab found traces of morphine from the broken syringe needle you sent them," Rogers began. "And just so you will know, I've been doing a little checking into morphine and discovered that in some cases it only takes about 50 mg of the drug to head a body towards death. It's considered a lethal dosage. For some folks, it does not require that many milligrams. Sometimes twenty-five to thirty would do the trick."

"Do tell."

"I did tell, and this is one of those ever-elusive clues you live for, right?"

"No doubt."

"Proves murder?" Rogers asked.

"Maybe."

"So you now know who the bad guy is?"

"I'm en route to the bad guy as we speak."

"By Jag?"

"No, by foot."

"What happened to the Jag?"

"Nothing. Rosey and I are inside the Peace Haven facility. Jag won't fit in here."

"A vain attempt at humor, love? So you knew who did it before I called you. You didn't need this information." She actually sounded disappointed.

"I need every piece of data you can discover."

"How's that?" she asked.

"Verification, love," I said. "We now have something to compare to other evidence which has come to our attention in the last day or so. If it matches, it puts our suspect in a very bad light."

"As usual, you understate this light of guilt for your suspect," she said.

"Just hedging my bets or refraining from counting my chickens."

"I get the betting metaphor, but I don't understand the chickens."

"My way of saying that there's several folks complicit in this mess."

"Lot of guilt going around," Rogers said.

"With surprises," I said.

"Oh, goodie. The case is nearly over and you can come home."

"Close. I should be home in another day or so. There are some loose ends to tie up, but it's just about finished."

"You can even bring the canine back, if you like. I actually miss you both."

"Nice to be missed. And Sam will be thrilled that you want him to come home."

I spotted the door to a closet open and I nudged Rosey and pointed in the direction of the closet just ahead of us.

"Signing out," I said and closed the phone.

"Good news?" Rosey asked.

"Evidence. The lab found traces of morphine on the broken syringe needle."

"Proof enough?"

"Some verification needed," I said.

No one was in the closet. We moved on.

I dialed the number I had entered into my cell phone for Dr. J. Miles Sinclair, the attending physician for J.R. Blair. He had given me his cell phone number after I had told him that this was a murder investigation. He said he was more than willing to help.

"Miles here," he answered.

"Doctor, this is Clancy Evans. I'm the one investigating Blair's suspicious death. One question. Did you have J.R. Blair on any dosage of morphine for pain management or any other reason?"

"Let me check. I have some patients on that," he said.

I waited while he apparently flipped through some files. It only took him a minute or so to find whatever it was he needed to answer my question.

"No. J.R. Blair was a healthy man in many ways. But morphine was not one of his medicines."

I thanked him and closed the phone.

"We have evidence," I said to Rosey. "Now all we need is a smoking gun."

After two unsuccessful excursions down two different wings of the complex, Rosey and I finally discovered another open supply closet door. We moved to the side of the hallway of the opened door and approached it cautiously. Rosey was ahead of me, so he was the first to peer inside. No one was there. The cleaning cart was stationed in the middle of the hallway. We could see no one in the area attending to it.

"I'll check the rooms on this side," Rosey whispered and pointed.

"Ditto over here."

We each began to check out the rooms on our chosen side of the hall. A short, fat woman emerged from a room two doors down on my side of the hallway. I didn't recognize her.

"We're looking for Joy," I said as we joined her at the cleaning cart.

"She's not doin' this wing," she said.

"Which wing then?" I asked.

"I don't rightly know. Lettme check my schedule," she answered reluctantly and removed a clipboard which was hanging on the side of the cleaning cart. "She's over in the west wing today."

"Thank you. You want I should call her?" she asked as she lifted her cell phone.

"No. We want to surprise her," I said.

"Okay, but it'll help to pinpoint her location," she said.

"How's that?"

"Well, when I's pushes this button to call her, she has to push another button to answer. Somehow in all that button pushing, this machine has a built-in whatyamacallit that tells us right here," she pointed and held up the phone for me to see, "exactly where a body is. Handy, huh?"

"Handy."

"So, you want I should push it for you?"

"No, thank you. But could I borrow it?"

"I don't know. I's suppose to keep this with me all the time, or so the boss says."

"Who's your boss?"

"Misrez Guinn, she be the big boss. Joy is my little boss."

"Well, I don't think your big boss would mind just this once."

"Okay," she said reluctantly. "But you will bring that back right away?"

"Consider it done."

She handed me the little black specialized cellphone and we headed off towards the West Wing of the Peace Haven Nursing and Care Facility.

"What do you intend to do with that?" Rosey asked.

"Decoy."

"Like ducks?"

"I've never hunted ducks. I wouldn't know what that's like."

"You use decoys. Painted, wooden ducks are floating along in the water. The hunters hide in the water and watch the ducks and wait for the real ones to come along."

"Sounds like a blast. You do this for recreation?"

"Used to."

"Why'd you stop?"

"Water got too cold. Reminded me of guerilla warfare in some bad spots around the globe. Ceased to be fun."

"I'd feel sorry for the ducks."

"Using decoys to trick them?"

"No. Having someone hide in the bulrushes always trying to shoot them."

"It's a hunter's thing," Rosey said.

"Truly."

It took us about four minutes to get to the West Wing of the building. We could easily see the entire length of the hallway. There was no cleaning cart parked anywhere along the corridor.

"We'll have to check each room," he said. "This could take some time."

"Not so fast, Mr. S.E.A.L. I have this modern device for hunting ducks."

Rosey rolled his eyes at me. "You couldn't catch a duck with that."

"But maybe a human," I said.

Rosey moved along the left side of the hallway about fifty

feet from where I was standing. It was impossible for us to cover ever spot along the entire hallway, but at least we were positioned in a more or less central location and ready to run in either direction. Joy was an older woman, so I figured we could take her in a long sprint.

I pushed the button the cleaning lady had shown me and spoke into the phone, "Joy."

We waited and I kept my eyes on the small window at the top which would provide me with a location when Joy answered.

"Yes?" an undistinguishable voice came back to me and the tiny screen displayed Room 336.

I looked for the room number closest to me. I was standing just outside of Room 315. Joy would be up ahead of us. I pointed in that direction and told him the room number. Rosey moved quickly along the corridor and then stopped outside Room 336 and waited for me to catch up. He had his gun drawn.

"Joy, this is Clancy Evans. We need to speak with you."

Joy emerged from Room 336 and first saw Rosey standing by the door. I was walking towards her.

"You figured it all out?" she said.

"Most of it," I said.

I thought she might run.

"I'm glad it's over."

"Why'd you do it?"

"Money and the threats."

"Threats?"

"My baby girl worked for the man. He threatened to fire her and ruin her life if I didn't do this. He called it leverage."

"But he did pay you each time, correct?"

"Yes, he paid me. I spent it on stuff for the grandkids. I never spent a dime on me."

"Why didn't you just have Marie quit?"

"You didn't know the power of the man. He had key people everywhere around here under his influence. They all thought he hung the moon. Know what I mean?"

"Yes."

"So there was nowhere to turn. It was like I had to do it to protect my family."

"Yes, I know about Henry."

"He did that on his on. He'd been doin' odd jobs for the preacher for years. Henry got Marie her job. It was his fault that Marie got tied up with that man. I blame him for a whole lot of this."

"Is that really fair to Henry?" I asked.

"Don't know nothing about fair. He didn't need to get my baby all messed up in this. He's responsible."

I wanted to defend Henry, but I knew that I might as well talk to the wall beside me as to convince Joy. Henry was her scapegoat.

We stood there for a minute or so in an awkward silence. Rosey touched my shoulder as if to remind me it was time to go.

"We need to go, Joy," I said finally.

"What led you to me?"

"The syringe that your daughter used to kill Robert Lee Rowland."

"He's dead?" there was obvious surprise conveyed by her tone and expression. "The preacher is dead? Hallelujah! This is a good day, Clancy Evans. No matter what, this is a good day. But what syringe you talkin' 'bout?"

"I believe that Marie accidentally killed Robert Lee Rowland when she borrowed what she thought was a syringe filled with B-12 from your supply. It wasn't B-12 at all, but for the moment I'm not sure what it was. I suspect morphine."

"But I don't take B-12," she said.

64

"She lied to me," I said to Rosey after we had deposited Joy Jones with Sheriff Robertson and had given him the information I had gathered from her. I also had Rogers fax him a copy of the lab report on the morphine trace found on the broken syringe needle.

The good sheriff was not happy that I had withheld evidence from him. However, I did dissuade his anger a little by reminding him that at the time that J.R. Blair died, Robby did not believe we had any case that proved murder at Peace Haven. We left him mumbling to himself about the number of people likely killed in this whole affair. He was not happy.

"People lie," Rosey said.

"But she seemed so sure of what she was saying, and I believed her."

"Okay. She's a good liar and you're gullible."

"Thanks."

"Hey, she duped you. It's not like it's the first time in your life. Are you thinking that Marie is not quite so innocent now?"

"I don't know what to think. Something is not quite right here yet."

"Joy confessed to the murders at Peace Haven."

"True. She was acting on orders from Reverend Rowland. But somebody killed the preacher. Somebody wanted him out of the way."

"I can think of lots of folks who wanted him gone. Right now the only viable suspect is Marie. You think someone is trying to frame her?" Rosey asked.

"Maybe. Maybe not. What if they only used her to do the dastardly deed?"

"*Dastardly deed*?"

"Poetic question."

"Like Edgar Allen," he said.

"Poisoning, whatever the type, is usually personal. Women generally like to use poison because traditionally women are not quite as violent as men."

"You wearing the Freudian hat now?"

"Evans school of thought," I said.

"Should have known. I don't think your thesis will hold water at the present time. You have Marilyn Saunders who would kill with any means. You have that female assassin lurking about wanting to do us in. And you have Joy working at the behest of Rowland and Saunders."

"But Joy chose poison as her weapon," I argued.

"Contextual method," Rosey said. "Poison is easier to use in certain situations, like a nursing home. Not as messy as bullets and knives."

"But it is personal."

"Well, the problem with that is Joy Jones didn't have anything personal to do with the ones she killed, except clean their rooms. The only patient she knew was Sarah. Maybe the Reverend himself chose the idea of using poison. His murderous rampage was personal."

"True," I said. "But whoever wanted him dead was also involved with him somehow."

"Nothing French here?"

"No. Just intimate knowledge or acquaintance. Knew him, worked with him, had dealings with him. Someone was angry with him and wanted him dead."

"Could be Saunders. Could be Joy. Marie is the first choice at present."

"A place to start," I said.

We pulled into the back of my mother's house and parked. Rosey went inside and I remained in the yard. I leaned against the Jag and called Rogers.

"What's happening?"

"You know that line about things getting *curious-er* and *curious-er*? Well, that's what's happening here."

"I believe the correct phrasing should be *more curious* and *more curious*," she corrected me.

"Joy Jones was the one who killed the patients at Peace Haven. Henry Smith tried to kill Sarah, and my mother, but failed. Mother got the drop on him. And, of all things, someone killed Robert Lee Rowland, the famous iconic preacher of Pitt County for the last fifty years."

"Do tell," Rogers said.

"I do."

"So what do you need now?"

"Research on Marie Jones, the youngest daughter of Joy Jones."

"Suspect?"

"Yes, but … yeah, she has to be the primary suspect at this point. I have nothing else. She lied to me about where she got the syringe. I think that the preacher was poisoned."

"Let me get this straight. She used poison to kill the man and yet you have some doubts about her being a suspect?"

"She said she was giving him his B-12 shot for the day."

"Oh. She's a nurse?"

"In training, she says. She's going to school, taking classes. But she's also the maid at Rowland's mansion."

"Sounds like a place for me to start," Rogers said.

"The mansion?"

"No, the classes she says she is taking. I'll look into it. Anything else?"

"There has to be a tie-in somewhere, something we're missing."

"This is the hard part of detecting, Clancy Evans. We seem to always be one step behind somebody."

"Thanks for the insight and the encouragement. Always good to talk with you."

"Same here."

She hung up on me. I think she thought she was paying me a compliment. It didn't feel complimentary. In point of fact, it stung as the truth often does. And she completely missed my sarcasm.

Rosey rejoined me at the car. We both leaned against it.

"Where to now, fearless leader?"

"Same as always, follow the clues."

"Marie."

I nodded without saying anything. I was reconstructing all that I knew hoping to find the missing puzzle piece. Nothing happened.

"You know this violates my ethics," Rosey said.

"What?"

"Leaning against my car. I should be chastising you. Instead, I'm leaning with you."

"I'm doing something terribly wrong here?"

"I never allow anyone to lean against my car."

"Except me."

"Except you."

"And you're joining me in this ethical violation."

"You're a bad influence, Clancy Evans. Must be your red hair."

AFTER SUPPER I CALLED THE SHERIFF'S OFFICE TO SEE IF Marie Jones was still being held as a material witness or something more. Ben Pickeral answered the phone.

"Sheriff Robertson decided not to hold her here."

"How long has she been gone?"

"Maybe ten minutes, probably less."

"Do you know where she was going?"

"I heard them talking and she wanted to go back to the Rowland's house, but the Sheriff told her she couldn't do that, it being a crime scene and all."

"Good call, Ben. So where did she go?"

"I reckon the Sheriff convinced her to let him take her home."

"What about Saunders?"

"The Sheriff locked her up. He's holding her for twenty-four hours while we do some background checks."

"Why didn't he hold Marie Jones?"

"His call on that, Miss Evans. I reckon he trusts her and all. They've known each other a long time."

"Really? How long, Ben?"

"Oh, I don't know. It's been several years, ever since I came to work as a deputy here. That's at least five years now, maybe six."

"Friends?"

"Miss Evans, I don't want to be talkin' out of school about my boss and all. I think you should ask him those kinds of questions."

I thought it was an innocent enough question to ask. Evidently I had hit upon something about which Ben wasn't too eager to provide details.

Rosey and I put Sam in the car and headed off to have a chat with Marie Jones. While en route, Rogers called to give me some news from her digging.

"Found something interesting on Marie Jones," she began.

"I'm listening."

"Seems she took out a loan for her college courses in nursing."

"That's normal."

"True. But she had to have someone co-sign the loan papers with her in order to get the loan."

"Okay. Most children use their parents to do that."

"Correct," Rogers said. "Marie Jones used someone else."

"Preacher Rowland?"

"No. Sheriff Robby Robertson."

I hung up and said, "Wow."

"Wow?" Rosey said.

"Yeah. A clue."

"We're getting lots of those of late. This be a good one?"

"Might be. Sure makes our investigation interesting, I must say."

"Well, you gonna tell me about the *wow*?"

I told him what Rogers had found. He was silent for a minute or so while he digested the information.

"So what's your take on this tidbit?"

"Why would a redneck sheriff help a poor black girl in a small, Southern town?"

"He felt sorry for her?"

"How would he even know enough about her to feel sorry for her?"

"You said a small, Southern town, didn't you? Everybody knows everything about everybody."

"Maybe, but I suspect that they travel in different circles."

"Well," Rosey said, "she is attractive."

"What does that mean?"

"That means the good old boy sheriff might be crossing cultural lines and seeing her on the sly."

"Seeing her? You mean dating?" I said.

"At least."

"Are we talking about the same guy we grew up with?"

"He was a few years ahead of us in school."

"But we still knew of him. And dating a black girl was not something he aspired to do."

"I don't recall him dating anybody back then."

"Wasn't a lady's man, that's for sure. He's never been married that I know of. We've been away from Clancyville for several years, so it is possible some things have happened we don't know about."

"Call your mother and see if she knows anything."

Rosey pulled the Jag over and parked in front of Queen's Court, the housing project where most of the town's poorer black population could afford to live. Joy and Marie's house was just a couple of blocks up the road from us. We decided to confer with my mother before proceeding.

I talked with Mother for a few minutes. She answered most of my questions. Sarah had some information as well. I related what I learned to Rosey. Sam was asleep in the back seat and paid no attention to any of what we were sharing.

"We were correct in our assessment. We did learn that

Robby almost got married about seven years ago, but the woman changed her mind at the last minute and called off the wedding."

"They give a reason?"

"No."

"They say who?"

"Yeah, it was Jessica Thompson's granddaughter, Sally Mae Franklin."

"She still live around here?"

"Don't know, but it's worth checking into," I said.

"Jessica would know," Rosey said and smiled.

We drove past Joy Jones' house but the Sheriff's car wasn't there. We turned around a mile or so past the house and then came back and parked close enough to watch the house without being too conspicuous. Jaguar, African-American male, red headed white female, large dog sleeping in the backseat – naw, nothing too conspicuous about that.

After an hour or so of nothing happening except Sam yawning and repositioning on his back seat bed, we left and returned to Mother's house.

"I'll call Jessica," I said.

"Brave person that you are."

"Well, along with everything else, she is a wealth of information."

"And this is her little granddaughter. I suppose she knows a lot."

"Since it is her precious little granddaughter, Jessica may be reticent to talk about what happened," Rosey suggested.

"Don't know I ever heard anyone use the words *reticent* and *talk* in the same sentence with Jessica as the subject."

"We'll see," I said.

"Better yet," Rachel interrupted our conversation, "I would recommend that you drive over to Mulberry Avenue and visit with Jessica instead of phoning. Some things are better asked and answered face to face rather than over the telephone."

It made sense so I headed out the door. I turned to see if Rosey was following.

"You going?" I asked.

"I'll sit this one out. That woman tires me out with her barrage of words."

"This could be important."

"No doubt. And if it proves to be so, I would imagine that my partner will fill me in on all the gory details with fewer words than Jessica Thompson could possibly ever use."

"A likely scenario, I'm sure. Come on, Sam. Oh, your keys?" I said to Rosey.

He tossed the keys to me and we left.

Jessica lived in a three story house on Mulberry Avenue. As we made our way over to that part of town, I recalled that Mother told me how Jessica would move her bedroom up to another story with each new decade from the time she turned seventy. Jessica said that she wanted the exercise and that climbing stairs was good for the heart. Climbing the long front steps of her house on Mulberry was sufficient for my heart.

I rang the doorbell and figured that if Jessica was upstairs in her bedroom, it would take a few minutes for her to get to the front door. I sat down on the top step and waited for Jessica to descend. I had time so I could afford to be patient. The case wasn't really going anywhere at this point. At least I had managed to stop all of the murders at Peace Haven, and in my mind, with Robert Lee Rowland now dead, there would be no more justice-killings related to his revenge. Since Sarah was the last juror from that 1970's case, I felt good that I had at least managed to save her life in the end. I corrected myself at some point in my thinking to give Rachel Evans the real credit for saving her friend's life. My mother had once again saved the day on a case I was involved with. Credit where credit's due.

I must have been completely absorbed in my ponderings on Jessica's porch because I failed to hear the front door open. The next thing I knew was that Jessica was seated next to me on the top step.

"Well, isn't this lovely, Clancy Evans. Do you know how long it has been since you came to visit me here at my house? Why, the last time you and I sat on this porch, you must have been no more than seven years old. You used to come over and visit with my daughters. Do you remember that? They were older than you, but you loved to come over and see them. They would be playing or doing something and you would just watch them and seem to have the biggest time doing that. They would invite you to join them, I recall, but you said you would rather just watch and learn. I loved that about you. You were always watching and learning by paying attention to others. Do you remember all of that?"

She paused and I decided that I had better jump into the fray or I would become very old sitting there before another opportunity might reveal itself for me to ask her anything.

"A little, Jessica. I remember some of that. I do remember your house and all. Quite lovely. Still is. But, listen. I am still investigating this case and I have some questions I need to ask you."

"Okay. I can't imagine how I could help you solve any ghastly murders, but I am willing to answer anything, if you think what I know is important," Jessica said.

"It's about Sally Mae and Robby Robertson," I said.

"Oh, that. Well, that was certainly a sad chapter in the life of this family. Sally Mae in particular. She loved Robby. I do believe she loved him a lot. And, well, I don't know. It was just so sad."

"Can you tell me what happened?"

"She found out he was seeing another woman. It was really that simple. He was getting ready to marry my grand-daughter, and that no good, trifling, scoundrel of a man was seeing someone behind her back."

"I'm sure that was upsetting to all of you," I offered.

"Upsetting? You have no idea. And that's not the worst of it."

"Oh?"

"No, not even in the least. He was running around with a black girl half his age."

By the time I arrived back at Mother's place, it was later than I had hoped. Jessica had had a lot to say, but most of it was opinion and editorial comments all related to what had happened. Of course, we discussed other subjects during the evening. That was Jessica's conversational style. I'd say, offhand, we discussed no fewer than a hundred different subjects. I don't recall many of them related to why I went over there in the first place. But that was Jessica Thompson. Revealing. Everything.

"So you learned nothing?" Rosey said.

"I wouldn't put it that way. I learned that another woman was involved and that she was black."

"No names?"

"No names. Some friend of Sally Mae's had come to town in preparation for the impending wedding. She told Sally Mae that she saw Robby and a young woman come out of the local motel one night. Sally Mae's friend didn't know the woman, but she recognized Robby."

"But we don't yet know Robby's side of the story," Rosey said.

"True, but it all sounds suspicious. If he were innocent, then why didn't he tell Sally Mae the truth about why he was with this woman and what they were doing coming out of a motel room."

"Logical, but sometimes people are not logical."

"I'll agree with that."

"Thank you. Was he the Sheriff at this time?"

"Yes," Rachel interjected. "I think it was his first or second year as Sheriff. That sounds right to me."

"Maybe he was doing something official at that motel," Rosey said.

"Or not," I said.

"You have a low view of people, Clancy Evans," Rosey said.

"I do. And it is well founded. Would you like a brief run-through of my history with the human race?"

"No, that won't be necessary. I just like to give folks an opportunity to explain."

"Well, let's sleep on this and then tomorrow we shall give the good Sheriff an opportunity to explain," I said.

My mother said goodnight and left us still sitting in the room adjacent to the kitchen. Sam was completely gone from the world. Now and then he would make some kind of unintentional noise to remind us that he was still close by.

"You think Marie was that woman?" Rosey asked.

"Could be. Makes for an interesting twist."

"That it do, Miss Clancy. That it do," Rosey said as he smiled wryly.

Several minutes went by before either of us spoke another word. It was one of those occasions in which everyone in a room seems to be mesmerized by the silence, or maybe engulfed in the silence and no conversation is needed. It also could be the times when everyone is lost in his or her own thoughts and no one desires to say anything until whatever cycle of thinking for them is done with. I was thinking of Sheriff Robertson and his involvement with this yet unknown woman and how that relationship had jeopardized his imminent marriage to Jessica's granddaughter, Sally Mae Franklin.

"I have a personal question to ask you," Rosey said, breaking the silence.

"You can ask."

"All of this talk about relationships made me wonder why you never had any relationships."

"So what's the question?" I said.

"Why didn't you get married?"

"Never found time and, more importantly, never found the right man."

"Did you look?"

"Not very hard. I knew somehow that I wasn't going to find Mr. Right here in Clancyville."

"Never found anyone you liked in Clancyville?"

"Besides you?"

"Besides me."

"No. But then, I knew I wasn't going to spend my life here either."

"You knew you were leaving."

"Absolutely. After my father died …," I didn't finish the sentence.

"What?"

"It's all history."

"That's true of everything. Your father's death changed something?"

"Me."

"You think you would have gone into another line of work?"

"Hard to say. I know he would have tried to persuade me

to go into something other than work that deals with criminals."

"But it was his passion, right?"

"Mine, too. I simply wanted to know the answers. It was that simple. Still is. That's why I keep poking and prodding and sticking my nose into things that are none of my business. At least I'm told that often."

"And it's true."

"Thanks."

"And no significant other is in that professional plan."

"None that I can see at the moment."

"Besides me."

"Besides you."

"But there's no romance between us?" he said.

"You want romance with me?"

"No. I think I care about you too much to become romantically involved with you."

"Like a brother?"

"Like a friend. I ain't yo brother, sister. Friend is much stronger for me."

"Scott and I are friends, yet brother and sister."

"Good for you. But who did you call when you needed help, Scott or me?"

"Has to do with skill sets. You got the skills and Scott does not."

"What skills? I drive a mean car and tolerate a dog sitting in the back seat. What does Scott drive?"

"Okay, you win. I have a weakness for Jaguars and Scott drives a Honda Civic."

"Yikes."

"Yeah. Could've been a problem."

"Especially for the dog."

"Let's go sleep on it. We have to find Sheriff Robertson or Marie tomorrow."

"Maybe we need to find both of them."

"That would be good. I'll settle for one or the other."

"Marie is still a suspect, right?"

"Well, if she is to be charged with murder, it would be up to the local law and the District Attorney in Dan River."

"At the very least she's a key witness."

"At the very least."

SHORTLY AFTER NINE O'CLOCK THE NEXT MORNING WE ARRIVED at the Sheriff's Office in downtown Clancyville. Deputy Ben Pickeral was manning the office along with Julie Shelton answering the telephones. Deputy Pickeral was sitting on the edge of Julie's desk with a mug of coffee in his hand when we arrived. They were laughing and chatting.

I needed information so I offered by best smile in an effort to win him over.

"Good morning, Ben," I said.

He sipped his coffee and offered nothing in return except a nod in my direction.

"You'll never guess who we're looking for."

"Sheriff Robertson," he said flatly. He took another sip. He offered us no coffee.

"Wow. Is he on the ball or what?" I said to Rosey. "This man should be promoted."

"All sarcasm aside, what do you want?" Ben said.

"You've already guessed it. We want to speak with the good Sheriff."

"The good Sheriff ain't available."

"Can you tell me where the good Sheriff is?"

"I could. I won't."

"Well, that does move us into a more honest conversation. Why is it you refuse to tell us where he is?"

"He told me not to tell you."

"Do tell."

He looked confused now. He sipped his coffee as a defense mechanism. He was at a loss for words. He slid from his perch on Julie's desk to a standing position.

"Ben, this case is not quite over with as yet. Are you not the least bit curious about how the preacher was accidentally poisoned?"

"Not unless Sheriff Robertson tells me to be curious."

"Oh. So much for self-development in your line of work, huh?"

"Beg your pardon?" he said. His mug was empty so he had no recourse but to talk to us or just look dumb. The option of returning to the coffee pot for a refill never occurred to him.

"No incentive for thinking for yourself?"

"I don't understand," he said.

"You know, using your own imagination and the clues at hand and coming up with your own theory of who did what to whom."

"Not my job."

"So besides sitting on the edge of Julie's desk, flirting with the office help, and drinking coffee from a mug, what precisely is your job?"

"Whatever the sheriff wants done."

"Well, good for you. Nice to have a solid job description. And I hope it all works out for you, all things considered."

"You know, Clancy, you have a smart mouth. I don't understand half of what you say, but I know that you are making fun of me."

"Not really, Ben. I'm just trying to get you to use the brain you have. That's all. The sheriff is not the only law enforcement officer in this town who can solve crimes."

"But he'd get mad with me if I did something without his permission," he said walking over to the coffee pot and filling his mug. He obviously had remembered where the coffee was. "He keeps telling me that he's the sheriff and that I'm the deputy."

"True enough, Ben. True enough. But he doesn't have to know everything you do. You have some free time to snoop around, you know."

"But I don't get paid for snooping around on my own time."

"True again. I see your point. Well, it's been nice talking with you. Good luck."

"Good luck with what?"

"Your future. Your job. Your options. Your flirtatious rendezvouses. I suspect that one day you will be the sheriff of this town. You'll need some luck. I wish that for you."

"Thanks, I think. You really think I'll be the sheriff of this town?"

"I have no doubt in my mind, Ben Pickeral. You are a prime candidate for the job."

"Thanks, Clancy," he said and smiled for the first time.

Rosey and I turned to go without learning anything of the whereabouts of Sheriff Robby Robertson.

"Where to now?" Rosey asked.

"Let's go see if the good sheriff is actually at his house?"

"What a novel idea."

"I thought so."

En route my cell phone rang and it was Rogers with an update.

"Marie Jones is taking classes and doing quite well. Smart young woman, to say the least. Top of her class. The records I found all confirm that she is an excellent student with great potential for becoming a nurse. Records also say that she is meticulous and rarely if ever makes a mistake. Thought that was interesting, don't you?"

"I do. Truly. Anything else?"

"Glad you asked. Of course I found something else, but I love it when you ask me."

I rolled my eyes and was grateful she couldn't see that.

"Okay, I ask and you now answer."

"I did some checking into her background."

"And," I said after too long a pause on her end.

"And, she was not born to Joy Jones."

"Whose child is she?"

"Don't know. But Joy Jones was not listed as the birth mother on the certificate I found at the hospital in Lynchburg. The Virginia Baptist Hospital was the place she was born."

"No birth mother was listed?"

"Not on the documents I found. Perhaps I can keep looking."

"Perhaps. See what you can uncover."

"I'm on it, Miss Sleuth," she said and clicked off.

I turned to Rosey and told him the news.

"We need to find Marie and talk further with her," he said.

"Precisely. Plus," I said, "Rogers discovered that Marie is quite the student. Straight A's and rarely makes mistakes."

"Wonders of wonders. So, you thinkin' that she didn't make a mistake with the B-12?"

"That's what I'm thinking."

"Motive?"

"I have no clue."

"You're not much of a detective, Evans."

"You're not the first to tell me."

"Maybe I should take the lead," Rosey said with a smile.

"Lead on, fearless one. I shall follow."

"Let's go see Robby Robertson."

"I'm with you."

"You know the address?" Rosey said.

"Not much of a leader, are you?"

6 8

Rosey was in a generous mood, so he permitted me to drive the Jag. Sam was in the middle of the back seat looking out the front windshield, directly in between the two of us, per usual.

"You clean and reload my gun?" Rosey asked.

"I beg your pardon?"

"The loaner, the Smith and Wesson?"

"Of course," I said. "Why do you ask?"

"Just checking. Some folks don't take care of their stuff."

"Not my stuff, but I take care of it anyway. That gun might be the difference between living and dying. My daddy taught me the daily ritual of cleaning the gun."

"Way to go, Daddy Evans," he said.

"He also told me to empty the chambers of all bullets, clean thoroughly, and reload with different shells. 'Each day is a new day,' he'd say to me, 'so start fresh.'"

"Fully loaded, fully ready."

"That would be the idea."

I drove us out to the Dairy Queen on Highway 40, what the locals refer to as going "up forty." We turned left onto

DeWitt Road and followed it almost to the end. Robby had a small, brick house nestled among a grove of trees on the left side of DeWitt before the bridge that crosses Humpback Creek. The Pitt County Sheriff's car was parked in the driveway.

I parked the Jag close behind the county vehicle so that it would be difficult for the county vehicle to be moved without moving the Jag.

"I hope he don't get mad at us and back into my Jaguar," Rosey said almost pitifully.

"Don't make him mad."

"You be the likely one to piss him off," he said.

"Must be my charm and my way with words."

"Must be that."

Rosey knocked on the front door. To our surprise it opened and Robby stood looking at us without much surprise. He unlatched the storm door and pushed it open for us.

"Come in," he said. "I figured you'd be on my tail soon enough."

The living room had a couch, a chair that matched the couch, a padded rocking chair, one end table which sat between the couch and the matching chair, a coffee table in front of the couch, and a floor lamp near the couch opposite the end table. He motioned for us to sit down. I took the rocker, Rosey sat in the matching chair, and Robby had the couch all to himself. Sam was still in the car resting from the long, twenty minute car ride.

"Where's Marie?" I asked.

"Safe."

"Safe from whom?"

"People who might want to hurt her?"

"You can't hide her forever, Robby."

"Why can't you just walk away and leave it be? She didn't do anything wrong."

"Maybe not, but there's an ongoing investigation and she's at least a witness."

"She didn't see anything. Her testimony is not that valuable."

He was looking down at the corner of the coffee table instead of looking at us when he spoke.

"Valuable enough for her to stay available."

"She's available, just not out in public."

"Why are you protecting her?"

"My job to protect the citizens of the county," he said. He raised his head and looked at me, then returned his gaze to the coffee table. I noticed an arrangement of cheap, plastic flowers in the center of the table. There was a large, ceramic elephant with a smaller one next to it. They both were painted and shiny. The colors were not typical for elephants. They had the Andy Warhol look about them.

"I want to speak with her," I said.

"You've done enough poking and nosing around."

"Apparently not enough. Still don't know who killed the preacher."

He lifted his gaze from the table to me. "His B-12 shots reacted badly. He likely died of natural causes."

"You have facts to support that?"

"My working theory. I'm gathering more evidence."

"No report on the contents of that syringe I found?" I asked.

"Not yet."

"You send it off to the lab?"

"You questioning my police skills?"

"No, just asking."

"I had my deputy take care of that."

"So why can't I talk with Marie Jones?"

"No need. I interviewed her and she has nothing more to contribute to this situation."

"I would just like to ask her a few questions."

"You have no official capacity in this case, you know. In fact, you have no reason to be here at all."

"Except someone tried to kill my mother and my friend."

"He's in jail in Dan River. And so is Joy Jones. Two prime suspects who will be convicted of murder, multiple murders. That's probably a solid case. I'd say you've done enough."

"What about Marilyn Saunders?"

"No real evidence against her as yet. There's an ongoing investigation. If we find something, then she'll be charged. I can't go around arresting people just because you have suspicions."

"I have more than suspicions."

"You catch her in the act of killing someone or attempting to kill someone?" He raised his head once more and looked into my eyes. He seemed to be gaining confidence. Eye contact lasted longer this time.

"She stole my dog."

"Misdemeanor. You pressing charges on that one?"

"She was associating with Henry and Joy," I said in defense.

"You have any proof?"

"I was an eye witness to her association with Henry. Rosey and I both saw her."

"That's not enough. I need more. The District Attorney would laugh at me if that's all I had on her. Besides, association is not nearly enough."

"Are you investigating her involvement?"

"I'm doing my job, lady. That's more than I can say for you. You're doing nothing now but causing trouble. I think you and Mr. Washington should leave my home. I have nothing else to say to you."

"You know I'll keep digging."

"If you get in my way, I will find a reason to charge you."

"I just hope you're not making a mistake here, Robby."

"That's Sheriff Robertson, Miss Evans."

"Walk carefully, Sheriff," I said as I stood from the rocker. I nodded in his direction. He was looking at me once more.

"I could take that as a threat, you know." He stood up and followed us to the front door.

"Don't. It's not a threat. Just a friendly word from someone who thinks you are making a serious mistake."

He opened the door and smiled. "And what mistake would that be, Miss Evans?"

"Protecting the guilty, Sheriff Robertson."

69

I DECIDED TO DRIVE OVER TO DAN RIVER TO VISIT JOY JONES and Henry Smith. I figured that the local police in Dan River might be more open to my continued investigation. I didn't actually drive this time. Rosey insisted that he drive us over there. Sam kept his spot in the back, ever vigilant with his watching and sleeping routine. Ten minutes into the drive, Sam was out and snoring.

Rogers phoned me when we were on the other side of Tightsqueeze heading south to Dan River.

"I finally found something that is interesting on Marie Jones. Perhaps I should preface my findings by stating that what I found could be related to my digging on Marie Jones."

"Okay. Tell me what you found."

"Well, coincidentally on the day that is given as the birth date of Marie Jones, March 17, 1975, a young woman gave birth to a baby girl and two days later that same young woman died of complications. There was internal bleeding and the hospital did not discover it in time."

"You find a name?"

"Annie Tilley."

"Okay. How does Annie Tilley figure into this investigation?" Nothing was clicking for me at the moment.

"Does the name Samuel Tilley ring a bell?" Rogers asked.

"Oh, the young man who was murdered by Preacher Rowland's son."

"Good guess, Sherlock."

"Brother and sister, then?" I said.

"That would be the connection. So, it appears that Annie Tilley is the birth-mother of Marie Jones. Wouldn't it be interesting if we could discover who the father was?"

"Maybe more than interesting. Any leads on that?"

"No. Apparently there are no files at the hospital with that info."

"What about names of nurses or doctors?"

"I'll get you a list. I'll call you back as soon as I have something."

"Anything on your end?" Rogers said.

"Yeah, stone walls."

I shared the information with Rosey. He actually showed some glimmer of emotion with this news. He raised one eyebrow.

"Me thinks that this case is about to break wide open."

"I hope your *thinks* is correct."

I first asked to see Henry, but the guard returned and informed us that Henry was in the infirmary of the prison. I took that to mean that Henry didn't want to talk to us on this occasion.

We turned our attention to Joy Jones and asked to see her. One of Dan River's finest escorted her into the visiting area a few minutes later. The policewoman remained by the door in the room. We sat with Joy at a gray table with gray chairs as far away from the officer as we could. Rosey and I sat on one side and Joy sat on the other. Her back was to the policewoman guarding the door.

"Didn't expect to see you again so soon," Joy said.

"We need your help," I said.

"And why would I help you?"

"Because you're a good person and probably wouldn't want innocent people being accused of murder."

"Not so good, I 'spect. I's in here," she looked around at the barred windows and pointed discreetly at the guard by the door without moving anything more than her thumb.

"Misguided," I said. "Doesn't make you evil."

"Why you think I was misguided?"

"Because you thought the money was important," I said.

"You ever been poor, Clancy Evans?"

"When I was young, living with my parents. We didn't have much."

"You had clothes. You ate regular. Your family had a car. You had shoes to wear."

I nodded, "Yes, I had all of that."

"Then you weren't poor. I grew up missing meals. I had one dress and no shoes. We walked everywhere, if we went anywhere. Lived in the projects and people whispered about us when they seen us. Poor, Clancy Evans, that's what we were."

"So you decided to kill people in order to stop being poor."

"Didn't want my grandchildren growing up poor. Money was important. I was used to poor, but I couldn't bear to see my grandchildren being laughed at. You understand that?"

I didn't say anything. There was no way I could understand the pain of what she had been through in her life. No use pretending that I could. I stared at her arms resting on the gray table across from me. I waited for a minute or two before I responded.

"I know that you have suffered in ways I can't imagine.

Still, you knew right from wrong and killing those people was at best misguided."

"They wuz old and going to die anyway," she said.

"But they still had some years left perhaps. It wasn't your right to decide when they died, or if. It wasn't your call. You trying to justify the money you were paid?"

"I wuz paid to make that call. You didn't understand the power of the preacher. He said he'd fire Marie and see that she never got another job if I didn't help out. He cudda' done that, too. If you doubt that, you know nothing about the power that man had over folks."

"You think maybe Marie killed him intentionally?" I said.

"No way. That child's got nothing mean in her. She's a good girl. She couldn't kill nobody, and that's the truth."

"So where'd she get the syringe if you didn't keep them at your place?"

"I don't know where she got it. I just know she didn't get it from my stuff. I do keep syringes and morphine in my house. Marilyn Saunders got me the stuff, but I keep it all in a locked cabinet. One place, one key, one lock, and I has the key."

"Would you be willing testify that Marilyn Saunders was involved in this?"

"What good would 'dat be? Gonna help my case? I'm the one who kilt those folks. Marilyn's nothing more than an accessory or whatever you call it. Wouldn't help me none."

"You told me earlier that you didn't take B-12 shots."

"I don't."

"So why would Marie lie to me about that? She said she borrowed a syringe from your collection in order to give Preacher Rowland his dosage. Why would she tell me that?"

"Don't know."

"You never told her what you were doing and what you kept in the locked cabinet?"

"Never. She knew nothin'. Only that when I started helping the preacher get rid of those people, he was a lot nicer to her. She commented on it to me now and again, but she never knew why. I never told her nothin'."

"Does she know that she's not your daughter?"

Joy's gaze moved from her folded hands lying in front of her on the gray table to meet my eyes head-on. Surprise was evident as she sought for the words to answer.

"She's my baby," Joy said as a tear followed a path down her right cheek. She wiped her chin just before the tear would have fallen onto the gray table.

"I know. But you didn't birth her."

"I did everything for her. I did it all. I cared for her like a mama. She was so precious. My sister Faith was dying of cancer. Her oldest, Ray, had joined the Navy. Then Samuel was murdered. Then Annie died. Two children dead, the other gone. I did it for her, too, you know."

More tears were coming and finding their way down both cheeks.

"You know who the father is."

"Of course I knows. I knows the whole story, Clancy Evans. I knows the whole, nasty story of growing up poor and trying to find a way out. You'll travel any road to get out. My sweet sister traveled one road. I traveled another. We both wanted out."

I waited to see if she would tell me. Sometimes I found it best to let the person you are questioning to find their own pace, their own rhythm for telling you what you need to know.

"That little baby was so precious. I had to help. I jest had to help Faith out. She cudd'na raised no child. That cancer was evil. Destroying her. So Marie became my baby, my little girl."

"Who was the father?" I finally asked.

"Oh, him. Well, he did help out. He'd come by once in a while, mostly at night so no one sees him. But he brought money, always brought money to help me. To his credit, I 'spect. It wudd'na done nobody no good for him to tell the world that Marie was his baby. It might'a hurt Marie, you know. If this town knew that her father was white. Naah…t was easy for us to keep that secret. Some secrets be good to have."

"Joy, I need to know the father's name."

"I know you do. I just not sure I wanna give it."

"You protecting him?"

She looked away from us, and her hands, searching for some answer along the dirty, gray walls of the room where we sat. I could tell that she was considering what might happen if she told.

"No way you can keep this secret," she said.

"Afraid not. I would if I could, but the truth is, I believe it has a lot to with this case."

"But I'm the one who actually kilt those people."

"True, but the preacher was behind it."

"He's dead."

"Dead enough. But someone has to answer for his death and you certainly don't want that person to be Marie."

"You think he did it? You think Marie's daddy did it?"

"I don't know until you give me a name and I check it out."

"You have no idea, do you?"

"His identity?"

"Yeah."

"No. But I could guess."

"Then you needs to guess. I ain't ever told anyone who her daddy is. I can't start now."

I nodded to her and looked at Rosey.

"Let's go," I said. "We have enough."

70

"I would have pressed harder," Rosey said as he increased the speed of the Jag along Highway 29 going north to Clancyville.

"I know."

"So why didn't you?"

"I don't think it would've helped."

"But you didn't try. I think her story got to you. Very unprofessional."

"I know."

"You feel sorry for her?"

"To a degree. I could never condone the murders. It's the other part that gets to me."

"The stuff we can't change."

"That would be the stuff."

"I would have pressed harder."

"I know."

"No argument, huh?"

"No need. When you're right..."

"Where to now, since we only know a little?"

"I know enough."

"Is there a next?"

"I'm going to visit my old friend Jessica Thompson, Mrs. Chatterbox herself."

"Does she know all this?"

"No. It would be all over town if Jessica knew it."

"So how can she help?"

"She knows something, but she doesn't understand what she knows. Perspective. She sees what she sees and knows what she knows but only through one view. That view has to do with her granddaughter. If she would ever move to another viewpoint, she could unlock this whole secret mess."

"You gonna tell her that?"

"Are you kidding me? I'm not stupid. No, I'm not gonna help her rethink all of this. I just want to know one thing from her."

"And she will tell you?"

"No question about it. She will tell me."

"And she won't figure it out?"

"I doubt it seriously."

We checked in at my mother's place and found everyone resting well. I left Rosey and Sam to interact with Sarah and Rachel. Birds of a feather. I went to see Jessica on Mulberry Avenue.

Jessica sat on the edge of the love seat which was across from the matching couch on which I was perched. Her knees were together and her back was perfectly straight, much straighter than I would expect for someone in their nineties. We were both drinking tea since it was early afternoon.

"So good of you to call again. It's always nice to chat with someone like you, Clancy."

I decided to let that one fall on the floor and die. If I reacted to everything Jessica ever said, I would never get to the subject I needed to discuss.

"Did you ever learn the identity of the woman who Robby Robertson was seeing?"

"You mean the one who destroyed my granddaughter's dreams?"

"You could put it that way if you like."

"I do put it that way. She did. But, like most Thompsons, Sally Mae endured and moved on," she said with an air of intended distinction.

I waited for Jessica to continue while I nursed the last few drops of my tea.

"You want some more tea, dear?" she asked.

"Another cup would be good."

She picked up a tiny bell and rang it. In a few seconds a middle aged black woman came into the sitting room and stood at the door without actually entering the room.

"Yes, ma'am?" she said to Jessica.

"More tea."

We were silent as we waited for the woman to bring us more tea. I felt uncomfortable, but Jessica was definitely in her element. In a few moments, the woman returned and poured both of us some tea.

"Will that be all, Mrs. Thompson?" she said.

"Yes."

The woman left and nearly took all of the air of the room with her. I took in a deep breath and slowly exhaled. Then I sipped my tea. It was very hot. Jessica smiled and sipped hers.

"Now, you were asking about that horrid situation long ago," she said.

"Not so long ago, I suppose."

"Well, no, I guess not. It is hard to forget."

"If this is too painful, Jessica," I began to say.

"No, no. I'm fine. You wanted to know if I know who the woman was."

"Yes."

"Well, I did some checking around after the whole ordeal had created such tumult in our family. My granddaughter was devastated. Simply devastated. You cannot imagine what she went through, learning that the man she was to marry was having an affair with a younger woman, and a black woman at that."

Her emphasis was obviously on the black part and not the young part. I sipped my tea instead of commenting. It was good tea.

"You sure it was an affair?"

"What? Of course it was an affair! Why else would he be coming out of a motel room with her?"

I decided that I didn't have enough facts to answer that one, but I knew that situations are not always what they appear. Still, I let it die.

"I thought you were a keen investigator, Clancy Evans," she almost laughed when she said that. She was wearing her condescending air.

"I look at all the facts whenever I investigate. Sometimes people, especially law enforcement people, have reasons for being where they are, and doing the things they have to do."

"True enough, but when questioned and confronted, he gave no answer. He told Sally Mae nothing. Said it was personal or some such nonsense. Personal, indeed. Why, Sally Mae was to be his wife, for goodness sakes. He could have at least explained it better. But then, well, you know men. I doubt if he had an explanation."

"So you don't have a name."

"I have a guess."

"A guess?"

"Some of my friends and I were talking one day, a few years later, and one of them said something at our bridge club meeting that sort of gave me the idea of who this woman was."

"Really." Hooray for the bridge club.

"Yes. It was an innocent remark, you know. And she certainly wasn't trying to dredge up the past or anything. We were simply sitting around playing cards and talking. You know, sharing stuff about the community and all."

I got the picture.

"She said that she had heard that Sheriff Robertson went to visit Joy Jones a lot and that she had heard rumors that maybe the Sheriff and Joy's daughter had something going on. But said that she had never seen anything or had no story to tell. Just an innocent remark, that's all."

Innocent.

"So your guess would be that Sheriff Robertson and Marie Jones were seeing each other?"

"Yes, but I have no proof or anything to back that up."

"Quite a few years difference in their ages," I said.

"I don't think that matters to a man, Clancy Evans. They're animals, you know."

"I found the name of a nurse who was working back in 1975 and called her while posing as you, Boss Lady. I hope you don't mind my subterfuge," Rogers said.

"Spilt milk," I said.

"What?"

"Water over the dam, Rogers. It's done. Go on."

"Sometimes I have no idea what it is you are talking about, and yet I am one of the smartest machines you know. Why is that?"

"Could it be that I am smarter?"

"Not likely. Not likely at all. Perhaps you have failed to program me properly."

"Tell me about the nurse you found."

"Oh, yes. She recalled the whole episode when I mentioned that the woman was black and that after she had given birth, she died a few days later. She said that it was a sad event. But she remembered that this black woman had been accompanied by a white man, a young white man."

"She remember a name?"

"She apologized for her memory saying that it was just too many years ago, but she thought his name was Bob or Rob or something like that. She said that she kept a diary back then while working in the pediatric wing of the hospital, but she had no idea where the diary was. She said she would look for it. It might contain something that would help. That's all I got."

"Might be enough. It's certainly enough for me."

"The puzzle coming together?"

"Yeah, but I don't like the picture that is forming. Call me if you get something else."

"Anything else I should be checking?"

"All of my loose ends."

"Now how am I to know what all of your loose ends are?"

"You're the smartest machine I know. Remember?"

She was silent as she processed my retort, so I clicked off. I would pay for it the next time we talked. The thing about Rogers and her intelligence was that she remembered everything, but she seldom held grudges for longer than a day or so. At any rate, I had more serious matters with which to contend.

Rosey joined me in my mother's backyard. I was sitting in the tire swing contemplating the whole mess that I was uncovering.

"You okay?" Rosey asked.

"Sure. I'm okay. Just sometimes I don't like my job."

"Which part?"

"The discovery part. Digging and digging, which I have to do; but, then I put this tidbit with that tidbit and the picture forms. Discovering the picture, putting it together … well, sometimes it is painful."

"Some dogs better left sleeping."

"Until they wake up and bite someone."

"Like in this case."

"This one is really complicated. Several dogs, lots of biting."

"So what has your tidbit collection formed?"

"Marie Jones is actually Robby Robertson's daughter."

"That be one of those deep, dark secrets better left buried."

"For this town? Absolutely."

"For most towns in the south. The cities are different."

"Depends upon one's circle of friends, I suppose," I mused.

"Is that all?"

"No, I think Robby is the one who switched syringes without Marie knowing it. She gave Preacher Rowland a shot of something that was not vitamin B-12. He used his own daughter to kill the man."

"Motive?"

"Working on that. I might have to go visit the good sheriff once more and ask some questions. It could be as simple as Preacher Rowland found out that Marie was his daughter and threatened to expose him. Leverage, you know."

"He won't be forthcoming."

"Suspects rarely are."

"He will resent you."

"It's a growing number. That's why you will be going with me."

"Body guard par excellence."

"And friend. Show him I have at least one friend left in the world."

"We could take the dog, too."

"Softening up, are we?"

"He already owns the back seat. Might as well let him ride along. I could charge him rent."

"Let's go."

I opened the back door and yelled to my mother that we were going visiting. She came to the back porch before she answered me.

"It's nearly supper time. Can't this wait?"

"Believe me, I would love for this to wait. But I need to get it over with."

I told her we were going to visit Robby. I let her in on the picture that had formed from my investigation. I offered my best deduction as Mr. Holmes might have done with this case.

"You have evidence to support all of this?" Mother said.

"Some."

"The rest is your insight, intuition, puzzle solving techniques."

"That would be the greater part."

"Be careful. He might feel trapped," she said in response. "If you're right."

"I suspect the man has felt trapped most of his life. At least the tiny part I know about. Having secrets has a way of trapping the best of us."

"You speak like a person of experience on that subject," Mother said.

"I think most people have some experience on that subject."

"So what are your secrets?" she asked.

"They wouldn't be my secrets if I told you, now would they?"

"And if you told me, you wouldn't feel so trapped. Would you?"

"Touché."

I turned and walked down the steps and got in the car. Rosey headed the car in the direction of Sheriff Robby

Robertson's house. Sam was sitting up, alert, looking out the windshield, and ready for whatever might happen. I wondered if my dog had any secrets in his life. No doubt he did.

We were heading west toward DeWitt Road to Sheriff Robby Robertson's house when I suddenly had the notion to go back to Dan River. My revelation came as we were passing by the Clancyville's water tower on the west side of town.

"Turn left after you cross the bridge," I said to Rosey.

"Why?"

"We're going to Dan River first."

"Shopping trip?"

"Is that a sexist remark?"

"Probably."

"I want to go back and visit Henry and see how he is feeling."

"He might not care if you know how he is feeling."

"My intuition tells me that he will see me."

"He wouldn't see you the first time. What makes you think he will see you today?"

"You're ruling out my all pervasive Clancy charm?"

"I suppose I was ruling that out," he said as he turned off of Highway 40 and onto the ramp which took us to Highway

29 South towards Dan River. "If he won't even see you, how will your devastating charm lure him into talking?"

"There's an old saying about not crossing bridges before you come to them."

Rosey made good time in the Jag and we were about to enter the visiting area of the Dan River Correctional Facility thirty-seven minutes later. We showed the man inside the well-protected and very secure barred booth our identifications. We put our firearms in the automatic metal basket that he sent in our direction like a bank teller at a drive-through window.

"You any kin to the prisoner?" the guard asked.

"He is," I said and pointed to Rosey.

Rosey always had a poker face and played along as if we had planned this strategy for days. The guard looked at Rosey and said nothing.

"How are you related to Henry Smith?" he asked.

"Cousins."

"You kin, too?" he looked at me.

"No, just friends." I smiled. I used just a little of that all pervasive Clancy charm. The guard did not smile back. Obviously, he had no charm handed down to him in his family.

"Go through the door on the right when you hear the unlocking mechanism."

We waited. A few minutes later there was a loud thud inside the right hand door. Rosey opened the door and we walked through. We walked into a large area with multiple rooms. The walls that divided these several smaller rooms were made of re-enforced wire. It afforded little privacy. Henry Smith was waiting in the second small room on our right along with a guard.

Henry stood up when we entered.

"You ain't my family," he said to us under his breath, and

moved towards the guard as if he were going to say something to the man guarding the doorway.

"We're as close as you're going to get today, Henry. Just talk with us for a few minutes."

Henry looked down at his feet, turned, and sat back down at the small table in the middle of the room. Must have been my Clancy charm. I sat down across from him while Rosey found a place to lean, directly across from the stoic guard.

"Marie Jones is not your sister, Henry."

"You tellin' or askin'?"

"I'm making a statement."

"Why you tellin' me something I already know?"

"So you'll know that I know. Marie is the daughter of Robby Robertson and Annie Tilley. Annie was your cousin."

"How you know this?"

"I'm a detective."

"So what you want from me?"

"I need you to fill in some gaps in the story of Robby and Annie."

"Talk to my dear, old mother."

"She wouldn't even tell me who Marie's father was. Family secret and all."

"Yeah, she like secrets. She's had plenty 'a secrets in her life to like. Plenty 'a men, plenty 'a children, plenty 'a time for everyone but me. That's my mama."

I knew some of Henry's story, but he filled in some of my gaps with details and pain.

"You has no idea what it's like to be a small boy and dejected by yur mama, do you?"

He looked at Rosey then back at me. I knew he meant *rejected*. I let it slide.

"No, I don't," I said to him.

"Well, it hurts. Hurts like hell. Won't my fault that her first boyfriend left her with me. But she blamed me. Treated me like I had leprosy. Fed me, gave me hand-me-down clothes, let me sleep in a back room, nothin' more than a broom closet, but never once told me she loved me. Never touched me except to wup me. I never had a real mama. Not like other folks. At least not much of one."

Rosey was still standing by the wire-wall to my right, opposite from the guard who was still stationary by the door. I turned my head slightly to the right to look at Rosey. He was composed, ever the stoic. My heart was breaking inside, but I tried to remain unmoved externally.

Henry was staring at his hands which were interlocked with the fingers. They were stretched out in front of him with his elbows resting on the table. He was silent, thinking about something long ago and far away, yet still close to him.

"I reckon she wanted me to be a secret. But I wouldn't let her. I didn't allow such. I made sure ever'one knew I wuz a son of Joy Whittaker as she wuz known back then. Some man named Smith came along and caused her eyes to dance. Never even offered to marry her.

"How old were you when Marie was born?"

"Ah, I don't know. Early twenties, I think. I wasn't livin' with my dear, old mama then. I was already on my own, trying to make it."

"Tell me about Annie."

He smiled for the first time and leaned back in his chair. I think it was the first time I had ever seen Henry smile. It surprised me. I didn't think the man any smiles left inside himself.

"She was a good person, a really good person. You know what I remember the best about her, Miss Clancy?"

I shook my head.

"She was kind. Kindness can go a long way, especially to a child that nobody wants. She was so kind. Didn't deserve what happened to her."

"Tell me about her, Henry."

"Annie had a twin brother, named Raymond. They had an older brother named Sam Tilley. I bet you heard of him before."

"Yes, I recognize that name. Do you know that story?"

"Course I do. I was there."

"What do you mean you were there?"

"I was at that hiding place in the woods when Sam and his girl were killed."

"You saw it happen?"

"Seen the whole thing."

"And why were you there?"

"Sam wuz my friend. He wuz also my cousin and he treated me with some respect, like I wuz a person and all. I knew about this secret place in the woods 'cause I spent a lot a time there when I wuz a kid. I could hide there and nobody wud bother me 'cause they cudd'na find me. Good hidin' place. Anyhow, I showed Sam the place, and that's where he and his girlfriend, that white girl, would go there to be together and nobody knew."

"J.D. Rowland must have known about it," I said.

He looked hard at me for a few seconds and then went back to watching his folded hands in front of him. He was thinking of something.

"That wuz my fault. He lied to me about being Sam's friend and all. Said he wanted to surprise him by showing up at the place. Said he knew all about Sam and Barbara Ann Smith, that white girl."

"So, you told him about the place?"

"No. I took him there. That's why I wuz there when he killed them. I brought J.D. Rowland to that spot where he gunned down both of them right in front of me."

"I suppose you're lucky he didn't shoot you as well," I said.

"I ran away. As soon as he fired that gun into my friends, I ran. I ran fast. I wudd'na gonna give J.D. no chance to shoot me. He wuz a mean sonofabitch. I shud'a known better. I can't ever forgive myself for that. It wuz my fault. I gots to live with it. As long as I live, I have to live with that."

"But you had no way of knowing that he was planning to kill them. It wasn't your fault, Henry."

"I shud'a known that J.D. wuz no good. Never had been. I let him fool me. Bad. I shud'a known."

I started to say something about J.D.'s father fooling Henry as well, but I thought better of it. Henry was carrying around enough guilt and grief. And pain. He didn't need me to put more on him.

"Robby and Annie were not there on that day either, right?"

"Naw, they weren't there. J.D. wudd'a shot 'em both. But then, if that had happened, there wudd'na been no trial for J.D."

"Why not?"

"I wud 'a killed him with my bare hands, or died tryin'."

"What do you know about Annie and the birth of Marie?"

"Not much. Annie and Robby didn't see each for a few years, but then all a sudden they were thick as thieves once more and next thing we know'd wuz that Annie wuz with child. She developed some problems giving birth and died shortly after Marie wuz born. That's 'bout all I know."

"What happened to Raymond Tilley, Annie's twin brother?"

"Oh, Ray, he joined the Navy, you know, to see the world. I spect he did. Saw more world than I ever saw. He came back now and again, but not often. Came back for the funeral and all. Never see much of him anymore. I think he lives in Norfolk, but I ain't too sure 'bout that."

"Robby Robertson never told anyone that he was the father of Marie."

"Naw, that wuz my mama's idea. She believed it wuz better to make that another secret. I told ya, she like secrets. So she made Marie her own. Mama took the baby since Annie's mama had cancer and didn't have no strength to raise a child. She died a few months later as I recall. Mama raised Marie like she wuz her own. Funny thing wuz tho', no matter how hard Mama tried to keep Marie from seein' me, knowin' me, that little girl wud come callin'. Just like her mama, she wuz kind. She liked me, too. I cud tell."

"Did Robby ever come around?"

"Yeah, at night. Protectin' the secret, you know. He wuz good 'bout that. I think he gave Mama money ever' month for Marie."

"Thank you for telling me this, Henry."

"Well, I don't mind as long as it hurts my Mama. I'm glad to tell some of her secrets to ya. Serves her right for tryin' to control it all. Some things you just can't control."

"Is that all you can tell me about Marie and Robby?"

"I reckon that's all I know... no, wait. I remember one other thing. Marie was seeing this low-life guy named Silas. He wuz no good. Lived on the edge of trouble all the time. In and out of jail, you name it, Silas Monroe did it. Quit school when he was sixteen. Man wud'na nuthin' but trouble. Never did know what Marie saw in him. Anyhow, I think Marie was secretly seein' him at the Clancyville Motel. I heard 'em talkin' 'bout Robby goin' down there and getting' Marie outta that place. But that's all I heard. Mama wanted to keep that a secret as well. Sometimes I wish there wuz no such thing as secrets. World might be a better place if ever'body just told the truth all the time."

73

HE SAT IN THE CHAIR LOOKING OUT THE WINDOW INTO THE late afternoon shadows. The rain clouds were moving too quickly in his direction. If lost was a true feeling, that's what he felt. She was on his mind, again. The truth is, her memory was never out of reach. What would life have been if she had lived? Living in Clancyville would have been out of the question. He could almost feel her touch. If he closed his eyes and let himself go, he could remember other intimate things as well. He dared not go there. It was never productive to do that.

He turned away from the shadows of the evening and concluded that life would have been much better if she were still here. Different and better.

He felt trapped. He had tried hard to stop this from happening. Sometimes life had a way of happening despite the best intentions. It was if the events of the last few days had a life of their own. He had thought he had some control. Maybe he never had control over anything. All through the years he had protected the secret, kept it at bay, and even showing great restraint at times. Now it seemed as if he had been guarding the wind, trying to keep it from blowing in the wrong direction.

The room was dark from the shadows of the later afternoon. It would be completely dark in a short while and he could sit and enjoy the blackness. Maybe the dark would hide him fully and he could feel safe again. Safe from the world of people, safe from the world of knowledge, safe from the world of revelation, safe from the secret.

He thought about running, just getting away and putting it all behind him. Where would he run? The more the idea appealed to him, the more he realized that he had no place to go. He was a prisoner of his own demons. The circumstances, as well as his actions, had imprisoned him. Tragic events, sinister plots, and now, finally, he had stooped to do the evil that he tried so hard to root out. He was a prisoner of his own actions.

He was no killer, he knew that. And yet, he had actually plotted the deed and done it. He would have to answer for that. Justice was still important. Despite the lack of justice he had experienced in his own life, justice was out there, albeit illusive, but nevertheless relentless. Slow in coming most days, it traveled at its own pace when it traveled at all. He now knew it would find him, much quicker than it found the good preacher.

She needs to take off that damn blind fold.

Even in the shadows he could see a part of the shiny metal object resting in his lap. His finger was on the trigger guard, just waiting for the right moment to move. As the room slowly darkened, his eyes adjusted and he could discern the outline of the danger in his lap. It felt heavy, much like the way he felt at the moment. He wondered if he had the strength to pick it up and fire it. That would take more than strength.

There was a sound somewhere outside of his small house. Was that a car door? Is someone coming to visit me? I don't want to see anyone or talk or think. I don't want to do anything except sit here and wait for courage. I can do this.

The knock on the front door broke whatever concentration he had mustered. He had first thought that he would just sit where he was and wait for the person to leave. The knock came again, louder this time. He opened his desk drawer and placed the instrument of death under some papers near the bottom. He rose slowly from the chair and made his way reluctantly to the front door.

Intrusions never cease. They will be the death of me. Somebody always wanting something. Why can't they leave a body alone? I'm just so tired. I just want to be left alone. Just leave me alone.

He moved the curtains carefully so as not to call attention to them. He recognized the woman detective and the black man who helped her. Maybe justice is not so slow in coming after all, he thought. This is my chance. Them or me. It would be that simple. An old fashioned showdown. How convenient life is if you wait long enough.

SHERIFF ROBBY ROBERTSON WAS OUR NEXT STOP. THE SMALL city of Dan River was behind us. Rosey and I had finished processing for the time being what Henry Smith had shared with us about Marie. Rosey turned off of Highway 29 North and onto Climax Road. DeWitt Road was just off of Climax about three miles from our turn.

There was still some fall color remaining, but many of the leaves in this section of the county had finally abandoned their distinctive hues. Now there was nothing more than dirty brown objects hanging lifeless from the thin limbs, waiting for the rain and the wind to finish their fall. A body could become saddened by the whole natural process if you thought too much about it.

"I have a question," Rosey said, interrupting my dreary autumnal mood.

"Okay."

"You think the Sheriff used Marie to kill Rowland."

"That's a question?"

"Setting up my question."

"Yes, that's what I believe."

"And you also believe that Marie is the Sheriff's daughter, unbeknownst to the great majority of the world."

"Unbeknownst."

"Why would he do that to his own daughter? Let's assume that he does love her and has tried to protect her from the Southern slurs all these years. Why would he make her the scapegoat in a murder?"

"You're saying that we're missing something here."

"Yes, we are. We're missing something really important."

I pulled out my cell phone to check for a signal. I had a good one.

"Turn onto that dirt road and stop," I said.

"Yes, ma'am."

He slowed the Jag to a stop. Sam moved to his alerted position between the seats ready for whatever might come. I got out of the Jag and called Rogers. She answered on the second ring.

"Rogers here."

"What if someone had stolen my cell phone and called my house and you answered that way? Our secret would be exposed."

"No one stole your cell phone," Rogers said.

"But they could have."

"But they didn't. Are you calling me to start a war?"

"No. I need your help."

"You have a fine way of asking me for help."

"My stress level is rising. I guess I was simply taking it out on you. I have some missing links. I need you to process some data and do some more research. I need it quickly."

"You always need it quickly, Boss Lady. As long as your humor improves, I will be glad to help you."

"I'm good. No more chastising. I need you to call the hospital and see if they have any records on Marie Jones as a young child."

"What are you looking for?"

"I don't know. Something. Anything."

"Well, that narrows the field. Can you give me a hint?"

"I don't have a hint. I believe that Sheriff Robertson used his own daughter to kill Preacher Rowland, and he did so without her knowledge. I believe he provided her with a poison while she thought she was simply giving Rowland his routine medicines. It would appear that he was framing her for the crime. The autopsy on Rowland and the lab report on the glass will most likely provide enough evidence to indict her for killing Rowland. It could be a perfect frame."

"I have already thought of that. In fact, I have done some research on the usage of medicines as poison."

"What lead you in that direction?" I asked.

"The fact that morphine was used to kill those people at Peace Haven."

"Then could you do some checking on potassium as a poison?"

"I have some information on that. Why do you choose potassium?"

"It was one of the meds that Rowland was taking."

"What else?"

"Insulin and B-12."

"That's it?"

"He had some heart pills and some vitamins, but nothing that seemed to be suspicious otherwise. I spoke with my mother's doctor earlier and she said potassium would be a good way to eliminate someone."

"She is correct, if used in the right dosage."

"So you know about this already."

"I know what I have unearthed."

"Do tell."

"I did some checking on Rowland and found everything you have mentioned."

"Why did you let me go on like that if you already knew what he was taking?"

"I was just testing you to see how thorough you were being."

"Great. My own computer is assessing my detective skills."

"Don't you think that is a good thing? I am keeping you on your toes, ever alert, vigilant, meticulous, and ready for anything."

"Whatever. What else have you found?"

"Potassium, if given in a large enough dosage, could easily shut down the vital organs and kill a person within minutes. No doubt about it. Of the meds that Rowland was on, potassium would be my choice."

"I know that Marie had access to all of the medicines, but did Robby Robertson have access to any of them?"

"He did. My research on him turned up some rather interesting stuff. It appears that Robby's mother has low potassium levels, so she takes it daily. He buys large quantities of potassium in order to save money. That's my working hypothesis. I discovered that Mr. Robertson has a standing order with the local Clancyville Pharmacy for potassium in a highly concentrated form. That concentrated form of potassium provides a neat weapon to exterminate someone."

"Robertson buys this stuff for his mother?"

"She lives with him. He is an only child. His father died in 1989. His mother required constant care sometime in the mid-nineties because of some dementia. He moved her into his own home a few years later. More complications developed in the form of breast cancer. Got through that with surgery and some doses of radiation. Then, last year more cancer came. This time it was ovarian. Her doctor called in Hospice earlier this year."

"This is certainly interesting, but how does this help me

prove Robby was able to kill Rowland without also framing his own daughter?"

"Let's connect some dots, shall we? With his mother now living in his own house and slowly dying, he likely has power of attorney, which means he can purchase her meds for her legally. He knows that his daughter is not only the maid for Rowland, but also is employed for her nursing skills. As a registered LPN, Marie Jones provides Rowland with whatever medicines he requires. When I checked on all of that, I discovered that Rowland began taking potassium last month. Perhaps Marie mentioned this as a passing remark, or they are complicit in this murder. It is possible that Robertson increased the dosage for Rowland without her knowledge."

"Explain to me how he could increase the dosage without her knowledge," I said.

"You know, for someone who is supposed to be such a top-notch, super-duper detective, you are sometimes slow on the uptake. Work with me here ... let's say Marie happened to tell her father that she needed to go by the drugstore and renew the prescription for Rowland because she had used up the first prescription. If she called it in, then Robby could actually be the one to go by and pick it up for her. He would have to sign for the prescription. Since he is the Sheriff, few questions would be asked. Just doing a favor for a friend. No one would suspect him of anything. He could simply fix a syringe for Rowland using the concentrate. The next thing she knows is that the man is dead."

"Sounds too implausible to me," I said.

"Implausible?"

"Yes, ma'am. Sounds like you have manufactured a story to fit the data you have discovered. Potassium is light sensitive. The syringe that Marie used for Rowland's dosage is amber colored. Protects the medicine from damage by the light. You suppose that Robertson knew all of this?"

"I am truly insulted. I am a mathematical, data processing piece of equipment. I gather facts and then present the obvious scenario to you. And you, of all people, should trust my highly reasoned and provable conclusions and deductions. I do not embellish, contrive, or create wildly imaginative stories just to please you. Drug stores keep records of all transactions and sales. The day before Robert Lee Rowland died, Robby Robertson signed for Rowland's prescription which included a box of generic bottles often used by people who dilute concentrated medicines. The other item that Robby Robertson purchased that day was a box of twenty-five amber colored syringes. I may be guilty of providing some extraneous information to you at times, but I never conjure up ways to make the storyline fit the data I discover. Do you want me to continue?"

I was duly reprimanded and contrite in the face of Rogers' revelations. She had been working overtime, discovering tidbits that actually proved my theory.

"Please, continue, and I beg your forgiveness for my insinuations concerning your research and processing."

"Insinuations? How about out and out accusations of jumping to conclusions and idle thinking? Sister, you owe me more than just some cheap verbal apology."

I could tell that she was enjoying this upper hand I had given to her. "Okay, my bad. Please continue with what you have discovered. I will never accuse you of such again."

"That's better. Since most of us know that I am rather thorough in my research, what I found next was most intriguing, even to me. Robby is color blind. The form of color blindness that he has is extremely rare. It is called protanopia and only one out of one hundred males have this. The rate is ridiculously low for females. In fact so low and so improbable that most folks would think it a complete waste of time to check to see if his daughter would have it. You know me. I leave no stone unturned until I find out every-thing that is to be found out. If there is a document trail for whatever, I will find it and bring it to your highness."

"What did you find?"

"I went back to the hospital in Lynchburg where Marie was born and they found some old records on Marie Jones, believe it or not. She is color blind. It's the same type of color blindness her daddy has. Since color blindness is inherited, it almost can prove that he is her father, if you need such proof. That's how rare the color blindness they share is. At the very least, they are related."

"And you're going to tell me more about this type of color blindness."

"Not really. The remainder of what I have added to my data base is not relevant to this particular case as far as I know. However, I shall retain the data and it will henceforth be available for all future cases."

"Henceforth. So, we have some circumstantial evidence, none of which can prove Robertson's guilt or Marie's innocence."

"That would be true. However, the facts I have presented to you are rather strange coincidences. As you have said before, there are no such things as coincidences in murder investigations. My position on all this is that it remains doubtful that Marie knew what her father was planning. If she were complicit, then there would be no need for dear old daddy to pick up that potassium concentrate at the phar-macy. With her knowledge she could have easily injected Rowland with a concentrated dosage and then wait a few minutes. I think daddy used her to kill Rowland, and then destroyed the evidence."

"What do you mean?"

"I think I remember you telling me that you gave the Sheriff all of the evidence you collected at the house, the drinking glass, the syringes, and the medicine bottle. Then Sheriff Robertson gave the evidence to his trusty deputy Mr. Pickeral. Didn't you tell me all that?"

"Yes, I did," I could easily follow her thinking. She was probably right. Ben Pickeral likely never sent that evidence to the lab for testing.

"If I were a betting computer," Rogers continued, "I'd say all of that incriminating evidence has mysteriously disappeared. Only Ben knows where. But, all is not lost. If I were a super sleuth like yourself, I would visit the good sheriff and check his house for potassium citrate. I'm betting that he has potassium in a concentrated form. As good as you are, you might even discover other clues that would link him to the crime."

"Sarcasm is not so becoming for you."

"Maybe not, but I believe you deserve it."

"Okay. I apologize for my attitude. You have been most helpful. If you are right, I will owe you one."

"Oh, Miss Super Duper Detective, you will owe me more than one. I want to know what you are going to do for me to make up all of your vicious insinuations and dubious doubting of my analytical and mathematical skills on your behalf for this most difficult of cases."

"I'll think of something. In the meantime, try to forgive me and stay on your game. Your acumen is staggering to say the least."

"Thank you," Rogers said and clicked off.

I climbed back into the Jag. I filled Rosey in on all of Rogers' fact-finding information and her assumptions as we continued on to the sheriff's house. I tried to make Rogers' assumption sound less assuming. I stole them as if they were my own.

Two cars were parked in front of Robertson's small home. One of them was the county sheriff's car. The other was a Ford Taurus from the nineties. There was a bumper sticker on the rear of the Ford that was advertising for Hospice.

The sun had played a type of dodge ball with the clouds for most of the day. It was now overcast. The clouds had finally won. There were some rain clouds over to the west and the slight wind was moving them our way. Nothing was happening at the moment.

Sam stayed in the car while Rosey and I approached the front door. I knocked and waited for an answer. Nothing happened. Rosey knocked harder. We waited. Again, nothing. It was my turn. I move my closed fist into position and the door opened. Sheriff Robertson stood behind the torn screen. He looked weary.

"Is this a bad time?" I asked.

"The nurse is inside seeing to my mother. She's pretty sick. I think the end is close," Robby said in a low voice, almost a whisper.

"Didn't know your mother was living with you."

"Long time," he said. "Most people don't know. I don't talk about it."

"This a hospice nurse?" I asked.

"Yeah. It's a good organization. They help a lot of people."

"I've heard good things," I said.

"Yeah, they're real helpful."

"I'm sorry about your mother," I said, not knowing what else to say.

He looked at me with searching eyes. I had no idea for what he was searching, but I could tell that he must have been satisfied when he finally nodded as he gaze fell to the ground.

"We need to talk," I said after a minute or so of strained silence.

He opened the screen door and shifted so that I could

pass in front of him. Rosey followed me into the living room. Robby was wearing his sheriff's uniform with his shirttail pulled out. He badge and firearm were not evident.

"Make it quick, Clancy. I'm not much in a mood to talk right now," Robby said without offering us a place to sit.

"Sorry this is a bad time, but I wanted you to know what I've discovered."

Robby was standing with his back to the faux fireplace. It was too warm for him to have the gas logs burning. It was merely a place for him to stand in an awkward situation.

"I hope this is important. I don't have time to waste."

"We know that Marie Jones is your daughter," I said.

He was staring out one of the front windows behind me and slowly shifted his eyes towards me. I thought I saw a tear appear in the corner of one of his eyes.

"Well, I guess my secret is finally out," he said.

"Not yet. I have no desire to tell the world your secret. But, the truth is, from what I have learned, you should be proud to have her as a daughter."

"I am. Make no mistake about that. But there's only two or three who know the truth, so I can't very well brag about her accomplishments. It would hurt her as much as it would hurt me if this town knew. Maybe more. I don't want her to be hurt and I certainly don't want to feed the damn gossip of this town. Let 'em talk about somebody else."

His tone and attitude seemed to indicate that Rogers was perhaps correct in that this man would not intentionally incriminate his own daughter in a murder.

"Agreed. But, you do have to answer for murder."

"You think I murdered someone?" he asked.

"I do. You gave Marie a concentrated dosage of potassium in a syringe for Robert Lee Rowland. She injected Rowland with concentrated potassium and it killed him. I can only guess that you were not trying to frame her. You had to have some plan in order to have her do it and get away with it. The truth is, though, you used her to kill the preacher."

At my mentioning of the potassium, Rosey moved effortlessly out of the small living room into the kitchen area to my right and to Robby's left.

"You're just guessing. You can't prove anything."

"I will."

"You'll need some evidence, and that will be quite impossible."

"You gave Ben Pickeral several items to send off for testing," I said.

"Ben seems to have lost it."

"Wow, imagine that."

"It happens. Evidence sometimes gets misplaced. You know the reputations of small towns."

"Well, that would explain why you were willing to let Marie use your mixture without knowing what she was doing. You had planned all along to destroy the evidence."

"That's quite a story. You have any evidence to support such a tale?"

"How about these two items?" Rosey said as he re-entered the living room from the kitchen holding two bottles. One was the concentrated potassium and the other was an amber colored syringes. "You left a mess in there, next to the sink where you created the stronger dosage for your daughter to use."

"That proves nothing other than the fact that my mother needs potassium and that's the way I buy it."

"How long has Hospice been helping with your mother?"

"What's that got to do with anything?"

"Hospice provides some medications."

The Sheriff smiled slightly, "But not potassium. That would be my responsibility."

"Seems that you have covered all of your bases, Sheriff."

"I simply have rational answers for your wild specula-
tions. You don't have a case against me. Nor do you have a
case against Marie. Why don't you just drop it? Leave it
alone, Clancy. There's been enough pain to go around
more than once. The preacher was a bad man. He used
people. He had people killed. You know he was no good.
Why don't you just walk away and keep your wild notions
to yourself."

Robby put his hands in his pants pockets and walked
across the living room. He was looking at the floor as he
moved slowly in front of me. He stopped in front of a large
cabinet, like an armoire. Its double doors were opened.
Robby had his back to me.

"I can't do that, Robby. Rowland was a corrupt man, and
he was behind the murders at Peace Haven. But you killed
him and you need to answer for that. We'll just have to rely
upon his autopsy to provide some evidence."

"Ah, the autopsy. Of course. Well, the problem there will
be that when I called his surviving children to get permission
to have it done, they all refused. It seems that the preacher
had this thing in his religious faith about autopsies. I think
he even had something in his will against one being
performed on him after death. I just couldn't convince his
children to allow such a thing to his body."

"How convenient for you."

"Appears to me that Preacher Robert Lee Rowland must
have died of natural causes, at least that's what I will have to
put into my final report. All you have is some information
that a bright, young African American woman is the
daughter of an aging, white sheriff in a Southern town. Tell
me, Clancy, what you are going to do with what your discovered about Marie?" Robby said as he took his hands out of
his pants' pockets.

"After I present what I know to the police in Dan River,

they'll likely want to conduct their own investigation into all this. You'll have some questions to answer."

"You could leave out that part about Marie being my daughter."

"I think it's germane. Goes to your motive."

"I killed him because Marie is my daughter?"

"You killed him because he threatened Marie somehow. Did he know that she was your daughter?"

"No," he shook his head. "He knew nothing of that. He was simply this powerful, self-made, ego-maniac who loved his own authority and tried to control everyone around him. Once I put two and two together from your investigation, I realized that he was the one behind all of the murders at Peace Haven. Marie told me about the Saunders woman coming out to his home on several occasions, and after I saw Joy talking with Saunders, I knew something was going on. Then you told me your theory about someone killing the jurors from that trial, and I knew it was Rowland."

"Why didn't you just work with me and help me put him away?"

"You didn't understand that man's power. You couldn't have put him away. He would have found a way to get around the justice system. He's been doing that for years. He had too many friends who respected him, no matter what he did. You had no hard evidence linking him to anything. He deserved what he got. Good riddance, I say."

The sheriff remained motionless with his back to me. Rosey was standing off to my right. I saw him put the two bottles on the small table next to the couch.

"I can't convince you to change your mind, can I?" Robby said to me.

"No."

"Let me show you something," he said.

On the shelf directly in front of him was a large television screen. Underneath that shelf was a series of four large drawers. He used his left hand to open the top drawer. He put his right hand inside of the drawer and stopped moving.

"I can't let you tell about Marie. This town will destroy me … and her as well. You know that. There is no mercy or compassion here for folks who violate some things. They will eat her alive. I can't let you do that, Clancy."

"You should have considered all of that before you killed Rowland."

"Didn't figure on you getting this far."

"Well, it seems that we have a conundrum here," I said.

"I don't know what that is, but I do have a couple of options for solving my problem with you two."

"I hope nothing too violent," I said.

My peripheral vision caught the slightest of movements from Rosey who had remained silent the last few minutes. He seemed to know intuitively what was happening before it happened. The next thing I knew, Rosey had a gun drawn without making a sound. Mr. Stealth.

"Not if you two come quietly with me," Robby said.

"I would suggest strongly that you remove your hand from that drawer," Rosey said. "Slowly."

I drew my gun from my back holster and pointed it to the floor while I waited on Rosey's lead. Rosey's gun was aimed directly at the right side of Sheriff Robertson.

"You two resisting arrest?" he said. His right hand was still inside of the top drawer.

"Something like that," I said.

"That leaves me no alternative," Robby said.

"Take your hand out of the drawer, Sheriff," Rosey said again.

"Okay," he said and turned abruptly as he removed his hand. He had the gun and no doubt was intending to fire it at me.

Perhaps he hoped to catch us off guard, to surprise us. The fact that both of us were armed and already suspicious of his intention meant that there could be no surprise. He was drawing against a full house and he had no chance. I think he knew that. I also think he knew that he was giving us no choice but to fire on him. He knew that we would shoot to kill. Maybe he hoped that at least one of us would shoot to kill.

Robertson turned to his left, away from Rosey and towards me. I can only imagine that if he believed me to be the easier target, he could in fact get off a shot, perhaps kill me, before Rosey would kill him. If that were his thinking, he misjudged Rosey's ability to shoot. Mine, too.

I heard one round discharge before I fired. Two more rounds followed my shot. Robby never had a chance to fire his weapon. None of our shots missed. I watched him fall as if in slow motion. Sheriff Robby Robertson was now dying on his living room floor. It was stupid of him to do what he did. He probably thought it was his only out, his way of exiting the drama of life. Suicide by detectives.

"I never had anyone," Robby said in a slightly muffled tone, "to back ... me ... up." He rolled his head slowly in Rosey's direction.

"Maybe you never asked," I said as I knelt over his bloody body after kicking his firearm away from him.

"I couldn't," he said. He was having a hard time breathing. One of the shots must have punctured a lung. "Too many judges in this town."

"They're other towns."

"Only good ... memories ... I ever had ... were here."

Rosey was on his cell calling for an ambulance.

"And your secrets, too."

"My secrets ... were ... my good memories."

I was leaning over him at this point. I tore off a large

portion of his shirt to use as a compress for the two wounds on his left side. I could tell that the two entry wounds were within a few centimeters of each other so it was easy to press on one spot to curtail the loss of blood.

"You …want … a confession … now?" he asked.

"That would certainly help Marie."

"If … I told you … it … was … all my … idea … you … would leave her … alone?"

"It would help her, but she still would have to answer some questions."

"You … could call it…. a … mercy killing … you know."

"Mercy for whom?" I said.

"Mercy … for all those … jurors … he killed … and mercy … for my … good … friends … Sam and Barb…, the teenagers … you know… the ones…he had his son … kill … decades … ago."

"Or would you rather call it justice, Robby?"

He smiled faintly, "No… this … was … for the … love of mercy."

It was the last thing he said. The ambulance arrived a few minutes later, but he was already dead. Ben Pickeral arrived after the paramedics and was asking Rosey lots of questions. I called Detective Anderson in Norfolk and told him that he had better call some friends of his in the Dan River Police Department. I suggested that they might want to come over as soon as possible to help Ben sort through some of this. Anderson thought that was a good idea.

I told Ben that Rosey and I would be at my mother's and we left. No sense running from the truth now. No sense at all.

THE DAY AFTER ROBBY ROBERTSON DIED WE ENJOYED
entertaining a Detective Rosenbaum from Dan River, along
with his partner, Susie Chong. In light of Robby Robertson's demise, the Dan River Police Department took over
the case for Pitt County. They did a credible job of investigating what we told them. They asked good questions for
the most part. They sorted through all of the information
we had and did some checking to substantiate our facts as
well as our stories. They told us after a week of sifting
through all of the muck that we really had no hard
evidence against Marie Jones nor Marilyn Saunders.
However, in light of the confessions of Joy Jones and her
son Henry, both Marie and Marilyn were what they
referred to as persons of interest. Ubiquitous terminology,
if you ask me. Surprise, surprise. So much for my detective
skills.

One might consider the fact that we had sufficient
evidence to indict the preacher Robert Lee Rowland for his
role in this sordid affair to be a good ending. I wasn't all that
satisfied. His death simply meant that all of those who were

injured by his hatred would never find any semblance of justice. Such is life.

The fact that the preacher's hatchet woman got away simply did not sit well with me. I knew that she was up to her eyebrows in guilt but she had been smart enough and illusive enough to escape the confines of the law, both the locals as well as the Dan River authorities. I had a nagging suspicion that like a bad dream she might likely come back to haunt me.

A week after our debriefing and exhausting interrogation with the Dan River detectives, Rosey, Sam, and I were back in Norfolk. It was raining and we were lounging around my apartment waiting on whatever it is detectives between jobs wait for. Sam was asleep on the sofa. Rosey was reading some recent issue of Scientific American that he had purchased on the way back to the coast from Clancyville. I was sitting by the window watching it rain and wondering about life and the choices we make, like choosing to be a detective.

My thinking was that some investigations just don't go by the book. You don't really solve them as much as they solve themselves sometimes. This was one such case. I was contemplating all of the loose ends we still had dangling. There were simply too many of them to count.

The phone rang. Whenever I was home, Rogers would let the phone ring as well. It ring several times before I decided I had better check to see if perchance someone important might be calling me. It might even be a perspective client. It was a long shot.

"Clancy Evans?" the voice said.

"Me in the flesh. How can I help you?"

"I'm going to help you."

"Okay. I'm game. What's up?"

"This is Diamond."

It took a moment for me to realize who was talking on the other end of the line. I remembered the voice.

"Diamond who?"

"Just Diamond for you."

"Oh. The mysterious assassin who tried to kill me and my partner."

"That would be me."

"Well, are you back in town?"

"No. I'm on my way to Los Angeles. I just wanted you to know that since you spared me, I dropped the contract on you."

"Didn't think you guys, excuse me, girls, offered rebates."

"No rebate. Just professional courtesy. You could have, maybe should have, killed me. But you didn't. I figure I owe you one."

"Well, seeing that your employer died during the ordeal, you weren't really going to get paid for the job anyway."

"I was paid. The money came while I was hiding away nursing my wounds."

"You were paid?"

"Full price."

"Wow. Won't this kind of charity hurt your business if word gets out?"

"I'll deal with that. Just wanted you to know that I won't be lurking in the shadows around you anymore."

"Until someone else hires your for a contract on me," I said.

"There's always that. I wouldn't worry too much."

"I don't worry at all. The way I figure it, you're lucky to be alive. And may I offer you a warning?"

"Me?"

"Yeah. Now that Rosey has seen you, I would make sure that you don't intentionally cross paths with him again. He won't miss next time."

"Is that a threat?"

"No. Professional courtesy. You're good and, well, I figure you deserve at least a warning. Now you have it. Thanks for calling."

The phone clicked without another word. The line was humming as I hung up the receiver.

"That was interesting," Rosey said.

"Truly."

"I got the gist of it. Any details I need to know?"

"Someone actually paid Diamond the full price to kill us both."

"You're thinking it was not the preacher?"

"Yeah. That's what I'm thinking."

"Then who? Marilyn Saunders?"

"Where'd she get that kind of money?"

"Can't say," he said.

"Could be someone else, you know."

"Hold that thought. Our list of enemies seems to be growing."

"Maybe we should take that Dale Carnegie course."

"Winning friends and influencing people?" he asked.

"That would be the one. Wonder if they have a section on the use of firearms?"

I poured myself a cup of coffee and returned to my seat by the window to watch the rain some more. It seemed to be raining harder now. I wondered where Marie Jones was and what she was thinking. She never did come out of hiding during the investigation by the Dan River Police. They listed her as a person of interest, but they had no real case, so there was nothing that they really wanted from her other than some information. I had convinced Detective Rosenbaum to let her go since she had nothing significant to contribute to what we did not know. I told him that Robby had confessed enough to me, and Rosenbaum believed me. It was enough of a white lie for me to feel comfortable with it. Robby would have wanted me to help Marie anyway.

I took a sip of coffee and offered a toast.

"May your life be better wherever you are, dear child," I said softly to myself.

A LOOK AT REVENGE (CLANCY EVANS PI BOOK 4)

Clancy heads to the mountains of Virginia to track her friend Rosey who failed to report to his office. Sam accompanies Clancy in the hunt and they run headlong into a serial killer who is seeking revenge for Clancy's recent interference. Soon the tenacious detective discovers that the killer wants more than Clancy's death. Rogers once again uncovers some data that leads Clancy to a Korean War sharpshooter and a fortune teller who knows too much. This time trouble is personal and Clancy finds herself protecting both friends and family from the vengeance of a clever killer.

AVAILABLE NOW ON AMAZON

ABOUT THE AUTHOR

M Glenn Graves has been writing fiction since graduating from college in 1970 but did not begin to work on novels until 1992. Born in Mississippi, he has lived in Tennessee, North Carolina, Missouri, Virginia, Costa Rica, and the Dominican Republic. He graduated from Mars Hill College with a BA in English and Religion. He received a Master of Divinity in 1977 three years after he finished his four-year tour in the United States Navy. Married to Cindy, they have three grown children – Brian, Mark, & Jenn. They also have three grandchildren – Jonathan, Matthew, & Phoebe. Glenn, Cindy, and Sophie, their Lab, currently reside in the mountains of western North Carolina where he is the pastor of a local church.

Find M. Glenn Graves at:
https://citylightspress.com/authors/m-glenn-graves/

www.ingramcontent.com/pod-product-compliance
Lightning Source LLC
Chambersburg PA
CBHW021843010726
47493CB00005B/1537